The Hydra

A NOVEL BY GRAHAM STULL

PUBLISHED BY RIBBIT BOOKS

*Copyright © 2015 by Graham Stull
All rights reserved.
The Hydra : a novel / Graham Stull – First Edition*
ISBN 978-0-9932650-0-6 (paperback) ISBN 978-0-9932650-1-3 (eBook)

This is a work of fiction. Names, characters, places and incidents either are the product of the author's imagination or are used fictitiously. Any resemblance to actual persons, living or dead, events beyond those which constitute objective historical references, or locales, is entirely coincidental.

Text edited by Bernadette Kearns

RIBBIT
BOOKS

To my Sweetums, Anna, for whom I shall always tell the Bad Lions of this world that she has gone to Suzie's house, and that she is certainly <u>not</u> hiding under the blanket.

And to Daniel, my main man, whom I shall never give up on. Not until I've drawn my very last breath.

Rates of Viral Infertility Syndrome Infection (2019)

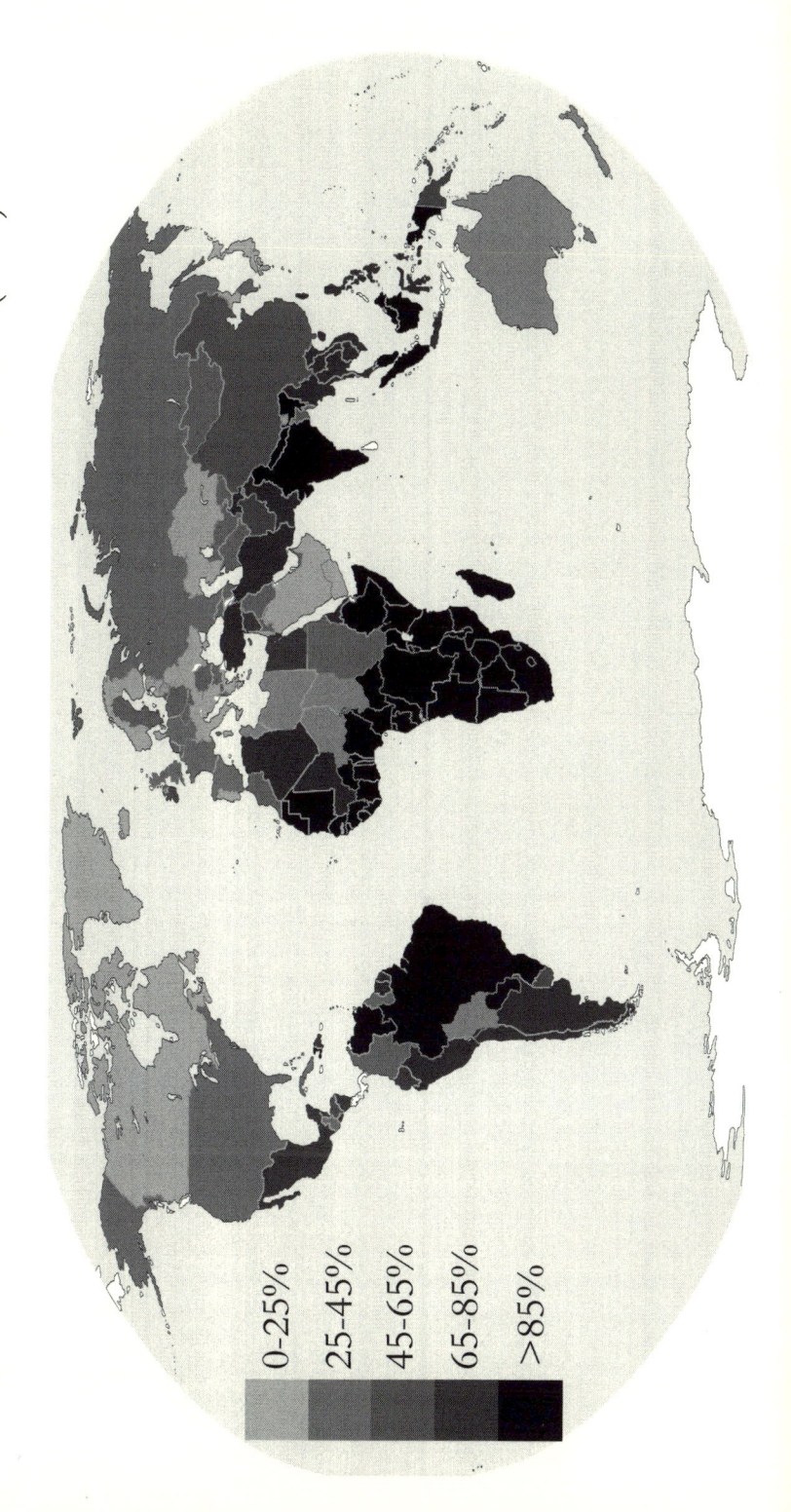

- 0-25%
- 25-45%
- 45-65%
- 65-85%
- >85%

» 1 «

On 7 July 2020 at 12:11 Central European Time, the world got its first clear view of Brian Matterosi.

Cameramen and news anchors were everywhere as he was paraded, almost ceremoniously, through an inner courtyard that connected two different parts of the International Criminal Court's new compound in The Hague. The ICC officials had him walk in a wide arc across the courtyard, so that the television cameras from all the different countries would have a chance to zoom in on his face. One billion people across the world watched him stare indifferently into one or other of these cameras.

Matterosi's defence attorney, Art Blume, was live-streaming the event on his tablet from the back seat of an armoured SUV, a sleek black vehicle slowly trundling its way along the bank of an industrial canal, heading towards the same complex. Art had wanted to be there with Brian the whole way through, but the ICC officials had ignored his request. *The defendant will undergo a separate security clearance procedure.* They were playing by their own rule book. And that rule book was sending Art a clear message: television cameras are more important to this trial than lawyers.

Art's SUV turned left, away from the canal, along a street lined with office buildings, all of which had been closed for security reasons. They were less than a kilometre away from the ICC court complex, but the vehicle's progress ground to a halt halfway up this street, blocked by a wall of protestors. The Dutch police seemed totally unprepared for the vast crowds: people of all nationalities who had made their way into the city to witness, to lobby, or to riot. The police escort vehicle in front of them had to pause every few minutes to clear a path through another stretch of crowded roadway. As they waited, Art could see the faces of protestors surge up over the wall of riot police. Their anger was like a living creature: its pulse could be felt in every corner of the city.

Art looked back down at his tablet. As the camera followed Brian Matterosi into the building, he tried to see this first glimpse of his client the way the world would see it. A second coming: but of whom? Christ or Hitler?

Actually there was nothing particularly vile, nor for that matter charismatic, about Matterosi's physical appearance. Slightly taller than average for a white male, he had dark brown hair, greying around the edges, a large, bulbous nose and sharp brown eyes. His body looked well developed and, maybe once, had been muscular, but was clearly wasted by illness in more recent years. His skin was pale and unhealthy in the way of people who avoid the sun as a matter of lifestyle choice. Someone had dressed him in a new suit, but they had been careful to ensure the sleeves were not so long as to hide the swollen wrists that were the tell-tale marks of VIS infection. People watching might call him a murderer, they could call him a monster, but they could not call him a hypocrite.

"Holy God!" A tremendous crash against the window sent Art cowering to the floor behind the front passenger seat, and the tablet spinning out of his hand.

"They're throwing paving stones at us," the driver told him. He was a rather droll Dutch fellow named Jeroen, who the ICC had explained would also act as Art's bodyguard for the duration of the trial.

"Don't you have, like, crowd control in this country?"

Art picked himself up and looked up at the window. The glass wasn't even cracked. Outside several of the protestors had broken through the line of riot police. Art could read the writing on the placard which one of them, an African man, was trying to use as a bludgeon: 'RACIST SCUM MATTEROSI HAS STOLEN OUR CHILDREN! WE DEMAND JUSTICE!'

"Normally The Netherlands isn't like this," Jeroen answered. *No shit*, Art thought to himself. "But don't worry, this thing is like a tank. We are safer here than in the hotel." Jeroen laughed. "Unless they have rocket launchers. Then we are screwed."

Art thought about the men and women he had defended over the course of his long career as a criminal defence attorney. There had been celebrities. There had been captains of industry. There had been drug barons. It felt like all those cases were just a warm-up act for what he was about to experience. As the SUV finally steered past the massive gates and down the ramp that led to the ICC's underground car park, that old thrill of excitement coursed through his veins. It was about to begin.

» 2 «

Leeton Kgabu, the chief prosecuting attorney for the International Criminal Court, sat in a second armoured SUV in the same convey, right behind Art Blume's. As he watched through the tinted windows, a young woman slipped in between two policemen and charged at Leeton's SUV. She got as far as to spit on the window, before being restrained by the two officers. Leeton just had time to observe her face, crazed with the anger of youth, her nose rings and her tattoos and poorly groomed, multicoloured hair. Above and behind the cops he could make out the elaborate signs and placards of the other protestors, demanding justice for the never-to-be-born and the dead alike. 'YOU MURDERED MY FUTURE' proclaimed one of the placards that flashed in the air above the police blockade. 'MY BODY $\neq$ YOUR SCIENCE EXPERIMENT' read another.

Their anger was understandable, of course. And yet it reminded Leeton only too well of violence in the South Africa of his youth. Though inspired by the noblest of motives, mob madness just as often whipped groups of young men into acts of unthinkable cruelty, as bad, if not worse, than the evil against which they were protesting. Caught up in such mobs, a younger Leeton had done things which he was now ashamed to admit even to himself. Leeton looked down at the notes for his opening speech. He tried not to think of how many people would be watching and listening to his words in an hour's time. How this speech would be recorded as a milestone in human history, not only because of the Matterosi case, but because of its place in new international Criminal Law.

Leeton had spent his entire career living with the frustration of watching corrupt dictators thumb their noses at the international community because of how "toothless" the old ICC had been. Now, finally, with the entry into force of the Abuja Treaty, there was a world-wide legal framework in place that would change everything. Such a pity it had taken something as evil as VIS, and someone as evil as Brian Matterosi, to bring about such a change. Even with the Abuja Treaty in force, there was no certainty that the court would have the courage of its convictions. All Leeton could do now was play his own part as best he could.

He took a deep breath and exhaled. His big hand clasped the ivory necklace he always wore under his tailored, cotton shirts.

"*Umama*," he said, using the Zulu word for "mother", "I will make you proud of me today."

***

When Art Blume emerged from his vehicle he was met by the four young lawyers he had picked to assist him.

"Any idea where Brian is now?" Art was asking Lisbeth, his most senior assistant, as they were ushered towards the lift. She was wearing tinted Internet glasses, so he could never tell if she was looking at him or at some screen.

"According to CNN, they've taken him into some kind of a holding room adjacent to Court One." Art thought about the madness of a defence lawyer having to rely on a news channel to find out the whereabouts of his own client. Brave new world.

The lift opened into a foyer, and they were led over to a battery of registration booths. This was the start of a long bureaucratic procedure to be issued with the access badges they needed to move about in the ICC complex.

"Your passport, please," a smartly-dressed court officer asked Art.

"What do you need my passport for?" he snapped. "Don't you watch TV? I'm Attorney Arthur Blume. By now everybody on the goddamn planet knows that."

"We require identification for all temporary access—"

"Why? Do you think I'm an impostor? This is nonsense. Where's my client? I want immediate access to my client."

"I'm sorry. I'm not authorised. You'll have to wait a second, please."

Art turned to protest the point to whoever was behind him. He thought it was one of his team, but when he looked around, he found himself staring straight up into the face of Leeton Kgabu. For a moment, Kgabu and Art locked eyes. Out of nowhere, a press photographer appeared and began snapping shots of the stand-off.

Physically, the two men could not have been more different. Art was Jewish in features and complexion, pushing sixty, short, thin and mostly bald, with plastic-framed glasses that had gone out of fashion in the late 1970s, while Kgabu was only forty-two, 192 centimetres tall and stocky, with the fierce dark stare of the Zulu warriors from whom he was descended.

"Tell me something." Kgabu's eyes did not waver as he looked down at Art. "How do you sleep at night?"

"Well, let me see," Art answered, doing his best to hold the bigger man's stare, "I turn out the light, put my head on the pillow and close my eyes."

» 3 «

Once both teams were seated in the briefing room, a pretty blonde named Rachel Hyberg, who introduced herself to the two lawyers and their teams as the "Trial Manager", began coaching them on procedure. Trial manager? Art had been in hundreds of trials before. The only "managers" were the court clerks and the judges themselves. He hastily scratched a note and passed it to Lisbeth. *Find out who Rachel is. Full bio for tomorrow's briefing.*

"Where is my client?" Art interrupted Rachel's little *spiel* to ask.

She smiled in that fake, PR way that such people do. "Mr Matterosi will be brought in after the judges have been sworn in. Then there'll be a one minute break. For commercials."

Art knew very well there was no reason for this dramatic entry, beyond entertainment. He recalled what he had read in the *Financial Times* last week: that the United Nations had sold live television rights to a syndicate of broadcasting companies operated by the media conglomerate, GlobalSix Entertainment. Far from being an expense, this trial would earn the UN millions. The trick, he thought to himself, would be to turn the media farce to his advantage. In this, Art would be in his element. High-profile court cases had, after all, been his bread-and-butter for over twenty years.

He looked across the room at Leeton Kgabu, who was absorbed in his notes. His big strong hands were trembling ever so slightly as he shuffled through the papers. Art observed the expensive shirts and the diamond-studded cufflinks. This man is young and proud. And scared shitless. *He'll make mistakes*, Blume thought.

"Okay, if there are no other questions, I'll just ask everyone to take their places in Court One. There are name tags on your seats."

Art and his team filed in to the courtroom. It was a far cry from the pristine and empty hall of justice he would have expected of a virgin court awaiting its first ever case. Instead, it was a hive of activity. Cameramen and -women were stationed in all four corners of the room. The packing tape was still stuck to the back of the upholstered blue chairs. Gaffers and key grips were performing last-minute sound and lighting checks. In fact, it was only from a certain angle that Court One resembled a real courtroom at all. Sure there were the twin flags of the United Nations and the International Criminal Court. There was the framed copy of the Abuja Charter above the judges' raised bench. There was the witness box and the benches for the prosecution and the defence, all in bright polished oak. And there was a semicircle of public seating—about one hundred and fifty places—where UN delegates from across the globe, as well as the media and other VIPs, were invited to witness the trial.

But these fixtures felt more like props on a movie set than the real thing. Elevated cameras, mounted on swivel podiums, could zoom in on any conceivable corner of the room. The ceiling was covered in scaffolding onto which hundreds of stage lights were attached. And behind them, overlooking the entire event, was the out-jutting glass enclosure of the television box, like the command tower on an aircraft carrier. Its tinted glass prevented even the judges from seeing exactly what was going on inside, but Art knew from the research his team had done that it was kitted out with dozens of monitors and hundreds of controls. GlobalSix Entertainment could control more than just the screenshot that would be beamed into every home on the planet. They could control the lighting, the sound on the judges' microphones, even the temperature in the room.

"Okay, we're about ready to go live." Rachel, the Trial Manager, had a speaker in her ear, through which someone else, presumably in the television box, was giving her cues. "In six, five, four ..."

» 4 «

Hello ... test recording, one, two, three ... this is the voice of Brian Joseph Matterosi. It is about one o'clock on Tuesday, the seventh of July 2020, and I am in The Hague, Netherlands, somewhere inside this crazy glass cage they call the International Criminal Court. It's day one of the trial, when all the swearing-in is supposed to take place. It seems right now the judges are being sworn in, and for some legal reason I can't enter the courtroom until they are officiated. So I guess that means more waiting. Five judges and each one has to read a ten-minute long statement to the court. So I guess it will be an hour at least. Time enough for me to start this recording.

Why am I making this recording? First, I need something to calm my nerves and occupy the time. They don't treat me badly, but they do keep me in a sort of solitary confinement, in an endless series of waiting rooms and offices with nothing to do. Beyond meeting Art and his team of hotshot attorneys, I basically have no human contact, and frankly I'm not sure lawyers qualify as "human contact"—even someone with the quirky charisma of Art Blume.

And of course they won't allow me to do any work whatsoever, which is how I am accustomed to spending my days. The endless waiting and boredom is driving me crazy; which, come to think of it, might be exactly what the UN is trying to achieve. So this is to be a way of killing time and keeping my head screwed on straight.

And secondly, I realised as I lay awake last night that there is nothing: no account of my life beyond what others have written. To be honest, I haven't read most of that stuff, but a lot of what I have seen by accident in newspapers and on TV is just plain wrong. So if they do sentence me to death, I would like some kind of record, something personal that I leave behind. I never used to think that would be important to me, you know. I always believed it was my work—my scientific work—that would be my legacy.

But I guess fear of death is a funny thing. It has a way of making you sentimental. And it's got me thinking about my past. Also, I want to be remembered as a person, a human being. Not just the monster they want to portray me as.

I'll see how far I get with this. If I start to run out of time I'll just skip to the juicy bits, the stuff that happened in, you know, the last few years. But my lawyer tells me it's going to be a long trial, so I guess I have time. Anyway, that was the background. I guess you'd call it my "introduction": now for chapter one.

Begin at the beginning I guess. Well, I grew up as an only child in a place called Watertown, Massachusetts, which is a suburb of Boston. Our house, the one I grew up in, was the last house on a quiet one-way street right on the border of Cambridge, Massachusetts, which is much more famous because of Harvard and MIT. Watertown is famous for nothing, as far as I know. Our house was typical for that part of Boston, a two-family with yellow vinyl siding, and me and my mom rented the upstairs apartment which was like a standard cookie-cutter two-bedroom. My parents were divorced, and when I look back on it now it seems to me I spent most of my early childhood in my pyjamas, eating bowls of sugary breakfast cereal on the 1970s carpet in the living room, watching cable TV.

Our "family", if you can call it that, was working-class Catholic. We were that typical mix of Irish- and Italian-American that made up much of white, suburban Boston.

My parents were about as ill-suited as two people could possibly be. So not only did it seem normal to me that they should be divorced, I actually found it hard to imagine how they could ever have come together. They never told me, but I'm pretty sure I was a complete accident.

My mother was second generation Irish, but my grandfather died when I was little and my grandmother went back to live with her sister on a farm somewhere in Ireland. My mother was always so proud of being Irish, like it was some great mark of achievement. And yet she'd never been to Ireland, and neither knew nor cared anything about the country or its heritage beyond the plastic leprechaun ornaments that adorned our fake mantelpiece.

She was a simple woman. When I say that, I mean she was stupid. Probably about as low an IQ as a person can have without being legally disabled. The child support she got from me and the "patronage" of her boyfriends were the only ways she had of paying the rent. Certainly she never worked a day in her life. When I got a little older I used to joke that she had three sources of income, and I was the only one that didn't fit into a push-up bra. I can see her now, with her dyed-blonde hair and one of those long white cigarettes she smoked, looking at me with her vacant blue eyes as I tried in vain to explain why she was throwing away exactly sixty-seven cents for every dollar she spent on the lottery.

"Oh Brian, ya' so smaaaht!" she'd say, and then pinch my cheek or something.

My dad on the other hand was a fast mover and a fast thinker. He made his living as a professional card player, which, as a child, I thought was just about the coolest thing in the world. I'd get his postcards addressed to me from all kinds of places, some having been written when he was on a post-victory high, some written while he was drunk and melancholy.

My dad paid his child support and alimony in lumps, presumably because that's how he earned his money. On the rare occasions when he was in town, we'd meet up in a hotel bar overlooking the Charles River and play cribbage, or he'd teach me card tricks. He usually had a flashy car and always seemed able to spend lots of money. I knew I had inherited my brains from him.

The fact that my dad paid his child support in lumps was not to my advantage, because it meant my mother used to spend the money in lumps too. To say I was neglected as a child would not be an understatement. My clothes were for the most part emblazoned with cigarette logos, because they were the free T-shirts and sweatpants my mother got when she bought cartons of cigarettes. She never cooked. But her make-up was impeccable any time her boyfriend came to take her out.

As for friends, well, I suppose you could say I was a solitary child. In fact, before junior high school, I really don't have many memories of friends at all. I used to just play by myself ... I don't know ... drawing elaborate mazes, and playing card tricks. Playing with my Commodore 64 computer. And, of course, watching TV. And that's how things remained until the start of high school, more or less.

» 5 «

Leeton Kgabu left an empty chair between himself and the rest of his legal team. He wanted this extra distance in order to concentrate, to focus completely on what was going on. The five judges were about to enter the court now, and he wanted to get a feel for them as people, in a way that the briefing notes could not give him.

Chief Justice Annabelle Wang entered first. Her black and velvet robe with the flat, white neckband that hung down the front was exactly the same design as the old ICC. Either a lack of imagination or a desire to maintain a sense of continuity, Leeton reflected. Nothing in her dress told the viewers that she was any different to the four other judges who followed her into the courtroom. The only difference was her greater sense of gravitas.

Wang was Hong Kong Chinese. Before the recent meddling from Beijing, she had served as Chief Justice of the High Court of Hong Kong; her fair, but outspoken, criticism of the Chinese mainland's policies had cost her a place on that bench, but won her international recognition and esteem almost everywhere else. Some saw her appointment to The Hague as a slap in the face to China for its refusal to ratify the Abuja Charter. Leeton observed her keenly as she stood at her bench and tossed to one side the little nametag. She herself was busy taking the whole scene in. She frowned heavily as she looked at the massive teleprompter that hung underneath the television box. Leeton turned his head and saw red digital letters scrolling past: *Chief Justice Wang, please take your seat.*

The other four justices followed right behind her. Two men and two women. They hailed from Sweden, Nigeria, India and Brazil. The Brazilian judge, in particular, was someone Leeton respected and admired. Luisa Gomes's name was synonymous with that branch of International Human Rights Law that Kgabu himself practiced, and which focused on using the law as a positive instrument to overcome the fundamentally racist nature of the post-colonial world order. All in all, Leeton found he was pleased enough with the selection of judges.

Once the swearing-in was done, Rachel Hyberg appeared out of nowhere and called out, "Okay, that's a cut!"

Wang stared at her in disbelief. "Excuse me?"

"Four minutes' break," Rachel explained, without losing a millimetre of her smile. "Then we can bring in Mr Matterosi." Leeton watched the tense exchange of eye contact between the two women with fascination, but also with a creeping sense of dread. The last thing the trial needed was tension between the UN-approved commercial partner, GlobalSix Entertainment, and the ICC's own judges.

Wang tried to wrestle back the control of the court by means of speaking directly into the microphone. But no sound came out. Rachel's team had put her on mute. Meanwhile the crowded courtroom began to jostle and chatter with the sound of a hundred and fifty excited voices. Leeton looked over to Blume, who was chatting with one of his assistants and pointing to something in the file. He seemed to be cracking jokes, like it was all some kind of game. *Arrogant little bastard*, Leeton thought. He knew this kind of man. It was typical of Americans. They used the law as a weapon to make money and achieve fame. Justice, actual human justice, meant nothing to them.

When Brian Matterosi entered the court, every one of the twelve in-court cameras turned upon him. Matterosi walked over to the defence bench oblivious, and only as an afterthought did he accept Blume's outstretched handshake. They are not deep in each other's confidence, Leeton mused, as he watched the two men settle back into their chairs. An interesting fact that might yet prove useful.

As Matterosi was being sworn in, Leeton scanned the crowd of approved observers who lined the rows of semicircular seating behind them. He was looking in particular at the ethnic composition of this supposedly global institution. Mostly they were Europeans. With the exception of the judges themselves, nine out of every ten people in Court One was a white person. Images flashed through his mind of mass graves in West Africa, in India, in the Native communities of South America. This was white justice for a white crime perpetrated against a brown world, he told himself, then made a note of that expression for later use.

After the next commercial break, the judges invited the prosecution to begin. Two minutes later, right on cue from Rachel, Leeton Kgabu rose and addressed the planet. Global viewership had risen to 1.6 billion at that stage. Leeton felt his hands shaking uncontrollably.

» 6 «

As Leeton stood, he caught a glimpse of himself on a tablet device which someone in the first row had resting on their lap. CNN was live-streaming. He thought the camera made him look powerful and confident. Perhaps even handsome. The image made him feel more at ease as he turned to the judges' bench and spoke the first words of Brian Matterosi's trial.

"We proceed directly to read to the Court the charges proffered against Mr Brian Matterosi. The charges are as laid out in ICC/2451/18, hereafter known as the First Schedule of Indictments, which I hereby submit for record to the Court."

"Thank you, Counsel," Wang answered. "You may now read your opening statement."

"Brian Matterosi, in his arrogance, believed he could control the destiny of mankind. He thought he was God. Caught up in this maniacal vision of self-aggrandisement, he unleashed onto our world his own sick version of Armageddon.

"Ladies and gentlemen of the Court, Honourable Justices, during the course of this trial you will hear the medical and biological evidence of the virus known as the Hydra and the disease it causes, known as 'Viral Infertility Syndrome'. This map—"

Here Kgabu paused and jabbed the button on the remote control which operated the projector. Screens on either side of the courtroom descended and lit up with a map of the world. The title of the map was: 'Rates of Viral Infertility Syndrome infection (2019)'

The US and Europe were a light green at 25 per cent. Russia was a pale orange at 45 per cent. Africa, South America, and most of Asia were dark red, showing over 85 per cent of their populations infected with the virus.

"—tells a story more compelling than mere words can convey. It shows a world divided, in which the poor of Africa, Asia and across the developing world have been made the victims of Brian

Matterosi's madness. Viral Infertility Syndrome will make almost every single one of them infertile. Their family legacies are gone. Their villages will die. Their cities will disappear. All because of this man. This map also tells you the horrific story of a racist agenda. Look at the map, ladies and gentlemen. It does not take a degree in geography to know that the areas where the infection was spread are predominately areas where human skin colour is darkest. Matterosi, like other genocidal maniacs who went before him, has a hatred of the other.

"In the course of this trial you will hear evidence that proves Matterosi acted in a premeditated, calculated way, planning his attacks with ruthless efficiency.

"You will hear evidence of the results of these attacks; evidence that demonstrates, beyond any reasonable doubt, that the consequences—medical, social and economic—with which we have all become so acquainted over the past years were the result of Mr Matterosi's deliberate, racist and cruel attempts at social engineering. National and international experts from countless countries, organisations, scientific disciplines, will explain to you beyond any doubt that the number of deaths caused directly by exposure to the Hydra virus is significant, and because they were targeted at specific populations, represent an admissible form of genocide under the new International Criminal Code.

"That Brian Matterosi is a genius, we have no doubt. That he has chosen to use his genius for evil, it is the thing we regret the most. We cannot undo this fact. But we can at least bring to the countless victims of his evil some small degree of justice, some sense that the international community is cognisant of their loss.

"Ladies and gentlemen, the country of my birth, South Africa, was once a land of deep division and injustice. The story of its recovery from oppression is one of hope. Beyond the efforts of individual heroism, it took the combined will of the international community to overcome these injustices, to help the victims heal and to create a lasting peace. It was not just the sacrifice of men like my father who gave their lives in struggle against the old regime. It was also white people in Europe and America who stood, in solidarity, for what was right.

"The crimes of Brian Matterosi will also leave deep scars. The process of healing will take many years. Your Honours of the Court, after hearing the evidence we will present, you will be asked, on behalf of the entire human race, to take the very first step in that healing process. You will be asked to bring justice to his victims, by finding Brian Matterosi guilty of genocide."

» 7 «

Hello, I'm back in the hotel now. Well, day one is over. I don't want to say too much about the trial because there'll be plenty of that in the newspapers and TV. But the prosecutor—what's his name … Kgabu?—his opening statement was a veritable diatribe, full of vitriol and emotion and pretty empty of content. If one of my post docs had gone on like that, I would have kicked him off my research team. But this is a legal circus, and it appears I'm the clown in the cannon.

My lawyer, Art, tells me he thinks Kgabu is an idiot. He says the only reason he got appointed was because of political pressure from the Indian government. Their new Prime Minister, Veedala Jhumi, is the mastermind behind the whole legal framework that's put me behind bars. And it seems he's also a personal friend of the prosecutor. Art thinks Kgabu will crumble as the pressure from the trial picks up. Maybe he's right. But from today's papers, that's sure not how it looks. In a special three-page spread, this morning's *Frankfurter Allgemeine Zeitung* describes Kgabu's open speech as a "masterstroke of courtroom drama". And there are reports of mass gatherings in Kinshasa, Cairo, Rio, of people celebrating this guy as some kind of a Third World hero. Which I think is weird. After all, all he's done is given one speech.

The camera thing is maybe the weirdest part. Everywhere there's cameras and reporters. Especially in the courtroom. I mean, even in my heyday, when I was one of the world's leading scientists, I could walk down the street anywhere in the world and pretty much no one would recognise me. Now my face is plastered on every newspaper on the planet. Anyway, enough about that. Let me get back to my story:

Where was I? Yeah, my childhood; I think I stopped when I was just about to hit puberty.

Puberty is the sort of biological and chemical change that's tough enough under the best of circumstances, but for me there were some really hard, added challenges. My dad, as I already mentioned, was something of an idol to me. Absence makes the heart grow fonder, and all that. And so a little after my fourteenth birthday, when he suddenly stopped writing or calling, or sending child support, it really rocked my world. I thought he had just given up on me, which turned out not to be true, but at the time it was how it seemed to me. Without any explanation, I had suddenly lost the one person I respected and admired from my life.

The most immediate effect of this on me was through my mother. Not that she cared about him from an emotional point of view: they'd been divorced for ever and there was no love lost. It was more a domino effect that toppled the admittedly fragile equilibrium of my domestic life. The child support money stopped coming. This created pressure on my mother, who at this stage was starting to show her age, it must be said. As I have already mentioned, she was not the kind of woman to do an honest day's work, and so she did the only thing she thought she could: she put pressure on her current boyfriend to give her more money.

The combination of a woman growing older and her growing more demanding produces a cocktail fatal for all but the most loving of relationships. And so, the boyfriend *du jour* dumped her (I can't even remember his name), and unlike his many predecessors, he was not so quickly replaced.

At this stage I had come to realise that my mother was not going to provide for me for very much longer. Food had never been very plentiful or healthy in the house, but of late the only contents of the fridge were mixers for vodka or gin. If I were inclined to cynicism, I would note that when the child support dried up, I went from being a good source of income to a liability, plain and simple.

It was summer and I managed to get a job at the local supermarket as a stock boy, which at the time paid the lavish wage of three dollars an hour. That felt like a fortune to a kid like me. I worked there as much as they would let me.

In September ninth grade started, which meant moving from Junior High School into Watertown High School. New teachers, new classrooms and an urgent need to form new friendship groups, if only to have someone to sit next to in the lunchroom.

My lunchroom table companions, and hence my clique, consisted of Spencer, Jessie and Rasheed, or Rasher, as we called him.

Spencer was a nerdy little geek with glasses and curly black hair. In a town almost exclusively Catholic (Irish and Italian) or else Armenian, his was the only Jewish family, a fact which no doubt contributed to his unpopularity. Besides being too smart to care about doing schoolwork, he was incredibly left-handed. He used to do elaborate drawings all over his notebooks of dragons and knights and stuff like that.

Jessie was kind of a general slob, with long, dirty ginger hair and lots and lots of zits. He always seemed to have a snotty nose which he would rub with little, disintegrating wads of toilet paper he kept stuffed in his pockets. It was unfortunate that his name rhymed with messy, because the description fit him so perfectly.

Like me, he came from a broken family and was, in fact, the only "latch-key kid" I knew in Watertown who, true to cliché, actually carried the key to his house around his neck on a string. His mother, who worked at some office job in downtown Boston 'til like a million o'clock at night, made him carry it that way because she was afraid he'd lose it. I guess she was probably right about that. Unlike Spence, Jessie was not very bright, but we hung out with him because, well, because he sat at our lunch table. Although he was actually bigger and stronger than the rest of us, he had a soft, gentle nature that, combined with his poor hygiene, made him a natural target for ridicule. He was the butt of many of our jokes, and I'm ashamed to admit we treated him as badly as the kids higher up in the social hierarchy treated us.

Rasheed was even smaller than Spence, and generally good-natured, but he had a vicious temper when provoked that we learned about early on. In retrospect I would put him in the category of a "frenemy": someone you socialise with but who just makes you feel bad and whom you would be better off without. But when you're fourteen, you don't really think about these things. A "friend" is just someone in your clique, not necessarily someone who is friendly to you.

In retrospect, our lunch table was probably the most interesting of the lot. I was the son of an alcoholic card shark, Spence was the only Jew and, like me, much too intelligent for such a place, Rasher was the only non-white kid, and the only kid who could speak some other language, while Jessie was probably the only person in that school with a genuine claim to heaven. That is, if you believe in such places. But let me not put some romantic spin on it: we were geeks, at the absolute bottom of the social food chain. And it made us resentful of society, of America as a country, of lower-middle-class suburbia, and especially, most especially, of the mind-numbing power of organised sports.

I've often thought back to those miserable hours in the hierarchy that was suburban High School and felt that it was truly the most honest expression of human nature. If you take any forced social scene in adult life—a workplace, a social gathering at an art exhibition, whatever—and you peel back all the layers of artificial civility, you will end up with a pecking order that resembles the lunchroom of a suburban American high school.

» 8 «

Leeton pushed aside his notes and switched on the television in his penthouse suite in the Paleis hotel in the centre of The Hague. France 24 had special live coverage of the protests outside the International Criminal Court and also outside his window at the Paleis, where Matterosi was reportedly being held prisoner. The Dutch authorities had eventually ramped up the security response, but not before several violent confrontations between pro-Matterosi protestors and anti-Matterosi protestors had left three people hospitalised. A reporter on the ground was interviewing some of the anti-Matterosi protestors, who were burning American flags.

"Why are you blaming the US authorities for the actions of Brian Matterosi?" She asked a man whose dark complexion was half-covered by a handkerchief.

"I will never be able to have children." He spoke with an Indian accent. "Nor my brother. Nor my sister. Do you understand what that means to my family? It is the end of us. All of us. India will die because of them."

"But the United States didn't release VIS."

"Then why aren't they cooperating with the International Criminal Court? Why are they trying to protect Matterosi? Do you really think justice is possible with—"

His voice was interrupted by shouts and shoves. A spray of water cannon hit the camera, and the camera shot flew up into the sky. Leeton went to the window and looked out. He could see the police truck with the water cannon, pushing the crowd back with jets of water. At least it was warm outside, he thought.

On the television, they'd cut to the newsroom. The news anchor was concluding that scenes like the one viewers had witnessed "… *highlight the need for a swift, transparent and, most importantly, a just outcome to the trial of viral engineer and alleged bio-terrorist, Brian Matterosi.*"

Skype was ringing on his laptop. Leeton switched the television off and returned to the desk. It was Caddie. When he clicked the green button, his son, Robert's baby face filled the laptop's screen. The boy's big eyes wandered around, and it was difficult to say if he was really focusing on the image of his father on the computer screen in front of him, or was simply bemused by the light stimulus. So handsome, Leeton thought with the swelling of pride he always got when he saw his son. He compared his own image in the little box in the corner of the screen with Robert's and decided they did quite look alike.

"It's Daddy! Can't you see him? There! Can't you see him on the screen? Say, 'hello Daddy!'"

Over on his side of the world, Leeton smiled and leaned into the camera. "Hello, my boy! You are growing so fast. Soon you will be able to pick me up and throw me across the room!"

Caddie's voice laughed at the idea, causing baby Robert to turn away from the camera in sudden surprise.

"Not for a looonnnng time. First he must learn to walk and talk."

"Well, hopefully, I will be home for all that."

Caddie's face replaced the baby's on the computer screen. She looked longingly at her husband, as if the qualification "hopefully" fell shy of her expectations. In preparation for the Skype call, she had dressed in her finest dress and put on her make-up and best jewellery, as she had done for their first wedding anniversary two months ago. That was the last night they spent together, on the lantern-lit pavilion of an Italian restaurant in central Bloemfontein. The next day he'd left South Africa.

Leeton felt a sudden pang of shame at just how much his wife loved him, but quickly pushed it back out of his mind.

"Are you eating well? Is Marambu taking good care of the house?"

"Yes, Sunshine. Don't worry about us, everything is fine here. You know, Robert and I watched you on television today—" Caddie began to say.

"Caddie, my Moonlight, I can't talk about the trial. Not on Skype. It's not a secure channel. Anyone could be listening."

"I know, my Sunshine. You don't have to say anything. I only wanted to tell you how proud we both are of you. To know that you are pursuing such a just cause—"

As if to protest against the idea that he, an eight-month-old baby, could be proud of a father pursuing causes he could not hope to understand, no matter how just, Robert erupted into a series of piercing screams, in that certain pitch that only human babies know how to achieve.

The picture on the South Africa end of the call broke down as Caddie juggled the baby around in an attempt to calm him. "I'm so sorry, my Sunshine, but I think he might be hungry," her voice said from somewhere behind the microphone.

In The Hague, Leeton turned to look at his clock. It was 21:43. His heart jumped. She said she would come to his room at 22:00. He had let time run away from him.

"It's all right, my Moonlight. It is quite late. You go feed him now. I have to read my notes for the trial tomorrow. We will talk again tomorrow night. Okay? At the same time."

They said their loving goodbyes against the backdrop of Robert's incessant screams. With a guilty sense of relief, Leeton clicked the red button and the screen went instantly quiet. He was back in his hotel suite, alone. Still fifteen minutes to go.

» 9 «

The first thing Leeton did was take off his ivory necklace and put it away, as if by hiding the talisman in the desk drawer, he could ensure Umama's spirit would not see anything she might ... misinterpret. Then he hid the pictures of Caddie and Robert, not because he wanted to hide the fact that he was married: after all, nothing inappropriate was going to happen. Still, he felt a strange sense of superstition that Caddie or his son might see something through the photos, and get the wrong impression. He applied an extra dose of cologne and considered whether he should put back on the soft blue silk tie he had worn during the trial, or just leave his shirt collar open. Open, he decided. He sat in the armchair by the door and waited, wavering between guilt and excitement.

At 22:07 there came a gentle knock. It was her. She had changed and now wore a black evening dress, trimmed with white lace. It was cut low around her cleavage. The softer lipstick she had worn earlier had been traded for a more aggressive red, and the warm professional smile was now a tad more daring. Her long blonde hair had been combed out and styled into buoyant waves that fell around her bare pale shoulders.

"I have something for you" she declared in her almost flawless American-English, with only a trace of a Swedish accent. She stepped into the room before he had a chance to invite her in. In answer to his puzzled look, she handed him a memory stick.

"Rachel, I wonder if this is—"

"I know what you're going to say. And you're right. It's inappropriate. Technically I'm not even supposed to take sides. But we both know there aren't really two sides to this case. The bastard's guilty, plain and simple. Just open the memory stick and see what's in there. If you don't want it, you can always give it back."

Leeton stuck the memory stick into his laptop. There was one MP4 file on it. He double-clicked on the file, and an image of

Brian Matterosi came up, sitting on his own in a featureless meeting room. Judging from the angle of the image, the camera must have been high up on the wall of the room, in the corner. On screen, the door of the room opened and Rachel appeared. She smilingly advised Matterosi that the judges were being sworn in, and it would be another little while before he'd be called to court. Left on his own, Matterosi produced from his pocket a digital recorder, like a Dictaphone, wrapped in a bundle of notes. He unfolded the notes on the table and ordered them. Then he switched on the recording device and said, "*Hello ... test recording, one, two, three.*" He played back his own voice and then resumed the recording. "*This is the voice of Brian Joseph Matterosi. It is...*" And on it went. Leeton clicked on "Pause".

"How did you get this?"

"We're a media company," she answered, with a coy smile. "Reality TV is one of GlobalSix's main areas of activity. Surveillance security systems are another." She leaned across him to the laptop and clicked on "Play". As she did, the full force of her perfume passed through his senses. "He seems to be recording a sort of ... autobiography. I think he might give away something that would be useful to the case. Anyway, it can't hurt, can it?"

As Leeton listened to the recorded voice, his mind began spinning with the possibilities. Not directly admissible as evidence, of course. But still, this was a gold mine. A private window into Matterosi's thoughts.

"Can you get me more of this?"

"Anywhere he goes, our cameras follow. Except where the defence attorney meets him. That room has been swept by an independent security team. But everything else he says, I'll give you."

"Why would you do this?"

"Like I said, he's guilty. But the conviction needs to be decisive. We owe that much to the world, don't you think?"

Now it was Leeton's turn to smile. "I don't know how I can thank you for this."

Rachel twisted a lock of golden hair in her finger. "Well, I *am* quite thirsty, now that you mention it." Before Leeton had even made it across to the minibar, she added, "champagne, please."

"Aren't you joining me for a glass?" she asked, when she noticed only one glass in his hand. Disappointment was writ large on her perfectly-featured face.

He looked from this face to the rest of her. Her thin frame was squeezed into the sparkling, silky evening dress, her smallish breasts pushed up to create the effect of a larger bosom. Where her smooth, pale skin emerged from the glittering black dress, it arched over well-defined shoulders into the slightest of necks, and finally back up into that sharp, delicate face, out of which her blue eyes sparkled like cold jewels. Though both women were what any man would call beautiful, the contrast between her and Caddie, with her soft, warm, brown eyes, her full generous figure and bright African dress, could not have been greater. Perhaps it was the very contrast that made this white woman seem so exciting.

"One glass," he conceded.

"Here, you do the honours, Attorney Kgabu."

She slipped over to the minibar to grab a second flute and squeaked with joy when the cork popped, as if it were the first time she'd ever seen a bottle of bubbly opened. Leeton knew it was all an act. But at some point the act is being so well played that you just stop caring whether it's real. He allowed himself to relax and they sat down together and made a toast.

"To justice."

He downed half his glass, while she barely sipped at hers. His was Dutch courage. Hers, just enough to leave a lipstick stain on the rim. Her bare silk legs were folded towards him, with most of her thigh exposed. The toe of her patent leather pump was less than two centimetres from his trouser leg.

"You know. When the trial began I wondered who they'd choose as lead prosecutor. Would they pick someone young and charismatic? Or would it be some crusty old fossil from the ICC's old guard?"

"You mean like Mark van den Buyten?"

They laughed together at the very idea of Mark van den Buyten leading the prosecution's case, and drank a toast to his questionable health. Van den Buyten, the icy relic of international criminal law, was the perfect ice-breaker.

Rachel smiled at Leeton and ran a red-painted nail along the condensation on the outside of her glass. "I'm so glad it was you who got the job. I have to admit I have a soft spot for ... powerful men."

Her look now told him there was no more need for pretence, or small talk. She sat, waiting for him to make his move. The wine and the smell of her perfume drew him in. He knew that if he touched her—on the hand, the hair, the face, anywhere—there would be no going back. And he was just about to touch her.

Clouds, which had obscured the sunset, suddenly parted, and a full moon, that had risen unnoticed over the low Dutch rooftops, exploded through the plate glass windows of the penthouse suite, throwing its pale light upon them. *My Moonlight*, he thought, and Caddie came rushing back into his mind. He was sure that the moonbeams were her love, reflected across the hemispheres, all the way from their house in Bloemfontein; as sure of it as if Caddie were standing there in person, watching him drink champagne with another woman. He arched back against the sofa.

"Rachel, I'm sorry but you'll have to excuse me. I'm very tired, and I still have to prepare for tomorrow."

She glanced down at her unfinished glass, yet managed to hide her disappointment masterfully. The perfect, artificial smile she had worn all day at court was back in an instant.

"Of course, I understand."

"But thank you ... for this."

She smiled one final time. "Goodnight, Attorney Kgabu!"

As the door closed behind him, Leeton let out a sigh of relief. He looked back out the plate glass windows of the penthouse suite and into gloom. The moon was gone again, as quickly as it had come.

» 10 «

One of the teachers in Watertown High School I'll always remember, and who had some relevance to my future infamy in a small and pathetic way, was my ninth grade biology teacher; a tall, thin, moustached man by the name of Mr Green. The guy was so obviously a dork back in his own high school days and was trying hard to make up for this by abusing his position of power. That's why we hated him so much. It was the way he sucked up to the cool girls in his class, and treated us with the same kind of contempt we got from the jocks. And so I would seek revenge in petty ways, by reading deep into the curriculum and showing up his superficial knowledge of high school biology. As you can imagine, this did not make me many friends in class, and it made me an enemy of Mr Green.

These high school tribulations were happening to me, I should say, against a backdrop of a continuously deteriorating domestic environment. My mother hardly left the house anymore. She had always been fond of drink, but lately she was drunk all the time, and would go into colic fits of temper, in which she would fire the contents of the house around for no apparent reason. By late November, as the first sleet announced the coming of a New England winter, it emerged that the rent had not been paid in two months. This was particularly upsetting to me, not so much because I was afraid we'd get evicted—I was still really a kid and had no concept of the practicalities of keeping a roof over your head (though I would learn this very soon)—the reason it upset me was because of what it meant in terms of our relationship to our downstairs landlords, Mr and Mrs Pezzoni.

You may find this hard to believe, but as I sit here now in my hotel room prison, thirty-one years later, and stare out a Plexiglas window onto a Dutch plaza full of people who see me as an incarnation of evil, the memory of how our relationship with the Pezzonis soured pains me more than all their mass-hatred put together.

You see, when I was younger (like, seven or eight), Mrs Pezzoni used to babysit me when my mother went out with her boyfriends. I'd stay in their downstairs apartment and fall asleep on their couch, and Mr Pezzoni would carry me upstairs when my mother came home. Their apartment was an amazing place, owing primarily to the fact that Mr Pezzoni was a master plasterer. He plastered enough fancy coving and cornicing into that cookie-cut two-and-a-half bedroom box to make the Palace of Versailles look like an army barracks.

Mrs Pezzoni treated me like the grandchild she never had. She loved my Italian last name and used to fill me with much the same kind of pro-Italian propaganda that I got from my mother about Ireland. She cooked fabulous meals, something I was otherwise unused to. I'm sure she did it mostly out of pity for me, knowing that I came from a disadvantaged home. Possibly there was a certain amount of guilt to it too, because my father had left us. As he was Italian, and he'd abandoned his family, she must have felt she owed it to the Italian-American community to keep an eye on me. I know for a fact the rent on the apartment was never raised above four hundred dollars a month, which was ridiculously cheap, even at the time.

But the advent of puberty dislodged me from the protective care of Mrs Pezzoni's motherly conscience.

Through no fault of my own, the hormonal surge that marks the beginning of manhood changed their view of me from a boyish victim into a juvenile offender, just in time for everything else in my life to fall apart. The bangs and screams of my drunken mother upset the quiet, old couple. And the fact that we stopped paying rent ultimately made us unworthy of the good faith we had been shown. I have a particular vision of returning home from my stock-boy job in the cold December rain of a dusky Saturday afternoon, and catching a glimpse of Mrs Pezzoni's face peering out behind the lace curtain. Her scornful glare hit me like a hammer—just a brief second of it—then the face disappeared into the safety of her baroque plasterwork and model Sicilian fishing boats. It was the face of what my world was becoming. The face of hostility and adversity.

I couldn't blame the Pezzonis for this and I was not yet ready to blame my mother or father, so I blamed the only person available: Mr Green, the biology teacher. Beating him, beating my sworn enemy at his own game, became my sole purpose and source of escape over that sad and sick Christmas break. I learned the theoretical foundations of gel electrophoresis as my mother smashed Christmas baubles and cursed her dead, abusive father. I studied the mechanics of electron microscopy as she muttered drunken Christmas carols and cried over old photo albums. I mulled models of dynamic equilibrium in homeostasis as she mulled her wine and smoked her long, white cigarettes.

By the time January 1988 had come, I'm convinced I knew more about cell structure and current theories in molecular biology than most college biology majors. Just as their hatred of me inspires romance and friendship amongst the protesters down in front of my hotel suite, my hatred of Mr Green inspired my future career as a biologist, with all its infamy and political consequence. Yes, in a way, this goofy, immature school science teacher of mediocre intelligence inadvertently played a formative role in radically changing the course of human history. The wings of a butterfly ...

But I digress.

My final "revenge" would have to be my class project. I knew all along this would be the ultimate showdown. Green would surely expend all his energy in attempts to find fault with my analysis, to mark down my work and justify the low grade he so desperately wanted to give me.

I chose a theme I knew would allow me to expand into all kinds of areas Green knew nothing about: the ubiquitous and life-giving *Escherichia coli* bacteria, topical at the time because of measures to clean up Boston Harbour, which had long been a repository for waste water from the surrounding municipalities (including

Watertown). I first thought to conduct a series of tests of E. coli levels in and around the Inner Harbour and the lower Charles River, but abandoned that project because I felt it would be too easy.

I needed more of a challenge. Green needed more of a challenge. That's when I hit on the idea of testing for various strains of the bacteria. E. coli, you must understand, is one of those foundation bacteria that mutates into many different forms. The process of mutation was not well understood at the time.

I took the bus into Harvard Square and knocked on the door of a professor whose paper on the subject I'd stumbled upon: Professor Gustav Gudjohnsson. He smiled pleasantly at first when I introduced myself and explained that I wanted some help for a school science project. At the time, Harvard was in one of its periodic phases where they wanted to dispel their elitist image and reach out to the local community. Helping a local kid with his science project was something an aspiring Nobel laureate like Gudjohnsson needed to be seen doing.

I talked generally about bacterial formation, commented on some widespread misconceptions floating around at school and even undergrad level. For a while he thought I was reciting something I'd picked up and learned by heart.

But once the Professor realised I had actually read his paper and understood his theory of bacterial conjugation, and the evolutionary game theoretical framework in which it had been cast, his attitude towards me changed.

"You are a remarkable boy. How old did you say you were?"

"Fourteen."

"I have postgraduate research assistants who know less about this than you do."

This was exactly what I wanted to hear.

"Then let me use your lab. I have an idea, but I can't test it unless I get access to an electron microscope. Needless to say, our school doesn't have one."

He smiled a smile which at the time I interpreted as benevolent.

"Have you ever used an electron microscope before?"

"Well ... no ... but I've studied—"

"I tell you what: I'll check with the person in administration who oversees the community outreach project. Let's see what would be possible. In the meanwhile, write up a research proposal. Tell me what it is you want; what this great idea of yours is. Here, take an envelope and send it to me in the mail. Maybe I can help you after all."

The Professor rose to signal the end of my interview, extending his big, fleshy hand to shake mine.

"In all events, it is truly encouraging to meet someone like you. You have a bright future, young man."

» 11 «

It was day two of the trial: a Tuesday. Art checked his phone messages on his way out of his hotel room. One unheard message.

"It's me," the message began. He wanted to hang up at the very sound of his ex-wife's voice, but the fact that she was calling him at all was so rare it kind of got him worried. *"I don't want to call you, believe me I don't. I have better people to call, like anyone on the face of the earth. But this isn't about me, it's about our daughter. I figured I had to be the bigger person. Yet again. And I know you like to forget you even have a daughter, but you do. And no matter what I tell her, she still gets disappointed when you let her down. Which you have done so many times now, that it's ridiculous. But this—this really takes the cake, Art. I have to say you've reached an all new low ..."*

What the hell was she talking about? And then it hit him. He threw down his bulging briefcase and began rifling through it, right there on the carpeted hallway of the hotel. There it was: a little white envelope with his name printed in elegant cursive letters. Inside, in gold lettering was the word "Invitation", and a little text with all the particulars, written in French and English. And the date: *Saturday, 27 June, 2020*. Two weeks ago.

"Fuck!" He rang his daughter's number, but it went straight to voicemail. There was no time to leave a message. He was already running late.

When Art stumbled into the briefing room he found Lisbeth, Anna and Chun were already nose-deep in the trial notes. Peter, meanwhile, was hovering next to the overhead projector.

"Here's the file on Rachel Hyberg," he said, handing Art a paper dossier before he'd even had time to sit down. *The kid's eager*, Art thought. *I like that.*

"Thanks, I'll read it later. First, let's do the press. Brian's arriving in five, and I want to get the press reports out of the way. Peter, hit it."

At this, the projector went live. One of Peter's jobs was to prepare a daily press briefing, which Blume had decided would be a useful way of starting each trial day. He had coffee and pastries brought up to the meeting room, and the team would listen to the briefing and then discuss strategy points. For the young lawyers, it would be a useful motivation tool and a good team-building exercise. For Art, it was to be a sort of brainstorming, a chance to let the young people throw stuff out and see if anything useful might stick.

The first clip was a round-up on media coverage from the first day of the trial. Most commentators seemed to like Kgabu's style. Next came a special edition of *Bild* newspaper, Germany's main tabloid. The special edition was called 'INSIDE THE LAB OF DEATH', and it had exclusive photos of the BetterWorld facility where VIS had been engineered. They had pictures of shit-encrusted jeans, which they claimed had been worn by Matterosi, the mad scientist who was too deranged to even go to the toilet while he worked. And, of course, they had a full spread on how the virus was perfectly adapted to render male sperm immobile and to accelerate the menopause in women. Just how they had managed to get in there was beyond Art, but it was clear they had got in. Only about a third of what they were claiming was made up. The rest was pretty accurate.

But the most interesting thing in the press was something Peter had selected from a Brazilian newspaper. The headline was: 'NOW WE HAVE OUR ANSWER', which struck Art as a bit odd. Only when Peter summarised the article did the point of it become clear: even though on a political level the reality of VIS had already moved mountains, a lot of people in developing countries didn't really even know what it was, much less who had caused it and why. It was easy to forget if you followed the news in Europe, where social and racial tensions had brought governments to the brink, but in rural Mexico, it just hadn't yet hit home. They weren't angry, because they didn't understand what they should be angry about.

"Which means two things," Art said. "First, the raw emotion we've been seeing in places like India is only the beginning. This trial is going to get hotter before it's over. But the second thing is that the public relations battle, which we all know is the real battle we're fighting here, hasn't even really begun yet. Which is good news, because it means we still have a chance to win it, if we can play our cards right." He paused and looked from one to the other of them. "Any thoughts?"

"We need to put Matterosi on the stand," Lisbeth said. "He needs to make a human appeal. He needs to show them who he really is."

Art was about to say, "*We'll have to see about that*," when a knock came at the door and the security goon ushered Matterosi into the room. Art's team rose and shook his hand. They introduced themselves to him for the third time. Once again the scientist seemed to have forgotten who they were.

"Sleep okay?" Art asked him with a smile.

"All things considered, yes."

"So I thought we could take this opportunity to go over the physical evidence again. Just to be sure we don't get any nasty surprises when they start talking about the lab stuff. If there's anything we're missing, feel free to interrupt."

"Sure," Brian answered, almost mechanically.

"Okay, Lisbeth. You're on."

She clicked a button on her tablet and began to read in her pristine, Oxford English. As she rattled through the descriptions of the evidence, annotated with her best guesses as to which witnesses might be saying what, Art watched Brian out of the corner of his eye. Nothing. No reaction. It wasn't just that he was like stone. Stony, impassive clients he could deal with. Art remembered, with a certain fondness, a company executive he once defended whose facial muscles never flinched in six long weeks. But Brian was different. It looked like he genuinely did not give a shit. And yet his life was on the line. The stakes could not possibly be any higher for him.

"Anything to add to that?" Art interrupted at some stage, as an excuse to get his client talking.

Brian slowly shook his head. "Sounds about right."

On the briefing went, until, glancing at his watch, Art called time.

Court reconvened in ten.

"Just do me one favour," he whispered to Brian, as they were about to enter Court One. "Try to look like it matters to you."

"Of course it matters to me," Matterosi whispered back at him, as they took their places.

» 12 «

Chief Justice Wang leaned into her microphone and called the Court to order before inviting the defence to submit its plea.

Art Blume rose. "Not guilty, Your Honours."

"Thank you, Counsel. Have you prepared an opening statement?"

"Yes."

"Then please proceed."

Art rose and spoke.

"Your Honours, ladies and gentlemen of the Court, people of the world. Brian Matterosi has never killed a single human being in his life. On the contrary, his work as a pioneer in genetics has led to several notable cures and saved the lives of countless afflicted persons. You will hear details of these miracle cures in the course of this trial. You will hear irrefutable evidence of how, since the very beginning of his career, Mr Matterosi has made it his mission to heal the wounds that we, as a society, have inflicted upon ourselves.

"The defence does not dispute that, in his quest for a better world, he engineered the retrovirus responsible for Viral Infertility Syndrome, the consequences of which will, it is true, be both massive and without precedent.

"Seen in isolation, his actions were ... extreme. That cannot be denied. But I urge you, ladies and gentlemen, *not* to see his actions in isolation. What Mr Matterosi has done, he has done in the context of a wider, more crucial, reality. The defence will present you with this full context: the context of a world so masticated by the twin evils of poverty and inequality, built on a foundation of overpopulation—a world of haves and have-nots. You will hear how some people suffer from infection, from lack of medicine, from lack of what should be a basic human right for all humanity. It is these people who face a heightened mortality risk when exposed to the retrovirus.

"The prosecution will attempt to argue that these poor unfortunate souls were at risk because they were exposed to a disease. On this point we can agree. But the disease in question, ladies and gentlemen, was not, *is* not, and never will be the VIS retrovirus. For, Your Honours, ladies and gentlemen of the Court, what you will *not* hear during this trial is any clear evidence that VIS was directly responsible for the deaths of these poor victims. Not one single human being was killed by VIS, and the defence will demonstrate this to you in due course.

"So what was it that killed them? What was the disease? Was it a disease engineered artificially by human beings to harm other human beings? Yes, it was, ladies and gentlemen. Was it a disease engineered by Brian Matterosi? No, it was not, ladies and gentlemen.

"So what was this disease?

"Poverty."

Here Art Blume paused for theatrical effect, turning a full 360 degrees to survey the courtroom before repeating the word.

"*Poverty*. The disease spread by the rich to infect the poor. The disease of a world that does not have the courage to face the real challenges before us. This is the real cause of death: poverty that cannot be dealt with until human populations have fallen to economically and environmentally sustainable levels.

"Ladies and gentlemen, in a world of injustice, a world crippled by its own inability to cope with the one true social problem of the age—overpopulation—we are seeking a scapegoat in Brian Matterosi. Why? Because he has had the courage to act.

"And equally, I am asking each and every one of you to show the courage needed to return the right verdict. The just verdict: that Brian is innocent. I know this is hard. Hard, because that verdict means we must all of us acknowledge that we have been guilty. Guilty of shirking our responsibility to deal with the world's problems in a structured, sustainable way. Guilty of leaving it all to one man to find a solution, however radical that solution might then be.

"In the past, men such as Brian Matterosi were never appreciated in their own time as visionaries. But thankfully, we live in more enlightened times. You, ladies and gentlemen of the International Criminal Court, have the opportunity to use the new legal instruments to demonstrate that the human race *is* more enlightened. Let's not make a scapegoat of Brian. He is more than a hero, a visionary and a saviour. He is a man deserving of justice. And most importantly, he is innocent of the crimes for which he stands accused."

The courtroom fell silent as Art Blume took his seat once again. The five justices, immovable as ever, seemed to take no notice of the message that appeared on the teleprompter in front of them. *Cut to a one-minute break. Then proceed to statement of evidence by prosecution.*

» 13 «

Day two of the trial is over. I'm back at the hotel and I've just had a hot bath. The news is full of images of riots sweeping across the world: India, Mexico City and across South Africa. They say Art's speech was like a red flag to a bull. All that talk of me being a visionary, a hero, a saviour. White South Africans are afraid to leave their homes now. Apparently the mobs caught this one Afrikaans guy and strapped him down and forcibly injected him with a syringe full of their blood. The idea was to infect him with VIS, but all he ended up with was HIV.

Even in the US, it has sparked race riots, which makes no sense, since infection rates are no higher for black Americans than white Americans. I think the whole VIS thing is just a convenient excuse to release the pressure of racial tension that's been building up for years. On BBC news this evening they had the Prime Minister of the UK calling for the television coverage to be cut off. But the media will never allow that to happen. Not until much more blood is shed. It sickens me to think about it. My best therapy now is this recording. So here goes: back to the 1980s.

Virtually all of my time and attention during the deep winter of 1988 was occupied by the application of Gudjohnsson's theory of bacterial conjugation to describe mutations in various strains of E. coli. The conclusion was, in essence, a testable hypothesis which I had fully intended to put under the electron microscope of Harvard's advanced microbiology laboratory. As it was, there was no way I could have managed the task in the time required. Testing the hypothesis would have required thousands of man-hours of applied research over numerous months. And for anyone who doesn't know who Gudjohnsson is, I should say now the entire theory was bullshit anyway. So I submitted the theoretical paper as my research project for freshman biology class, and sent a copy to Gudjohnsson as a kind of research proposal.

I'd guess Green didn't even try to read it. He gave it a C minus and returned it without comment. This, I felt, was the ultimate slap in the face. I wasn't going to take it sitting down.

"Excuse me, Mr Green."

"Yes, Brian" he answered in an indifferent, hurried way.

"Can I ask you about my grade?" He was walking away when I said this. My inner alpha male wanted me to shout *"Don't walk away from me when I'm talking to you!"* Instead I followed him stubbornly.

"You got the grade you deserved," he informed me over his shoulder.

"I don't see how. This paper is original research on the frontier of microbiology. I think you either owe me an A plus or an F."

"You didn't read the instructions carefully. You were asked to summarize a topic, not try and do high-level research."

"I did summarize the topic. That's part one. The introduction."

"For which I gave you some marks. But then you went on with twenty-five pages of material not even covered in the course. You exceeded the word limit by ... I don't know ... at least five thousand words."

"I had a lot to say."

"Yeah, you had too much to say."

So then I squared myself up to the fullest of my fourteen–year-old manhood, and said something like: "Let's be honest, Mr Green. How much of it did you even understand?"

Green stopped and turned abruptly. For a brief moment, I thought he was going to punch me in the face. Maybe I even winced. But he just stared at me, and from within the steely glare I could see sadness in his eyes. He was a weak man after all.

"You have to learn to play by the rules, Brian."

As the whole world already knows by this stage, I never learned to play by the rules. Else I might be a school science teacher right now, flirting with fourteen-year-old girls and wondering why "they" don't do something about the problems of the world. None of these people gathered outside this Hotel would have come to know

Brian Matterosi existed. Nobody would be rioting in Cairo today. And an overpopulated planet would be slowly sleepwalking its way to its own doom.

As it happened, Professor Gustav Gudjohnsson never got back to me about my research proposal. After my stand-off with Green, we seemed to reach a kind of truce, and my excitement and interest in microbiology began to wane. In my memory, the months that followed were filled with games in Spence's attic, Dungeons & Dragons and board games and the like. The fantasy world these games enabled me to inhabit became my great escape, and I clung to it as to a lifeline.

At the same time as my mind was thus preoccupied, my mother was progressively losing hers. She would get all dressed up and wait at the door for her boyfriend to pick her up, just like she used to when I was little. But there were no more boyfriends to pick her up. She would wait for hours and hours, then eventually give up and go into her bedroom and cry. And, of course, drink.

I would leave food out for her which I'd bought or stolen from the supermarket where I worked (I remember I once stole an entire deli turkey breast from the fridge and smuggled it home for her). The Pezzonis had begun formal eviction proceedings against us, but I'm not sure my mother cared or even understood about this.

There was a brief and painful period in which a man started hanging around the house. He'd kind of shown up out of the blue, and seemed to have "claimed" my unattached mother, like so much chattel. He called himself "Eddie" and told me he was my mom's new boyfriend. There was something instantly unsavoury about him, and I could see my mom had genuine fear and loathing of him, simple-minded though she was.

She left the house with him, all right. On more than one occasion they went out. But when she came home her anxiety and her temper were even worse. She got very drunk and violent and screamed at me for no reason.

"Look at this place, it's a fuckin' mess. Why don't you do something to clean this place up, Brian?"

"What are you talkin' about, ma? What don't you do something? You're here all day."

"I got enough to do already. You don't do anything to help in the house. Ya so fuckin' lazy, Brian."

"Look who's talkin'! You're just a stupid, drunk old whore."

She slapped me hard. I fell backwards.

"HOW DARE YOU TALK TO YA MOTHA LIKE THAT! You ungrateful little shit! After all I done fer you!"

My cheek stung. My body shook. All my life I've abhorred physical violence, but to be struck by my mother like that was unbearable. I crawled backwards against the kitchen cabinet, clawed open the drawer and took out a big kitchen knife.

"Oh, you gonna stab me? You gonna stab yahr own motha? Go ahead Brian, stab yahr own motha! Do it! Do it! Stab me through the haaaht."

I was backed into the corner, holding her off at knifepoint. The knife trembled in my thin, pale hands. "I know what Eddie is, Ma!"

"You don't know SHIT Brian! You think yah so smaaht, but you don't know shit about the real world."

"Oh, like you know so much, Ma? That's why you haven't paid the rent in six months?"

"To hell with you, Brian! Where's yah fatha? How come he don't send no more money? How can I take care of a kid and pay everything at the same time?"

"Take care of a kid? That's bullshit, that's such bullshit. You neva took care of me, ma. Neva. I've been takin' care of myself eva since Nanna left fer Ireland."

At this, her face contorted. In one of those rapid, chemical mood swings, her drunken anger imploded into drunken self-pity. Her eyes filled with tears and streaked the mascara and make-up covering her forty-something face. "Why do you think I'm goin' out with Eddie? You think I like doin' that? YOU THINK I LIKE IT? I'm doin' it fer you, Brian. So I can pay the Pezzonis, and they don't stick you in a … fuckin' … home." She started to cry. "I'm just tryin' to keep it all togetha. I know I'm not a great motha, *but I'm tryin'…."*

She was about to collapse. I dropped the knife and took her in my arms and she sobbed.

That moment, I think, marked a turning point in my life. As I stood there and held that weak, small and feeble women, reeking of booze, I knew that there was no more pretence of her being my guardian. My childhood was over.

» 14 «

Around that time a letter came to say my grandmother had died in Ireland. The cottage she lived in was hers, we thought, but there was no Will and nobody with the presence of mind to claim it. Ireland was a million miles away; a foreign planet in those days. I can't remember who had sent the letter either, and later on I would find myself wishing that letter had not gone missing. The letter included a cheque for six hundred pounds, which had belonged to my grandmother and must have been about a thousand bucks back then. Not knowing what else to do with it, I gave the money to the Pezzonis to pay the back rent.

I don't think they were very pleased with this, because they naturally assumed we'd had the money all along and were just playing cat-and-mouse with the eviction proceedings. Anyway, I doubt they were short on cash: they just hated us and wanted us out of their house. However, Massachusetts law being what it was at the time, this payment in arrears made it virtually impossible for them to evict us, and they closed the proceedings without conclusion.

The death of my grandmother didn't affect me that much at the time. At least, not directly. She had looked after me in my infancy, but your infancy is never so far away as when you are a teenager, and I only had the vaguest memories of what she even looked like. I know she sang to me when I was a baby: those sad, Irish songs about the Famine and young men leaving their true loves behind, and maybe that's why I still love that kind of music. Beyond that, I didn't remember more than certain fleeting moments, though more have come back to me of late.

But for my mother, it proved the final straw in her passage into idiocy. The Friday night following the bad news, she was supposed to be going out with Eddie, but, by eight o'clock, she hadn't even bothered getting dressed. Instead, she sat on a chair in her bedroom sucking her thumb and listening to a little music box from her childhood. When Eddie showed up, she didn't budge. This annoyed him, and he grabbed her roughly by the arm, pulling her to the door. He didn't seem to care, or notice, that she was still in her dressing gown.

Some instinct in me, or maybe it was my new-found sense of manhood, made me leap to my mother's defence. "Let her go!" I shouted, with all the chivalry of a fourteen-year-old son. I made a grab at him, but he flattened me with one jab to the throat, leaving me reeling for breath on the hall floor. From this low vantage point, and with stars dancing in front of my eyes, I could just see him dragging my mother down the stairs by a fistful of her dyed-blonde hair. She was whimpering, "No, Daddy, don't. Please, Daddy, don't." Between the drink and the pain and the mental instability, I don't think she even knew where she was.

Phoning the police was the last thing on my mind. Instead, I spent the next few hours pacing the apartment floor, plotting Eddie's murder in careful and gruesome detail. I would exact such awful revenge on him that his entire family would quake with fear. I'd beat his head in with a brick. Cut his penis off with a bread knife. Use pliers to extract his teeth one by one.

In the end, none of that stuff happened. I never even saw the bastard again. Around midnight, there was a screech of car tyres on our quiet one-way street, and a car door slammed. When I looked out the window I saw a sleek Camero driving away, and my mother lying in a heap on the bare sidewalk. I ran down to get her. With a strength I mustered from God knows where, I hauled her up the stairs and into her own bed. In the lighted room the damage could be seen: she had two black eyes; her face was badly bruised; she was missing a tooth and bleeding from cuts to her cheeks and from her broken nose. A lump of her hair had been torn out.

Perhaps surprisingly, my fury and bloodlust melted away at the sight of my poor, pathetic mother. I got a washbasin and carefully cleaned her, set her nose as best I could, and drew the covers around her. As much as I wanted to kill Eddie, it was not in me, even if I had had the opportunity. I was not a killer. People may laugh at this, given everything that's being said about me, but it's the truth nevertheless.

That night I left my mother to rest, went into the living room and switched on the TV. I remember it was the *Return of the Jedi*, the final instalment of the Star Wars trilogy, which was showing on cable TV.

The summer started hot and quick. My mother was more or less in bed all the time, except when she needed more alcohol. Physically, she deteriorated rapidly. Her nose never set properly and hence was crooked. She lost weight, and her skin became shrivelled and dry, with burst blood vessels showing all over her pale face. More and more, I began taking care of her, making sure she got what she needed so that no one on the outside would find out what was wrong. The last thing I wanted was to be taken away from my home and stuck in some institution.

And that was the state of my life on my fifteenth birthday. My mother sick in bed, mumbling to herself as the fan oscillated across her shaded bedroom in the long, sticky afternoon of early July. There was no more money left, but out of my job I managed to pay the electricity bill and the cable bill and to buy food. I also bought vodka in cheap plastic bottles for my mom, something that was surprisingly easy for a fifteen-year-old to do back then. The Pezzonis said and did nothing more to get us out, and I suppose I just planned on keeping going that way as long as I could. Maybe I intended to drop out of school at sixteen and get some kind of a real job. If I had any real plan at all, I can't remember it now.

When I think back on it, it seems to me like the authorities should have been notified about a family like ours. My mother was, for all intents and purposes, an invalid, and I was just a minor. We weren't paying any rent; I had skipped weeks of school towards the end of the year and had furnished only a badly-forged letter from my mother by way of excuse. But despite all this, no guidance counsellors intervened. No social workers got involved. No concerned neighbours raised any red flags. The truth is, as long as I kept myself and my mom out of serious trouble, nobody really cared. That's the way it was in America in the Eighties. Maybe in Sweden or some place I would have been looked after, socialised, and made into a normal kid again. Then I never would have ended up doing what I did, and the whole world, Swedes included, would have been left to their own highly socialised doom. But where I grew up, in the land of the Free and the Brave, you just had to be both.

As the summer months wore on, with all my friends away, and the pending shadow of school grew nearer, I became obsessed with the idea of escaping. Not surprising, really, when you think about my life. Another letter had arrived relating to some effects belonging to my grandmother, and it occurred to me that there was a place out there, my family's place, where I could actually go and live. In my own mind, I quickly fashioned this cottage into a cosy dwelling, with the smoky fire of some ancient hearth warming a deep armchair in which I sipped at a hot cup of tea. My long-term goal was to make it there, to establish a comfortable, safe and sane home for myself in another world, far away from the Boston area. And yet it remained a dream. A dream I took with me into my sophomore year in high school.

» 15 «

Day three of the trial began with a group of FreeMatterosiNow.org protestors storming into the foyer of the ICC building, chanting *"Can't feed 'em, don't breed 'em!"* in canon. How they got past security was anyone's guess, and it took the ICC officials several minutes to call in the Dutch police to arrest them.

Art, Brian and the team watched the whole thing on BBC World on Lisbeth's tablet, as did the rest of the people in the court. Only Leeton Kgabu appeared entirely focused, not looking up from his notes even when his own team tried to show him what was going on downstairs.

"Silence, please," Chief Justice Annabelle Wang began, speaking louder into the microphone in an attempt to focus attention on the proceedings. "Please switch all devices to mute. The prosecution will call the first witness. Please proceed, Counsel."

"Thank you, Your Honour," Kgabu said. "The prosecution calls Mr Vinay Kumar."

Art shot to attention and looked at his list. Vinay Kumar was not the first name on the list. In fact, he wasn't even on the main list. He was on the second supplementary list. Art looked over to Lisbeth who passed him her tablet. She had already pulled up her file on this guy. It was seven pages, but Art hadn't had a chance to read it. *Fuck*.

"Objection, Your Honours! This witness was not announced to the defence."

Leeton Kgabu, clearly expecting the interruption, swivelled and rested his deep, staring eyes on Art. He addressed the judges, but his eyes never left Art.

"Your Honours, Mr Kumar appears on the prosecution's supplementary list of deponents. He has been sworn in. There is no legal reason not to hear his testimony now."

Art watched as Wang conferred with the other justices. They had their microphones switched off, but Art had mastered the skill of lip-reading early in his career. He could see Gomes, in particular, advising the others that this testimony was perfectly in accordance with both the Abuja Treaty and the ICC Court procedures.

"The witness may be seated," Wang announced at length. "Objection overruled."

"That's fine, Your Honours," Art added. "If the prosecution wants to play little tricks instead of an open and honest exchange of the facts, that's fine by me."

"Are you done, Mr Blume?" Gomes asked, leaning into her microphone. Art sat down.

In stature, the witness was small and his only distinguishing features were a carefully groomed moustache and the tell-tale swollen joints of a man who had suffered from an early strain of VIS. The prosecution had evidently dressed him in a thin cotton T-shirt so that the cameras and the court could see his disfigured body. Kgabu spoke to him gently and with softness.

"Mr Kumar, for the benefit of the Court, can you please state your full name, age and where you are from?"

"Vinay Kumar, from Pendeshwar, India. I am thirty-four years old." He spoke in staccato, like an old-fashioned typewriter. But that wasn't because his English was poor. It was nerves. And maybe emotion.

"And you are a victim of VIS?"

"Yes."

"Tell us how you got the disease."

"They say it was from the water. But we could not taste anything different. It came upon us suddenly. All the people in my area. At first, they tried to tell us it was a sanitary issue. But I knew this was something different. The older people died, and we wept for their passing. But now, now I think it is a blessing they have not lived to see the rest."

"What about you?"

"I had a fever. First it lasted for a week. And I sweated and went to the toilet all the time. Eventually the fever passed and I was, I thought I was, healthy again. But the fever came back again and again. It is not so often anymore, but the main problem for me is the joint pain."

"Which joints hurt you?"

"All of them. My elbows, my wrists, my knees. I cannot sit without pain. I cannot walk without pain. Only on my back. I can lie on my back. Everything else hurts."

"How has this affected you?"

"Of course, we cannot have any children. For me, I do not care. I think that with this disease I will not live very long. But for my wife—"

Here he broke down and started to cry. Kgabu placed his big hand on the witness's shoulder and comforted him. The court sat silently as he sobbed like a child.

"—who will take care of her when she gets old? When I am dead? It is a disaster for us. For all of us."

Kgabu sighed and allowed the cameras a minute to remain on the man's tear-stained face, as he tried to compose himself in front of the entire world. As he did so, Kgabu paced around the expert witness box, stopping briefly to cast a withering stare at Art Blume, before returning his features to their former benevolence.

"Mr Kumar, I would like to show you a picture."

Kgabu handed him a picture. As he did so, he said to the judges, "Physical evidence, piece ICC/432-a," The five women and men on the judges' bench nodded and took note.

In the television box, the editors cut the camera shot to the full-screen scan of the image in seamless synchronisation with the courtroom action. Art could see it on the big projector screen which scrolled down from the wall, but the resolution was higher on the CNN live-stream on Lisbeth's tablet.

The picture showed what appeared to be a mass grave, reminiscent of scenes from a concentration camp, with the bodies of older men and women piled lengthways upon one another.

"Can you describe for us what you see here?"

It took Vinay Kumar a minute to gather himself sufficiently to respond.

"It is my village. The people here are the older ones, who died from the infection. We wanted to give them proper funerals, according to the rites. But there were so few of us to do it. And so many dead. The healthy ones were afraid of the virus, so they stayed away.

"Now our village is a sad place. We will have no children. There is no future there. Just the memories of death and the emptiness. He—" and with this he pointed across the courtroom at Brian Matterosi, his voice swelling in anger and indignation, "—has taken everything away from us."

Art wrote a single word on his spiral notepad. *Bullshit.*

» 16 «

My attitude to school and to authority continued to deteriorate. It got me roughed up by the jocks and it also got me into detention. And the more "they" were against me, the worse my attitude got.

In the end it was the detention, combined with some issues around stolen jars of Gerber banana baby food, which cost me my job at the supermarket. A job that was my family's only form of income. Five days to Christmas, and all I had was sixteen dollars to my name. The phone had been switched off. The cable had run out. Boston Edison had sent us a "final notification" and, worst of all, we were nearly out of heating oil. I had sold my mom's jewellery for a miserable one hundred and eighty-five dollars, which went on electricity, food and vodka. But that was it.

Right around then it got so cold that every global warming theory seemed suddenly ridiculous. I already had the heating switched as low as it would go, but that wasn't going to be enough. I needed money for an oil fill, and I needed it badly.

There is an expression "necessity is the mother of invention", meaning when you are most put to it, you will find a solution to your problems. Unfortunately, it's not really true. In fact, most progress is made in periods of human history when invention is least needed. Thus, the Enlightenment and Renaissance followed periods of relative peace and abundant harvests. Conversely, the Great Famine in Ireland did not result in the invention of a better system of allocating food on the island. Instead, people simply starved, and the political consequences led to the establishment of a Free State that impoverished its people for another hundred years. And management science studies show businesses that are already doing well are the ones most likely to come across innovative cost-cutting measures.

In my case, the dire need of the winter's cold and poverty was not an impetus to find a solution to my family's problems. It just made me depressed, sullen, angry at the world and, if possible, more prone to masturbation. I would make outrageous comments in class, phrased in Shakespearean English or in scientific jargon, which quite often got me beat up or harassed by the jocks. The only thing I did that might have had some positive impact on our circumstances was to write a letter to my father, begging him to send us some money. I sent it to the last address I'd had for him, with no confidence he'd ever read it.

Spence, who was a pretty close friend at this stage in my life, was in my confidence, and after our usual discussion of Dungeons and Dragons, I told him some stuff about what it was like at home. I remember we were walking slowly away from school on the last day before the Christmas break, watching our frozen breath in the still, icy air as our feet made impressions in the white, crunchy grass.

"I guess they're going to stick you in a reform school or something," he said, more matter-of-factly than I would have liked.

"Not if I can help it. I'm gonna run away if I can."

"Where to?"

"I don't know, maybe some place where it's warm. Florida, maybe." This was a deliberate lie. I intended running to Ireland, to the cottage in Leitrim. But for some reason, I just didn't think I could trust Spencer with this secret. "Heat is the main problem right now. If I just had the money for one heat fill. Even just three hundred bucks; that would get us through the winter."

"Dude, I wish I could help you, but ... I really can't do that."

This struck me like a hammer. I mean, I *was* half-asking, in a way. But I wasn't *one hundred* per cent asking. And the way he just came out and said that stung me somehow. It was like he took me for some cheap beggar. And I knew Spence had money too.

"You mean you could if you wanted to, but you just don't want to."

"Look, whatever, okay? It's not my fault your family's all messed up."

Escalation. Not the way to talk about my family.

"That's not the point. The point is you're Jewish."

"What's that supposed to mean?"

"Everyone knows Jews are cheap."

"Just like everyone knows Irish are always drunk. Like your slut mother." He said this and broke into a run before I even had time to react. To say my mother was a drunk and a slut was perfectly true, but Spence knew right away he'd crossed a line. Honour has little to do with the substance of that which it defends, and much more to do with projecting power.

A red curtain of rage descended before my eyes, and I gave chase. All my anger at the world, at the injustice of my life, was suddenly directed against Spencer Stein, whose best friendship had just been lost.

Spence could sprint, being the small and nimble type. I wasn't so quick, but I had more stamina, and he lived a long way away. I think if I had caught him, I would have beaten him as badly as my fifteen-year-old body was able. I saw him round the corner onto Fayette Street—his usual route home—and knew I'd catch him by Waverley Avenue at the latest. But he was thinking one step ahead. He turned a tight network of curves, and I just managed to keep him in sight, which brought him out onto Main Street. I knew he was losing breath fast.

He ran into the police station a step before I got him. I stood outside catching my icy breath and watched him spin some bullshit story to the desk sergeant on duty. No doubt he'd get his mom to drive down and pick him up. My rage faded away and I left.

An hour later I arrived home to the sight of a fuel truck parked in front of the house, with the big hose going around to the basement fill point. For a brief second, I thought some benefactor had decided to give my family a Christmas gift, and there would be heat after all. I thought it might have been Spence, trying to make up for his insult.

But I quickly saw my error. It was the Pezzonis who had ordered the oil for their own apartment, and whose fill point was right beside ours. A thick, Sicilian guy with dirty earmuffs and a Red Sox baseball cap was standing there looking at the gauge on the hose.

"Hey, I live upstairs. I wanted to get a fill for our apartment too, while you're here. It's that one, there. You can bill us for it."

"You gotta talk to the office, kid. I just go by the ordah list."

"Can't you just fill it now, while you're here? And send us a bill?"

"Sorry, kid, it don't work that way. Call the office."

I went upstairs. The apartment felt even colder than outside. I turned the electric oven on to heat the kitchen a bit. Then I went in to check on my mother. She was in her usual catatonic state, wrapped up in the blankets I had thrown over her that morning. A trickle of drool escaped her open mouth and ran down into her pillow. An empty two-litre bottle of vodka lay on the floor. I knew she had bedsores, but I didn't want to think about that. The scene with Spencer replayed itself in my mind, and it hit me again and again.

I walked into the living room and switched on the TV, forgetting the cable was gone. It was too cold to watch TV anyway. I went back into the kitchen and thought about eating some plain rice and corned beef from a tin. Suddenly my spirits sank. What had been holding them up 'til then I don't know. But they sank. Completely and utterly. For the first time in my life I was filled with absolute despair and hopelessness. I truly saw no way out. No way of keeping going. Without even thinking, without even knowing what I was doing, I left the apartment and walked away. As I heard the screen door slam behind me I decided that I would end my own life, right then and there.

» 17 «

"The defence will now have an opportunity to cross-examine the witness."

"Thank you, Your Honours." Art Blume stood slowly and deliberately, "the defence would like to request a few minutes to prepare questions for this witness."

"Objection, Your Honours!" Now it was Leeton Kgabu's turn to rise to his feet. "Mr Blume has had the exact same amount of time to prepare for this case as I. If he uses that time badly, this should not result in a delay of justice for the victims of VIS! The planet is demanding justice, while Mr Blume seeks to play for time."

A stir went around the courtroom. Art glanced down at the notepad and read the word "bullshit". Next to it was the seven-page file on Vinay Kumar. He was a fast reader, but, still, he'd only got as far as page five of Lisbeth's briefing. That would have to do.

"On second thoughts, your Honour, I'll proceed. My client deserves to have his innocence demonstrated swiftly."

Blume then approached the Indian man in a gentle way. "Sir, let me begin by saying that I am very sorry for the loss you have endured. Your situation, in common with the situation of a great many people on this planet, is one of difficulty and hardship. This trial, I hope, will shine a light on just how unequal the world has become. This is a responsibility we all share."

The judges were exchanging whispers.

"Mr Blume. Can you please just ask the witness a question? This is not the time to make broad statements of opinion."

It was Gomes, again, who spoke. Art nodded.

"Thank you, Your Honours, I was just getting to my first question. Mr Kumar, can you tell us a little bit about your village?"

"I have told already what happened when the virus struck."

"Oh, I know that. But I mean in general."

"What do you want to know?"

"Well, is Pendeshwar a prosperous sort of place?"

"Not prosperous, but we had our community. We were happy."

"Tell us a little about the sanitary conditions."

Kumar winced with shame. He evidently didn't want to talk about the sanitary conditions.

"We are very poor."

"Right. But, precisely, what does that mean in terms of sanitary conditions?"

"What question are you asking me?"

"How do people go to the toilet in Pendeshwar?"

"The same as everywhere else, Mr Blume. Believe it or not, Indian people have the same biology as your people in America."

"Oh, I know that. But in New York, we have flushable toilets in every apartment, in every house. When you press down on a lever, there's a system of pipes and sewage that flushes the faeces out of the toilet bowl and down underground, until eventually it reaches this massive sewage processing plant, which we New Yorkers sometimes refer to as 'New Jersey'. Have they got a system like that in Pendeshwar?"

"No."

"So how do you go to the toilet?"

"We leave the village. We dig holes in the ground and then cover them up again."

"And how far outside the village would people go? Would they sometimes not go very far, say, if it was raining, or if it they were old?"

"I find your questions distasteful."

Art shrugged. "It's not a pleasant subject. But let's move on. You have lived in Pendeshwar all your life? All thirty-four years of your life?"

"Yes."

"Then perhaps you remember what happened in August 1992?"

Vinay Kumar shrugged. "I don't know of anything in particular."

"No? Really? You mean you don't remember the heavy rains?

When the sewers overflowed in the nearby city of Kumbharwada?"

"I was a child."

"Yes, but I'm sure such an event would have been talked about for many years. The sewers broke and the water from the stream became polluted. But the people from Pendeshwar drank it anyway. They got very sick. Many died."

"I was only a child then."

"In fact, from the records left by the doctor who treated the villagers, the sickness, produced by an exposure to E. coli bacteria, had a very similar profile to the recent deaths you described in the village."

"If you say so. I am not a doctor."

"No, I'm not either. But isn't it possible that the recent deaths you have attributed to VIS were caused by something else? Something like raw sewage from the nearby city? Or just the lack of sanitation in the village itself?"

"The people died from the virus he released! Don't you understand? Our future has been murdered."

"How can you be so sure? After all, you just finished telling me you're not a doctor. However, on the other hand, I have here the medical records of Doctor Shewanar, who *is* a doctor, and treated several people from your village; the cause of death of these people is—and I quote the coroner's report—*'unknown, but likely related to sanitary conditions exacerbated by the spread of an unknown influenza-like virus.'*"

Vinay Kumar sat in silent rage. Blume paused, and took stock of the atmosphere of the courtroom. There was that nervous tension of a crowd with divided opinions.

Wang finished writing some kind of note, slid her glasses half way down her nose and shot a glance at Art. "Counsel, perhaps you could ask the witness questions which are within his sphere of knowledge to answer."

"Well, maybe if the prosecution produced some witnesses with actual medical or scientific knowledge I could do that, Your

Honours."

"Do you have further questions for *this* witness, Counsel?"

"No, Your Honours."

"Then the witness is dismissed. Thank you, Mr Kumar."

It was only when Art got back to the defence bench that he saw a handwritten note from Lisbeth. It read: *mention the WHO medical report. On page six!*

Too late now.

» 18 «

By the time I left the house that evening, it had already gotten dark. Those are the darkest days of winter and by four-thirty the light is pretty much gone in Boston. I followed the road towards Fresh Pond imagining ways of committing suicide. I settled on the idea of throwing myself in front of a truck or bus or car.

I am not a religious person. Needless to say, my parents didn't make me into a very good Catholic, and I would probably be the first to dismiss the possibility of guardian angels or divine intervention. But what happened, happened. And I cannot deny, looking back on it now, that it had all the appearance of an act of God. If you were one of my supporters (I don't mean the official FreeMatterosiNow.org campaigners, I mean the Bible-bashing variety everyone thinks of as a "Red-State Matterosi apologist"), you might even argue that God intervened to ensure I could carry out my mission years later. But I don't really believe that. My life's work was done because of, and with the aid of, hard science. God—if He even exists—has never been more than a mere observer of the fragile little planet He created for us. He might have been curious to see how things would turn out with me in particular, who knows? He may even have been rooting for me, but I doubt He has such a cynical disregard for science as to tamper with an experiment in progress.

But I digress.

Back to the winter of 1988: somewhere in that aimless suicidal ramble, I found myself on a busy, four-lane stretch of road known as Fresh Pond Parkway. This particular road is full of fast-moving traffic, and I positioned myself on the margin strip at an especially speedy stretch. The next truck or big vehicle—that's all I needed. A minute passed. No trucks came. A couple of cars whizzed by on the inside lane, too far to dive in front of. Then I saw the bright headlights of a big-sized car coming at me on the outside lane. This was it.

But just as I braced to make my dive, the car slowed, almost as if the driver could read my mind. He not only slowed, he stopped. Right in front of me, with hazard lights on. It was a big, white Cadillac, shiny and new, with New Jersey plates. The passenger-side window rolled down, and a man leaned over to me. He had that kind of Californian yuppie accent you got from Infomercials, but which you never actually heard on the streets of working-class Boston in those days.

"Excuse me! Are we in … um … Watertown, here?"

"No, this is Cambridge."

"I'm looking for … it's a place called Sexton Street. Do you know where that is?"

"Sexton Street in Watertown? Yeah, I live there."

"Oh, really? I'm looking for number 44."

"That's my house."

"No kidding? Are you Brian?"

"Yeah. Who are you?"

"My name's Jeff. You don't know me, but I'm a friend of Leo's. I mean, your dad's. You're Brian Matterosi? I can't believe I found you this easily. I mean I called the phone number your dad gave me, but it seems to be disconnected. Then I was like, how am I ever supposed to find this place? And here you are! What a coincidence. I was actually just about to give up. Hey, hop in. Are you hungry? I haven't eaten since Newark. Let's grab a bite at that place across the road."

We ate at the Ground Round, a diner I had often walked past and longingly smelled the burgers cooking. Jeff was a clean-cut, tall, long-faced Mormon-looking guy. So different to the grubby Bostonians I knew. He was the kind of person you could never imagine saying "fuck". And yet, there was something quick, something shifty about him that sort of reminded me of my father.

He talked a lot. About my father. It seemed Jeff and my dad were part of the poker ring. A "coalition of card-playing professionals", as Jeff euphemistically put it. But he was more the behind-the-scenes guy, the administrator. It was from him that I learned that my dad had got into trouble with the Mob. The way Jeff put it, the Mob guys claimed he was cheating. "We weren't technically cheating, but there's a fine line between playing really good poker and stealing from the house. And the guys who run casinos sometimes aren't too particular about where exactly that line is."

Jeff went on to tell me my dad had been physically attacked by some "pretty mean dudes, definitely East Coast mafia. Reeeal Italians. No offence. But he's in a first class facility. In a place down in Princeton, New Jersey."

"I wasn't actually in AC at the time," he went on, talking between bites of his steak sandwich. "I was taking care of the financial end of things. We had just finished a successful stint in Vegas, and I was down on the islands making a deposit. How they found us out is a mystery to me. I think they must have bugged the hotel rooms."

"Tell me about my dad. How's he doin'?"

"He's ... he's not the same, Brian. They figured he was the leader, so they gave it to him pretty bad. I'm not sure it would be a good idea for you to see him. But don't worry; the place he's in is A1. I mean, no expense spared. He's really being well looked after."

Unlike me, I thought wryly. And as if the guy could read my mind, he snapped his fingers and reached for a briefcase.

"Now comes the important part. Your dad said you wrote to him saying you were a bit low on cash. He wanted me to give this to you. As a Christmas present."

He handed me a thick envelope, which I opened immediately. It contained wads and wads of bills: hundreds, fifties, twenties. Jeff beamed at me from across the table. "Merry Christmas, Brian." Then he added in a stage whisper, "It's five thousand dollars."

I was speechless. An hour ago I would gladly have given my left arm for a hundred bucks. Like magic, this guy arrives in the very car I was going to throw myself in front of, and hands me an envelope containing an unbelievable sum of money.

Of course, it didn't occur to me at the time that the whole thing was really very suspicious. Who was this guy, and how come he was carrying five thousand dollars of my dad's money? Where was the rest of my dad's money? On mature reflection, I'm sure Jeff had pocketed the whole thing and only paid out those members of the ring who were recovered enough to ask for their money back. After all, if the bookkeeper was driving a new Cadillac, how much had the ringleader been earning on the scam? And—though I didn't know it at the time—my dad was a complete vegetable, so he wasn't about to be making any demands. But Jeff, I reckon, had had a pang of conscience and put dad in the care facility. Then he had another pang of conscience and decided to stop off in Boston and give the poor bastard's son a "big" gift. He couldn't have known how dire my situation was at the time, and he must have figured that was more than enough money for a kid like me.

I probably could have stopped right there and said *"Stuff your five grand. I want my dad's entire share, and if I don't get it, I'm calling some people in Atlantic City and I'm going to see that you get what everyone else in the 'coalition of professional card players' got."* Who knows, he may then have handed me a half a million. But I was just a kid, naïve and scarred by poverty, by circumstance. I wasn't thinking big. I was thinking of buying heating oil, of reconnecting the cable and the phone. And so I just sat there, fingering the money in absolute amazement.

"Wow, look at the time!" Jeff announced suddenly, while I was recovering from the shock. He was looking at a Rolex-clad wrist that had shot out from under a crisp, cuff-linked sleeve. "I'm actually on my way to Vermont for some skiing, and I wanted to get there before midnight, so I'd better be making tracks. Listen, Brian, it was great meeting you and uh … Merry Christmas, okay?" He threw down a fifty to cover the bill and told the chirpy little waitress to keep the change. We shook hands and that was the last I ever saw of clean-cut Jeff whom fortune had favoured at the expense of my father.

They say money won't make you happy. But as I waltzed out of the Ground Round restaurant on that cold December evening, with my belly full of cheeseburger and steak fries and my pockets full of cash, you could have fooled me. I began singing Christmas carols into the wind. I thought of all the things I would be buying for Christmas: a Nintendo, a new computer, some cool sneakers, maybe some stuff to cheer up my mother.

The next day I bought heat (I had to pay an additional fifty dollars to get the boiler restarted, but who cared about that), I sent money orders off to reconnect the cable and the phone; I even left a money order for two months' back rent for the Pezzonis. I bought my Nintendo and I bought a new dress for my mother. I bought a Christmas tree and decorated it with all the old decorations from the attic. And I still had almost three thousand dollars left. By nine o'clock that evening the apartment was toasty warm again. Two pizza boxes were open on the carpet, with a few slices remaining, and I was banging away at Super Mario Brothers, gathering virtual gold coins faster than I'd been spending the real ones.

Christmas wore on in much the same vein. I thought about my father lying in some hospital, but it would be a lie to say I felt much grief for him. In fact, I was more relieved to find out that he hadn't just abandoned me. Maybe that was because I had no real conception of his suffering, or maybe it was just the supreme selfishness of being a teenager. I don't know.

» 19 «

I spent the Christmas break playing Nintendo or reading up on higher maths: matrix algebra, techniques for optimisation, algorithms for determining numerical solutions to difficult integrals.

Back in November, I had come up with a general method for solving systems of linear equations using Jacobian determinants. I had submitted it to my maths teacher in lieu of actually doing the homework. I explained to him that solving simultaneous equations was idiot work, once you understand the basic principles of matrix algebra. He failed me on the homework, even though I showed him how the method could be used to produce the right answer. But he insisted I suffer the tedium of solving the dull, repetitive end-of-chapter problems by means of substitution, simply because he himself didn't grasp what matrix algebra was.

As I read *A Compendium of Advanced Mathematics* (a book I got for free from the throw-away bins of the Watertown public library) I was intrigued, though a bit disappointed, to find that my method wasn't original, and, in fact, had been in use for a hundred years. On New Year's Eve I hopped onto a 78 bus into Harvard Square with a pocket full of twenties and found myself a book called *Great Mathematicians in History*, which I devoured over the course of the next few days. These two books between them, read over a Christmas break at age fifteen, have provided me with the entirety of my textbook training in mathematics. I can well and truly say that the only thing public school in America taught me about mathematics was that the vast majority of people—maths teachers included—have no understanding of it.

My learning was a solace to me, it's true. It occupied hours of my time, and made me happy. It still does. I think it was my thirst for knowledge and my belief in the power of knowledge that kept me away from drugs and alcohol, a route that might have tempted me otherwise. In all honesty I never touched drugs in my life, nor smoked as much as a single cigarette, but I'm sure if I had done so I would have become the worst kind of addict imaginable. While I did drink, it never had quite the lure it held for my parents.

But no man is an island. And books are no real companions for the soul. I missed Dungeons and Dragons; I missed hanging out with Spence. The jokes, the day-to-day camaraderie. The loss of his friendship grieved me sorely.

Just how sore this loss was, I was only to find out when school restarted. Spencer was sick for a few weeks, which delayed the confrontation until the end of January. In this interim time, I was the nominal group leader, and there had been some tensions between me and Rasher. He didn't accept me as leader at all.

In the evenings Jessie was not available, and I generally smelled a rat. It was pretty obvious they were playing Dungeons and Dragons without me.

When Spencer finally did come back to school, it was a Monday morning. We avoided eye contact in German class. As Frau O'Reilly babbled on with her "*Wie geht's*" and her "*Ich heisse Jackie*", I wondered what would happen at the lunch table in an hour's time, when Spencer and I would be facing off over a barely edible Salisbury steak.

When the time finally came everyone was in their normal places. My place was empty, as I would have expected. But when I went to sit down with my lunch tray, Rasher authoritatively placed his folder down on the hard, bum-shaped plastic seat.

"It's taken," he announced. I looked at him. He glared back. I turned to Jessie. He looked a bit sheepish, but the group dynamic lent him strength of purpose.

"We don't want you sitting here anymore, Brian," Jessie announced. "Go find somewhere else to sit." This was the ultimate betrayal. My whole clique turned against me. Rasher had never really liked me to begin with, I knew that. But Jessie! *Et tu*, Jessie? As pathetic as my last-place friendships to these fellow outcasts had been, it was all I had: the only barrier between me and total social isolation.

I couldn't help but glance over at Spencer, who had so obviously orchestrated this little coup. What intrigues and false promises had he made to win over Rasher and Jessie? Who would take my place at Dungeons & Dragons now? In a way, it was predictable. Spencer had a house and a strong family structure. The playroom in the attic. His parents buying pizzas for the gang on Sundays. He also had a kind of charisma that made him the natural leader of the social group, though I was always a co-chairman. In the event, I had clearly underestimated his power, and now was paying the price for challenging him unsuccessfully.

It may be difficult if you didn't attend a suburban high school in America to comprehend just how awful being kicked off the last lunch table was. There was formal recourse, to be sure. I could have gone to a lunch room monitor (read: teacher on duty) and explained that I needed a place to sit. They would have sat me somewhere where I didn't socially belong. But this was not a practical option. You just couldn't, *couldn't* sit in the wrong place, with a teacher placing you there. The reality was I had nowhere left to go.

What did I do? To be honest, I was quite at a loss. Despite all my scholastic aptitude, I've never been able to react to situations like that quickly. I think I just stood there for a while, watching as my group pretended to be talking about something else. After a while other kids started noticing me, realising something had happened down at the geek table. It seemed to me then that the entire lunchroom had taken notice of me. There I stood: the absolute object of social ridicule for the entire second period lunch.

A blush took charge of my face, which only made matters worse. I heard some kid say, "He don't even got no place to sit." Eventually, I managed to regain enough command over my body to place the lunch tray on one of the clear-up racks and walk out. A teacher tried to stop me in the hallway, but there was no chance of that. I started running, out the door and all the way home.

Inside the house, everything was just as I'd left it. My mother was just coming out of the toilet, sick from drink. She looked at me blankly. Her eyes were so bloodshot she probably couldn't even see.

"Don't you want to know why I'm not at school?" No answer. Despair and anger welled up inside me. "You didn't even know I'm supposed to be at school today, did you?" Still no answer. "SHIT!" I kicked the wall, as hard as I could, bursting the plaster. That futile act was enough to quell my anger again.

When I'd calmed down enough, I followed her into her room and said, "Ma, I'm leavin'. I can't put up with this any more. You're gonna have to fend for yourself somehow."

Still no reaction. I left her and went into the living room. The old pizza boxes were still on the floor, along with an empty tub of ice cream. The Nintendo was sprawled out on the carpet and the Christmas tree was still up, now wilted and brown and shedding pine needles. These things that had brought me so much joy only a few weeks ago seemed so shallow and pointless now. It was time for a resolution. To leave that day and never come back.

I found an old suitcase in the attic and set about packing the essentials. A few beloved books, my birth certificate, some documents relating to my mother and father (their marriage certificate, divorce papers, my mom's birth certificate, etc.). I may have packed in some clothes too, but probably not many. My clothes were mostly rags at this stage. Of course, I took all the money. And the very last thing I packed, on a whim, was a little plastic leprechaun that had been sitting on the mantelpiece for as long as I could remember. He was green with a buckle on his thimble hat and a pipe in his mouth. And the pedestal he sat on bore the inscription, "Happy St Paddy's Day!"

When I passed by the door to my mother's bedroom she was sitting on the side of the bed weeping. In a hoarse whisper I could hear her crying, "I'm sorry, Brian. I'm so sorry." For a moment I almost went to her, to hug her and say goodbye. But something held me back.

So instead I just left. I left the yellow two-family house that had been my home for as long as I could remember, determined never to come back. It was 6 February 1989, around two o'clock in the afternoon, and I was fifteen-and-a-half-years-old.

» 20 «

"Dr Andrews, can you please describe for us the process by which the Hydra virus infects the human body?" Leeton asked.

The doctor cleared his throat. "Well, there are different strains, you know. The gamma strains associated with the Asian epidemic were slightly different to the African and South American strains, which were more localised. They were the betas and the deltas and the epsilons."

"What was the difference?"

"Mainly in the degree of infectiousness. Take for example, Hydra-gamma8, which was rampant in India at the beginning of the epidemic. Well, gamma8 was highly infectious because the receptors were not just cone-shaped, but were anchor-shaped. This allowed them to cling to the host much better. Also the virus multiplies more quickly and—crucially—it was lighter, so it could be transmitted through the air. That's true of all the gamma strains, but the other strains were really just waterborne."

"For clarification, Doctor, when you refer to the betas, gammas, deltas, alphas, you mean the engineered strains. The ones Brian Matterosi actually genetically crafted? Whereas the numbers, like the thirty-five in 'beta35' or the eight in 'gamma8', those refer to the natural mutations that occurred once the virus was released?"

"That's correct, yes."

"So in terms of Matterosi's intentions, what we're looking at here is essentially, 'Hydra-alpha1', 'Hydra-beta1', 'Hydra-gamma1' and so forth."

"We can basically break it down into two groups: the strains developed in the BetterWorld laboratory, and the strains which originated in the University laboratory. From the files we found in the BetterWorld laboratory, it seems Mr Matterosi's understanding of the mutation trajectories of each strain was fairly primitive before the anchor-shaped breakthrough."

"Can you explain in simpler language what the 'anchor-shaped breakthrough' was, Doctor?"

"Em ... yes, you see, Mr Matterosi knew the strains would mutate. He planned it that way. But the cone-shaped receptors didn't have the necessary velocity."

"Meaning?"

"Meaning they didn't mutate frequently enough to develop along a stable path that would give them a chance to overwhelm a person's immune system."

"Is there any indication that Matterosi was relying on this feature of the virus for the infection to spread?"

"Yes, I think so. First of all, it would be consistent with many of the 'mutating cures' he developed for other aspects of his biomedical research."

"Can you explain that, Doctor?"

"Before VIS, Mr Matterosi—then Professor Matterosi—was well known in the biomedical world for pioneering bacterial and viral cures for certain illnesses. There is a whole range of cancers that no longer pose a threat to human life because—"

"Thank you, Doctor, but let's stick to the question, please."

"Well, in his research, Matterosi famously posited that the most effective way to groom a cancer-fighting virus was not to develop it through RNA splicing, which is too difficult, but to estimate a likely mutation path and allow the virus to develop within the human body itself. In this way, the hosts would become the Petri dishes, allowing the development of benign viruses on a vastly accelerated scale."

"So you're telling us, Doctor, that the anchor-shaped strains of the Hydra, the gamma1s, were designed to mutate into the more effective 'gamma8s' and 'gamma35s' your team has linked with the wider fertility crisis?"

"In my opinion, yes."

"Let's talk about the outcomes, Doctor. What does the Hydra do to its victims?"

"Again, symptoms vary by strain. But, generally, most of the strains cause reactions similar to a dose of influenza. The virus spreads rapidly throughout the body, targeting host cells aggressively and multiplying. Eventually, the body is saturated; the victim usually has a temperature, headache. He or she might feel weak, dizzy, you know, often with a sore throat. Eventually the body will develop an antibody and the spread will be contained. The infection never really goes away, but the virus continues to exist in a latent state and the victim can function normally."

"What about the joint pains? The recurrent fever?"

"Those symptoms are actually relatively rare. We have seen some such reactions for exposure to the alpha6 strains, particularly in male patients. But, to my knowledge, in the later gamma strains those effects have not occurred."

"Dr Andrews, considering the direct viral effects of the Hydra—by which I am not referring to the permanent loss of fertility, but to the flu-like symptoms already described—would you say that it was able to kill its victims?"

"Oh, yes. That is to say ... certain strains are deadlier than others, but the Hydra, as a retrovirus, is a potent pathogen in any of its forms, make no mistake. Infected persons suffer high temperatures and without the right care they can easily die. Especially the elderly or children."

"Which strains are the most deadly?"

"Alpha6, as I just said. But gamma8 is certainly the most deadly from a population point of view. Without a doubt. Because you see ... because it is so infectious. It attacks the body very quickly. Anyone who is not very strong will take some time to develop the antibodies. In this period, which can last up to seventy-two hours, the immune system is very weak and susceptible to a whole range of ancillary infections."

"You have analysed the WHO data on VIS infections worldwide, is this correct doctor?"

"Yes, I have studied the epidemiological spread of VIS in some detail. Though I should stress I am not an epidemiologist."

"Thank you for this clarification. This caveat notwithstanding, can you estimate the number of deaths attributable to VIS?"

"Well, of course, we cannot be sure. Because there are many factors. And there are many strains. The cycles of infection differ across different environments. There will always be a wide margin of error."

"Your best estimate, please, Doctor."

"Our best estimate is fifty thousand, worldwide."

"So you would estimate that fifty thousand human beings have lost their lives directly because of infection from a virus which was engineered and released deliberately by the defendant, Brian Matterosi?"

"Yes, that is correct, yes."

Leeton paused to let the effect of that statement sink in. He threw his gaze up to the judges' bench, across to the public gallery, and finally over to Brian Matterosi himself. It was as if to say, do we even need to continue the trial beyond this point?

"And that's even before we consider the infertility effects?"

"Yes, correct."

"I have no further questions, Your Honours."

Wang turned to Art Blume and invited his cross-examination. The rest of the courtroom seemed to do likewise. Leeton did not turn. He was conscious of the fact that Camera Six was focussed directly on him. This was a moment to appear cool.

Blume's voice barely rose from a whisper as he said, "I have no questions for this witness, Your Honours."

That caused Leeton to look. No questions for this witness? Was Blume insane or just stupid? He saw the dark-haired girl—Lisbeth Larsson was her name—sliding a note along the table to where her boss was sitting. But Blume just shook his head at her and continued reading his notes.

It wasn't until the next morning, when a message from the senior clerk arrived at his hotel suite with the morning post and papers that Leeton managed to make sense of this. Art Blume was going to subpoena Dr Andrews as a separate witness for the defence. *He's playing for time.*

» 21 «

I stood at the front desk of the Princeton Arms Hotel: a place much less splendid than the name would suggest. The main thing that attracted me to it was its proximity to the bus stop, where I'd just been dropped off. It was nearly midnight, and the night clerk looked like he'd been sleeping when the bell rang. Judging by the number of keys hanging on the hook, you could hardly blame him.

"I need a room for the night, please."

"Oh yeah? How old are you? Like twelve?"

"Fifteen."

"What'd'you do, run away from home or something?"

"No. I'm visiting my dad."

"Shouldn't you be in school?"

"There's heavy snow in Massachusetts. School's been cancelled."

"If you're visiting your dad, why don't you stay with him?"

"He's in a nursing home." The guy looked at me for a second. He was young, like a college student, and I had the feeling he saw right through me, but just didn't care enough to make an issue out of it.

"Write your name and address on this card here. It comes to fifty-two dollars, thirty-five with tax. Cash or credit?"

"Cash."

The next morning I left my suitcase in a locker in the station and made my way out to the Longwood Care Facility, at the address Jeff had given me two weeks ago. Despite his claims of the place being an "A1" care facility, it looked more like a dump to me. The residents were mostly decrepit people, who'd been stood up on a date with death. The luckier ones hobbled around on walkers, while the unlucky ones sat in wheelchairs and looked vaguely in the direction of wall-mounted televisions. The halls smelled of old people and chemicals. Everything clanked with stainless steel sterility.

It had been nearly two years since I'd seen my father last, and I was shocked at what he looked like. He sat in a wheelchair and barely acknowledged me when I greeted him. It didn't seem as if they were taking particularly good care of him either. His hair was greasy and unkempt, and the gown he had on looked like it needed a good wash. There was still scar tissue on the side of his head, as if his skull had been broken and had grown back together, but not quite properly.

Eventually, he turned and addressed me slowly, "How'ya' doin' Bri'?" "Bri'". That's what my dad always called me. My heart surged out in a moment of filial love. He was still inside there—somewhere.

"I got s-s-sstung, Bri', ne-va, ne-va, ne-va … s-s-s-s-ssaw it comin'. What … the … dooooooo …. d-d-d-doooo—"

I started saying something just to interrupt him. I couldn't bear to hear him babble like that. "Dad, I saw your friend Jeff. He came to see me. Brought me some money."

But I didn't get a response. It was like his brain was stuck in some kind of internal cycle. He was a broken machine.

I thought back to how he'd taught me to count cards. How quick his mind used to be. He could tell you the odds on a poker hand in seconds: straight odds, crooked odds, bent odds—that's what he called odds that took into account the bluff factor. He claimed you could quantify the likelihood of a bluff. Everything was just numbers to him. He drove his car fast and had razor-sharp reflexes.

Now he was nothing but vegetable, just like my mother. I knew I should have been expecting this, but it still took me by surprise: the extent to which I was on my own in the world. My eyes suddenly filled with tears, and, before the sobs set in, I ran for the door past a concerned-looking attendant, and out of there.

Outside, I swallowed my tears, like the man I was not yet, and went back into the town, determined to keep my thoughts focused on what lay ahead.

What lay ahead was the university town of Princeton, New Jersey, which is a nice place to visit as an esteemed academic. I say this because I have visited Princeton several times as an esteemed academic since. Usually in the autumn, for some reason.

The campus is full of leafy maple trees, and when you are a Nobel-track researcher, they have friendly, pretty research assistants to compliment you on how good your latest paper was, and take your coat when you go in to eat a four-course meal in one of the nineteenth-century dining halls as the honorary guest of some tenured crustacean.

But in 1989 Brian Matterosi had made no significant contributions to microbiology. He was just a kid no one cared about. And so I found a little café and ordered a hot chocolate. It was the first moment of relaxation I had known since the lunchroom incident back at my high school. College was just back for spring term, and all around me the tables were abuzz with talk of future courses and past exams. No one took any notice of a smallish, unassuming boy with a backpack sitting on his own. I didn't feel in the least out of place.

I sipped my hot chocolate and took out *A Compendium of Advanced Mathematics*, just to look more like a student. I certainly wasn't paying any attention to the chapter, which was on homothetic transformations. But it was the moment I wandered into a lecture—Physics I think it was—that I was hooked. It was the feeling of being there that I liked. University was a place where deep and lofty knowledge was important, where it was rated highly. The people here cared about the truth, about knowing more, and they respected you for that; whereas my high school was a place where being smart was a sign of "uncoolness". A university, I determined, would some day become my home.

» 22 «

I hung around Princeton like that for the rest of that week, staying in the Princeton Arms Hotel, and spending most of my time in the student café, reading used textbooks which I bought or found lying around.

I attended various lectures, including the second lecture of the Physics 101 class I had stumbled into before. I went to smaller classes too (called "preceptories" in Princeton). You were noticed in small groups, but all you had to say was, "I'm auditing this class." At the time, I didn't know what that meant. I had a vague idea it had something to do with being part of a student evaluation corps that was checking up on the lecturers, since that's what the word "audit" meant to me.

The biology class was the one that interested me the most, since I was already at college level in that subject. In the class on microbiology I answered all the teaching assistant's questions and became an instant class pet. For my part, I would have liked to do some heavy petting with her: Karen O'Hara was her name and she was really gorgeous. She had that "black Irish" look: long black hair and pale skin with bright green eyes.

"Hey, did you, like, do biology before?" The question came from behind. It was a girl, following me down the corridor. She was not what Spence and I would have called a "fox", this girl: medium-length brown hair, glasses, kind of fat and short. But she had breasts, and she spoke to me, so I was just about on cloud nine.

"Yeah, I did it in high school last year." Perfectly true.

"So you're a freshman too? I am too. I did college level biology last year in high school. You must have too, right?"

"Yeah, exactly."

"I mean, I got an A in school, obviously. But you're like, really good."

"Thanks," I smiled at her. She smiled back. I was already in love with this as-yet-nameless fat girl.

"My name's Martha," she said, offering me her hand. I took it. It was soft and chubby and slightly moist, and wonderfully, oh so wonderfully, warm. A girly bracelet dangled around her pale wrist. The scent of her perfume reached me. I love you, fat girl named Martha.

"I'm Brian."

"It's nice to meet you." We stood there for a moment in awkward silence. It was one o'clock on Friday. She was probably just as nervous as I was, but that didn't occur to me at the time. Eventually she mustered up enough courage to ask, "Are you ... going to the cafeteria for lunch?"

My heart sank. The student cafeteria had a turnstile entrance which needed a Princeton student card to get through, a hurdle I had already fallen in front of. A very long second passed. Martha mistook my hesitation for rejection.

"Um ... I guess I'll see you later then." With that, she turned and started walking away.

"No, wait ... I, I just forgot my student card. So ... do you want to come eat some place off campus?" This time my advances were rewarded with a smile.

My heart was racing as we settled on a popular diner called The Carousel. This was my first date, and the first real chance I'd had to talk to someone since my big blow-out with Spencer, which seemed like a lifetime ago. Besides being incredibly desirous of female flesh, I was also starved for human contact. I was hungry too.

"So how are you finding Princeton so far?" Martha asked as she sipped at her Diet Coke.

"Oh, so far, so good," I answered. "How about you?"

"Well ... fall term was okay. I got a lot of compulsories out of the way. Except my science course, which is biology. Everything else is elective right now. Creative Writing. Psychology. Women's Lit. What courses are you taking?"

"Oh, mostly science subjects. Physics. Biology. Math."

"Wow, I'm impressed," she said. "You must be incredibly left-brained. Did you do your Arts compulsories last term?"

"Well, I wasn't here last term. I was in ... Harvard. I ... I transferred down."

"You made the right choice, Brian. I got into Harvard too, you know. But really, Princeton Undergrad is way better. My mom is happy too because we're from Pennsylvania, and this is a lot closer to home. She and my dad really miss me already, even though I go home, like, every other week. After Christmas they were, like, in tears."

The lunch proceeded along that vein, with her telling me details of her scholastically outstanding, but socially retarded life, while I skilfully dodged any questions that might reveal me as the high school sophomore I really was. At one stage she even asked me how old I was. I told her seventeen-and-a-half, and she said that explained it: I did look very young. Which was not something I wanted to hear.

"But cute," she slipped in innocently, which set my heart pounding again.

Even in mid-burger, I was getting distracted by intense sexual fantasies. Of running my fingers through her straight brown hair, which at that moment seemed like the most wonderful hair a woman could possibly have. Of kissing her chubby, pale skin all over. Of massaging her big, wobbly breasts ... I wanted the lunch to last forever, but eventually the waiter cleared off our plates and presented me with the bill. It was time to go.

"So maybe I'll see you again?" I suggested shyly.

"Sure. What dorm are you in, by the way?"

"Um ... what dorm? ... Um ..." I started to blush.

"It's okay, you don't have to tell me if you don't want."

"No, it's not that. It's just that, to tell you the truth, I haven't found a dorm yet."

"You mean they didn't assign you one?"

"Well, there was a mix-up with my file. Because of the transfer."

"So where are you staying?"

"In the Princeton Arms Hotel. It's just down the road."

"Wow. That's kinda weird." Well, yes. But then, everything about me was kind of weird.

"I'll get it straightened out next week." We were walking down Nassau Street, in that awkward post-date amble where every step is marked by the uncertainty of when or how the imminent parting is to come.

"So—" We both spoke at the same time. She giggled.

"You first."

It was the entrance to the campus. She was going in, I had no certain destination.

"So I guess I'll see you later, then."

"Sure. And thanks for lunch. It was really nice." I watched her as she disappeared into the campus, behind a beam of fading afternoon sunlight and across a path of crunchy, half-frozen leaves. Her big ass moving in the loose jeans that rode up over her jacket. I love you, Martha, so bad it hurts. I found the first toilet stall I could and masturbated violently, whispering her name in throes of reverent ecstasy.

There is a kind of sinking feeling that occurs in the period immediately following male orgasm (which is known as the "refractory period") in which men sometimes come to feel that the sexual activity or fantasy which they so enjoyed only seconds previously is dirty, ugly, even horrible; particularly if the orgasm was achieved by means of masturbation, homosexual or "socially deviant" activity. Some psychiatrists have dubbed this a "post-climax mood swing", and I know of at least one peer-reviewed study which attributes the phenomenon to the complex interaction of orgasm-related hormones (oxycontin, prolactin and dopamine) with psycho-social elements of sexual repression and taboo prevalent in Western society. As a biologist, I have my opinions on this theory, but this is neither the time nor the place to give them voice.

Suffice it to say that, after achieving a mind-blowing orgasm in the handicap toilet of a Sunoco gas station on Route 1 in Princeton, New Jersey, the ensuing refractory period was marked with a considerable dose of "post-climax mood swing" of the type just described. As I sat there on a dirty toilet seat with my jeans around my ankles and my spent penis slowly wilting in my left hand, the reality of my situation struck me forcibly, just like the proverbial dark cloud descending over my head.

The great "success" amounted to nothing more than having lunch with a girl who was, let's be honest, not exactly Miss America. I would probably never even see her again, and even if I did, she would sooner or later find out the truth about me: a fifteen-year-old runaway high-school drop-out, living in a hotel, pretending to be a student at a prestigious Ivy League school, spending money and hanging out in student cafés.

Talk about spending money! In less than a week, I managed to drop 550 dollars. Plus the back rent and everything else I'd been buying. Of the 5,000 dollars Jeff had given me, just under 2,300 dollars remained. I couldn't even account for how most of it got spent. It made me shiver to think what would happen when that money ran out in the not-so-distant future.

The next day, a Saturday, I was sitting in my favourite café. It was nearly empty now, because, although the building was open, the café itself was closed on the weekends. So no hot chocolate. I was reading a novel and eating Oreo cookies I'd brought with me, totally oblivious to the world outside Victorian London, when a voice recalled me to the present.

"Hi."

I looked up, and my heart jumped with joy. It was Martha. I smiled up at her.

"Oh, hi. Want a cookie?"

"No thanks, I don't eat junk food." Fat girls, it seems to me, never eat junk food.

"So how are you doing?"

"I'm good. I ... I saw you earlier ... and ... um ... I was wondering if you wanted to study biology with me. We can go to my room if you want 'cause my room-mate's not even here this weekend."

"You sure it's not a problem?"

"Oh, yeah, it's fine. We're allowed to have guests. Anyway my room-mate Jen, her boyfriend comes over all the time—" Martha blushed, realising too late how uncool a thing that was to say.

For the first time, I actually saw the situation from her point of view: an unpopular girl at school who'd made it to Princeton and was completely lost. No friends, no contact with boys. And though she might have seemed a universe older than me at first, the truth was she'd only just turned eighteen. She was almost as much a kid as me.

To me, her dorm was about the coolest, cosiest, neatest place in which you could possibly live. There were two bedrooms, occupied by two girls each, and abutting a kitchen cum living room, with a nice little table for eating and a couch area. Man, this was the life. Hanging out in a dorm like this, studying elective courses and wandering around a campus full of scholastic overachievers! Martha made us tea, and then we settled into orthogonally-positioned couches and started studying biology.

Thankfully, there was only one copy of the textbook between us (yes, she had a complete set of textbooks for all her courses!), which meant I had to slide across and lean over her shoulder. I started explaining to her the principles of cell composition, but at that moment all I cared about was the smell of her perfumed flesh, the texture of her shiny brown hair. The thought that, in all likelihood, her pubic hair had the same colour.

There were two counteracting forces at work here. The first was my desire and instinct, which was compelling me to make a move. The second was my fear and shyness, warning me not to. Caught in this tense stand-off, we studied on. We studied until the tea went cold.

"… which is the function of the endoplasmic reticulum. But bear in mind this only describes the more basic prokaryotes. We still have another class of cell altogether to talk about, the eukaryotic cells. I'll get to that in a minute—I think it's the next chapter, actually. But what's interesting from an evolutionary perspective is how structure informs the mutation processes for these different types of cells. It's almost like Nature knew how to get the optimal genetic development paths for each type of organism, and set out separate cell structures to suit."

Martha turned and looked at me. Our faces were inches apart. "Brian, you are, like, sooo smart. I'm amazed."

I held the eye contact. Her eyes were big and brown and watery. I looked at her skin, so smooth and soft. Her mouth was just ... just like a perfect little bud. And the smell of her sweet perfume captivated me, surrounded me, pulled me closer to her like an olfactory winch. In an instant, I threw caution to the wind. I reached for her far shoulder and craned my neck to her and ...

The movement was clumsy and agitated. I tilted my head one way, she the same way and our noses mashed together.

But we kissed. My first kiss. Her first kiss too. The feeling of her soft lips against mine. It was so wonderful. My arms encompassed her. There was her entire body, entirely within my sphere. I felt her hands on my back, and we kissed harder. I could feel her bra strap as my hands roamed across her back. Oh, sacred bra strap, symbolic fabric of womanhood! Thy Lycra and frilly lace border are a gateway into the land of bliss!

My hands went from her back to her head. I ran my fingers threw her silky hair, and it threw up a mild perfume of Head & Shoulders. God, I could have devoured her dandruff, her snots, her earwax, anything. All the while, we kissed and kissed.

When it finally came time to part, we said our awkward goodbyes and I skipped "home" in a state of absolute bliss, with the taste of sweet Martha Shumer still on my lips.

» 23 «

"It's really not looking good."

Art Blume, flanked by Lisbeth, Anna, Chun and Peter, was on one side of the table. Brian was on the other. It felt more like an interview panel than a prep session taking place in the middle of a trial.

Art went on. "We went over the depositions again. These witnesses they keep digging up. From a legal point of view, it's a joke. But we're losing the public relations battle, Brian. We need you to testify."

"I don't want to testify, Art."

"They need to know what kind of a person you are. They need to see the human side to the defence. You saw what they did with this little Indian schmuck this morning. The prosecution's going to treat us to one sob-story after another. Every poor bastard and their dying village in the whole goddamn Third World is gonna be in that witness stand. Christ' sake, Brian, I can't cross-examine these people. You heard me today. What am I gonna say? That they should have gotten retirement insurance? We need some human side too, Brian. We need you in the witness box."

"I've been recording a statement. It's kind of like an autobiography. I'm going to put it on the web. It really tells my story."

"Why not just take the stand? You can tell your story on the stand."

"I want to tell it my own way."

"Don't you want to win this trial? Don't you want at least a lighter sentence? You told me you had so much more to give to science, to give to the world. Don't you want a chance to do that? Christ, Brian, you can write your autobiography when you're eighty."

Art Blume tried to read his client's expression, and not for the first time. He was still not giving anything away. From what Art knew of him, Matterosi only ever became animated when he talked about his science. Too many hours spent with his head in a test tube, maybe. It's worth a try, Art thought.

"It could be an opportunity for us to mention some of your big discoveries. You know the cancer wonder drug. What's it called? Taxatram?"

"Traxamat," Matterosi corrected.

"Yeah, that's what I meant." Art had known the name of the drug full well, of course. But at least that got Brian talking. "You could explain to people what it does. How hard you worked on it. How much you wanted to save the world. All that shit."

"There's plenty of others who can talk about my research. Anyone who's anyone in med tech knows all about it. I can recommend a dozen names."

Art glanced down at the notes again. Try a different track.

"You know, Brian, even if we do win the trial, there will still be a lot of anger out there. Your safety—"

Art's eye skimmed over the briefing, and he caught sight of the name "Laura Schneider".

"—as well as the safety of the people you love—"

For the first time, Art got a reaction. Matterosi also looked at the briefing note and seemed to catch the name as well. He shifted ever so slightly in his seat. Discomfort.

"— will depend on convincing the world that what you did had to be done. The court of public opinion never really adjourns. But if we can get some convincing testimony—that could really make a difference."

"Okay," Art tapped the table, as if nothing had happened. But he made a mental note to look into Laura Schneider in a bit more detail. "We have to move on here. Let's park this issue for now. Just tell me you'll think about it."

The mask was back. Matterosi's gaze had drifted off to somewhere outside the meeting room.

"I'll think about it, Art." Art noticed Matterosi's hand was inside his pocket, and he seemed to be fumbling with something. "Listen, can I go now? There's something I want to do before Court restarts."

"Sure, whatever you want. We work for you."

Art hit the button to call security, and a minute later his client was gone.

"Peter, let's hear some press reports." Art shoved half a chocolate croissant into his mouth, and sipped absent-mindedly from the first coffee that was within his reach—which turned out to be Lisbeth's. The projector lit up to a screenshot from the British *Daily Mail's* website. It was a picture of Vinay Kumar in tears, and the headline read: 'OUR FUTURE HAS BEEN MURDERED'. In London a hundred thousand people, mostly of south Asian descent, were marching for justice. "Justice", in this context, meant Brian Matterosi's head on a platter.

Art was only half-listening to the rest of the briefing. He had one eye on the dossier they had prepared for him on Rachel Hyberg. Born 1989. Father Swedish, mother Canadian. Upbringing in a middle class suburb of Stockholm. Two siblings. Honours Degree in Psychology from the University in Lund. A stint with Volvo. Then on to Chicago for an MBA with a focus in Communications. HR manager for a Swiss pharmaceuticals company. Promoted to head of HR. Started work for GlobalSix as HR manager in 2018, switched to production management in January 2020. *Which makes her a newbie, though you really wouldn't know it.* Fluency in Swedish, English, French, German. No known romantic attachments. *Strange, doesn't fit the profile.* Hobbies: table tennis, decorative arts, including interior design, jogging and marathon running ... *wait.* Art flipped back a few pages. There it was. HR manager for a Swiss pharmaceuticals company called Medi-Discover Technologies. Art was sure he'd never heard the name before in his life. And yet, a little alarm bell was going off.

He scrawled another note to Lisbeth. *Find out everything on Medi-Discover Technologies.*

» 24 «

It would be easy for me to dismiss the love I legitimately felt towards Martha Schumer in those tender winter weeks as an amalgam of sexual desire, loneliness, and a need to find my place in a world lost to me. After all, I am a biologist, and in no other discipline, save perhaps economics, is the legitimacy of the concept of love treated with greater scepticism. We can break it down to the level of hormones; we can describe attraction, monogamy, sexual deviance, even divorce, in terms of evolutionary function. We can find eerie parallels between the biological function of mating rituals as practised by low mammals and the much-touted manifestations of so-called love in the human species.

But then again love isn't something that *can* be observed. It's a subjective feeling in the Kantian sense, which may well have its foundations in the cold reality of hormones or of mutual dependence, but in the heart and soul of the lover it takes on a context and definition of its own. Of course, it is possible for anyone to break love down into its constituent parts; anyone, that is, who is not himself in love.

And during those wintry weeks in 1989, I was completely and utterly in love with Martha. Walking through the crowded streets and thinking I caught a glimpse of her, and feeling my heart jump with joy, only to discover it was someone else, at which my heart would sink back down again. Feeling a surge and pulse just by writing her name absently in a notebook during some boring lecture. And then the precious moments when she would appear, walking towards me with her backpack and a book under one arm. I adored the way her nerdy glasses would fog up when she came in from the cold. How her cheeks and ears turned bright red when we went for our long winter walks along Carnegie Lake.

I'd managed to get myself out of the overpriced Princeton Arms Hotel at this stage, and was staying in a motel down on Route 1 which offered me a much more attractive rate: one hundred and fifty dollars a week. This still wasn't a long-term plan, but it kept me close to Martha, and that was all that mattered to me.

She didn't like coming down to the motel though, which was on a highway strip, well out of town. It was dingy and didn't at all have the "campus feeling" Martha thought appropriate for Princeton students. On top of which, our relationship very quickly reached the point where I was constantly trying to get between her legs, and she was resisting.

I continued making up lies about dorm room availability and forms getting lost in the mail. There was even an embarrassing moment in which I suggested we might somehow sneak me into her dorm. It was a cringe moment, in which I realised that love, after all, could not conquer all.

How I managed to fool her for as long as I did remains a mystery to me. My suspicion is she knew damn well, but lied to herself for the sake of not rocking the boat.

The other thing that changed was that Martha started to develop a wider circle of friends. She'd joined the drama society, and met a bunch of girls there who introduced her to smoking and beer and parties and invited her to have lunch with them.

Instinctively, I resented the loss of my monopoly, because my love was a selfish love. And so, instead of embracing her circle, and helping her to find a place within the student world, I shrank away from it, thereby driving a further wedge between us.

The preceptor for Microbiology 202 was Dr Karen O'Hara; I believe I mentioned that already. She was a genuinely attractive woman, but my involvement with Martha bled her and the rest of non-Martha womankind of all feminine charm. And as if to punish me for this unjust lack of admiration, it was Karen O'Hara who was my ultimate undoing.

The time had come to organise lab sessions and, of course, Martha and I had put our names down together. The following week, class was just finished, and Karen appeared before us as we were packing up.

"Excuse me, you're Brian, right?"

I nodded affirmation, already uncomfortable at where this was heading.

"You signed up for the Monday at three lab session?"

"Right"

"It's just that, I don't actually have you as being registered for this course."

"Oh," I responded too quickly, "that's because I'm an auditor."

"A what?"

"I'm auditing the course."

Karen paused. "So you're not actually registered?"

"No … well, I am … but … I'm sort of registered."

"Either you are or you aren't."

"It's because I transferred …"

"I mean, there's no way you can do the labs if you're not on the course. Technically, you're not even supposed to be in the classes."

"Sorry, I didn't know that."

Dr Karen O'Hara looked at me for a hard second. I must have been blushing. "Actually, what's your name? Brian … Brian what?"

"It's okay … I'll talk to the registration office."

"Um, yeah … can I see your Princeton ID Card?"

"I forgot it. I'll bring it in next time. Come on, let's go, Martha."

Dr Karen O'Hara watched our retreat with a disapproving, authoritative eye.

We made it out and walked together in silence. I wanted to break the silence, but the sense of something bad about to happen choked down anything I might have said. Our route took us down the paved campus path that led out to Nassau Street, as if we were going to eat at The Carousel, our usual dining spot. But Martha abruptly veered off to the left towards one of the dining halls.

"Where are you going?"

"To the Dining Hall." We never ate at the Dining Hall. I followed her speechlessly, but she refused to look at me.

"I'm going to eat with all the real Princeton students."

"What's that supposed to mean?"

She stopped and turned to face me. Her big brown eyes that I loved so much were filled with tears. Her breath was fast with emotion.

"You think I'm stupid, Brian? If that even is your real name. You think I can't put two-and-two together? No college dorm, no course registration, ID card for the Dining Hall always forgotten. You're not at Princeton, are you? You're a fake."

My heart sank with each word. I never quite thought of myself in those terms. But when she put it like that, it was true. I was a fake. And now it was all unravelling, as I knew it had to, sooner or later.

"So even if I'm not a Princeton student, does that make me a lesser person somehow?"

"That's not the point," the tears rolled freely off her precious, pudgy cheeks. "You lied to me. You've been lying to me about everything. Just so you could *fuck* me. How do you think that makes me feel?" She started really sobbing, and instinctively I went to take her in my arms, but she just brushed me away and marched off.

Of course, she was right. That's exactly what I'd done, no bones about it. But at the time these accusations seemed entirely unjust. Remember, I truly loved her. I was spending all the money I had to my earthly name to be close to her. I had given up my plan to go to the cottage in Leitrim, given up on the idea of returning to Boston, given up—it seemed to me—everything for Martha. And as long as I had her love, I just assumed it would all work out in the end.

I wanted to run after her, to tell her what my feelings for her were. But I guess I knew it wouldn't have mattered. We were always worlds apart. And, as if for dramatic effect, at that precise moment it started to rain in big, heavy drops. What am I doing here? All of the sudden it all seemed so ridiculous. Me standing in the middle of a place where I didn't really belong.

How weak our bond was in the end. How much I was, after all, alone.

» 25 «

I have just returned to my luxury prison: the Paleis hotel in the centre of The Hague. Outside the tinted Plexiglas windows, I can see the crowds forming everywhere. They have definitely gotten bigger since the trial started. The Dutch police seem to be better organised. They've corralled my supporters into one small part of the square below the hotel, which wouldn't have taken long; there's sadly only a few dozen of them out today. There, on the left, at the corner of my line of sight, I can see the main body of the protestors, who are all against me. Easily a thousand of them. If this sample is anything to go by, I'm doomed.

Certainly Kgabu's doing a good job of portraying me as a racist, a maniac, whatever mud he can throw. Judging from the kinds of tweets coming in, it would appear it's working. I just saw the Facebook page for 'BRIAN MATTEROSI'S ROTTING CORPSE', which a hundred million people have "friended".

And as if that's not cheering enough, my joint pain is killing me today. Maybe it's because of the change in the weather, I don't know. It's got so hot and muggy these last few days. Global warming. Seven billion people all wanting meat and fossil fuels. Someone should do something about that. Anyway, enough about that. I'll just get back to my story.

When I left Princeton after the fight with Martha, I was in a state of complete emotional trauma. I felt more lost than ever before. In my mind, she had rejected me, just like my mother and Spencer and my father, and the whole goddamn world. I cried, nominally for the loss of my lovely Martha, but really out of deeper, general self-pity. I could feel myself falling into that dangerous place called victimhood.

I hopped on a Greyhound to New York City, more by default than anything else, and roamed the streets contemplating where to go next. Such famous sights as Fifth Avenue, Carnegie Hall, Times

Square, passed before my eyes in a blur. One minute I was resolved to return to Princeton and plead with Martha to take me back, the next to return to Watertown, apologise to Spencer and humbly ask for my place back at the lunch table. I thought about my mother: whether she was still alive; idle memories of happier childhood moments followed me down the broad Manhattan sidewalks.

In a dirty puddle I saw an image of my mother's smiling face. My father was behind her tickling, her sides as she squirmed in delight. She had on a bikini and was young and very pretty. It was a holiday we'd had together, long ago. One of the few memories I had of an intact family. Somewhere warm, it must have been, like Florida. They had money, and they were young and their lives were still fresh and full of hope. Where had it gone wrong? Why had they been so easily defeated by the world? I felt a sudden longing to return to my mother, to try and rekindle some of the hope my mind reflected onto that dirty puddle.

But the past was dead. I guess I knew her life was too broken to be fixed by me. Running away was the easier option. The option of escaping to my grandmother's cottage seemed like the only one left to me. I went into an Aer Lingus ticket agent and inquired about the price of a flight to Dublin. Four hundred and sixty dollars—round trip. I had about fifteen hundred dollars left. I was halfway through booking a flight when I realised I didn't have a passport. No passport, no passage to Ireland. It was dusk, and the city was looking cold and inhospitable. I needed time to plan.

There was a tourist hostel uptown in Manhattan that only charged sixteen dollars a night in the off-season, which I thought was a good deal for a bed. It was cheaper than Princeton. There was a kitchen for self-catering, and I had the place more or less to myself. Having a decent place to stay was enough of a reason to remain in New York for a while, I decided, and so I stayed. It was a place to apply for a passport, and wait until the warmer weather came. After a week, I became friendly with one of the assistant managers, and we cut a deal whereby I could stay in a bunk for free if I manned the desk and did a few other little tasks, like taking out the trash and stuff. I had told him I was eighteen, which he pretended to believe.

It was late April and the weather had softened. A German tourist—one of many—had befriended me, and we were leaning on the railings of the ferry that takes you across the harbour to the Statue of Liberty island. His name was Matthias.

Seagulls were dancing in the sunlight, and I was chomping on a knish which Matthias had bought me. I had spun him a yarn about who I was. Not a runaway kid from a broken home, but a professional poker player, and was just in the process of telling him an anecdote made up from things my dad had told me and stuff that just sprang into my imagination. Since a lot of the stuff my dad told me was made up too, I doubt it sounded very authentic. The anecdote was reaching its climax, with me being involved in a shoot-out with a bunch of mobsters.

At some point this tall, straight-faced German swallowed a lump of his knish, and said,

"You just think out this story. Maybe so you can impress me. So to make me believe you are cool American."

This was very insulting. No one hates being called a liar more than a liar caught in the act of lying.

"Well, if you don't want to believe me," I huffed, "there's no point in even talking to you." With this I walked away to the other side of the boat. As I had been discovering, it's very easy to walk away from people you only just met. But Matthias wasn't giving up that easily. He came over to my side of the boat and leaned against the rail next to me. I thought it would be silly to move again, so I pretended to ignore him, as he rolled himself a cigarette and stared out into the sea.

"I think maybe you think out stories ... how you say it ... adventures, because you are a bit afraid people do not like you if you don't say vhat is true." No response from me to this perfectly correct guess. "I think, maybe you are ... not yet eighteen, yes? Maybe you run away from home? So you come to zis big city, yes, and you look for vhatever—I don't know—job or for becoming famous? It's right, yes?" No response from me to this partially correct guess either.

How dare this stupid Kraut challenge me like this? I looked out for another minute at the view of Staten Island in the distance, not turning to face the German even once. The engines bucked, and our ferry started pulling in to the pier. Eventually, I heard Matthias heave a sigh, and say, "Goodbye, Brian." And when I turned my head in that direction he was long gone.

I walked around the little island, not bothering to go inside the stupid Statue of Liberty, the symbol of a country I hated and was trying to escape from. There was a picnic bench which afforded a good view out over Lower Manhattan, and I sat there with my head in my hands thinking dark thoughts.

Incidentally, I find that very true about telling lies. My theory is that most lies people tell are not told out of greed or malice. Rather, it is when we are most uncomfortable in ourselves, in who we really are, that we turn to lies. Lies, you see, give us control over a world which is largely outside our control. And so we lie in much the same way as women apply make-up. Whether it does or does not make them more attractive is secondary to the control it gives them over their physical appearance.

That evening, I was on desk duty, reading a book on philosophy or politics, I think. Matthias came by on his way to the lounge room, as impassive as the cliché would have it. I caught his eye and said hello.

"Hi," he answered plainly, as if nothing had happened.

"I just wanted to say thanks for the knish."

"You already did thank me once for this. It was my pleasure."

"Did you enjoy the Statue of Liberty?"

"It was all right. It's not zat what for I come to see in America."

"What do you want to see in America?"

"Yeah ... most of all the nature. I wanna hike on the Appalachian Trail. Here, I show you." He took out a map of the Shenandoah

National Park in Virginia. Eventually we sat down together in the thick armchairs of the lobby, as if our fight had never taken place. We talked about hiking, about wildlife and trails and camping and lots of stuff. Matthias was a very calm guy, patient of manner and entirely without guile. The confrontation on the ferry somehow cleared the air, and allowed us to be more open with each other.

He explained to me how his carefully planned-out trip would unfold.

"Sounds like a great plan," I said absently. "I envy you."

"So why don't you come with me?" he asked. "I vill leave tomorrow by bus for zis town ... Damascus. From there goes the trail."

"Okay, yeah ...that'd be kind of cool. But can you give me an hour tomorrow to get my passport sorted out?"

The passport situation was a bit of a mess. I had been into the Passport Authority in New York and had "made a hames of it", as the Irish say. There was a proviso on the issuance of passports to minors that said you had to have parental consent. Instead of coming in with the permission right away, I told the official woman my mom was waiting in the car, went outside and came back with a hastily-forged letter. But at this stage she was suspicious, and told me I'd have to come back accompanied by a legal guardian. I tried sneaking up to another counter a few hours later, but the woman spotted me and reported me to her colleague. Things looked like they were going to get ugly, so I left in a hurry.

Fortunately I had a back-up plan: my Irish passport. I had learned that, since my grandmother was Irish, I was entitled to Irish citizenship, and it seemed it was pretty easy to apply for. I'd already been to the Irish Consulate and they'd sent me away to get a money order and some photos. All I had to do was drop back the next day. Little did I know that my life would one day come to depend on the decision to apply for that Irish passport. The passport of a country which would later ratify the Abuja Treaty.

» 26 «

The next witness in the "Direct Effects" phase of the trial was a World Health Organisation doctor, whom Leeton would patiently and diligently ask to explain the basic infertility effects of the virus. It was important to ensure the physical evidence was voiced in open court, not only from a legal point of view, but also from a public relations point of view. This trial, Leeton had come to realise, was an important part of a wider human catharsis. He needed to make the world understand exactly what Matterosi had done, so that when the conviction came, they would at least benefit from the sense of justice it would bring. Compared to what they had lost, it was perhaps not much. But it was all Leeton could give them.

"Dr Simms, please explain to the Court exactly what Viral Infertility Syndrome does to the human reproductive capacity."

"The invasive virions that cause the actual infection—called the Hydra—vary according to the strains. I believe you have already heard evidence concerning these. But what is common to all strains of the retrovirus, and what is utterly unique in the known viral world, is that when the virus reaches the maturation phase, a second type of virion is released through lysis with those host cells that have the right coding, and following a sort of programming engrained in its mRNA. This second type of virion, which is the part that is actually shaped like a 'Hydra', has a series of tentacles, each one with anchor-shaped receptors which are perfectly-sized to attach to the flagella of human sperm.

"In men, these Hydras attach to the sperm and render them immobile. They don't actually kill the sperm, but they stop them from moving, which makes them useless in terms of getting to the egg. In women or girls, the spearhead front part of the Hydra becomes active as they approach the ovaries, specifically they latch on to the cells containing the DNA repair gene BRCA1, causing it to malfunction, thereby leading to a vastly accelerated decay in ovulation."

Leeton smiled generously. "I'm afraid, Doctor, you've lost us. Can you explain all that in simpler language, perhaps?"

"When the virus has saturated the body, it releases a second type of virion, or viral body. This viral body is specially designed to attach itself to sperm cells and stop them from travelling. The same virion also enters the ovaries of women and attacks their in-built repair system, making it impossible for them to create new eggs. It basically forces women, even girls, to enter the menopause as soon as they get the infection."

"And in your opinion, is this infertility effect a deliberate design feature of the virus?"

"Oh, without any doubt."

"Why without doubt?"

"Well, for one thing, we have the logbooks from the BetterWorld labs, which show that Brian Matterosi drew pictures—by hand—of the shape of these Hydras before he went about cultivating the viral RNA that would make them come into being.

"And then we have the 'dot r-o' files from his replication software that show the results of the cultivation process. The 'factory', as he refers to it in his notes. Billions of individual mutations, each one registered and recorded by his computer system and compared with his prototype design, until he chanced upon just the right sequence of code to create what he had already sketched out on paper."

"Would you say he got lucky?"

"No. With enough repetition, achieving a given result becomes a statistical certainty. Once you create the system to encourage the mutations, sooner or later you will get what you are looking for. We know from the files and the records that it took Brian Matterosi a pretty intensive six months of trial, with advanced instrumentation and three thousand separate samples, working around the clock, to make the Hydra do exactly what it does."

"A deliberate, calculated effort, expending enormous resources, in order to create a virus perfectly adapted to stop human beings from having babies. Is that what you are saying?"

"Yes."

"Thank you, Dr Simms. Your Honours, I have no further questions for this witness."

"Thank you, Counsel. The Court will adjourn for lunch. We reconvene at 14:30."

» 27 «

Once my passport was sorted, I bought a sleeping bag and some boots and went to Virginia with Matthias the German. For weeks we hiked the hills and mountains together as the days grew long and warm. Nature was alive and verdant: the science of real life. I think that hiking trip did much to stimulate my true love of biology, not just the theory of textbooks, but the actual biology that thrives around us at all times. This was the stuff of field scientists; something I would have scorned a year previously as the refuge of naturalists—only one step above bird watchers.

Of course, such snobbery is foolish. For all science begins in observation and wonder, and that is what is best in nature: to sit and observe a chipmunk or a robin; to poke a big fat porcupine with a (very long!) stick, as it sits on the low limb of a knotty oak tree; to have the clear cold water of a mountain brook drain all feeling from your toes. It was a whole new world to me; a complete escape from the suffocating living room carpet and the endless HBO movies of my former childhood.

The weather was nearly perfect, rising to just above 27 or 28 degrees in an afternoon sun that baked away your trail sweat as you rested on some island of rock and ate a granola bar. And yet it was cold enough to leave most of the mosquitoes (those suckers-away of the life's blood of outdoor tranquillity!) unhatched in their colonies of eggs. We camped in Matthias's tent and cooked pasta on Matthias's little gas cooker. Sometimes we stayed in trail huts.

I have seen much in the way of natural beauty in my travels around the world, but there are few places that can top the Shenandoah National Park in Virginia. It has a lushness that speaks of the South, and yet a ruggedness that speaks of Northern wilderness. Matthias and I walked together for days on end, sometimes chatting non-stop, sometimes hardly speaking a word, just enjoying the splendour of nature. Shenandoah means "the princess of the stars" and in the evenings, Matthias played his flute by a campfire, while I lay on my back and watched those distant suns twinkling in the black firmament. Even now, when I see a clear night sky (something that does not exist in Western Europe, due to all the light pollution), I close my eyes and think of those cool nights in the Virginia Mountains, and I hear the soft notes of that flute drifting through my mind again.

This was a happy period in my life. The woods are a world unto themselves, a world that didn't judge me, demean me, or force me into some social grouping. I found out I had a natural hardiness and resilience to cold that made me suited to the outdoor life. My feet grew hard and callous; my skin turned the rusty gold of my father's Sicilian forebears. I stood 5 feet, 11 inches and in perfect physical condition. For a while, I forgot about my silly dream of going to Ireland; of running away to a country completely alien to me just because there was some cottage out there. Matthias had shown me a forest path which seemed to be taking me somewhere happy and safe.

Grown men you meet as a teenage boy and who want to travel with you, want to spend time with you, want to spend their hard-earned money feeding you and providing you with shelter are usually either one of two things: Jesus freaks or homosexuals. And it's usually the latter.

I don't mean to sound homophobic, but if you are a wayward teenage boy you do get to thinking all men are gay, simply because these are the only men who will have anything to do with you. The other kind, I suppose, are spending time with their traditional families, getting hen-pecked by their wives or hitting on their secretaries at work.

Matthias, as it turned out, was both a Jesus freak and a homosexual. I found out about the Jesus bit first, being the less private and embarrassing issue for us to broach. It became the subject of many serious debates between us. I was the proponent of hard science, explaining to him how religion was a repressive social instrument based around a bunch of flimsy fairy tales and constantly being adapted to suit the expediency of its paymasters: guarantees of eternal life to the impoverished peasants, while the so-called holy men lived lives of gluttony and sexual abandon, laughing into their silken habits at how well the pyramid scheme was working.

"You think of Jesus and Mohammed as prophets. But let's take an evolutionary perspective on this. Imagine Christianity and Islam were just two biological systems. Systems of Faith. The question is which system will thrive? Answer: the one best suited to the habitat of its followers.

So, down in warm Arabia and the Maghreb, Christ says, "God alloweth ye to eateth pork!" What happens? His people eat pork in the festering heat and are more likely to contract trichinosis and die. Over time, the non-pork-eating followers of Mohammed start outbreeding the trichinosis-infected Christian competition.

Meanwhile, up in Roman Gaul, Mohammed says, "God forbideth eating pork!" Since home-fires burn year round in cold, fuel-abundant Gaul, meat tends to be well cooked and the risk of getting trichinosis is negligible. Colder weather conditions also help preserve the meat longer. So, therefore, Jesus's followers enjoy the relative advantage of being able to keep and eat the flesh of the versatile and efficient farm pig, and so they outbreed the Muslims up there. What's the result? Christianity spreads in cold, Northern Europe; Islam spreads in the warm Mediterranean and Middle East climates. This is biology, not the Word of God."

Matthias looked long into the fire, unmoved as I concluded my homily with this triumphant turn of phrase. I rewarded myself with a satisfying bite into a lump of our trail bread. Body of Christ.

"I think … " he began slowly, "that one faith can blind you to the presence of another, if you are truly believing in this, yes. For you, biology is a faith. My faith, it is the Word of the Gospel. Why you seek to have this science as truth? This is because you want something … strong … something you can trust to be a certain way. You have had maybe a difficult time as a boy, Brian. You are seeking some kind of strong ... thing, yes, to believe in. For you now, science is such a strong thing.

"But also you can trust in love, Brian. The love of Jesus Christ for us is something strong. At the core of Christianity is the message of Christ: that he died for us, suffered for us, because of love. If you would live life by this message, it would make you strong."

"Hold on, you say I have faith in science because I'm looking for something strong. What if I have faith in science because it just makes sense?"

"And love? Does not it also make sense? Forgiveness, sacrifice, healing? This things do not they also make sense?"

"No. I mean ... maybe ... but that's not the point. Look, if you love someone who has a serious infection, you want them to have antibiotics, right? Did Christ conjure up antibiotics? No, it was hard science. Microbiology, in fact. You can't deny this."

"But what brings us this ... all this medicines and so on, if we wouldn't have the love? What for a world is it, in which we are having all this ... materialism ... but not any love? Jesus spoke of this materialist world, because it has not too much changed in our day, you know. Of greed, or this success, yes. Back then the Romans and the Persians fight for controlling the world; today it is the Americans and the Russians. But God tells that we must live above this.

"Look at us now, here. You and me. We live so simple, just sitting on a down tree, yes? A little bit to eat—not too much, yes? Some little music, and just to live in the nature. This is what it means to walk in the path of Jesus. What for a world do you think would be better? If everyone would be living like us now, but without the antibiotics? Or if everyone would be living with the antibiotics, but there would be also only war and greed and hatred?"

"Why not have both? Antibiotics and peace?"

"Yes, maybe this. If it would be possible."

We returned our gaze to the slowly smouldering flames which to me were an exothermic oxidizing chemical reaction, and to Matthias the light of the Glory of God. But to both of us they were hypnotic; for a man who is at peace with himself desires no more distraction than to stare absently into a fire.

» 28 «

Leeton watched with mounting annoyance as Art Blume began his cross-examination by trying out his cheap, American trial tactics on yet another world-renowned, well-respected witness.

"Dr Simms, you mentioned that Brian Matterosi took nine months to develop the Hydra retrovirus. This was from September 2015 to May 2016, correct?"

"Yes."

"So if he had the virus fully developed in 2015, why did he continue to develop the different strains? Why was he still at work in the University in 2016, if all this was done already back at the BetterWorld lab?"

"Well, the Stage Two virion—the Hydra—was developed early on, as you say. This piece of the puzzle he could then slot into the primitive virus as a separate string of mRNA—"

"Sorry, Doctor. Can you explain what mRNA is?"

"mRNA is the code which makes the virus do what it does. It's sort of like a string of very specific instructions. These instructions are written in their own special language: the language virologists speak. And Brian Matterosi speaks it incredibly well."

"Thank you, that's a little clearer. Please continue."

"Well, as I said, he knew how to make the Hydra work early on. But what Matterosi apparently struggled with, was finding a form of infection through which he could spread the infertility-causing cells. A launching pad, if you will."

"And these were the various strains of influenza he cultivated?"

"Yes. They were, in effect, adaptations of the flu virus."

"Surely isolating an influenza virus is a pretty easy thing to do?"

"Well, yes, but getting it to do exactly what you want is not so easy."

"What do you mean?"

"Flu viruses are very hard to control."

"Like the old saying: they can put a man on the moon, but they still can't find a cure for the common cold?"

"Exactly. Presumably Brian Matterosi was experimenting with ways to achieve more control."

"Do you mean because he was afraid the Stage One virions would not do the job of spreading the infection throughout the host?"

"N … no … I don't think that was a problem. Pretty much any flu virus will do that very effectively."

"So then why would he have been so obsessed with control?"

"Well, I don't know. I wasn't there. However, he's sitting right next to you. So why don't you just ask him?"

A murmur and some laughter went around the courtroom.

Art just smiled.

"Because, Dr Simms, you're the one giving testimony right now. You're the expert witness, and I want you to answer the question, not Dr Matterosi."

"And I told you I don't know."

"But you can speculate?"

Dr Simms shrugged. "I wouldn't like to do that."

"What about the logbooks. You've read them. Was there any indication of why he was playing with the Stage One virions for so long?"

Dr Simms shrugged again.

Blume asked again, "What do the logbooks tell us about why he was casting different strains of the virus?"

"There is no clear description of what he was doing in the logbooks."

"Oh, come on, Doctor, you're playing games with me now!"

"Mr Blume, I'm answering your questions as accurately as I can."

"Fine, then let's try it this way around. Does it seem probable that Brian Matterosi experimented with different strains of the influenza virus because he was trying to find a form of the infection that would minimise any risk of unintended casualties to the infected persons?"

"That's speculation."

"But is it probable?"

"I don't know what's probable. He's a madman. Anything could have been going through his mind."

"Do the log books support the conclusion that he deliberately infected himself with certain strains to test their potency on the human body?"

"He deliberately infected himself, yes. As to why, ask him."

"And can you read, for the benefit of the Court, the entry from 3 May 2016?"

The court clerk passed Simms a copy of the log book.

Simms put on his glasses and read: *"Injected 20 ml of VB23=H into vein, right arm, at 16:32. Body temperature normal. Blood sample taken 21:20 shows infection evolving at beta-squared 16 mms. Respiratory effects so far minimal. Temperature rising to 38.5. Pain is acute, likely from inflammation in the lower back and shoulders."*

He stopped and took off his reading glasses. Art motioned for him to continue reading. With a frown he read on.

"4 May 2016. 05:36. Blood sample taken at 05:10 shows infection at saturation. Temperature elevated to 40.3. Respiratory effects normal. Virulence of inflammation unacceptably high. Abort use of this strain."

"So Brian Matterosi infected himself with a test strain and found it to be too dangerous to use as a launching pad for the Hydra. In other words, he put his own life at risk to avoid risking the lives of others. Is that a fair assessment, Doctor?"

"I think that's a very twisted way of putting it. He didn't have to develop the virus at all, if he didn't want to risk people's lives."

"And yet, given he was developing the virus, the evidence suggests he really did try to avoid casualties. No further questions for this witness, Your Honours."

» 29 «

I found out about Matthias being gay by degrees, I guess. It was little things he said, the way he kept looking at me when I went skinny-dipping in a mountain stream. He took a lot of pictures with his Polaroid camera, of me, posing with my back to various scenic vistas. In fact, I still have one of those pictures, and, now, as I speak, I'm looking right at it. It shows a smooth-skinned boy with a sun-browned smiling face, not quite fully bearded. His cheeks are still childishly pudgy. In all, he looks a lot less manly that I remember feeling at the time.

And the boy is wearing cut-off jeans and a loose-fitting, worn-out Marlboro T-shirt, a last relic from the cigarette carton days. He's leaning against a big rock with something scratched into it that cannot be read. It is hard not to see the homoerotic dimension in the way Matthias positioned the camera on me, and maybe I knew what his motives were even then, but I was not entirely honest with myself either.

One night as we were lying in the tent, I had one of my impossibly itchy hard-ons. I was pretty sure Matthias was asleep, and so I slipped my left hand down into my sleeping bag and attempted to relieve myself in as inconspicuous a manner as possible. Though it was dark, I closed my eyes in order to better visualise whatever sexual fantasy I was indulging in that particular night, and attempted to keep my body from rocking too much. The climax came and I felt the tension ease away.

As I lay there, I suddenly realised Matthias was wide-awake beside me. I don't know how I knew this, for it was pitch black. But I knew it; I knew he had witnessed my entire masturbation episode in studied silence.

It made me quite uncomfortable. Gayness was something totally dirty and forbidden, something no one in my home town would even mention in anything, but a jocular, derisory context. The very thoughts of him being gay scared the wits out of me, I think. It also cheapened the context of our friendship somehow. I suppose I felt the way women often feel, when men see them merely as sexual objects: the way Martha Shumer must have felt, for that matter.

It was early June, and the very next day true summer broke down on us unexpectedly. We were on a trail deep in the Shenandoah Valley close to the border with Pennsylvania. Around midday we came across a cool, mountain stream, and as we bathed I became aware of his attention. Embarrassment and confusion drove me out of the water and back into my shorts and T-shirt.

At night it was hard to get comfortable. If you stayed completely in your sleeping bag, you'd sweat and itch; if you lay uncovered, the sweat would dry into a cold film, and you would shiver in a sudden breeze. The mosquito netting was the only thing between us and being buzzed out of our minds. At first, I slept lightly, half-hearing the sounds of the muggy woods through my dreams. But fifteen trail miles is a great sedative, and eventually I drifted off into my usual deep slumber.

My body bucked in response to an unexpected touch upon my bare skin. A hand underneath my T-shirt, gliding over the contours of my back. It was a caress so gentle I thought of Martha. And the sweetness of being touched like that came before the realisation of whose touch it was, and what it meant. A gay hand on my back.

My heart jumped at the thought. But there was no battle of conscience. Or at least if there was, it was so brief I don't remember it. We were, after all, a hundred miles from the nearest human settlement; it was completely black inside our tent, and I was an anonymous runaway in a world that never particularly cared what I did. Whether out of pure lust, curiosity or cowardice, or maybe just that basic human need of having physical contact with another human being, I took hold of that hand and guided it down to my raging-hard penis. The hand became a mouth, and a few thoughtless moments of pleasure later I was no longer a virgin. As the hand returned to touch my skin, I was already regretful of what I'd done.

My body twisted away in disgust. And the hand retreated, leaving me to a minute's spent, dirty regret, before I drifted back off to sleep.

That morning there was a very embarrassing avoidance of eye contact. We walked in silence until the afternoon.

Though I had believed us to be in the deepest depths of forest the day before, we were in fact quite close to a cleared, settled valley, dotted with horse farms. A dirt road led to a paved road which led to a town. It was a colonial Virginian town, painted white with cannons on the lawn in front of the town hall. It was the kind of place overpaid Federal government workers retire to after a career in Washington DC. Matthias went into the village store and bought us some treats. Oranges, cold cuts, fresh white bread, chocolate bars; these are the things you crave when you're walking on a trail for a long time. He set them out on the floor of the gazebo in the town square, along with his backpack, and walked off to find a toilet.

The food just seemed like a detestable bribe, like payment for the blow-job he had given me. My appetite faded. As he crossed the road I saw the patterned sweat stain of his T-shirt where the backpack had hugged him, outlining the muscled contours of his powerful, twenty-five-year-old back. Gay! A queer, a faggot! And he did it … to me. It didn't bear thinking about for more than a second.

Exactly what ideas and feelings were rattling around inside me during those long three minutes I can no longer say for sure, but somewhere in that porridge of fifteen-year-old hormones and fears I must have felt that the only way to reclaim my straightness was to punish Matthias for what he'd done. To betray his kindness and friendship. And I gave it no more thought than that.

I reached for his backpack and fished through the various items which were by now utterly familiar to me. There was his wallet. Together with the key to the locker containing my suitcase in New York I took it and ran as fast as I could away from the town, down the road in the direction of the interstate.

There was a sickly pleasure in leaving behind my own backpack, with my own few threads of worthless clothes and my dirty sleeping bag and baggies with their half-eaten contents of dried food. The very items that had weighed so heavily on my physical frame all those footsore miles were just gone—abandoned—like the rest of my life. It gave me false power to know I could escape from things that easily.

I hitched a lift to the next big town, all the while peering around for police or an angry Matthias. But no one came after me. I cast one last glance around as the doors of the Greyhound bus closed, and the bus engine roared into action. On the next bus somewhere on I-95 outside of Philadelphia I dared to open his wallet for the first time. It contained a hundred Deutschmarks, three hundred and fifty dollars and a bunch of cards and tags in indecipherable German. It also contained the aforementioned picture of me against the big rock.

At the time I'm sure I thought of Matthias as a villainous sexual predator; a fully grown man in complete control of his world and his emotions. He had money, opportunity and complete security in life. The notion that he was little more than a boy himself, confused about his feelings and struggling to find his own place in a big, scary world: this idea never occurred to me for a second. I felt no guilt at what I did to him. I just took the money and carried on, leaving Matthias on the growing tab of people left behind, alongside Spencer, my mother, my father and Martha.

Two days later I boarded an Aer Lingus 747 Jumbo jet at JFK airport. A smiling stewardess took the boarding card from inside my brand new Irish passport. It was 12 July 1989, the eve of my sixteenth birthday. The sun cast slanted rays through the little aircraft windows, reflecting off the stainless steel seat belt buckle which sat on top of yet another raging hard-on. The captain mumbled something about runway clearance into the PA system. Runway. Runaway. I was running away again.

» 30 «

The next witness was a detective with the German Federal Criminal Police. She was blonde and somewhat pretty, though very Germanic. Leeton decided he would get through her quickly enough. She was just there to testify to one thing and one thing alone.

"Detective, please describe for us the scene you found at the microbiology laboratory in the University of Göttingen when you entered the facility at 04:34 on Friday, 11 August 2017."

She answered in German, causing all five judges and almost everyone else in the courtroom to scramble for their headsets. In the simultaneous interpreter's booth overlooking Court One Leeton could see a middle-aged woman with headphones on. She was stooped into a microphone and fed them back the words in English.

Rachel Hyberg was the only person who seemed prepared for this linguistic transformation. She had arranged for the simultaneous interpretation to be fed straight into the live camera stream, so that, at the same time as the judges, Leeton and the rest of the world could hear Chief Inspector Jana Schroeder of the Göttingen police say:

"We entered the facility, yes, as you say it was 04:30 in the morning, and it was still dark. The offices were mostly empty, but in a few there were scientists working. We asked that everyone remain in their places and not move, but also not touch anything they were working on. The scientists seemed very surprised to see us. We had photographers, and they took pictures of everything right away. The man who had answered the door to us, to whom we had shown the warrant, directed us to the virology facility of the lab on the second floor, where we found Mr Matterosi. Here we paused to allow the technicians to take clean samples. The Court Order and the mandate were very particular on this point. Then we entered.

"At first we did not see him. He was lying, curled up inside a metal cabinet, in just a T-shirt and shorts. His clothes were soaked in sweat and he stank."

"Of what?" Leeton interrupted.

"Excuse me?" the German policewoman seemed a little confused by the way the simultaneous interpretation worked.

"You said Mr Matterosi stank. What did he stink of? What was the smell?"

"Of vomit. And urine. It was so strong you could smell it even through the bio-masks." She paused, but as Leeton asked no further questions, she went on.

"We could also see dried vomit on the cabinet shelf. He did not lift his head. At first we did not know if he had noticed us or not. But then he said, in quite good German, almost no trace of an accent, 'I'm guilty. I did it. Arrest me.' He held out his wrists, and for a second I did not understand why. Then I realised he expected me to put him in handcuffs."

"And did you?"

"Of course not. He could barely move. There was no chance that he would run away. We called the medics. They had fresh clothes. His T-shirt and shorts were removed and kept as evidence."

"Did he say anything else?"

"Yes. He said the masks would not be much use to us. I asked him what he meant by this and he answered 'You are probably already infected.' Then he fell unconscious."

» 31 «

When you first come to a different country, what strikes you most is the sheer, delightful newness of little details. I remember emerging into the arrivals hall in Dublin airport and seeing the different advertisements. In the little newsagents there was a rack of chocolate bars I had never seen nor heard of before: something called a Double Decker. Another one called a Twirl. A Lion bar. None of that existed in the States. The girl in the newsagents wore a funny little uniform too. No one in newsagents in Boston had uniforms, I thought. The shape of the plastic seats in the arrivals hall and the clothes people wore were different. Even the lettering used on the signs in the airport was in a font I had never seen before.

And that difference was something wonderful to me. They say you cannot run away from your problems, but as I arrived in Ireland, it sure felt like I had done exactly that.

When I stepped outside to where the buses stopped, the cold rain hit me. My last outdoor experience had been entering the terminal building at JFK airport, where temperatures were over thirty degrees. And so my body was completely unprepared for the temperature change.

It was also a different kind of rain to anything I'd known before. The close sky was bright and boisterous all around me, with vast low clouds threatening rainbows between patches of clear blue. From no cloud in particular a rain-like vapour fell, as if the air itself was raining instead of the clouds above it.

In America rain is a separate phenomenon to atmosphere, but in Ireland it falls with the air, as one, bound to the very oxygen you breathe. It sits on top of your clothes like an outer layer of garment. It moistens your eyes without you having to blink. It penetrates somehow into your bones, making you cold even when the temperature doesn't warrant it.

But it is soft, the Irish rain; just like the grass it keeps green four seasons long. Soft and somehow forgiving, like the accent of the person I met as I sat on the double-decker bus for the first time, an old man who passed me the time of day the way Irish people used to do back then.

The suitcase was a real burden. It was not only heavy, it was also awkward to lug around, having that uncomfortable shape that made it bang into your leg as you walked. I was on a road on the outskirts of Abbeyleix, County Laois, hitchhiking my way through the hedgerows and villages of the Midlands: the flat, largely forgotten centre of Ireland. I was conscious of how the suitcase made me look less like a dynamic young wanderer, and more like a homeless person. Really, I needed one of those giant rucksacks the Canadian summer tourist kids always sported.

But the Ireland of that time was actually a good place to hitchhike. Though cars were few and hitchhikers many, you didn't wait long for a lift. There were all kinds of odd people on the narrow roads that cut and banked through the steep, verdant hedges. They drove old cars strewn with rusty tools and newspapers caught in the ripped upholstery of the passenger seat. They had farmed in Monasterevin, laid bricks and blocks in London, drove taxis in New York and somewhere in between they'd learned an awful lot about the meaning of life.

One character who stuck in my mind from that journey was a lonely bachelor farmer I had a meal with. It was in the sitting area of the grubby two-room cottage and he was cooking sausages on a type of stove known as an "Aga", which ran on solid fuel and was his only form of heating and cooking. His method of preparing the food I shall never forget. He spat in the frying pan to moisten the sausages. Out of politeness or some warped sense of wanting to fit in, I forced myself to eat them from the dirty plate he offered me as he told me stories of his chequered past in the British Merchant Navy. It was impossible not to look at his fingers: the long, claw-like nails and the pulps of his fingers were completely stained yellow from decades of smoking unfiltered cigarettes. If this was the

Ireland I had imagined, my imagination had edited out the smell of an old seaman rotting away in a crumbling cottage miles from the sea, the foul breath of his dying sheepdog and the knottiness of his arthritic knuckles. And yet for all that, his hospitality was infinitely superior to what a sixteen-year-old runaway could expect to receive from Irish people nowadays, now that they've got a little bit of money in the bank.

I drank his tea and listened to his stories. That night he let me sleep in his shed, and I had my first introduction to that most Irish of wild animals: the rat. The Irish countryside is festering with these ingenious rodents, more human than animal in their spirit, their omnipresence and their insight. I am convinced that if our species fails—and despite my interventions it must inevitably do so, sooner or later—then the next dominant species will evolve from rats. It was not our much vaunted human intelligence that enabled us to spread our presence across every corner of the globe, nor even our opposable thumbs; it was what we share with rats: our exceptional ability to adapt.

That short July night was punctuated with a half-dozen visits from one or more of those beady-eyed creatures. I can still recall that moment, lying breathless in the hay and watching one small eye gleam with a thin sheen of light.

» 32 «

"I don't want you to mention her, Art, okay?"

This was the most animated Blume had ever seen his client.

"Right, yeah, I know, Brian, but just listen. This isn't about your love life. It's about putting together the best defence we can. And because of Laura Schneider's association with the lab, her management role ... if we can cast any kind of a shadow of a doubt over who did what at BetterWorld—"

"There is no doubt, okay? I confess. I did it. I acted alone. I ran the lab and I engineered the virus. The log books show my signature. My fingerprints are all over the goddamn vials. She was never even in that room, okay? Anyway, most of the engineering of the active strains, the ones responsible for mass contagion, took place in the University lab, after I'd left BetterWorld. I told you that before."

Art marvelled at how Brian remained stubbornly loyal to this woman, after all that had happened. *We guys are such schlemiels,* Art thought.

"The thing is, Brian, we've found inconsistencies in the—"

Brian hit his fist against the table, causing Peter to look up from his notebook in alarm.

"Drop it, okay? No mention of her. That's non-negotiable."

"Okay. Okay, if that's how you want it. It's your neck in the noose. But she could come up anyway, you know. The prosecution might even subpoena her."

"Why would they do that? Didn't you just say her involvement makes the case against me more complicated?"

"Depends on the evidence she presents. I mean I can't really one hundred per cent say, since you won't tell me what actually happened. I'm kinda in the dark here, Brian."

"I've already told you what happened."

Art winced and shook his head. "You told me an edited version of what happened. But I know you're leaving stuff out. The thing is; I'm your lawyer, Brian. I need to know everything in order to be able to help you. Especially if she ends up testifying for the prosecution."

Once again, Art observed the movement in Brian's otherwise impassive expression. An extraordinary person he must be, who cares more about protecting others than about his own defence. When he finally did answer, Matterosi had managed to regain his composure.

"We'll cross that bridge if and when we come to it. But as far as our case is concerned I want us to be perfectly clear on one thing. I don't want you to mention her name or ask any questions of witnesses that cause her name to be mentioned. Otherwise I will fire you and get a lawyer who listens to my instructions. Is that understood?"

Art nodded soberly and shrugged. "Understood."

» 33 «

Day broke with no discernible dawn, and as I thought to slip away unnoticed in that pale grey light, the old man appeared in front of me with a broad grin. Something about my night in the hay shed amused him. I declined his offer of a breakfast, which I imagined would be fried in the same trusty old pan, and so we parted ways. Several footsore miles punctuated with an arse-sore lift on a tractor got me to the town of Mullingar, roughly in the geographic middle of the island.

Here I had my first introduction to an Irish council housing estate. For anyone who has not seen them—and I believe they have not changed much in the intervening years—Irish housing estates are remarkably dull, with endless terraces of identical stucco-fronted, two-and-a-half bedroomed houses surrounding open plots of grass in which a whirlwind of plastic bags blow perpetually in all directions. They were built, "on the cheap", by the government to house the "lower class" of society: the welfare recipients and those generally dealt a losing hand in the great card game of life. Social housing looks crummy everywhere, but in Ireland it looks both crummy and miserably cold at the same time.

In every such Irish housing estate, there was a local gang of ruffians who made mischief and terrified the old people. Sometimes bands of responsible men got together and "sorted them out", but in the late 1980s most such men were still over in England, America or Australia, stacking bricks for union wages.

With their gel-slicked hair and their shiny track suits, the youths congregated at factory gates and sought out opportunities for potential mischief. When a scruffy-looking, tanned sixteen-year-old with odd clothes wandered into their sights, lugging a suitcase awkwardly, it was like a holiday from the dull routine of their usual hooliganism.

I was not alert to the danger, because I had not yet been culturally acclimatised to know which neighbourhoods meant which kind of trouble. But that didn't stop the trouble from finding me.

"Are you goin' on a trip? Ya' missed the road to th' airport, boy." I only half-understood the heavy accent, and just ignored it.

The next thing, a sharp pain seared through my left leg, followed by the thud of a stone on the footpath in front of me. It took me a second to realise where the missile had come from. As I looked to that location, and saw the gang of four townie teenagers, my first reaction was they don't look very dangerous. They were relatively small and weedy and seemed somehow ridiculous in their shiny Adidas tracksuits. In my American eyes, urban danger was black and big, not stunted, pale and Irish.

No doubt these local Midlands ruffians wouldn't have fared particularly well in a turf war with the black gangs of 1980s Boston, but that fact was of little avail me then. I saw an arm cocked and another rock whizzed by my head.

I decided the best option was to walk away briskly. They followed. "Here! You boy! I'm talkin' to you, boy." I broke into an awkward run, limping into my suitcase with every stunted stride. They had no trouble catching up to me. The boldest of them body-checked me.

I tripped and released my suitcase, screaming "Just leave me alone!" in a voice that betrayed my sense of panic.

"Are ya American? Fuckin' hell, lads. Yankee fuckin' Doodle, right here in Mullingar, boy." He stood right in front of me and glared at me with clear blue eyes set deep in his pasty, zitty face. His short hair was jet black and waxed down against his pale white skull. You could see the zits that grew even under his hair.

An old lady was walking along the other side of the street. She was pretending not to notice, even as my heart begged her—or anyone—for help.

"What's in the case, Yank? Have ya' got loads of Bruce Springsteen records and tapes in there?" They all laughed at this, though it didn't strike me as either clever or funny.

"What's wrong, Yankee. Can ya' not even fuckin' talk?" He

pushed me hard, and I tripped over the body of another one of them, who'd got behind me on all fours, in the classic push-and-trip manoeuvre. As I lay on my back, a third loomed over me and the kicks began in earnest.

The kicks weren't particular hard, because they weren't particularly strong boys, but it was enough to make me cover my face with my hands. I mumbled, "Stop, please, stop!" as the Nike runners rained down upon me again and again.

Eventually they disengaged, and when I looked up with the one eye that would still open I saw them sauntering away, swinging my suitcase with an arrogant swagger. My suitcase!

And then a change came over me. I picked myself up from that wet, dirty footpath, my hand grasped a lump of rock, and with something resembling a battle cry I charged down my attackers. It was the prospect of losing my suitcase—my last few possessions in that lonely world—that filled me with such violent desperation as I had only known before in that ill-fated chase of Spencer into the police station.

I believe I must have been frothing at the mouth. I no longer knew pain: indeed my very fear of death was gone in that moment, and like some savage German tribesman charging madly at a Roman legion, I was quite resolved to imminent death at the hands and feet of these merciless thugs. My only goal was to hurt, and, if necessary, kill, as many of them as possible before I met my fate.

They turned and stared. Instead of meeting me head on for the anticipated counter-attack, they dropped the suitcase and fled like dogs, screaming "Legger, lads, legger!"

I chased them halfway across a grassy field, then let fly my rock at the retreating figure of the slowest. The momentum of pending victory propelled the stone faster than my arm alone ever could. It caught him on the leg and he fell heavily. I watched with great satisfaction as he upped and limped away, in haste and obvious pain.

I paused for breath beside my suitcase. The vision from one eye was still semi-opaque, blood trickled down my damaged face, and a feeling of triumph spread across me. There was the dull throbbing sensation of the physical injuries, to be sure, but it was not pain: only elation and victory. I had beaten local ruffians on their turf, outnumbered, alone and in a completely foreign country. The lion had survived the onslaught of the hyenas.

» 34 «

Leeton Kgabu closed the door of his hotel suite with a heavy, tired hand. He had been at meetings all day with officials. First, technical meetings with scientists from the WHO, and then the one he hated: the "policy" meeting with the ICC Special Committee for Criminal Justice, chaired by no lesser asshole than the Secretary General, Michal Sobiewski.

To say that meeting had not gone well would be an understatement. Sobiewski began by reading excerpts of Leeton's speech and asking him to tone down the rhetoric.

"Are you asking me to lose this case?" Leeton finally asked, with a measure of indignant pride swelling in his breast.

"There's no need to be dramatic, Mr Kgabu. We're not in a courtroom," the grey-haired Polish chairman told him. As a mark of his power, Sobiewski insisted on smoking cigars during the meetings, even though the UN buildings were technically smoke-free everywhere, save in designated smoking rooms.

Leeton Kgabu said nothing, but instead glared indignantly at the Pole from across the table. He knew his stare had the power to intimidate physically smaller men. It was a weapon he had often wielded in his career.

Sobiewski, however, seemed unperturbed, and just stared back at him with his little cold blue eyes. "Of course you should continue to do your best to prove him guilty. But what we are trying to make you understand here is that there are also political considerations. If we make this case about racism, then we risk dividing the world. It's a particularly divisive issue in the United States—"

"So that's what this is about. You've struck a bargain with the United States? If the ICC only does a half-hearted job of prosecuting Matterosi, they will agree to ratify the Abuja Charter? Is that right?"

"Don't be ridiculous. No one has pushed harder than I to ensure the Abuja Treaty has 'teeth'. But let's just say this. Our best way of getting the United States on board is by convincing them the ICC is colour-blind. At the moment, polls show 85 per cent of black Americans support ratification of the Treaty, against only 23 per cent of whites. The whites distrust the ICC. And your rants are a big part of that."

"My rants? Are you seriously suggesting you believe VIS was not designed to cull the black and brown populations of this planet?"

"What I think doesn't matter, Mr Kgabu. The world has to live with the consequences of VIS, and there are two things we can do to make that happen. The first is to convict Matterosi in a fair and impartial way. That's your job. The second is to unite the world under the banner of a new United Nations. Black and white together. And given your profile now—that's also your job. The Committee's message to you is this: tone down the sharpness of your rhetoric. No more grandstanding about racism. No more self-righteous vitriol."

Leeton felt anger rising within him. As he stood up to go, he clenched his fists and asked, "Will that be all?"

"No," Sobiewski replied, taking a leisurely puff of his cigar. "There's more. I saw from the protocol you intend to subpoena new witnesses. You never told us this."

"I am building a case against Matterosi. I will call all the witnesses I require to do so. You have no authority to tell me to do otherwise."

"These witnesses are high-ranking executives of the Swiss Pharmaceutical company Zextra and former staff of BetterWorld. They have cooperated already and provided us with all the material evidence we need. Why do you need to call them to the stand? Matterosi has all but confessed. The material evidence is overwhelming. We don't need this. It can only weaken the case against him."

"That's for me to decide," Leeton snapped, and turned his back abruptly on the Committee. On his way out of the room, he caught one last glare which Sobiewski let linger. It was a withering stare. And then the door slammed shut.

Now back in the hotel suite, Leeton replayed the conversation over in his head. He found himself growing irrationally angry at the constraints being imposed upon him by disingenuous politicians, who never seemed able to play a straight game. Then he got angry at the facetious mannerisms of defence attorney Art Blume, which left him feeling as though he were being mocked.

His final anger was reserved for Brian Matterosi himself. Rachel Hyberg had been as good as her word and given him several more instalments of the recording, most filmed from a hidden camera in Matterosi's locked hotel suite. Leeton had listened to the recordings with a sense of addictive fascination. At times he had even caught himself getting sucked in to the murderer's way of thinking. Matterosi was a sad and pitiful man, it was true. But it was equally as clear to Leeton that the attempts at making his childhood seem horrible were an artificial ploy designed to garner sympathy at a later stage in the trial. *It's not really my fault. My bad upbringing made me do it.* This was all a game Art Blume was playing. Leeton was sure of it.

He had just switched on one of the 24-hour news channels to watch some of the trial coverage when the Skype ring tone sounded on his iPhone. Even without looking he knew it was Caddie. Mechanically he opened the laptop and fired up the full version of Skype. The computer took a while to boot up, but Caddie would wait. She always did.

Her face beamed with pleasure when the connection was finally made.

"Hello, my Sunshine!"

"Hello, Moonlight."

"Are you okay?" she asked, in response to his lacklustre greeting.

He forced himself to smile. "Yes, Moonlight. I'm just very tired."

"Of course you are. It is very taxing, what you are doing. And to know how much depends on you." She smiled coyly and added, "I only wish I were there with you, and I could give you a nice, long, massage."

He forced himself to grin and reciprocate this wish. Guilt and the pride he felt at being a devoted husband prevented him from showing any trace of the fact that in his heart, he really didn't wish she were with him.

"How is Robert?"

"He misses his daddy," she replied. "I fed him early and put him to bed so that you and I could talk together without him crying."

"But I wanted to see my son."

Caddie's face fell. She always tried to please him. This reprimand stung her to the quick.

"I'm sorry, my Sunshine. Tomorrow I will make sure he is awake to see you."

He forced another smile to show her he was not really cross, which faded into a sort of awkward silence.

Silence. This was what he had come to dread in their Skype calls. The fact that, given they were not able to discuss the trial, they had nothing left to talk about. Had it always been like this between them? Was his career their only common interest? Why had he not noticed it during their first year of marriage?

"How is Claire? Have you seen her?" he asked, more because he needed something to say that because he cared about Claire or whether Caddie had seen her.

"Yes, we went shopping today." Another silence. "I bought a new dress for myself."

"Did you? What does it look like?"

"I'm wearing it." Her face fell as she said this.

Only then did he realise that she had deliberately repositioned the camera a degree downwards, so that her full body was visible in the screen. It was another colourful, African dress, but with a different pattern to the other one she had worn. And much more green and yellow. To his own surprise he found himself thinking how European women would consider such a dress clownish and tacky. An image shot through his head of the sort of clothes Rachel Hyberg wore. He forced himself to concentrate on Caddie.

"It's very beautiful. It suits you perfectly."

She gave no answer. She didn't need to. He knew tears were forming in her soft, brown eyes.

"I'm sorry, Moonlight. I ... it's just that I'm so very tired, you have to forgive me if I'm not as observant as I should be."

At this she brightened up again. "Of course I forgive you, Sunshine. And of course I know how tired you must be. The weight of the world is on your shoulders now. And even with such strong shoulders, my Sunshine must feel the weight sometimes. But I do miss you, so very much. It's not easy to be without you for so long." One single tear escaped down her cheek, which she caught in her wrist in a deft movement of the arm.

"I miss you too, my Moonlight."

"So I will let you rest now. My parents send their regards. Also Walter from the University."

"My regards to them, too."

"Goodnight, Leeton, my love. Sleep well."

"Goodnight, Moonlight."

Leeton went to the minibar for a drink. He had a sick feeling inside him that he could not place, a sort of manic loneliness mixed with hunger. But it wasn't hunger, exactly, for he had eaten well that day. Perhaps a beer would help, he thought without any conviction. He'd never been much of a drinker.

Next to the bottle of Heineken he was about to grab, his eyes fell upon a bottle of champagne. Something in his groin stirred. All of the sudden, he was able to place the feeling.

He walked over to the telephone and dialled 7-3-3.

"Hello?" His heart began pounding at the sound of her voice.

"It's Leeton."

"Well, hello, Attorney Kgabu. To what do I owe the honour? Have you watched the latest episode?" She had already sent him another Matterosi recording earlier in the afternoon.

"Not yet. But that's not why I'm calling."

"I'm all ears."

Leeton cleared his throat. "The other night when I was so tired

... I'm afraid you never had a chance to finish your glass of champagne. I wondered if you had time tonight ..."

There was a silence on the other end of the phone. Leeton rubbed the sweat from his palm into the fabric of the armchair. He did and he did not want her to say no, to take away this temptation, once and for all. On the other hand, a part of him reasoned, she was providing him with vital material now, and he needed all the allies he could get, especially now that Sobiewski was acting up. In a way it was a sacrifice he was making for the sake of international justice.

"Just give me a minute to freshen up. Then I'll be right over."

In a surreal state of anticipation Leeton moved about the hotel suite. It felt to him as though his actions were being governed by an outside force. That external force drew the blinds completely and lit the table lamps. It then removed Umama's necklace and put it away in the desk draw, together with the photos of Caddie and Robert. Finally, it doused his face in aftershave.

Then came the soft knock on the door.

» 35 «

As the massive, low clouds tumbled across the small Irish sky above me, spitting rain and sunshine in roughly equal proportions, I made my way across fields and farms. My shoes sank into mud. My trousers got caught on barbed wire. I was attacked by sheepdogs and even escorted off the lands of one shotgun- brandishing farmer. Astoundingly, my suitcase survived all these travails, and somehow—footsore and exhausted—I arrived at my destination, which was a place called Drumnaslew.

Drumnaslew is an anglicisation of the Irish *"droim na sluaite"* meaning "the hill with crowds of people on it". The hill in question is quite clearly to be seen from the road up out of Ballinagleragh. It is a bulbous, slightly elongated glacial hill or "drumlin" rising out of the otherwise low grassland that runs off from Lough Allen, to the north and west of mid-Leitrim. Topographically, this is the area where North Leitrim joins County Sligo, just below the mountains which make up the country celebrated by the Irish poet, William Butler Yeats.

Where the "crowds of people" bit fits in is less clear. There is only one cottage at Drumnaslew: "Whelan's Place" and it is halfway down the bare-peaked slope, hidden by a forested patch on the southeast facing side, and with no clear view of Lough Dreen. It may be that there were once numerous houses dotting that bleak hillside, before the Famine and successive waves of emigration robbed Leitrim of her people: my own maternal grandparents—the Whelans—being the last to abandon this particular spot. But it is equally likely that the name is more ancient still, and refers to a time when the pagan people of Ireland would host ceremonies on such hills, gathering in crowds to dispel evil or to worship some godly benefactor.

Whatever its precise etymology, one thing is clear: Drumnaslew, Drumeen, County Leitrim is a place whose infertile soils have, since time immemorial, been scratched, coveted and clung to by desperate and humble human beings. This was something I could feel like an omen, as I trod the overgrown gravel lane that led to the old cottage.

Smoke rose from the chimney to announce that this would-be homestead was a homestead already: something I was unprepared for.

For a brief, insane moment I imagined that perhaps my grandmother was still alive. But before I could dispel that utterly impossible thought for the fantasy it was, an angry bark stopped me in my tracks. A dog came charging around the bend in the lane, all snarls, something mongrel-like, but with enough Alsatian in it to strike sudden fear in my heart. No retreat was possible; nor was there time to grab a stick, and in that blinding moment of panic I did the only thing a sensible person can: I barked back, stamping my foot and attempting to imbue my voice with as much authority as possible.

Against dogs on which this trick doesn't work, you really don't have much chance anyway. But this particular beast was civilised, or cowardly, enough to give me the benefit of the doubt. He stopped, semi-crouched, and snarled a deep warning at me, trying to figure out just who I was and whether or not he ought to savage me.

"You all right?" A British accent asked me. It came from a thin man who'd brusquely called off the dog and replaced its aggressive posture with his own. What I didn't know at the time was that when British people asked you "are you all right?" in that certain tone, it meant the exact opposite of concern for your welfare. It meant ... roughly what the dog's snarl meant.

"I'm fine, thanks."

He looked from my suitcase to my bruised face to the physical stature I possessed, which was only slightly less manly than his.

"The village is that way."

"I'm looking for Drumnaslew. Whelan's Place."

Whelan's Place. That's what several people along the way had told me it was called, and it was my mother's maiden name.

"Got it wrong here, mate. This is Chet's Garden, this is. No

Drum-of-whateva' or Whelan here. So off you go, right."

"Oh, okay."

But I didn't budge.

"It's just that ... I'm pretty sure this is Whelan's Place. Everybody told me it was here, and this is the only house I can see. So if you're here by mistake, that's cool, but, you see, it's *my* house. My grandmother left it to me in her Will."

"Look." The dog raised his eyes as his master took a threatening step towards me, though his body language told me he wasn't entirely convinced of the threat himself. "I'm not gonna tell you again, right. Piss off!"

It was enough temper to scare me back away, and his confidence grew in proportion to my reticence.

"And don't come back or else, got it?"

Oh, but I would come back.

My first thought was to get help from the proper authorities. The police station in Drumshanbo was a stone building with iron bars on the windows, glistening in their fresh black paint. The funny little Garda Síochana lantern made it seem quaint and vaguely friendly. However, the Guard at the desk was unhelpful and off-hand. Bullish thickness and the physical power of the official state oozed out of his broad, pink face and under the shiny rim of a police hat held snug by tufts of snow-white hair.

With a keen blue eye that took me in quickly and thoroughly, he listened to about half of my story, then interrupted me to suggest it was a land dispute and he couldn't intervene unless he had a court order to do so. When I pressed him to do more, his face set into something a little more menacing and told me at my age I had no business anywhere but at home with my mother. He might just ring the welfare board.

"Now go on home wherever home is, and don't be causing trouble bigger than you can swallow."

I left discouraged and wandered down the village street with no more sense of purpose. Had my quest ended this quickly? Was the cottage simply gone? Had I just been too slow?

On a bench next to a statue there sat an old man dressed in one of those worn suits and grotty caps. He eyed me curiously. I nodded politely, and that was enough for him to beckon me over and start speaking. Although "speaking" seems a bit exaggerated. From what I could make out from his heavily-accented, slurred voice, he was claiming he'd known my grandparents, my aunt and her husband. Improbably, he seemed to know already who I was and what I had come for, and he strongly suggested the best way to get back the cottage was to use main force.

"Claim the land, lad. Do you hear me? Claim the land. I knew your grandfather and I'll tell you, no English fucker would have got the better of Joe Whelan. Claim the land!"

"But the policeman said ..."

"Ah, fuck the police. Fuckin' shower of Free State gobbeens, don'tcha' know. If you want that cottage back, take it!"

"How?"

"Do ya see this?" He waved his stick and squinted his eyes furiously. "That's how."

His stirring words notwithstanding, I might have given up anyway, if I had had any other options left to me. But there I was, in the middle of Ireland, with nothing and no one to go back to. That cottage was all there was for me in the world. I thought of the hyenas I had defeated and felt the lion swell inside me.

The taste, the sounds, the feeling of Watertown, Massachusetts was erased from my mind. The meek nerd from the bottom lunch room table was transformed into a feral animal now, and nothing, neither mores nor fear of something to lose, was left to restrain him.

I spent a night in a hostel not far away, planning and considering my next move. I would go back to Drumnaslew and face this man in Chet's Garden once again. Only this time I would come to lay siege. If it cost Chet, or whatever his name was, his life, then so be it.

» 36 «

Leeton drank coffee all the way through his morning briefing. He even brought a take-away coffee—American style, in a paper cup—into Court One with him. He needed to be attentive, despite the lack of sleep. This witness was one of the crucial links in the case and he needed to ensure, not just the content, but the emotional impact of the questioning came across clearly and well. It was also the first African witness to appear in the witness box. "This time is for Africa," someone had said to him in the hallway. Leeton reviewed his notes a final time and approached the witness box with a sense of fraternity.

"Doctor, could you be so kind as to state your name for the Court record?"

"Martin Dsulanga."

"Dr Dsulanga, you worked as a travelling doctor in the Kerio River Valley region of Kenya, is that correct?"

"Yes, sir, that is correct. For nearly ten years I travelled a radius of 50 kilometres, serving the villages. I treated mostly poor people. They are generally small farmers in little villages. A population of 2,500, for which I was the only doctor."

"That is very noble work, Doctor. It is a shame more do not follow your excellent example."

"Thank you, sir."

"So, during your work, you came into contact with the VIS virus?"

"Yes, I did."

"When did you first diagnose VIS?"

"It was after the short rains in late 2016. I was approached by a shaman, a village medicine man from Mogotio, who told me of an infection that had appeared in his village."

"How did the village medicine man describe the infection to you?"

"He said it was the wrath of an angry white demon, which had been summoned to punish his people. This demon, he said, flew on a winged lion and spat poison into the water. All who drank the water would grow feverish and forever remain barren.

"He blamed me, because he said I had brought the white man's medicine to his tribe, which had greatly angered the spirit world. He said the spirits of our ancestors had summoned this demon in retribution."

"Well ... let's just stick to the medical facts, shall we? Did you examine the infected villagers?"

"Yes, I did. They showed symptoms similar to malaria, though not as severe. Many vomited and were weak. During the 'hot' phase, which lasted only a few days generally, patients broke out in cold sweats and shivered. Then, the infection seemed to go away and the lucky ones were as normal. But what was different was the swelling of the scrotum among the men, and the women reported unusual menstrual pain and prolonged bleeding. The inflammation remained for many days after the fever had abated, causing discomfort in the genital region. I was intrigued by the infection, because I had never seen this before."

"Were there any deaths?"

"Yes. At least twenty three people died while in the 'hot' phase of infection. This was over a week. I stayed in Mogotio the whole time. I took blood samples from them, and from a great many more patients, and sent them to the lab in Kinshasa for analysis."

"What was the result of this analysis?"

"At first, nothing. They were testing for known viruses, so they found nothing. Later the samples were sent on to the WHO lab in Stockholm and VISbeta3, beta2 were identified in nearly all the samples. That's when the WHO became involved."

"So the twenty three patients you treated, who displayed symptoms which later were determined to be consistent with VIS infection, died of this illness, and were subsequently found to contain active Hydra-beta2 and beta3 virus cells in their blood samples?"

"That is correct, yes. At least twenty three."

"Is there any chance that their illness was not caused by VIS? Any chance they would have died anyway?"

"There is always a chance. But in my professional opinion, they died because of the infection with the VIS beta strain."

Turning in the direction of the judges' podium, Leeton treated Camera Two to a broad, satisfied smile and pronounced, "No further questions for this witness, Your Honours." He felt his body relax as he took one final sip of stone-cold coffee.

» 37 «

Second-generation, anticoagulant 4-Hydroxycoumarin, or "rat poison" to the non-scientifically minded among you, is an especially effective means of killing all kinds of animals, not just rats. This is because it is tasteless and odourless, a necessary precondition for them to don their culinary bibs and chow down, and also because the active poisons in it are delayed-action, allowing them to enter the bloodstream before the target can effectively vomit. Rats don't vomit, but they do nibble. Other animals vomit. Either way, delayed action is required to ensure the poison gets to the blood.

At sixteen, I already knew this from my studies of biochemistry. I also knew that the proteins and steroids in minced beef would react synergistically to expedite the progress of the antibacterial agents used to further suppress the coagulation through colon failure.

Armed with my science, I stooped over a makeshift campfire on the banks of Lough Dreen and carefully crushed the rat poison pellets with the flat of a pocket-knife blade. The little white balls crumbled to lumps and eventually to powder. I added the powder to the twenty little meatballs I'd prepared, each enclosed in its own individual foil wrapper. Then it was time to brown the meat, but carefully so as not to overcook it, lest the anticoagulant agent be harmed. It was just to get the aromas and the juices flowing; to make it as tasty as I possibly could.

The soggy, clay-ridden earth of Drumnaslew was no stranger to cold, hungry people clinging to its infertile soil. Generations of my ancestors had done just that. Likely this was not the first land war that had been fought over it, either. It seems to be one of those perverse rules that the more wretched, the more impoverished a piece of land is, the harder human beings fight with one another for its occupancy. And so, in the early dawn of a wild, windy and sunless Irish day, I crawled up through the fields of marshy reeds and scutch grass, over ditches and brambles, up towards Chet's Garden, as close as I dared to get.

The siege would begin with catapult fire. From all sides of the ancient hill called Drumnaslew I lobbed poisoned meatballs high in the air and towards the cottage. At one point I hit a window, and the barking began. Remembering this dog's snarl, I beat a hasty retreat, all the way back to my campsite. I was well out of range before Chet could awaken, before he could let the dog outside, where the poor creature would sniff around and enjoy his Last Breakfast.

Day broke across the choppy, opaque surface of the lake. As is so often the case in Ireland, the veil of cloud suddenly lifted, and what I thought would be unending gloom magically exploded into the brightest, clearest light imaginable. Ireland is known for its cloud and rain, but what I remarked on that morning was that the power of its sunshine is very much underappreciated. Perhaps it is because of the cleansing effect of the Atlantic on the air. Perhaps it is because the high moisture content somehow magnifies and refracts the sunlight. In any event it is hard to find a place where the sunshine—rare though it may seem at times—is quite as splendid as in Ireland.

In the sun, it was warm enough for me to strip down to my T-shirt. And then to strip naked. Standing on the water's edge, the surface reflected back at me the body of a sixteen-year-old boy. I watched him through the ripples for a moment, thinking about who and what I was. A boy or a man? Then, without reaching any conclusion, I took four swift strides into the lake, merging my physical being with its reflection and plunging into the icy shock of bitterly cold water.

The air felt much warmer after the swim. Breakfast was bland cheese and traditional stoneground bread, toasted on the embers of my dying campfire. By the time I'd finished eating, Chet's dog would be dead.

It wasn't until late in the afternoon that Chet found the dog. I knew it because I heard him scream, "You bastard. You sick little bastard. Come and fight me like a man."

I let three more days pass after poisoning Chet the Englishman's dog. And in that time I drew steadily closer to my prize, encircling the cottage behind hedges and trees, until eventually its occupant could see my form moving around the back of the hay shed and the outbuildings. The outbuildings all belonged to me now. Soon the cottage would too.

I threw rocks at all the windows, mostly at night, until I'd smashed in every one. The tin roof was also constantly bombarded by my rocks. I imagined the sound it would make at night, the rocks hitting like a crash of thunder, then rolling down. Always hitting at perfectly random times. It was a form of psychological warfare, designed to drive him mad. Once, Chet, in a fit of drunken courage, showed his face in the clearing in front of the cottage door, loudly screaming at me that I should show myself, if I was a man. Ever the man himself, he was armed with a baseball bat.

I was not far away, but still concealed, and I had a heavy oak staff into which I had whittled a knobbly-spiked tip. I held it at the ready, just in case he charged me. But we were both afraid of a direct confrontation: like two kings on a chessboard that can never get too close to each other. Instead, I gave him a volley of rocks from over the outbuilding's roof, and he retreated inside, leaving me with a string of curses.

That was my trump card, I thought, as I lay amongst the leaves watching a rat pick away at the carcass of the dog, which Chet (in his love for the beast) had carelessly fired out one of the broken windows. I had absolutely nothing to lose.

Eventually, on the fourth day, I heard his car's engine fire up. The car, an old Vauxhall with the yellow and black registration plates of the UK, was the one thing I hadn't touched, because, of course, I wanted him to leave, and he'd need his car for that. From my vantage point I saw it hurtling down the lane at a dangerous speed. Maybe he was hoping to run me down. For me, the important thing was the fact that the back seat was stuffed with bags of clothes and a guitar. It sure looked like he was moving out.

When I was certain he'd gone, I cautiously approached the main dwelling and saw that the door was swinging open. He'd not even bothered to close it behind him. Filthy with dirt, freezing cold and raw from hunger and gnat bites, I entered my ancestral cottage at Drumnaslew for the first time and took possession of it. I must have looked wretched, but it mattered not. No military conqueror in history—not Caesar crossing the Rubicon, not Napoleon entering Vienna, not Hitler driving through the Arc de Triomphe in Paris—felt prouder and more triumphant than I did at that moment.

Inside, I quickly closed the door and drew the bolt. There was no obvious key, but as long as I was inside, he wouldn't be getting back in. Then, I took stock of the place that was to become my home for the next two years.

The front door opened to a sitting-room area with an open fireplace. Doors led off to the back, left and right. I knew already from my siege that the kitchen was to the rear and the bedrooms to the sides.

It was small, and Chet had left the place in a holy mess. Cigarette butts strewn on the floor; pots half-full of week-old baked beans; empty cans of cheap beer, old clothes and rags in heaps on the two-seater sofa. There was dog shit wrapped in newspaper flung into the corner of the kitchen. But I could see beyond the Englishman's filth, to what the place could become: the haven of happiness and comfort I so longed for.

I could see myself staring into the fire over a hot cup of tea, pondering the deep thoughts of my work. It was the cosy home I had dreamed of for so many years. Happiness filled me as I began to take stock of the potential of Whelan's Place. Matterosi's Place, it was now.

» 38 «

Shortly before Art rose to begin his cross-examination, he decided on a whim to stick one of Lisbeth's earbuds into his ear and listen to the Fox News commentary from the live-stream.

"*What we know of Blume from his previous cases, and I'm thinking in particular of* The State of New York *versus* Cantelloni, *is that he can be cutting, witty and really take witnesses by surprise.*"

"*But we haven't seen this so far, have we?*"

"*No, we haven't, Leticia, but I have a feeling Blume is pacing himself ... and I think it's fair to say that with this witness, he's really got to be careful. I mean, Dr Dsulanga is exactly the sort of person who has earned so much respect since the outbreak of VIS, because he's one of the guys who's right there on the line of scrimmage. If Blume tries to attack him in his usual way, it could really backfire—*"

Art removed the earbud and rose. *Let's see how much respect the world has for him in twenty minutes times*, he thought.

He began by rubbing his eyes, as if to get the sleep out of them.

"Dr Dsulanga, at the time, you were the only doctor operating in the Kerio River basin, which has a population of nearly 2,500, and stretches over a hundred kilometres from north to south. Is that correct?"

"Yes it is."

"You must find it hard to give your patients the care and attention they need?"

"Africa is a poor place, Mr Blume. We do not have the money for medicines and for care. Doctors on our continent do the best they can with what they have."

"Oh, sure, I understand. In Europe and the US the ratio of doctors to patients is about one to three hundred. You have to deal with one to 2,500 and that makes a big difference, right?"

Kgabu shouted out, "Objection!" With a broad sweep of his big, open hands, he asked the bench, "Where is this testimony going to,

Your Honours? Mr Blume is not dealing with the issue, which is the death of the victims by infection with VIS in Mogotio."

The judges conferred for a moment, after which it was Gomes who spoke. Clearly it was she who had pushed the point.

"Mr Blume, are you going to deal with the deaths of the victims in Mogotio or not? Once again, we have to remind you that this isn't the place for speech-making."

"Yes, Your Honour, I know. This is about the Mogotio people. Just give me a moment to make the case."

"Continue, Mr Blume. But please keep it to the point."

"Dr Dsulanga. Where were we? Ah, yes, the ratio of doctors to people. Would it be a benefit to the people you treat if there was six times the number of doctors per thousand, like there is in the West?"

"Of course it would be a benefit, but it would not have saved the lives of these victims of VIS."

"No? Why not?"

"It is not just doctors we lack, but also medicine. Equipment to analyse blood samples. Even needles to take the blood samples."

"Okay, so it's money and doctors. In other words, if we had been able to engineer a substantial improvement in the material quality of life of your patients we could have saved them from VIS, not to mention malar—"

If she had been in an American court, Chief Justice Wang would have had a gavel she could bang in frustration. But here, she could only brutally tap her microphone.

"I'm not allowing it, Mr Blume. And furthermore, I'm warning you not to try this again. It's speculative and indirect. If you want to address wider social points, please do so with witnesses that have been called for that purpose. Questions should address the immediate point being raised and should be within the scope of expertise of the witness who is currently on the stand."

"Fine."

Art strolled again, stopping at the defence's desk to drink a sip of water and give Lisbeth a mischievous wink.

"Dr Dsulanga, you mentioned you consulted with the village shaman before treating the victims. Was this something you did regularly? Consult with the local witch doctors?"

"I take exception to the term 'witch doctor', sir. It is a racist term conceived by the white man to describe things he holds in contempt, but does not fully understand."

"Okay, well, let's call him a 'medicine man'. Is that okay? Do you consult with 'medicine men' a lot when you travel to villages?"

"Yes, I often do. They are the ones the villagers come to first, so they have a good overview of the situation."

"Do you believe in their magical powers?"

Dr Dsulanga paused for a second. He had a proud, strong face. His smooth black skin shone in the bright lights of the camera even more than that of the prosecutor Kgabu. But he had none of Leeton Kgabu's arrogance and grandstanding. He had an honest countenance. The countenance of a defender of virtue, and of the poor.

"I do not say I believe or disbelieve in traditional medicines. But there are many things we do not fully understand. And the culture of the ancient ways is very old. There is wisdom in things that have stood the test of time. You cannot discount it, simply because it doesn't appear under your microscope."

"So ... you're saying you don't know whether a witch doctor's—sorry, medicine man's—spiritual incantations and stick-shaking and all that stuff ... you're saying you don't know whether it's actual, real magic or just pretend, make-believe magic?"

"I'm saying there are many things we as practitioners of medicine do not fully understand. Ask any doctor—"

"I'm not asking any doctor. I'm asking you. The doctor who is a witness for the prosecution. Whose testimony is trying to convict my client of murder. Do you believe in witchcraft, yes or no?"

"Yes and no."

"That's not a clear answer, Doctor."

"Some questions cannot be answered clearly."

"Funny, you were pretty clear in your diagnosis of VIS."

Chief Justice Wang let out a heavy sigh and motioned with her hand that this testimony was going nowhere. Art got the hint.

"Moving on. You told us that you sent a sample to a lab in Kinshasa. How does that work? Do you, like, pay to get a lab analysis?"

"It costs money, yes."

"But I thought you told us you didn't have money for samples? You said you didn't even have the money for the needles. How come you had the money to take over a hundred blood samples in Mogotio and get them analysed in Kinshasa? Just to satisfy your curiosity about some guys with swollen balls?"

"I ... had some money. For those samples, I could pay."

"Really? How much were they?"

"I can't remember precisely. This was years ago."

"That's weird, Doctor, how your memory works. I mean, you could remember everything about the witch doctor's story of an evil demon riding a winged lion and spitting poison, which was also years ago. But you can't remember spending an enormous amount of money on blood samples when, according to your own testimony, you didn't even have money for needles?"

"Believe it or not, Mr Blume, not everyone is as obsessed with money as you are."

"I don't believe it."

At this, Art Blume provoked a round of muted laughter.

"And I'll tell you why I don't believe it. I called the East African Medical Centre, where you got the samples tested, and they told me they charged 1,500 Kenyan Shillings for a comprehensive blood test that includes malaria and HIV. That means you would have spent nearly 3,000 US dollars to get all those samples checked. Could that be right, Doctor?"

"I wasn't charged."

"You weren't charged? But you just told me you paid for the blood samples?"

"I don't mean I wasn't charged. I mean I may have got a discount."

"A discount? Why would they give you a discount?"

"Perhaps to support my work. Perhaps to help the poor people of Africa."

"Perhaps. So after finding nothing in the blood samples for which they gave you a discount, the folks in Kinshasa decided to send this 'random sample' on to the WHO lab in Sweden. On spec. Did you pay for that too?"

"No."

"So I guess you don't know how much that cost, either, huh?"

"I guess the lab in Kinshasa paid for that."

"Guess again, Doctor. Here's a copy of the annual accounts for the East African Medical Research Centre for 2016 and for 2017. Could you take a look at them and tell me if you see something unusual."

"I am not an accountant, sir."

"I know that, Doctor. And I'm not a Michelin Star chef, either. But I can tell a plate of spaghetti from a chicken Caesar salad. Look at the accounts. Tell me what's different."

The African man put on his reading glasses ponderously and bent over the papers for a minute.

"This one, for 2017, has a larger balance. Here ... under 'receipts'."

"Bingo! 300,000 Shillings of bonus revenue. And here's the bank account statements I subpoenaed. Read the highlighted entries, please, Doctor."

"*235,000 Shillings, international transfer from Sweden ... November 23, 2017.*"

"So I guess it was the WHO that paid to have the blood samples airlifted to Sweden where they tested them for VIS?"

"On request ... I mean ... I suppose that it must have been ... because of ... suspicions."

"So let me get this straight: a lab in Kenya receives a huge batch of blood samples from some rural doctor who believes in magic. A rural doctor who, in the first place, took the samples on the advice of a witch doctor. Sorry, 'medicine man'. The lab decides to cut you a special deal and test the samples at a rebate. They find nothing. Instead of deciding to cut their losses at this obvious waste of time and money, they send the samples on to Sweden, paid for by the WHO? And low and behold, an beta strain of the Hydra shows up, at the lab in Malmö!"

"Yes."

"They were looking for VIS, weren't they?"

"Maybe so. The international community was already concerned about the situation in India at this point in time. It is natural they would be interested in similar cases elsewhere. There is nothing wrong with that."

"So if the folks in the WHO were looking for the virus, why did they make you pay 3,000 dollars for the initial samples?"

"I don't remember exactly how much it was … the initial samples. Maybe they didn't charge me when I told them that … that I suspected VIS."

"What about the needles and vials? Did they supply you with those?"

"No. It was my own equipment."

"Really? We're talking a pretty big sample here, Doctor. You carry around hundreds of needles and vials, routinely?"

"I often have supplies in reserve."

"I thought you said money was tight? I thought you said you didn't have enough needles and medicines?"

The doctor provided no further answer, but the warmth and joviality which had marked his countenance were slowly disappearing.

"Do you know what I think, Doctor? I think the WHO paid you to go to Mogotio and take those samples. They supplied you, bought your gas and sent you out there to find VIS. They knew—or suspected—VIS would appear in the early alpha strains for which the Swedish lab had reliable tests, because they had retraced Brian Matterosi's steps, and they knew he had been there with the BetterWorld research mission beforehand. You expect this Court to believe you're some kind of do-gooder volunteer, helping your poor

African brothers and sisters. In reality, you're a 'stethoscope-for-hire' bought in on a UN-agenda to cherry-pick evidence in order to convict Brian Matterosi. Isn't that right, Doctor?"

"No, it is not."

"They said, 'go out and find a village with a lot of dead people and make sure they had VIS, send us the samples and we'll pay you for it'. Isn't that how it was?"

"No."

Art Blume strolled around again, but this time not as close to the prosecutor.

"Are you sure, Doctor?"

"Objection, Your Honours," Leeton Kgabu interrupted. "The witness has already answered the question twice. It is pestering the witness to keep asking the same question."

"Sustained. Mr Blume, a new question, please."

"Dr Dsulanga, do you know a Ms Deirdre Carter?"

"Yes, I do."

"How do you know her?"

"She is a friend of mine. I met her when I was a student in the UK, in Nottingham, studying medicine."

"When was that?"

"In 2005."

"And you've stayed friends ever since?"

"Yes."

"Then you know she was in Kenya in 2016 and 2017? Working as a medical technician in Kinshasa?"

"Yes."

"And you knew she was working for the East Africa Medical Centre, the very lab you sent the samples to and got such a great discount from?"

"Yes."

"It's a small world, isn't it, doctor?"

Dsulanga shrugged his broad shoulders at this.

"How would you describe your relationship with Ms Carter?"

"That's none of your business."

"Oh, I beg to differ. You, Ms Carter's former employer and the WHO are trying to implicate my client in the deaths of twenty-three people. And I'm trying to show he's innocent. That makes your relationship to her very much my business. So now, do you have an intimate relationship with Ms Deirdre Carter?"

"None of your business."

"Fine, will you confirm to the Court, at least, that you share an address with Ms Carter at 16 B Street, Apt 33, in Lower Manhattan?"

"I confirm nothing."

"Here is a photograph that was taken last week on ... Saturday morning at 09:13 ... of you and Ms Carter leaving the building hand in hand, on your way to a local coffee shop for breakfast. Will you confirm that this is a picture of you?"

"How dare you!"

"Ms Carter's career is doing quite well, now, wouldn't you say? Astonishingly well, in fact. After getting only a 2:2 degree in Earth Sciences from Nottingham Polytechnic, and working a number of years, on and off, for NGOs in London, Ms Carter followed her boyfriend back to his native Kenya and got a crummy desk job in a med tech lab in the big city. Then, all of a sudden, last year, she's appointed Project Leader for the United Nations African Redevelopment Fund. Which according to the job description posted on their website, offers a tax-free salary of 250,000 dollars. Wow! That's quite a big job for someone in her early thirties, with no management experience, a patchy resume and a pretty poor academic track record. How did you think she pulled that off?"

"Why don't you ask her?"

"Because you're on the stand. And you're her boyfriend. And I'm asking you. How did she get that job, Doctor?"

"I have no idea. Ask her."

"No? You guys never chat about stuff like that while enjoying your Saturday morning bagels and coffee? Sort of like, 'oh, guess what honey, did I tell you about my new job? It comes with a 2,000 per cent salary increase over my old job!' She forgot to mention that one, huh?"

A wave of subdued laughter went around the court. Dr Dsulanga glowered back at Art.

"Well, let's speculate. Maybe the big UN job was her pay-off for getting her boyfriend to forge a case against Brian Matterosi?"

"You are just crazy. It's nonsense."

"You know, Dr Dsulanga, I live in Manhattan too. Lower East side. Only a couple of blocks from you and Ms Carter, in fact. It's a great location, isn't it?"

"If you say so."

"Of course, I grew up in the South Bronx, which you know, is not such a great location. More like Kinshasa, with snow. But, being a greedy lawyer, as you pointed out, I made it to the nice part of Manhattan. The part of Manhattan people get to live in, who worry about money all the time. Funny how you and I live in the same neighbourhood, isn't it?"

» 39 «

Before I'd even made a complete tour of my new home, I started cleaning up. I was humming an Irish tune; one that sprang into my head from some deep place where the memory of my grandmother still dwelled. On a foolish whim I took out the plastic leprechaun I had brought with me from Watertown and gave it pride of place on the new mantelpiece, before returning to work. *Rubbish in this bag, dishes in the sink, a bucket of fresh water to wash the stone floor. I'll just move this chair into one of the bedrooms to clear some space ...*

And there she was. My heart nearly stopped when I saw her. On the floor, huddled in the corner, clutching a lump of duvet to her chest, was a girl, about sixteen or seventeen years old.

We just froze, facing each other in shock. For me, it was the shock of an unexpected human presence. For her it was pure terror, as if I was going to kill her. I leaned the staff against the wall and took a step towards her. Her already defensive posture became almost foetal; her lips quivered and tears welled up in her eyes. I saw now that she was deathly pale. Her dark brown hair was matted and uncombed. Her ghost-like skin was bruised here and there. She had a black eye and her lips were swollen and cut.

"Hi," I offered, in what I hoped was a friendly voice. She wouldn't answer. Just stared at me, wide-eyed, like an animal in a trap. After another minute, and because I couldn't think of what else to do, I went back into the sitting room and started cleaning up again.

It was extraordinary that in the four days of my siege I hadn't seen this girl once through the windows. I'd seen Chet dozens of times, but it was as if she had spent the whole time on the floor. She had, in fact, spent the whole time on the floor.

An odd situation to say the least, with her crouched in the corner, and me scrubbing the floor in the adjacent room. It occurred to me too that her presence might mean Chet would be back soon. This thought caused me to drop my floor cloth into the bucket and approach her again.

"Is he coming back?"

She was still staring at me, but the terror had subsided.

"Is he coming back?" I repeated, louder.

She shook her head, and with that tears welled up in her eyes and her body quaked. She was sobbing in silence, and it soon became clear to me why. He had abandoned her here.

Instead of pitying her, as I ought to have, I felt dizzy with a surge of power. She was thin, frail and not really pretty, but she possessed the one quality my maternal home had taught me to find attractive in a woman: weakness. In a rush of sexual energy, I reached out a cautious hand and placed it on her shoulder. My hand glided from shoulder to shoulder blade. There was no bra strap under the pink T-shirt she wore. I touched her brown, greasy hair, then her face, which was still wet with tears. Her body was cold and tense.

And then another part of me—the better part of me—took hold and made me withdraw my touch. Weak women that I could control aroused me, but it felt dirty. It was pathetic and shameful.

Confused, I left her suddenly and returned to my household chores in the other room. I washed the dishes as if in a blurry dream, and the excitement returned when I saw that she had followed me to the kitchen. She was standing at the threshold, watching me with unblinking eyes.

"I'm Brian." I offered her my hand, but she recoiled, as if she still expected I might strike her. With her reticence, my confidence grew.

"What's your name?" I repeated the question three times, but she still would not answer. It was only when I took hold of her chin and lifted her eyes to mine that she softly said:

"Linda."

"Pleased to meet you." When I smiled she looked away, and retreated into the other room. Sounds came from the bedroom and I knew that she was packing. She came back out with just one bag slung over her shoulder.

"Are you going now?"

Linda nodded, looking at the floor.

From the threshold I watched her retreating around the bend in the lane until, on a sudden impulse, I bolted after her.

"Wait. Where will you go? Have you got any money?"

She wouldn't or couldn't answer. She just stopped and stared at the ground. The weather had turned again, and a thin film of rain clung to our faces.

I took her hand. Linda's little hand. Small, pale, clammy and weak. My hand was strong, full of the vital energy of victory and warm with my blood.

"Where are you going?"

At length she answered, "Home."

"Where's home?"

At this she started to cry. Instinctively, I put my hand on her shoulder again, and when she did not resist I drew her into a comforting embrace. The sexual arousal returned. Linda stank of cigarette smoke and her body was not very clean. But then again, I was probably no bed of roses myself.

"I can give you some money to get a bus," I promised in a sudden rush of chivalry. "Twenty pounds." She looked up at me with some strange kind of admiration in her eyes, but said nothing. At length it became apparent she was waiting for me to give her the money.

"Let's have a cup of tea, first." I took her hand and led her back into the cottage.

And so I found a few unused teabags and made us tea on the gas cooker, which amazingly still had some gas left in the bottle. As we sat and drank our tea I observed her and slowly began to piece the puzzle together. Chet had met this girl, God knows where, but she had an English accent, so likely in some godforsaken council estate in the North of England. He'd taken her here to enjoy her sexually for as long as the money and the beer would last. My arrival was probably just the catalyst for him to depart. He had probably never intended to take her with him when he left.

When the tea was finished she asked, "Can I have the money

now?"

And I nearly did open up my wallet and hand her twenty pounds. But something inside me was stirred by the scene, and instead I said, "It's too late to get a bus today. The bus leaves Drumshanbo in the morning. Stay tonight and you can go home tomorrow."

She looked at me wide-eyed as she considered this proposition.

"Did you poison the dog?" she asked.

"No," I lied. Too quickly, but Linda also wanted to be fooled.

I occupied the rest of the afternoon and evening in cleaning and salvaging things from the mess. Linda was tasked with removing rubbish out to the shed, and I made busy fitting some clear plastic to cover the broken windows. In all, I could hardly wait for the evening to come.

It was not yet dark when I called her to bed. She was crouched back down at the floor in the spot where I had found her. I crawled into the single bed expectantly.

"Aren't you coming?"

She shook her head.

I lay there, burning with desire, uncertainty and frustration, as the light finally faded and her crouched form began to blur into obscurity.

"I'm not giving you the money unless you get into bed with me."

After a brief pause, I heard her scamper over. I felt out into the darkness and took hold of her wrist. I guided her into the bed.

"Take your shoes off."

As she crouched forward to do so, I ran my hand over her braless back and felt the knobs of her spine. She lay back, flat on her back, with her arms strapped across her chest. I moved them and felt her small breasts. The nipples were erect. My body lit up with desire, and my hands searched for further parts of her body.

"No," she said.

"I'll give you forty."

She didn't answer. I pushed her hands away and felt at her jeans. Eventually the button came undone and I pried a hand down between her clasped legs.

"No," she said again.

"Forty pounds."

She didn't answer, so I took that as a sign of acquiescence to the deal. Slowly I inched her jeans down her slender hips and wedged my fingers in between her legs. Eventually, I could feel her vagina, and I ran my fingers all over it, as if by doing so I could make her suddenly want to have sex with me.

At length, I became aware of her gentle sobs. With my other hand, I reached out and touched her cheek, which was wet with tears. These tears extinguished my lust into a sudden puff of shame. I released her and turned onto my side, away from her.

"Okay, but you only get twenty pounds."

As I drifted off into sleep, I could still hear her sobbing gently. And there came the sound of rain drumming against the plastic I had put over the window.

» 40 «

"Psst! Turn around!"

The woman sitting at a table in the front row of the cafe terrace glanced up from her phone and over her shoulder to look at the bearded Arab sitting behind her. He had on sunglasses, and was dressed in a traditional thawb.

"*Non, merci*," she replied. From the dismissive wave of her hand, it was clear she was used to guys hitting on her on the streets of Paris, and this guy looked like a real freak. And he was old.

"Jessica! It's me!" the "Arab" hissed. "Your father!"

She stared for one shocked moment, before realising it really was him.

"Dad! What the *fuck* are you doing here? And why are you dressed up like Aladdin?"

"I came to see you. And the reason I'm in a disguise should be pretty obvious."

"What? You got, like, death threats?"

"Hundreds of them."

Jessica turned her chair and sighed. "Why am I surprised? You know I've had to change my phone number and erase my Facebook page; I even changed my last name, just to keep the journalists away."

"That's probably why I couldn't find you. So what'd you change it to? Céline's name?"

"No. Simmons."

"I'm sure your mom's delighted at that."

Jessica shrugged. "Not really. She's had reporters buzzing around her for weeks now. Her PA's even advised her to hire a bodyguard."

"Yeah, well, she got enough money out of me. That's the price you pay for screwing your husband out of millions in the settlement."

"You know, if you just came here to insult my mother, you can go back to The Hague. I don't wanna hear that shit, okay?"

Art Blume sighed and raised his hands defensively. "All right I'm sorry."

They sat for a second in silence. Art scanned around to make sure nobody was eavesdropping. But it just looked like the usual collection of Sunday morning patrons at a cafe in the 16th *arrondissement*: old women with miniature dogs and Chanel handbags, rich internationals reading the *Financial Times* in their Sunday sportswear. *Paris was starting to look more and more like New York*, Art thought.

"So is the trial over?" Jessica asked.

"What do you mean is the trial over? Don't you watch TV? No the trial's not over."

"So how come you have time to come here?"

"It's the weekend."

Jessica nodded briskly.

"How have you been?" Art asked.

"Good."

"Enjoying life in Paris?"

"Yup."

"Where's Céline?"

"Why do you want to know?"

"Well, I dunno. I mean, are you guys still together?"

"Jesus Christ, Dad, we just got married! Yes, we're still together! Sorry to tell you, but I'm still gay. And I will be the next time you ask too."

"Okay, that's fine. I'm perfectly fine with that. I always have been, as long as you're happy. I only asked 'cause you're here in a cafe alone during a period of the week that most people consider ... prime couple time, and she's not with you."

"She works, okay?"

"On Sunday mornings?"

"She's a doctor. Doctors work on Sundays. How come every time I talk to you I feel like I'm on trial?"

Art Blume sighed and looked down at his espresso. All the way on the train he had thought about what he would say to his daughter.

Of course, he'd imagined a much happier conversation. Memories of times when the family was still together, jokes, anecdotes he could tell her from the trial, the juicy stuff the press didn't know about. He thought she'd laugh at his ridiculous Arab outfit. He even imagined she would be a little proud to have a father who was so famous. He also wanted to apologise to her, and to Céline, for missing their wedding.

But whenever they actually met, there was always the same tension. As if there was some intangible barrier between them. So many issues that never got dealt with. Half of it was her mother's fault; she had made it her life's mission to poison Jessica against him. But deep down, Art knew that was only half the story. The rest was his own doing. He had not been a good father to her. Secretly, he believed this was the reason why she had turned out to be a lesbian. Which meant he had no one but himself to blame for the fact that he'd never become a grandfather. That was bitter.

"Here," he said. "I got you guys this."

"What is it?"

"A wedding present."

"A little bit late, wouldn't you say?"

"I know. But I thought, better late than never."

"What is it?"

"Open it and find out."

She did. It was the *Complete Traditional Jewish Cookbook*. With over 250 recipes for all occasions. Sixth Edition.

"I figured I'd get you something to celebrate your heritage. So you could make a nice dinner for Céline. Something your Grandma Ida used to make. I dunno, matzos or something."

"Thanks, but ... actually Céline does most of the cooking at home. I don't really know how to cook."

"I know that. That's why I got you a cookbook. If you knew how to cook already, you wouldn't need the book."

Despite herself, Jessica smiled. It was a clumsy and stupid gift, but at least he was trying. She looked up at him.

"You look ridiculous. What did you do? Dye your skin?"

"Yeah, it's like ... fake tan. Comes in a bottle. Makes me look more authentic, don't you think? And, hey, what do you think of the beard? It kinda suits me, huh? I was just petrified on the train ride down that some Saudi Sheik would come up to me and be all like *Allahu akbar*! That's why I had to wrap the cookbook. Didn't wanna provoke, like, a diplomatic incident or anything."

They shared a laugh.

"So ... what have you got going on today?" he asked her.

"I'm meeting some friends. We're having lunch, then I've got an opening this evening."

"Really?"

"Really."

Art tried to find something to say about the Paris art scene. But despite his name, he knew absolutely nothing about the art world, neither in Paris nor in New York.

"So it's like an opening ... in your own gallery? Here in Paris?"

"Yup. Which means hours of work to make sure my gallery's ready."

"Who's the artist? Anyone I ever heard of?"

"Her name is Maia-Liise Zbavno. She's Serbian-Swedish. Her work uses everyday household objects to reinterpret gender roles from a post-modernist feminist perspective."

"Really? Wow, that's ... that's interesting."

Jessica smiled sarcastically. "Actually, it is."

"I just thought ... maybe later on, you and I could go to the supermarket. Get some stuff. Maybe cook a meal from the book back at your place. Then, when she knocks off work, we could all eat dinner together. You, me and Céline. What do you say?"

Jessica heaved a sigh of frustration. "I just told you I had plans."

"I know that. But given I'm here now, risking my heavily tanned neck to see you—"

"Dad, I have an opening. What don't you understand about that?"

"Well, cancel it! You probably have openings all the time. How often am I around?"

She snapped her fingers, "That's it! That's exactly it. How often are you around? Because I can sure tell you when you're not around. You're not around when I have my depression. Not around when I graduate college. Not around when I open my gallery—which was a big deal for me. What about when I got married? Where were you on the most important day of my life? Oh, not around. Then, all of a sudden, you decide to show up, and I'm supposed to drop everything else in my life and be your devoted little daughter for a few hours. Well, guess what, Dad? It doesn't work like that."

Art felt the old anger welling up inside him. These were her mother's words. Almost verbatim. His therapist had warned him about this before, this waging of a proxy war against his ex-wife every time he saw Jessica. But in the heat of the moment he just couldn't help himself.

"Oh, right, but you have no problem taking the money, do you? Your mom's there all smiles for the graduation, but who paid the fifty thousand bucks a year in tuition? Ivy League don't come cheap, you know. So your mother goes to the gallery opening, but who gave you a hundred thousand dollars to open it? Sorry, SO SORRY, if I was out actually earning that money, unlike your saintly mother, sitting on her fat ass all day—"

Jessica was already leaving.

"Hey, where are you going?"

"You never change, do you? Call me after you've missed the next important event in my life."

"Hey, hey, you forgot the cookbook!"

"Give it to Brian Matterosi. He'll cook you some matzos."

Art watched her walk away with a sort of helplessness that had characterised his entire approach to family life. He wanted things to be different, but there just didn't seem to be any way to change the pattern. Everything was stuck in a rut, as if the way they spoke to each other was scripted for them by the Fates.

"Wow, that's really harsh, Blume. I was hoping maybe you would at least get to have dinner with her. And her wife. Or female husband. However you say it."

Art looked across at Jeroen, his bodyguard, who was sitting at the table on the other side of him. He had been listening to the whole thing. From Jeroen's flippant way of speaking, Art could tell that he found the whole thing very amusing. He certainly wasn't going to give the Dutchman the pleasure of showing him how upset he was.

"Hey," Art shrugged, forcing a smile. "Whaddya goin' to do? Kids are a pain in the ass at any age."

"In the Netherlands we have a little saying that goes: 'sometimes you win, the rest of the time you learn.'"

"Right. C'mon, let's get back to the train station."

» 41 «

In my mind's eye, the winter of 1989/1990 was all one long, dark evening spent in an armchair in Drumnaslew. On the side table, a plate licked clean of the potatoes and cream I had prepared for dinner. Next to it, a hot mug of tea resting on a tower of scientific journals, which the librarian in Sligo Regional Technical College had given me for nothing.

In front of me, a smoky fire, composed of the turf which I'd cut and dried in September, smouldered away before me. Leitrim turf was schizophrenic, unable to decide whether to consider itself fuel and burn properly like a pine log, or whether to consider itself dirt and just fade into a smouldering mass of turd. However, it was plentiful and free in exchange for labour, and it kept me somewhat warm.

I had made such minor improvements to the cottage as were absolutely indispensable to render it habitable: reconnecting the electricity, putting new glass into the windows, a rug for the sitting room floor and a small refrigerator (not to keep the food cold, but to keep the rats away from it.)

Then I was comfortable and could read the journals carefully and critically. Those that were of no interest were fed unceremoniously to the fire, leading a brief and explosive rebellion against the smouldering pessimism of the turf, before dying as spectral sheaves of ash.

The ones I found interesting I kept, and these were in the majority, for my interest in science grew with every passing article. As much as the past summer had been an opportunity to fall in love with the macrobiology of nature, the cold, perpetually rainy winter was a chance for me to indulge again in my appreciation of the little things in life: viruses.

Viruses really are amazing. As far as "life" forms go, they outnumber us (organisms) ten to one at least, if not 100 to one. The fact is, science has still only scratched the surface of the viral world, and to this day I remain convinced that all of the solutions to man's problems lie in the proper understanding of those little mysterious beings that link the organic with the inorganic world.

As the 1980s drew to a close and the communist world was disintegrating, the world of microbiology and virology in particular was expanding rapidly, in no small part due to a huge increase in funding for research to understand and combat the HIV retrovirus.

As early as 1976, American scientists had completely sequenced RNA strands. This had led to as many new questions being asked as old ones were answered. To get their heads around HIV, researchers had to go back to the very basics of virology. We needed to observe. To categorise RNA sequences in viruses; to see what was happening to them over time, how they evolved. How did antibodies cope?

One thing that blew everyone away was how rapidly some viruses could evolve, making the job of the immune system's antibodies nearly impossible. It's like that X-Men bad girl who keeps changing shape just as the cops come to arrest her. And so it was with HIV. And the flu. And lots of other viruses. For a while, they just seemed to be way ahead of us.

At around the same time, in 1988, a team of researchers in the US was working on a project involving petunias. If memory serves, they were trying to make them more colourful, or better smelling, or something. In the process of introducing a new gene, they found that, in effect, the original plant genes could be shut off. Instead of turning the flower from red to purple, they ended up bleeding it of colour altogether.

The specific mechanism at play was a phenomenon known as "post-transcriptional gene silencing". Basically, this was a means of cracking in to the RNA strand—the actual sequence of proteins that makes the plant tick—and altering its profile, without the whole strand breaking down completely. From something as simple as a mistake, the whole foundations of genetic engineering began to emerge.

As yet there was no link with the science of virology. But it occurred to me, one rainy night in December 1989 as I read an article by R. T. Salinger in *New Microbiology*, that the logic of the RNA sequencing could be applied to viruses too. Sex was complicated, but virus reproduction was not. By altering the genetic sequencing of a virus, it might be possible to shut down some of its properties too. These alterations could be dynamically transcribed to set in motion a chain of quasi-organic evolutions.

It was thinking outside the box on a cosmic scale, because up to that point, virology had concerned itself with beefing up the body's defences, through antiviral agents or with the development of vaccines. The idea of attacking a virus the same way it attacked cells—by invading it and altering its properties—had never really occurred to anyone.

So for HIV, I thought, instead of worrying about a "cure", what we really needed to do was find a way to "tame" it. Create a strain that was more prolific, but also more benign, than its ancestors. A super-HIV strain. Then AIDS might become like herpes. Nearly everyone you know has it, but it just isn't that bad.

I dreamed of discovering just such a process. Of cracking the inner code of viral RNA that made HIV do what it did, and rendering it pacific to the human organism. From within the deep folds of a torn and stained, duvet-covered armchair in the endless night of an Irish winter, I determined that I would one day become the father of modern virology.

» 42 «

Leeton played with his pen and pretended to listen as one of his assistants briefed him on procedure. When Blume had refused to cross-examine Dr Andrews last week, it had left Leeton feeling nervous and unsure of himself. Dsulanga had not gone well, and now that Andrews was back on the witness stand, Leeton's instincts told him the little American had something similar up his sleeve.

Without meaning to, he found he was indulging in brief glances at Rachel as she went past. Today, she had on a tight white skirt with black stripes, and a silky cream-coloured blouse that hinted here and there at the black lacy bra he knew she was wearing underneath. He wanted her. A part of him could have taken her right then and there. *Stop it*, he told himself. *That was only nerves.*

Chief Justice Wang turned to Art Blume and said, "Counsel for the defence may now begin his examination of the witness. We recall that the defence declined a cross-examination following the witness's first appearance on the stand; a special supplementary examination is deemed permissible under Article 57 of the ICC's rules and procedures."

Blume ambled towards the witness box, his hands buried in his pockets and his gaze fixed on his shoes. Today, he looked particularly scruffy, almost comically so. After all the man's blunders, Leeton was now finding this casual shabbiness hard to take seriously. He had read more than a few newspaper articles complimenting his own good taste in suits, and commenting that Blume seemed to pay as little attention to his case as he did to his taste in clothes. Perhaps Art Blume used to be a great lawyer, Leeton reflected, but he'd lost it somewhere on the way to the bank.

"Dr Andrews," Blume began, "when last you were on the stand, you mentioned that you estimated fifty thousand deaths as a result of VIS infection. Can you provide us with a breakdown of casualties by strain?"

"Well ... the estimate is not precise, you know."

"Yes, I know, you explained that already. It's an estimate, so there's a margin of error. But it's nevertheless a number. A number you threw out. And I just want a breakdown of that number."

"Well, it is an estimated number. It could be thirty thousand. It could be a hundred thousand."

"Could it be zero?"

"No ... no ... not possible. There are verifiable cases. Particularly with Hydra-gamma8. A lot of work was done on that in India. Thousands of people were treated by the Indian Ministry of Health in their VIS programme."

"Yes, we've seen the reports on gamma8, but what about the other strains. The African strains. Say, beta1, or even alpha1?"

"The problem is these early strains had a very localised range. And the virus had not yet been identified. By the time the infection had been identified, most of the victims were immune. It's possible, even likely, some had died, but this would be indiscernible from other maladies. We cannot say for sure."

"What about gamma1? The Indian government, even the WHO, was on to that pretty much upon inception? How many verifiable deaths are attributable to gamma1?"

Dr Andrews let out a sigh of frustration. "Well, you know, the relative number of gamma1 infections in the Indian epidemic is quite small. Perhaps 0.03 per cent of all Hydra infections are gamma1."

"Okay. And how many of them were verifiable casualties?"

"That's not the way we conduct our analysis. We don't look at particular cases associated with that exact sub-strain."

"In other words, Doctor, you're telling us that for all the 'one' sub-strains: alpha1, beta1, gamma1, epsilon1, delta1—the sub-strains actually engineered by Professor Matterosi, either in the University in Göttingen or in the BetterWorld lab— there is not one *verifiable* case of fatality?"

"Eh ... verifiable ... I mean, you're playing with words, Mr Blume. Of course, there were fatalities for these strains too. But the virus mutated. Hydra-alpha6 was very deadly. We're talking about nearly seven billion infections. You must understand the difficulty in pinpointing individual cases."

"But you must have pinpointed individual cases, in order to come up with the fifty thousand casualty count?"

"This is only an estimate. I have already explained this to you."

"So, of these fifty thousand people, how many can we name?"

"Among other things, the estimate is based on extrapolation from a panel study in Bangalore. Here we have four hundred casualties. If you must name victims, there are four hundred victims in Bangalore that we can definitely name."

"And these four hundred victims were infected with which precise sub-strain?"

"Hydra-alpha6."

"So when we talk about 'direct effects'—the millions of casualties the media has told us about so often—what we are actually talking about is four hundred people who died from 'flu-like' symptoms, which doctors attributed to a virus that was five mutations away from what Professor Matterosi actually engineered back in his lab in Germany."

"Four hundred human beings! Even if that were all, you cannot simply dismiss them, sir."

"I have no intention of dismissing anyone, Doctor. These four hundred people, have you studied their actual medical reports?

"Yes I have."

"And what was their patient profile?"

"They were poor, mostly."

"Average age?"

"Thirty-five."

Blume paused for a moment, and then allowed himself a little smile. He wagged his finger playfully at the witness.

"Now, now, Doctor. If I take the average age of one baby and one septuagenarian, I get about thirty-five, don't I? So, let me ask you the question again. What was the average patient profile of the four hundred people in the Bangalore report? Give me an ethical answer, please."

"Most were either very old or very young, if that's what you're getting at."

"So ... the kinds of people who are most at risk in an environment lacking proper sanitary conditions and access to medicine. And they died from ... VIS directly?"

"They died from VIS, yes."

"That was their actual cause of death? That appeared on their death certificates?"

"It's not a question of what appears on their death—"

"Yes it is! 'Cause that's the question I'm asking. What was the cause of death on their death certificates?"

Andrews was silent for a second.

"Well, it just so happens," Art went back over to his bench and Lisbeth handed him a thick file, "that I have the death certs right here. Physical evidence, ICC 447. Should we go through them and read out the cause of death, doctor? If we did, how many would say 'died from VIS'?"

"Mr Blume ... the point is, the Hydra retrovirus weakens the immune system, leaving the victim vulnerable to bacterial infections or other viruses. Pneumonia is the most common secondary illness. That's what you'll find listed as the cause of death in the majority of cases."

"So, in fact, VIS didn't kill these people at all. They died of pneumonia, or malaria, or—"

"Well, let's not be pedantic here, all right? The Hydra virus was the cause."

"But could you not say other things are also the cause? Like, for instance, lack of access to antibiotics? After all, pneumonia can be treated with antibiotics. Or perhaps, lack of adequate care? Poor nutrition? You could say, could you not, that the poverty caused by living in a heavily overpopulated country was as much the cause of their death as was Hydra-alpha6?"

"Crap! You're talking pure crap! That's like saying, if I shoot you, then it's not the bullet that's to blame, it's the lack of a bullet-proof vest. You're talking crap."

Blume took a stroll around the courtroom. Leeton watched the reactions of the judges to see what this testimony was doing. It didn't help to have Andrews lose his temper that way.

"Dr Andrews, let's take a different approach to this. You estimated the direct effects of VIS to be fifty thousand casualties. This is out of an overall infected population of how many?"

"I don't have the precise numbers off the top of my head."

Art smiled, "Estimate, Doctor, estimate. That's what we're doing anyway."

"Perhaps 6.9 billion."

"So out of a population of 6.9 billion—nearly 85 per cent of the entire global population, only fifty thousand are estimated to have died. That represents a casualty rate of ..." Art whipped out a calculator for dramatic effect, "only 0.000079 per cent."

"If you say so."

"Oh, I don't say so, Dr Andrews. I'm just a lawyer. You're the expert witness here. You and the calculator say so. Dr Andrews, are you aware of the guidelines your organisation, the World Health Organisation, offers to national food and drug administrations on acceptable levels of fatality risk in its medications?"

"No."

"Allow me to read them to you. 'WHO Guidelines on Medication', October 12, 2014. Load Code DAR-145-S-354-2014. Page 240-241. I quote: *For the dispensation of medications which are deemed life-saving or invaluable to the protection of the general health, the recommended fatality risk is not to exceed 0.002%.*' In other words, your organisation tells countries to give out life-saving drugs in cases where the risk that these drugs will kill their patients *is not greater* than 0.002 per cent. That's two hundred and sixty times greater than the risk of death by VIS, based on your own estimates, which I stress, have not been verified on an individual patient basis."

Dr Andrews stood up, barely able to contain his rage.

"You're ... you're twisting everything. You can't make that comparison! For one thing, people weren't given the choice as to whether they'd get VIS. They didn't go to the doctor and sign up for a risk. That bastard just infected them, whether they liked it or not! And anyway, you're talking about life-saving medications. VIS isn't a life-saving medication. It stops lives, it doesn't save anyone."

"That, Dr Andrews, is just where the defence is going to prove you wrong. Thank you, Your Honours, I'm done with this witness."

» 43 «

Agriculture in County Leitrim does not suffer from the chronic water shortages of equatorial Africa which I observed when I travelled there to spread VIS in 2016. In the West of Ireland in 1990, the opposite problem existed. At times it felt to me like it would never stop raining. The importance of adequate drainage became clear as I struggled to pull a potato harvest from my ancestral lands. My first attempts at subsistence farming were, to use a pun, a damp squib.

My paid employment went a little better. It consisted of the fabulous art of "grinds", or hourly tuition to secondary school children. In this, I would travel the area by bicycle and help the sons and daughters of local farmers with their preparations for the dreaded "Leaving Certificate" State examinations they would have to face in June. These exams mark the end of secondary school for Irish children and unlike in other countries, they are the sole deciding criterion for entry into third-level education. In other words, your entire schooling boils down to one set of examinations.

The fact that I myself was a high school dropout and had never even attempted the exams was no real obstacle in this. Armed with my Italian air of maturity, the beard I had let grow, my American accent and my ability to tell convincing lies, I easily fooled people into believing I was twenty, although in fact I was not yet seventeen. There was something about being American, I discovered, which made me seem somehow important and special, more mature. Perhaps it was the natural inferiority complex of a small country of oppressed people, I don't know. But it was a strength I quickly learned to play to.

"Trinity College, Dublin" was another magical phrase that evoked awe and humility in the Leitrim catholic peasantry. In 1990 it still represented a world of power and knowledge they felt they could neither aspire to nor fully comprehend. I, of course, did not share their inferiority complex.

Using my old trick from Princeton, I explained to them that I was a Trinity student taking a year "off books", and that I was well equipped to help their children with any science or maths subjects that might be giving them trouble. This latter statement was, in fact, perfectly true.

As it happened, I was operating in the best tradition of ad hoc rural tuition, which predated the establishment of a state education system in Ireland. For centuries, Irish hedge school masters traversed the countryside, setting up schools in rough shelters in fields (hence the appellation "hedge schools") and on terms not unlike my "grinds". Such schoolmasters often exaggerated their qualifications, and while some were genuine scholars, most were charlatans who pawned off false verbiage on an ignorant and gullible audience.

By the time of my arrival on the scene, the hedge schools of course had long been replaced by a formal system of education, nominally run by the church, but paid for by the State. And yet the Leitrim folk had long memories. As with many dubious traditions, the locals guarded a special affection for this kind of door-to-door scholarship in which my unique personality seemed to find its own special niche. There was something that appealed to them in my rugged form braving the foul weather on an ancient bicycle, along the twisting little country lanes with grass growing down the middle of them. My association with the Whelans also gave me a stamp of belonging, which a pure outsider could not have obtained in thirty years of residence.

And so they welcomed me into their homes with hot meals and cups of tea, and they welcomed me into the minds of their offspring with hourly tuition fees.

In defence of my deceptions, I don't think I was a bad tutor. Of course, biology was a walk in the park, but really so was maths and physics, once I familiarised myself with the curricula. If I was guilty of anything, it was of inciting their minds towards thoughts that were greater and deeper than the rigid, mnemonic state curriculum could accommodate, or (in some cases) than their weak minds were able to grasp. I don't mean to sound like a class snob here: the problem of prescribed curricula and stupid students has followed me from Keshkerrigan right into the lecture halls of some of the world's leading universities.

The pay for a "hedge school" grinds tutor in 1990 Leitrim was not great (I think I usually got a pound an hour), but with my turf reserves, bags of potatoes and sacks of porridge, my only real bills were bottled gas and electricity.

By degrees my accent became Irish. I developed Irish mannerisms and attitudes and was soon acting like I'd spent all my life in "Lovely Leitrim". Such was my contentment with having successfully re-forged my identity according to plan, that for a time, I forgot about my real roots. On the rare occasions when I speculated on Watertown High School, on my mother, or on my father, it was as if I was remembering a different person's life. Details of things that had been so real to me only a year and a half ago seemed vague when remembered through the mist of soft Leitrim rain. Images of my past occasionally stirred in the flickering flames of my turf fire, or in the half-remembered guise of a dream. Still I convinced myself, or tried to convince myself, that it was, after all, possible to run away from misery and to find happiness far, far away.

The Trinity student myth became a sort of self-fulfilling prophecy. So often had I announced that I would be returning to my studies in Dublin in September, that as the summer wound down, I found myself getting ready to depart.

It was true, too, that I had itchy feet. The Leaving Certificate results were in, and several of my tutees were heading off to Dublin to start university themselves. The idea of another long winter cloistered in Drumnaslew was unappealing. The hobbit hole had grown dull. I wanted to be in a more challenging environment, one in which people understood science the way I did. I also wanted to get access to a real lab with an electron microscope, so I could put into practice things I knew only from reading others' results. And so I packed up my rucksack, locked up the cottage and took myself and my old rusty bicycle off in the direction of Dublin. The last time, in Princeton, I was young and unprepared for the challenge of successfully impersonating a real student. This time, in Trinity, I was determined to succeed.

» 44 «

"It's nowhere in her deposition. Nowhere in her bio. Nowhere!"

Art shuffled through papers he'd already looked at a hundred times: the complete transcript of Professor Jennifer Amery's deposition; her publication record; her media interviews. Everything she had ever said that had been caught on a microphone or camera. He needed to know if they had missed something, more for pride than for anything else. His paper-flicking became manic, and, in the end, he tossed a whole ream of it across the table.

"Fuck. Shit. Fuck and shit!"

Peter looked up from his press folder in astonishment.

"Excuse my French."

"We could just not put her on the stand," Lisbeth suggested.

"Right. And then the first thing Kgabu's gonna do is ask himself why I'm withdrawing my star witness at the very last minute. And the second thing he's gonna do is poke his nose into her research until he finds this."

Art's finger jabbed at the tablet. A pdf version of Professor Jennifer Amery's latest working paper glowed to life. It had been published on the university's website that very morning, buried at the bottom of a long list of publications. The title gave nothing away. There wasn't even a hyperlink, but Lisbeth had still managed to find it in the University of Chicago's digital archives, which were technically open only to students and staff. Probably no one else in the world even knew it was there. If Art wasn't so pissed off right then, he would have made a point of congratulating Lisbeth for finding such a needle in a haystack.

"And the third thing he's gonna do is—"

"—call her as a witness for the prosecution." Lisbeth finished Art's sentence for him. "Except he never subpoenaed her."

"No, but we did. Why means she's cleared to testify." Art read the paper's astonishing conclusion again.

"I say we call her anyway," Chun said. They all looked around at him. It was rare for Chun to make such strong statements on strategy. "If you listen to the deposition, Amery tends to give very precise answers. She's kind of like a machine. The main thing is to just ask closed questions. Then hope the prosecution overlooks her latest findings. At this stage, it's our best hope of burying her and making this go away."

Art could feel his blood pumping. He looked at the clock. 09:37.

"Okay, let's take up positions, guys. What's our client doing, by the way?"

"He's in his holding cell upstairs," Anna told him. "Doing his recording."

"Good. We keep this to ourselves. This is need-to-know information, and right now, Matterosi doesn't need to know."

The Court session opened with something of a drama between Chief Justice Wang and Rachel Hyberg. Art watched it play out with interest. *This has been coming for days*, he thought. Wang had been refusing to follow the instructions on the teleprompter. She would order five-minute breaks when Hyberg was calling for ten-minute breaks. Art couldn't quite catch what they were arguing about now, but he heard Wang reciting an article of the Abuja Treaty, and Hyberg countering with threats to refer the matter to Sobiewski, who was pretty much everybody's boss. This really seemed to antagonise Wang, who abruptly turned her back on Hyberg and engaged the other judges in a private consultation at the bench.

Out of the corner of his eye, Art caught sight of Kgabu, still sitting on his own. He too was absorbed in the Hyberg-Wang drama. Good. Anything to keep him distracted.

"Alright," Wang began once the Court had been called to order. "We have reached the point where the defence will call witnesses for the 'Direct Effects' segment of the trial. Before we go on, let me recap on the process, going forward. The prosecution will be afforded the opportunity to cross-examine each of the witnesses for the defence in turn, in accordance with the agreed procedure.

After this, the defence can summarise their case concerning the direct effects *only*. Then, lastly, the prosecution will be invited to summarise the evidence they have presented to the Court, again on the direct effects case *only*.

"At that point, we will move on to the 'Indirect Effects' case, where the procedure is largely the same. Finally, the judges will confer on all the points raised, and vote on a decision. If the decision is unanimous, it will be presented as such. If the decision is not unanimous, the judges will hold a special séance to deliberate, calling witnesses for direct examination, as may be required. We will seek unanimity again, and finally a third time. If no unanimity is reached, we will take the third and final vote as binding. Note that in accordance with Article 63, Section 1 of the Abuja Treaty, the structure of sentencing depends on whether the vote was unanimous or not. Only in the case of a unanimous guilty verdict on the specific charge of genocide can sentencing be carried out in accordance with Article 63, Section 1."

Article 63 of the Abuja Treaty: the most controversial legal provision passed since the Nuremberg Trials. The mere mention of it made Art Blume's toes curl. He reflected on how far the world, and Europe in particular, had come in allowing that part of the Treaty to pass. Technically, nothing in the Treaty or the implementing Resolutions, actually talked about a death sentence. Article 63 was their moral escape clause. It provided for sentencing to be carried out "in accordance with the national laws of the victim member state." But because so many signatory countries to the Treaty had the death penalty, this effectively amounted to a global mandate to execute Brian Matterosi.

The main "victim member state", in this case, was always going to be India. And India was always going to sentence Brian Matterosi to death. Their Prime Minister, Veedala Jhumi, was reason enough to make Art cynical. The man had so blatantly seized on the whole thing to orchestrate a collapse of the Indian government and bring himself to power, that it made Art sick. Brian's execution was Jhumi's sceptre. *And not just Brian*, Art thought with a shudder. Behind the legalese, the Treaty was setting up a global court with the power to press charges—and to issue a death sentence—on anyone on the planet. Brave new world, indeed.

» 45 «

From her special place behind Camera One, Art could see that Rachel Hyberg was visibly seething at Chief Justice Wang's speech. Once again, Wang had ignored the teleprompter and explained things her way. Art had to admit there was something about Wang he really liked, even if she was a part of this vicious machinery, and, he suspected, not nearly as impartial as she ought to be. Still, she had that kind of drive to her: that quiet self-belief that emanated from her presence. She was the kind of judge who would protect a sausage from a pack of hungry wolves in a winter forest, if she felt the wolves had no legal right to it.

"Mr Blume, you may call your witness."

"Thank you, Your Honour. The defence calls Professor Jennifer Amery."

Jennifer Amery was a thin, short, but intense-looking blonde woman in her late forties or early fifties.

"Professor Amery, could you explain to the Court your background and qualifications?"

"I'm a professor of epidemiology at the University of Chica—"

"Sorry to cut across you there, Professor. Could you just explain to the Court what that is: 'epid—mology'?"

"It's the study of the spread of infectious diseases. How diseases spread in populations; how many people die from them. All that stuff."

"Diseases like VIS?"

"Yes, VIS, HIV, Bird Flu. All of the above."

"And you've been working in the area for …?"

"Twenty-six years."

"You're considered a leading expert by your peers?"

"I was voted Harvard's 'Academic of the Year' in 2015. I hold honorary doctorates from Berlin's Humboldt University, University of Beijing, and University of Bologna. My publication record in the field compares well to anyone's."

"So, when it comes to epidiam ... epidemiomo..."

"Epidemiology," she added helpfully.

"Yeah, when it comes to epidemiology, it's fair to say, you wrote the book on it?"

"I have written or contributed to quite a few of the leading textbooks in the field, yes."

"Okay, let's not beat around the bush here, Professor, now that we've established your credentials. Please tell the Court, how many people have died from VIS?"

"The truth is, it's impossible to say."

"Really? Well the prosecution just got through telling us fifty thousand. Then they said hundreds of thousands. Then they said twenty-three people for sure. Then, in the end, they just seemed to be saying 'lots'. And now you're saying it's impossible to know?"

"Well, I think the prosecution's evidence is based on some assumptions which could easily be questioned."

"Such as?"

"The models they used to trace the disease progression were designed for infections with obvious fatal consequences, or for which permanent debilitations followed infection. But VIS doesn't work that way. There's a 'hot' phase, as you know, in which heightened mortality risk exists, but after that the body adapts—actually it spurs on the development of antibodies. Recent tests have shown a lowered risk of infection by influenza in the six months after infection, due to the presence of the antibodies. If you were to look at a post-infection VIS population, say, four months after it was hit, you might observe a lower incidence of mortality from symptoms consistent with 'hot' VIS. The WHO, in their analysis, simply treated them as if they weren't infected populations, but they were."

"So VIS is a cure as much as an affliction?"

"Well, yes. And also, because VIS behaves like a bad dose of the flu virus, you can never tell in a given population, if it's the VIS causing deaths or something else. Just because someone who died had VIS in their blood doesn't mean they didn't also have some other virus as well. Or a bacterial infection."

"But what about the four hundred people in Bangalore, which the Indian Ministry of Health diagnosed with VIS and who all died?"

"Well, I mean, what they did is, they went out and found four hundred people who were highly feverish, you know, who had pneumonia, were dehydrated, weak, malnourished. Basically, who were coping very badly with the effects of a localised viral infection."

"But they had VIS?"

"Well, yes, but so did the millions of other Indians who weren't put under the microscope. You can't cherry-pick a sample of victims, diagnose a cause of death within that sample, and then extrapolate this onto the rest of the population. A population, remember, which you deliberately excluded from your sample in the first place. That will yield biased results every time. The fact is, in a country of 1.4 billion like India, people die all the time, of lots of things."

"So you're saying the WHO cherry-picked their evidence?"

"Yes, absolutely. It's bogus science."

"But there was a heightened casualty rate in Bangalore, wasn't there?"

"Oh, sure there was. But, I mean, if you look at any part of the world at any given time, you'll see mortality surges. Some of these are demographic trends; some are just statistical anomalies. 1.4 billion is a big number. If you were to create a continuous line of 1.4 billion random letters, you'd probably get a few recognisable sentences in there. But that's not poetry either."

"So, what's the correct way to tell if VIS is a killer?"

"You would need to monitor the death rate in a predefined, random population over the course of the infection. Since VIS never really goes away, you would need to establish an outer bound for the infection. In our published research, we had set this outer bound at a year, since the effects of the antibodies are greatly diminished after that."

"And, if you do that, what do you get?"

"Well, there are surges which correspond to the 'hot peak': the statistical point in time when the largest number of people are in the 'hot phase' of infection. So there, the mortality risk goes up. But then, it falls quickly to a point below where it started."

"So after a population has been infected for a year, their mortality risk actually goes down below the level it was at before infection?"

"Yes."

"Why?"

"Because the infection works like a vaccine."

"A vaccine against what?"

"Against influenza."

"So there we have it. Far from being a killer, VIS is actually making the world healthier. Thank you, Professor. I have no further questions."

Art did his very best to look smug. He was almost positive that no part of his inward cringe would be visible on the outside. He even threw an arrogant smile at Kgabu. But Kgabu wasn't looking at him. He was looking at Lisbeth: more particularly he was looking at Lisbeth's hands. With a creeping sense of dread, Art followed the prosecutor's line of vision and quickly realised why. She was gripping the corners of her tablet so tightly her knuckles were white.

» 46 «

The first week in Trinity College Dublin—Freshers' Week, as it was known—captured my imagination completely, and if there had been any doubt in my mind as to whether I had made the right decision in leaving Leitrim, it was gone within an hour of crossing the threshold of Front Arch and entering into the stately, cobbled grounds of Front Square.

Student societies ranging from the Atheists Society, to the Dublin University Water Polo Society, to the College Historical Society Debating Club used this first week as a chance to bolster their membership. There they were, all jostling for the right to sign you up as a member. This was combined with the old buildings and the general, studenty feel of the place. I was hooked.

I did quickly discover how low the standard of teaching was there, compared with Princeton, which came as a bit of a surprise. Perhaps the awe and reverence in which the natives of Leitrim held the place had been infectious, and had prejudiced me to look with a certain unwarranted favour on what was, in fact, a second-rate State school.

The student societies turned out to be not much better. They were for the most part an excuse for their members to gather in dark rooms provided by the college, smoke cigarettes and get drunk. Some, like the Business Society, were networking tools for the middle-class kids from South Dublin to maintain and improve the associations they had already formed in their private secondary schools. They spoke and acted with the self-assurance of an elite that fully expected to be running the country in twenty years' time. I'm sure several of those very kids are now senior officials in the Irish Government, responsible for facilitating Ireland's full and unconditional ratification of the Abuja Treaty, which is how I (as a dual Irish/American citizen) am now subject to prosecution.

But what Trinity had to offer, and what I soon came to see as its only real asset, was its amazing library. Besides being a warm and comfortable place to sit until ten o'clock in the evening, Trinity was also one of a handful of 'copyright' libraries, which meant effectively that any book published in the English language had to send a copy to Trinity. Nowadays, with the Internet and the ready availability of information, this may not seem like such a big deal. But in the early 1990s, the Internet effectively did not exist, and so the vast catalogue of information at my sudden disposal felt like a cornucopia of academic knowledge.

Robert Dunlop was my first friend in college. We met in that casual, informal way people do in college—I guess it must have been through one of the student societies—and by degrees we became close. He was studying science too, but had no interest in it. Really he had wanted to do arts, but his ambitious father, a GP doctor, had forced him to study medicine. When he failed to get the requisite points in his Leaving Cert, he was shoved into science as the next best option, having got just enough points for that. Robert hated science nearly as much as he hated his father. In truth, he had no real ambition for arts either. He wanted to spend his time playing his guitar, smoking pot and meeting girls.

I had come to spend a lot of time sleeping on the sofa of his flat, mostly because we would stay up late discussing politics or religion or else just strumming the guitar and singing songs. Technically, I was still staying in youth hostels and sleeping in parks, but as the term wore on, and the weather grew colder and my bank account emptier, I effectively lived on that couch. This arrangement only became formalised one evening as we were sitting around, and Robert announced to me that if he failed First Year, and had to repeat, his father would punish him by making him stay in "digs".

"Digs" was the form of student accommodation that was universally dreaded at the time. It meant you lived with a local, Dublin family from Monday to Friday and had to take the bus home to your parents' house on the weekend. No drinking, no smoking, no girls, no staying up all night, and no weekends partying in Dublin.

Also, quite obviously, no chance for your quasi-homeless American friend to stay on your couch.

"So you'll just have to pass your exams," I said, shrugging.

"Easier said than done," Robert countered, taking a swig of beer from his can, and pushing his long, greasy mane of hair back out of his eyes. He had missed almost all of his lectures up to that point and would face the Michaelmas term exams in early December, with no hope of passing. "I'm not like you, Brian. God gave you brains and the ability to study. He gave me family money." Robert uttered this last sentence with bitterness, as if free money from your father and a stable, loving nurturing home were a curse.

"So let's barter," I suggested.

"What do you mean?"

"Well, since you never go to lectures, none of the lecturers know what you look like. I could just sit your exams for you."

"And what about your own exams? You're doing the same subjects as me. You can't be in two places at once."

And it was then that I told him the truth. That I wasn't even registered as a student; that I was only sixteen and had run away from home. That I had no money and no family and nothing, except a desire to educate myself.

The deal was struck. I pretended to be Robert Dunlop, and 'lost' my student ID card, then had another one made up with my picture on it. That was easily done.

Armed with my new ID, and keeping myself in the quietest corner of the exams hall, I sat exams in biology, physics, chemistry, geography and maths for Michaelmas Term, while Robert lounged around the flat in Harold's Cross and took drugs. The only difficult part of the exams was ensuring the answers I gave were not so good as to raise suspicions.

» 47 «

In the poor neighbourhood of Durban where Leeton had grown up, poker was a popular past time. It was a way for the gangs to while away the hours in their shanty HQs, in between the fights with the white cops or with rival black gangs. Leeton had become good at it—in fact, good enough to pay his way into college—though he had always hidden the fact from Umama, who disapproved of gambling almost as much as she disapproved of gangs or alcohol. Leeton had mastered poker by adopting a very simple strategy: he never played the cards, but always the opponent. Of course, this was hard to do with a cagey old shyster like Blume, but the American had an Achilles heel: his team of young lawyers.

The whole time Professor Jennifer Amery had been on the stand, Leeton could see the bluff written all over their faces, especially the posh English girl. They were nervous. Scared that Amery might say something, perhaps? And so, seconds before he began his cross-examination, Leeton shoved aside his notes and decided to go completely all in for this witness. Instead of trying to discredit her, to refute her, to challenge her findings, he was just going to let her talk. It was time to go fishing.

"Professor Amery, I find your insights into the spread of diseases really fascinating."

"I'm glad my life's work entertains you." She was cold and sarcastic. Not in the least intimidated by the fact that two billion people were watching her live. The court let out a laugh. Leeton swallowed his pride and allowed himself to join in good-naturedly.

"Is there anything more you think the world should know about VIS?"

Amery shrugged. "How to cure it, maybe?" Another laugh.

"I meant about your research. Do you have any further insights into the spread of the disease? Was there anything my esteemed colleague, Mr Blume, might have missed in his questioning?"

"Well," she began, "our research is ongoing. So ask me again in a month and I might have different answers."

"In a month this trial will be over."

Amery stared blankly. Leeton hazarded a final glance at the English girl, and wished it were her, not Amery, on the witness stand. Then he cast his final line and bait.

"Can you tell us a little more about your ongoing research?"

"What do you want to know?"

"Anything major in the pipeline? Any new ... research papers due out?"

She delivered the "Yes" in so flat a tone, Leeton almost mistook it for a "No".

"Yes? As in, you have got something new?"

"In working paper form, only. So nothing published."

"But is it of relevance to this case?"

"That's not my job to judge."

Leeton raised his hands in frustration. "Well perhaps you can tell us what it is, so the people whose job it is to judge can judge. Namely, the *judges*."

"Well, as I say, it's not published yet, so really I'd prefer not to."

"But given that you are under oath and have sworn to divulge anything that might be relevant to this case ..."

Amery sighed. "Fine. But it's important to understand we're talking about a *working* paper. The results are not final."

"I fully accept that, Professor. Please continue."

"Our latest studies are showing mortality surges in infected populations re-emerging after one year of infection."

"Mortality surges? Are these significant?"

"The latest data shows they are significant and, moreover, will become much more significant in time."

"Do you know the cause for this? Is it through reinfection?"

"No. It appears to be caused by elevated suicide rates."

"Objection!" Blume shouted. "That is an 'indirect effect' and is not permissible in this phase of the trial. Suicide is not a symptom of VIS contagion. Rather, if at all—and the defence disputes it is—it is indirectly related to the fertility ... to the social effects and clearly has no place in this part of the trial."

"This witness was called by the defence, Your Honours," Leeton countered. "I'm following directly on from the defence's own line of questioning. Professor Amery was introduced by the defence to testify on the spread of VIS and the mortality risks brought about by the infection. Professor Amery mentioned suicide as part of those risks."

The judges conferred for a moment. In particular, Justice Gomes seemed animated and adamant on the point. After a moment, Wang announced that they would take a short recess and confer. This was not scripted, and Rachel Hyberg ran into the television box to improvise a commercial break. In the few seconds it took her to do so, a camera remained focused on Brian Matterosi, who was trying to make eye contact with Art Blume. Blume had retreated across the room and was conferring with his legal team. Leeton cast an eye on the live-stream he had on his tablet next to him. It looked to all the world as if Matterosi had been abandoned by his own lawyer.

When the judges returned after twenty minutes there was a certain stiffness in their manner that told the world there had been a lively discussion, if not an outright row.

"We will allow the Counsel for the prosecution to continue the line of questioning as regards the testimony introduced by the witness on the mortality drivers of VIS infection. The reference to suicide arose naturally from a discussion of the scope of the infection, and can therefore be taken to be within the predefined terms of reference of the trial to which both—"

Blume was on his feet in an instant.

"But this is ridiculous! If we're going to talk about suicide here, why don't we talk about global warming? Why don't we talk about food shortages? Deforestation? This is out of scope, out of place and outrageous!"

"Enough, Counsel," Wang said in an icy tone. Leeton had been waiting for days for her to lose her temper with Blume's Hollywood antics. Finally the point had arrived. "One more word out of turn, and you'll be sent out of this courtroom, do you hear?"

"Continue, please, Mr Kgabu," she added at length.

Leeton felt a surge of power as he rose and walked towards the witness, passing provocatively close to Art Blume and his team.

"Tell us about the mortality risk arising from suicide."

Throughout all this, Amery had sat like stone, the image of an immovable speaker of hard, scientific fact.

"Basically, suicide rates among people infected with VIS increase dramatically, about a year after infection."

"Why is that, Professor?"

"Well, I'm an epidemiologist, not a social psychologist, so maybe I'm not the best person to answer that question. But, I mean, even for a casual observer, it seems obvious."

She pushed a lump of her shoulder-length, blonde hair behind her ear and went on.

"Reproduction is an important human function. If people are denied the possibility of achieving it, they get depressed. They drink, take drugs. They commit suicide. That much is well supported by previous research which has shown suicide rates tend to be higher for people without children. But what we are finding, and what is surprising, is just how much of these psychological effects seem to be frontloaded in afflicted populations. Even for people who are unmarried or quite young, the effect is just as pronounced. It's almost as though people sense that their intergenerational contract has been broken, and they despair."

"So if we take into account the heightened risks of suicide, by how much does contracting VIS increase your mortality risk?"

"Well, as I said before, it all depends on your timescale. Technically, VIS doesn't kill at all. In the 'hot' phase it weakens your immune system. Then, in the virion phase, it strengthens your immune system. After about a year, it can be linked with an elevated risk of self-harm, and suicide, in particular. So far, that suicide risk doesn't appear to go away over time.

"So if you look at seventy-two hours, the mortality risk rises by about 1 per cent over the baseline of 'no infection'. If you look at one month, the chances of death are about on par with the baseline. If you look at four months, the chances of death go down by about 1 per cent. After thirteen months, they're about at par again. After sixteen months, up 1 per cent. After two years, up 2 per cent."

"And after that?"

"Well, we really don't know yet, because we just don't have data. Our most recent data covers the cohort for two years of infection. And, furthermore, we may never know. The fact is, since 90 per cent of the developing world has VIS, we are rapidly losing our baseline as time goes by. The psycho-social characteristics of populations in the developed world are probably too different to allow for any useful cross-country comparisons. I don't doubt studies will be done, but I think the results will be quite ambiguous."

"But let's just assume the two-year timescale. How many deaths could we associate with VIS over this period?"

"Well, that's arbitrary—"

"Just answer the question, please, Professor."

"I mean, it's a dumb question."

A loud laugh rippled throughout the courtroom at her cool impudence, but Leeton didn't mind. He was landing body blows here. A short little jab like that didn't matter.

"Thank you for your critique of my intelligence. Now, please answer the question. If we assume the two-year timescale, how many deaths can we ascribe to VIS infection?"

Professor Amery sighed again and thought for a second. "I would have to do calculations based on that timescale, but roughly ... well ... maybe 120 million. Maybe more."

"So you're saying that at least 120 million people can be considered to have died from suicide as a result of VIS infection?"

"If you assume an arbitrary two-year baseline against which to measure it, that would be the mechanical conclusion. But to do so, as I just told you, doesn't really make any sense. Because why not look at the effects over three years? By then it might have gone back down again."

"But is that very likely?"

"Who knows? We have nothing to measure it against."

Later in his hotel suite, Leeton watched the media coverage of the segment. Some pundits picked up on how Amery thought he was stupid, but the basic message that came across was that he had pulled a masterstroke out of the bag. It felt like he had out-Blumed Art Blume.

Just before he went to bed he examined the supplementary list of witnesses once again. The ones Sobiewski had told him not to call. His eye settled on one name in particular, whom he decided he was going to subpoena in the morning. Tadeki Mateki.

» 48 «

It was three days before the Christmas of 1990 when the feelings of depression and isolation gripped me, and gripped me hard. The Trinity Library was closed for the break, and all the students, including Robert, had gone home to their families. Robert had left me the key to his flat in Harold's Cross, so I had a bed to sleep in now. I had taken books out of the Library and bought a bottle of gas for the Superser heater to heat the little flat. I had even done a big clean-up in Robert's piggy absence and had used coins I found under the sofa and scattered around the bedroom floor to buy some festive food to enjoy over the break. But the mass exodus to the home fires of a family Christmas made me feel so alone. All at once, the thoughts of my mother, my old home in Watertown, my failed life as an American, came back to haunt me.

It is a curse to be so absorbed in one's work that you tick along as if nothing else existed and miss the chance to form relationships and bonds; you miss your place in the human social order. Then something happens, like Christmas, and you realise you are on an island, cut off and without a soul to care for you. We are, after all, social creatures; even the most abstract-minded of us. Even scientists.

I sat in the armchair and tried to focus on the journal I was reading. It was a study of plant RNA sequencing being carried out in the Soviet Union, which that country's collapse had unfortunately brought to a premature end. The lead researcher had published the findings such as they were. It was inconclusive and poorly written up, and so had gone largely unnoticed by the scientific community. But I saw the merit in what they had been doing. Only the day before, I had been totally absorbed in it.

The onset of depression robbed me of all my interest. Depression is like a veil that descends over your eyes and blocks out the colour of the world. If you are not awake to it, you can fail to even realise it is affecting you. It removes the joy and hope, which most people, most of the time, take completely for granted. And so it was for me that Christmas. I sat looking at the pages of that journal wondering why I had ever cared about any of it.

The next day was Christmas Eve, and the depression got worse. I found myself haunting the wet streets of Dublin, stumbling about close to tears with no precise destination, realising that if I were to fall and die, no one would know, or care, who I was. I bought a phone calling card and tried to dial the old number in Sexton Street from a public phone booth. It was disconnected. In a state of almost desperation, I dialled the only other number I could remember: Spencer Stein's. He answered the phone with a voice I almost didn't recognise. Deeper and more manly, but it was him.

"Hello?" the voice asked again. I hung up, and tears ran down my cheeks. There were still a few units left on the calling card, but I left it sticking in the slit. I had no one else to call.

» 49 «

Art Blume couldn't keep his attention focused on the daily press briefing. Something from the trial yesterday was eating at him. Something he could not quite place. He tried to block out Peter's whiney voice, which was distracting him.

"... *the main newspaper in Russia reported. Russia seems to have taken up the story of the mass suicides in Sudan and given it much more prominence than Western European media outlets. Russia Today, for instance, gave it first-place billing on its website yesterday, running the headline:* 'VIS SUICIDE DEATH TOLL LEAVES SOUTHERN SUDAN RAVISHED.'"

What had happened yesterday? There had been the interruption; the adjournment; the Amery debacle. But there was something else: something that had caught his attention. It had to do with the interruption. What was it? If only Peter would shut up for a second.

"... *of course ran with the suicide testimony of Professor Amery. Their focus was a little bit different, with page three devoted to a full analysis of the five judges and speculation on how they dealt with that crucial decision ...*"

Peter liked to enhance his presentation with a slideshow containing media clips. As he spoke, an image from the CNN website flashed up on the screen behind him. It showed Rachel Hyberg rushing to speak to Chief Justice Wang amidst the general commotion in Court One. On the extreme left of the picture, Blume could be seen motioning to one of his team members. On the right of the image, the face of Leeton Kgabu could be made out. His attention was turned to the disturbance at the judges' bench, but, oddly, the way the camera caught him, he seemed not to be looking at the judges at all.

That's it! Art realised in an instant. He leapt up from his chair, causing everyone to turn towards him and Peter to break off his report.

"Um, it's okay," Art said hastily, "just keep going. I have to do something urgent, but ... but this is really good stuff. Just go on without me. And for God's sake, people, eat some pastries. Look at this! We got cinnamon swirls, we got chocolate croissants, we got almond croissants ... Are you guys all on a diet or something? C'mon, Lisbeth, Chun, Anna, dig in, all right? I'll see you all at our usual spot at eleven, okay?"

Art raced down the corridor, checking to see if anyone was watching him. There was a security guard outside the meeting room door, but he did no more than give Art a curt nod and return to the screen of his smartphone.

Art paused at the fire-exit door at the end of the hall, and looked around again. He casually pushed open the door, and the plush, blue carpet of the ICC's central hallway was immediately replaced with the bare concrete walls and floor of an emergency stairwell. It led straight down to the underground car park.

Art shot down the six flights of stairs with surprising dexterity for a man of his age, and slipped out into the subterranean garage as quietly as possible.

Jeroen Clijvers sat in the SUV listening to dance music. His mind appeared to be on nothing at all. This was how he seemed to spend his days during the trial: waiting patiently to drive Art Blume safely back to the hotel at six o'clock, ten o'clock or at two in the morning. It was all the same to him.

When Art Blume reappeared, tapping madly at the window of the SUV, only half an hour after they had arrived, it would have come as a surprise to most people. But not Jeroen. As the tinted window wound down, Art was greeted by the same sarcastic smile he got from the Dutchman every day.

"Done already? That was a nice short day."

"Unlock the door."

Jeroen did so, and Art got in.

"Roll up the window."

Art scanned the sleek interior of the SUV. Suddenly he had second thoughts about confiding in Jeroen inside this car. The ICC had provided the vehicle, and he had never had it swept by his own security team.

"I ... dropped some of my notes on the way in to Court just now. Can you help me look for them?"

They walked around the garage for a while, weaving in and around the fleet of jet-black BMW SUVs and estate cars that the ICC used for official business. Art wasn't sure he could trust Jeroen, but there wasn't much time to shop around for an alternative. Plus, there was something about the man that inspired confidence, and Art knew that whenever he was in doubt, it was best to go with his instincts.

After a few minutes, he took the big Dutchman by the arm and craned his head up to his ear. "You told me before you used to be a private investigator. Is that right?"

"Among other things."

"So would it be possible to hire you for a private job?"

"Does it have anything to do with the Matterosi trial?"

"Of course. Does that mean you won't do it?"

Jeroen smiled. "No. It just means it's going to cost you a lot of money."

» 50 «

My depression lifted somewhat when term began. There was even a brief, happy reunion of friends, when I was greeted by a jubilant Robert Dunlop, and the news that he had aced his exams. He could not thank me enough. There was fresh beer and fresh marijuana and lots of songs and trips to the pub.

Still, I was demoted back to my old place on the sofa. After the relative comfort of a fortnight's worth of proper beds, and with a growing sense of entitlement, this seemed less than I deserved. Why, after all, should Robert Dunlop enjoy the privilege of the bedroom simply because he had had the good fortune to be born the son of a wealthy Protestant doctor, while I, the only one of us who had achieved any tangible academic results, was relegated to the status of a servant? In the abstract, Robert was clear in his contempt for the class structure and the injustices it entailed, but yet he never seemed to make the connection between that and the unequal relationship that existed between us.

As is so often the case when unresolved issues cloud a friendship, I didn't have the emotional maturity to deal with my feelings directly. Instead I kept it as a secret grudge against him, and left it to fester in my heart.

Eventually, it all erupted over a girl. Máiréad was her name. She had silky, dark-brown hair and smooth, perfect skin; bright blue eyes and cherry-red lips. Her body was that perfect voluptuousness that many Irish girls possess. She came from Templeogue, and belonged to that social class that had risen a generation ago from poverty, but was, as yet, not so firmly rooted in the middle class as to feel itself entitled.

We met her together, but Robert was slicker and more self-assured, and made his move before I had even thought it possible to try. From the bar stool, I watched jealously as they snogged in the corner booth of the dingy student pub called the Buttery. Behind them on the towpath that ran along the canal to Harold's Cross, I watched jealously as they giggled and held hands all the way home to the flat. And from my bed on the sofa, I listened jealously as they squeaked and grunted during sexual intercourse in a bed I felt should have been mine.

My mind was dark with anger as I lay there, and watched the rain pelt against the window panes. Robert got sex simply because he was lucky, despite being both stupid and lazy. I was hard-working and intelligent, and yet, because of my circumstances, I was left to curl up on the sofa, forgotten like a dog.

As the weeks went by, and the three of us hung out together, I found myself getting more and more vicious against Robert, especially when Máiréad was around. He had evidently boasted to her that he had aced his exams, and, at one point, when we were sitting around, and she was praising him for his brilliance, I felt a temper surge up within me.

"Of course, you only got Firsts because I sat the exams for you. So, really, I was the one who got those Firsts."

Silence. His fingers hovered over the guitar strings for a moment as Robert stared at me in disbelief. I had broken the most sacred part of our pact, which was not to tell anyone, under any circumstances, of our deal. I had also embarrassed him in front of his girlfriend.

Máiréad looked uncomfortably from one of us to the other. "I guess I'll head home—"

"No," Robert interrupted her, placing a proprietary hand on her bare, white shoulder. "I think Brian's the one who's going home."

"I don't have anywhere to go." I stared in anger at him.

"That's not my problem."

And so, in silence I gathered up my few possessions and left his flat in Harold's Cross.

"Good luck in your end-of-year exams," I said bitterly, as I slammed the door on our friendship and walked out into the February rain.

Sadly, this experience taught me nothing at all about how spite and anger were destructive to one's own self interests. That was a lesson I would not learn for many, many years. Instead, it hardened my resolve to succeed at Trinity and to lord my superiority over Robert Dunlop, who had now become my avowed enemy.

Two days later I was back in Drumshanbo, knocking on the door of the principal's office at the Christian Brothers' school. This man I had known from my hedge school days, and he had treated me with a certain kindness. I can't now recall his name, but I remember him as a keen-witted schoolmaster, with a streak of kindness he kept hidden from the lads in order to preserve discipline.

"I want to sit the Leaving Certificate. Can I do it here?"

He looked at me with surprise. "But I thought you were in second year at Trinity?"

"I am. But I want to do my Leaving Cert again. To repeat it and get higher marks."

He paused and looked hard at me. I could tell then that he saw through my lies. "Well, for repeats we'll have to see a copy of your original Leaving Certificate, you see. You need to register using the same CAO number, which is your student ID number at Trinity."

I stared at the floor. It was an impossible web of lies. The system was locking me out any way I turned.

"Unless, of course, you were a first-time applicant. Then we could apply for a new CAO number for you."

I looked up at him hopefully.

"I won't say a word to anyone about it," he said, in answer to my unspoken question. "But you'll have to play it straight with me, Brian. And you'll have to get me your records from the States. From now on you tell me the truth, do you hear me? The whole truth."

» 51 «

Leeton Kgabu leaned across and looked the witness deep in the eye. Leeton's eyes were big and brown, and even the whites were dusty, framed by his broad, strong face. Tadeki Mateki, who was Japanese, had smaller, Asian eyes that seemed watery and weak. His stare was uncertain; his pupils shifted constantly.

He was a witness for the prosecution, but there was something in his deposition Leeton distrusted, something about him he felt was unsavoury. His court experience had taught him to trust his instincts, and his instincts were telling him to give this man a grilling.

"Did you work at BetterWorld laboratories under the supervision of Brian Matterosi between August 2008 and April 2016 in that company's research facility in Göttingen, Germany?"

Mateki answered hesitantly, clearly not expecting the violent accusatory tone with which the question had been posed.

"Yes."

Leeton paused. "Tell us something about BetterWorld."

"What do you want to know?"

"Were there any African scientists working there?"

"No. None that I can remember."

"What about from India or South America? Were there many from there?"

"I'm not sure. I don't think so."

"Why do you suppose that is?"

"I have no idea."

"Who selected the staff?"

"Professor Matterosi. Together with Frau Schneider, of course."

"Of course," Leeton repeated. He glanced at the next batch of questions on his list. "Did you have access to all parts of the lab?"

"Do you mean the lab where I worked?"

"I mean the whole facility."

"I don't know. I suppose so. I never encountered any restrictions.

But I did not exactly go exploring either."

"So Mr Matterosi trusted you?"

"I think so, yes."

"Were you aware of the Hydra project?"

"No."

"Did you ever ask Mr Matterosi about it?"

"No."

"No? You mean you had no suspicions that something big was being planned?"

"Well ... no, I didn't question ... it's true that near the end, he spent a lot of his time in the Delta section of the laboratory. The rest of us were left to sort of ... self-manage. I thought this was because we had earned his trust."

"So you were not aware of Brian Matterosi's special project, even though he had been discussing his approach to dealing with global population problems with anyone who would listen?"

"You have to understand that the atmosphere in the lab at this stage was very strange. We were all living in a sort of anxiety."

"Why?"

"Because projects would be cancelled. Professor Matterosi was having personal problems. There were issues in his home. We knew vaguely of this. But the best thing was to concentrate on one's work. We were scientists, you must understand."

"But he worked on the Hydra project for over half a year. He even kept records. One third of the BetterWorld facility was occupied with it, in what you call the Delta section! Surely you knew something about it?"

"I am a scientist. Those things did not concern me. And as I said, the Professor had personal problems. So we did not ask too much about his work. We left him alone."

"Did you notice when *Mr* Matterosi got sick?"

"Yes."

"Tell the Court about his illness."

"There is not much to tell, really. It happened on a few occasions, as far as I can remember. He told us he had accidentally contracted a virus, nothing serious, but we should stay away from him. He always took the necessary precautions not to infect anyone—"

At this, Leeton Kgabu let out a sarcastic guffaw.

"—I mean, not to infect anyone in the BetterWorld lab. He always wore a facemask and avoided the common areas."

"And you never questioned him? You never asked, what was this virus that he had contracted?"

"No."

"You never went into the Delta section of the lab?"

"No. He always worked alone. We never disturbed him."

"Didn't you find that a little strange?" Leeton watched the man's reactions carefully as he gave his next response. The pupils flickered up to the left.

"We were given to understand that the Delta section was reserved for commercially sensitive pilot projects. The fewer of us that knew what was being done, the less chance there was of a leak. Industrial espionage is a constant concern in med tech."

"Did Brian Matterosi ever ask you to work on the VIS project?"

"No, never."

"Did Mr Matterosi ever talk to you about his plans for the developing a Hydra virus?"

"No. Usually we just talked about what I was working on."

"What were you working on?"

"Glycolytic enzymes. We were trying to encourage them to attack cancer cells. As a cure for pancreatic neuroendocrine cancer."

"I have here a series of email exchanges you had with Brian Matterosi. They date from February to April 2016."

Leeton paused, pretending to be rooting around in his papers to produce the evidence. In reality he was studying the reactions of the defence. Art appeared to be scribbling in a bored fashion. Either he didn't care about this testimony, or he was doing a very good job of pretending. He allowed his glace to drift casually across the others. No, he decided, they did care.

"Yes," the Japanese man pronounced at length. "The exchange concerns the enzymes I told you about. There, it says so right here—"

"That's fine, Doctor. But the one I am concerned about is the email from fifth March. Can you read it for us?"

Mateki read, *"Brian, I have finalised the preliminary findings. I just need you to sign the report. I know how busy you are—I'll pop over to you on my way out. T."*

"So you 'popped over to him'?"

Mateki stumbled and paused. "I guess so ... I mean, I don't remember."

"Where did you 'pop over' to him? Was it his restricted area of the lab—the Delta section? The one you told me you'd never been inside?"

Mateki gulped and looked agitated.

"I can't remember. It might have been his office."

"And how did you know how busy he was? I thought you said he isolated himself from the rest of the scientists?"

"That's just ... that's just a polite way of speaking. In Japan, you must always compliment someone you work with by telling them they are busy."

Leeton let his stare linger on the witness for a few extra moments. The scientist shrank visibly into the deepest recesses of the witness box. The prosecuting attorney was looking at Tadeki, but was thinking about Art Blume. Would Blume take the bait? Would he risk a cross-examination that could only drive home the message that Brian was guilty, all the more guilty for trying to deny he acted alone? After an eternity of six seconds or so, Leeton abruptly declared, "No further questions for this witness," and turned his back.

Art read a note that his assistant had slid across the table to him. He shook his head briefly before addressing the bench. "No questions for this witness, Your Honours."

"Five-minute break, then the prosecution may call its next witness please."

» 52 «

In the break, Leeton stepped out to use the toilet. He passed Rachel Hyberg on the way out, but did his best not to be seen noticing her. She was talking to another GlobalSix person about the social media buzz. The only words he caught were *"... sense of drama. Viewers love it."*

As Leeton approached the urinal, he let his thoughts wander to Rachel Hyberg, until a voice interrupted him.

"What was the purpose of calling that witness?"

The man standing next to him was Michal Sobiewski, the General Secretary of the International Criminal Court. Leeton hadn't even been aware that he was present that day. Though, on second thoughts, it wasn't really a surprise.

"He was a witness testifying to material evidence."

"You were grilling him."

"Because I think he was hiding something," Leeton answered at length.

"Who cares if he's hiding something? He was there to tell us Matterosi locked himself in the lab and created the virus. Material evidence. We want a conviction of Brian Matterosi. We don't want to cast doubt over our own witnesses."

Leeton felt anger surge up inside him. He didn't like this man's tone one bit. It felt like another condescending white man looking down at him. Leeton also remembered that Sobiewski had done his best to block his nomination as Chief Prosecuting Counsel.

"Let me make one thing clear, Mr Kgabu," Sobiewski continued. "You work for me. No more witnesses from the supplementary list are to be called without my express prior approval. Is that clear?"

Leeton could feel his rage cooling under the Pole's calm persistent gaze. He nodded submissively, instantly ashamed of his own contrition in front of this arrogant little white man. A lump was forming in his throat. Sobiewski nodded and turned to leave.

Leeton's mood did not have a chance to improve. No sooner had Sobiewski left than Art Blume entered. The defence attorney was humming a little tune. Madonna's *Like a Virgin*. It grated on Leeton's nerves.

"You look flustered, Leeton," Blume said out of the blue. He was breaking the unspoken code of men's toilets: never speak to the guy at the urinal next to you.

Code or no, that comment didn't deserve a reply. Leeton wasn't about to allow Blume to play any of his mind-games on him. Still, the old shyster went on talking as if they were having a genuine conversation.

"Yeah, you look really healthy. Vigorous, I would even say. It's almost like you're getting more exercise. Which is great to see, you know, because a lot of guys in your position—I mean, family men—they don't tend to do well when they have to go away for long periods of time. No one to cook; no one to iron their shirts. I mean, as you can probably tell from the state of my shirts, it doesn't bother me, but then again my personal life is a complete mess—"

"What are you trying to say, Blume?"

"Oh, nothing. Just that your wife, Caddie, she must really miss you. And the baby, what's his name again?"

Leeton sprang at Blume and pushed him against the wall.

"Woah, woah, take it easy!"

"Don't ever speak of my family again. Do you understand?"

"Calm down, Mr Prosecutor!"

"Just so we're clear. I despise you as much as I despise your client. I rejoice in the fact that he will be brought to justice and pay the ultimate price for his crimes. I only regret that you, his lawyer, will be able to walk away from yours."

Before Art had a chance to respond a man who might have been a reporter entered, and both men disengaged and tried to look casual.

Blume smoothed down his lapels and greeted the young man, who was doing his best to pretend he had seen nothing. "We were just having a private consultation. It's the only place us hot-shot lawyers can go where cameras don't follow." He scanned the ceiling. "At least, I hope so. I don't really wanna see my schlong on the nightly news. For that matter, I don't think anyone does."

Left alone, Leeton washed his hands and took a deep breath. In the mirror, he saw his own face. But it was no longer the face of that proud, handsome man who had won Caddie's heart. He vowed to himself that he would end the affair with Rachel that very night.

» 53 «

"They say suicide is a sin," James told me, as he flicked the ash of his cigarette into an empty beer can. "They say it's an act of cowardice. I say it's the most courageous, ambitious and holy thing a person can do."

"Really?" He'd been talking a stream, and I hadn't been paying attention to him up to that point. I was thinking about Robert Dunlop's girlfriend, Máiréad, imagining the feel of her ample breasts in my hands as our lips met for full and gentle kisses. But James's last comment was sufficiently off-beat to catch my attention.

"How do you mean?"

"We're all driven by the will to live. The 'will to live' is another way of saying the fear of death. I mean, like, that's the most basic part of our being. You know, love, greed, hunger, friendship, whatever you fancy; it can all be reduced to fear. Fear of death, at the end of the day."

"Even sexual desire ... lust?" I asked lazily, Máiréad's anatomy floating once again across my mindscape.

"Yes. Lust is a reproductive function. You lust because you want to make babies. You want to make babies because that's a way of continuing your existence, advancing your DNA. That's back to the fear of death, right?"

"Right," I acquiesced. I could think of a few objections to this line of reasoning, but I really didn't care enough to argue with James at that precise moment.

Just why and how I developed the fascination with Máiréad Hannigan, I can't say. In truth I had barely known her, and from the safe distance of a hundred miles, the jealousy I had felt back in Dublin seemed puzzling to me. Why then, was I unable to get her out of my mind? Was it nothing more than revenge and the simple desire to take something precious away from Robert Dunlop?

James was the only new addition to my narrow and shrinking

pool of friends and acquaintances. He hailed from a farm not far from Drumnaslew, and I had tutored him in Maths the previous year. With a middling Leaving Certificate, he had made it as far as the Regional Technical College in Athlone, which was a place as prosaic as it was mediocre. James, though, had the heart and soul of a poet. He was the only person, besides the Christian Brothers' school principal, to whom I told the truth of who I was and how I'd come to be there. And that was the moment when we had become true friends.

Now, whenever the work was done and the bourbon cream biscuits had been cracked open, James would spend long hours by the fire with me, expounding his theories on religion, or why Gaelic football should be adopted in place of soccer as the new global sport. Or, in this case, on the virtues of suicide.

"Right, so it follows that in terms of freedom, you know, you're always a slave to your fear of death. Everything you do is ultimately because you're afraid of death. It's the ultimate constraint to freedom.

"And so to overcome that, you know, to escape that fear of death, is the only true act of freedom a human being can achieve."

Here I did interject. "Doesn't it depend on the motives, though? Lots of people who commit suicide aren't facing any fears. Generally, they're running away from their fears. I mean, isn't it true that people sometimes commit suicide because they're more afraid of life than of death?" I was thinking of the night when I nearly jumped in front of a car on the Fresh Pond Parkway.

James paused, his ego slightly injured, perhaps. He threw his leg over the back of the little couch and took a drag from his cigarette.

"Well, I can't speak for everyone, can I? Maybe some people do run away and commit suicide. But if you are a thinking, philosophical creature, you must be afraid of death. I'm absolutely convinced of that. To jump over that wall of fear, it's the most amazing thing. It has to be. Let's put it this way, suicide is like jumping over a wall of fear. The better your life is, the higher the wall. Maybe there are some people whose lives are so shite, they can just step over it and into the abyss of death. So that's really what I mean by fulfilment through suicide. First you have to be happy, you know, have a great wife, some kids, a happy family, money, all that shite. Or a successful career. Or whatever it is that makes you happy. Then, as you're at the peak of your happiness, when the wall of suicide is at its highest, if you jump over it, then you have become superhuman."

I laughed.

"You're wasted in Athlone, man, you should be doing feckin' philosophy in Oxford."

He laughed and said, "With all those fuckin' Brits? Are you jokin' me?"

And then he grew serious, and a shadow passed over his face. "I don't know, Brian. I don't know what the fuck I'm doin'. Maybe I should emigrate. You know, just, get the fuck out of here. America or some place."

It seemed strange that he should want to run away from his life, and travel in the exact opposite direction to the one I had taken in running away from my own. I thought about telling him that he couldn't run away from his problems, but who was I to give that kind of advice? Really, I just didn't want to lose him as a friend.

A pine log we had thrown onto the fire caught and crackled into life. It would liven up the smouldering turf for a few handsome minutes.

"What is it you want?" I asked him after a brief contemplation of the flames.

He sniffed. "I don't fuckin' know. That's the problem."

I had no answer for that. The log collapsed to one side, shifting the centre of burn out to the left and causing a tremendous spark to leap out of the fire and land on the rug. Instinctively, James licked his big, calloused forefinger and reached out to extinguish it.

My mind wandered back to Máiréad. I decided that as soon as I had finished my Leaving Certificate exams, I would go back to Dublin and try to win her heart.

» 54 «

Jeroen Clijvers usually left Art where the concrete floors of the underground garage ended and the plush carpet of the building's formal working spaces began. This was also where ICC security was ever present, so the Dutchman's role as bodyguard was technically no longer needed. If someone were watching them closely—for example, someone who had access to the CCTV security system that covered the building's corridors—they might notice if Jeroen were to start walking alongside Art for longer than usual. This might raise alarm bells, and that was not what Art wanted. So he was very careful to ensure they parted at exactly the same point every morning. This gave them a few moments to talk, if they parked far away and walked slowly.

"Have you had any luck?"

"No. I have had *success*. But no luck. Luck has nothing to do with it." Even through the whisper, Art could hear his flippancy.

"What have you got for me?"

"Nothing yet. But by this evening, I promise you, you'll get your money's worth."

No time for any more questions. The guards nodded as Art flashed his ID and stepped onto the carpet.

"Thanks again for the safe driving. See you later."

"You're most welcome, Mr Blume. Have a nice day in Court."

» 55 «

Court began with the first witness for the prosecution's "Indirect Effects" case: that is, the phase of the trial which was to deal with any secondary consequences of VIS. It was here Leeton intended to leverage the Amery testimony on suicide, most especially from the man who was currently on the stand.

Dr Arthur Polet was a sociologist and a leading light on "psycho-social infertility trauma": a new field, and one of many in which a growing number of "experts" were making their living from research grants studying the social consequences of VIS.

As Dr Polet took the stand, Leeton Kgabu attempted to rub the sleep out of his eyes. He instantly regretted doing so, as a flash drew his attention to a photographer clicked away in the corner. He knew it would be this image emblazoned across every newspaper on the planet tomorrow. He concentrated on stopping his hands from shaking as he shuffled through the notes on the witness.

"Dr Polet," Kgabu began, reading directly. "You heard the testimony of Professor Jennifer Amery earlier regarding VIS-related suicide?"

Arthur Polet nodded, clearly expecting the question.

"I did. And it is very welcome to finally hear an epidemiologist recognising that which, in my field of study, has been obvious for some time now."

"What do you mean, specifically?"

"Well, the infertility effects of the virus destabilise the careful balance between the sexes that holds together most societies. Suicide is one, but not the only, logical consequence of this."

"When you say 'balance', what do you mean?"

"I'm talking about the family structures which give most of us our purpose and place in this world, particularly those in which women gain status from their role as the mothers of the children that men then see as their heirs. By taking away that fatherhood role, the men lose focus and turn to suicide, while at the same time, incidences of rape and abuse of women rise. The consequences for society are dire, economically and politically."

"And how would you respond to critics who say these trends of social disintegration have been happening anyway?"

"I would respond by saying that the rates of rape, family disintegration, divorce, crime, have been vastly accelerated. To claim these are simply social trends is to deny the large body of sociological evidence that is now emerging. What is interesting is that, while most people focus on women, because their natural child-bearing role as mothers is the most obviously impacted function, men are more likely to suffer VIS-related trauma. They suffer from the lack of fatherhood acutely, much more so than had been mooted at the outset. One of your previous witnesses noted the rise in suicide rates among afflicted populations and, in fact, what we're seeing is that male suicide rates have risen twice as sharply as female rates."

"So, you're saying it is men who are the true victims of VIS?"

"Everyone suffers from VIS one way or another. For example, we also observe an increased incidence of violence against women."

"In which parts of the world are these effects showing up?"

"Right across the developed world. In Cameroon, for instance, reported rapes have tripled since 2016, although the actual impact is probably even higher. In Brazil, they have invented a new word for the practice of dumping older people on the side of highways, because their families no longer see a need for them."

"How many suicides can we attribute to infertility trauma, Doctor?"

"Of course, it's only ever going to be an estimate. And we must also consider the secondary effects. If your country is falling apart with high crime rates and economic collapse, this heightens the risk of suicide. Our best estimates are in the region of 130 million a year."

"130 million a year? Every year?"

"Well, eventually the base from which we are drawing will be vastly diminished, so there won't be as many people left to kill themselves. But for the foreseeable future, it will be around that figure, we think."

"What about other types of violent behaviour, including violent crime?"

"Yes, this is also a huge problem. However, the studies are still quite raw in this area. What we can say for sure is that, when we control for all other variables, VIS-infected populations show a heightened risk of lawlessness. What we've seen is a complete breakdown in the conventional social order in these areas. Marriage rates have plummeted. Children no longer care for their parents, because the generational contract has been broken. Grandparents are important carers in many cultures, but now they have completely lost their function. This is linked, we believe, to the new problem of acute depression among elderly people. We are now seeing people in their seventies and eighties committing suicide."

"And from the urban/rural perspective? Where, would you say, are the problems worse?"

"I would say they are worse in urban areas. Men who don't form families, often tend to form gangs. Gang activity has spiked since the onset of VIS, and is now a real problem in Mexico, Haiti, Brazil, and right across Africa and Indonesia also. Western India has broken down completely into a patchwork of gang-controlled regions. Utterly lawless. In China the problems are less acute, but only because the government has been so brutally effective in restoring order."

"Can we put a number on the deaths caused by VIS-related violence?"

"Oftentimes, no. The scale of the problem is incalculably large. There is no one on the ground to tabulate these catastrophes. In the largest city in America, Mexico City, a census was scheduled to be held this year. But the government cancelled it because they just don't have tabulators willing to go into the areas that have been worst affected. Mexican statisticians don't believe it's possible to count the living, never mind the dead.

"What we know, and all we know for sure, is that millions have fallen victim to the rising violence linked with the infertility effects associated with VIS infection. How many millions is hard to say."

"A low estimate?"

"Well, let's put it this way, the US government has a satellite tracking system in place which can estimate human populations by heat sensation. By that estimate, the global population is dropping by 350 million a year. If you allow for a natural mortality rate—by which I mean non-VIS—of 150 million, and then adjust for births of about 10 million, then the rest is due to VIS. How you divide that up between suicide or violence or other causes is difficult, but most studies tend to put it at a ratio of about 62:38. Meaning, we estimate 130 million suicides and about 70 million 'other', which includes murders, accidental deaths, and so on. I should stress, though, that these are what we refer to in the field as 'top-down' estimates. What we lack are 'bottom-up' estimates, but I think that in time the data will start to feed through. I know for example there are researchers doing some interesting metadata studies which draw inference from a wide range of indicators—mobile phone usage, changes in water pressure, supermarket shopping trends—in order to find out what is going on. And new census data is slowly coming through for many countries."

"What's your prediction for the future?"

"I predict things will get worse before they get better. We'll see more violence. Governments will collapse, similar to what we have already seen in India. The other big issue is how subsistence farming will continue without child labour. In many countries, children are important labour inputs. Once their labour is taken away, entire agricultural systems are threatened. This has implications also for the food supply in many countries …"

Leeton's tired mind wandered as Polet rambled on. He thought of a little boy, aged seven, set to work in the fields: sent to carry water like a mule in forty degree heat, for crops that failed as often as not. The gruelling, blistering poverty of what amounted to little more than slavery; that was what this ivory tower academic blithely referred to as "important labour inputs". It would all be different when they went to the city, Umama had told him. She was right, of course; the slums of Cato Manor were nothing like the Umgeni countryside. They were much, much worse.

"… and, of course, the big problem is what happens to all the old people in ten, twenty years' time. There is no intergenerational contract anymore. No one to care for the elderly, in the way they cared for their own parents and grandparents."

For a second Leeton was lost in his memories. He flicked through his notes until he found the next prepared question.

"What about the concept of 'cultural genocide', Doctor? Can you explain what that means?"

"Yes," Polet answered. "By 'cultural genocide', we mean the destruction of populations, which is so extreme that whole cultures cease to exist. The culture lives as a conduit, a vehicle for transferring knowledge and social norms from one generation to another. Once a generation is taken out of that chain, the link is broken. Sure, there are books and videos and what not, but these things are no substitute for the visceral sensations of family continuity. Right now, VIS is threatening to annihilate the cultural experience of most of this planet's human inhabitants."

» 56 «

The summer of 1991 was a summer to remember. It was a rare year of sunshine in Leitrim, and the days seemed endless. James and I had become best friends. I helped him around his father's cattle farm. We borrowed tractors, and he taught me how to drive a car. There were also boats and fishing and long evenings of bonfires with some of the other Leitrim kids. The rest of the time we spent looking after a tourist hostel, which a local publican had opened in nearby Ballinamore.

It was at this hostel that I finally lost my virginity to a girl. Two Australian girls were staying there, on the prowl for adventure and boys. James and I joined them in a drinking game involving an incomplete deck of playing cards, cheap vodka and juice mixers. In that easy way of young, careless sex, we naturally sorted ourselves into two couples: I ended up with the slightly fatter one, who had mammoth tits and a really nice smile.

The first night we had sex in the hostel in that rushed, frantic way of bodies that do not know each other well. As with most sexual experiences of that kind, it felt too hurried to be a truly pleasurable experience. The next night I took her back to Drumnaslew, while James entertained her friend. We spent the best part of a day in bed, and the sex got better and better. I even convinced her to come down to the lake and skinny-dip with me. Although I can no longer remember her name, I can still see her squealing in shock and delight as I splashed the cold water over her big, naked breasts and onto her hairy crotch. And then we kissed on the shore, still naked, and I grew erect yet again.

When she finally moved on to her next adventure, we said our goodbyes and exchanged addresses on little slips of paper, promising in that empty, youthful way to stay in touch. I wonder if that girl—now a middle-aged woman—remembers me still and knows she once had two days of carefree sex with the most infamous villain of the twenty-first century?

At some stage in all that, my Leaving Certificate results came in. I got 585 points out of a possible 600. Irish was my only weakness: not because I'm not good at languages, but simply because I had no inclination to learn a dead, useless language which I would never need in my future career as a microbiologist. Anyway, 585 points was more than enough to get into biology in Trinity. I could also have chosen University College Dublin or Galway, or even put in an application for Oxford University, which would have made more sense from a strictly academic point of view. Without admitting it to myself, I chose Trinity because of Máiréad.

And so it was, just after my seventeenth birthday, that I returned the form confirming my place in Trinity. With the student grant from Leitrim County Council for which I was now eligible, I made my way back to Dublin to begin my academic career in earnest.

» 57 «

Before proceeding with cross-examination, Art Blume blew his nose into the monogrammed handkerchief he kept in his breast pocket. The little cloth hanky didn't catch all of the discharge, however, and a single dollop of snot was left hanging from the bottom of his septum, gathering itself into a droplet to fall onto the court's polished floor. At the last second, as he arrived in front of the witness box, Art wiped the offending fluid into the sleeve of his jacket, where it would remain as a shimmering stain on the fabric for the duration of the cross-examination.

"Dr Polet, do you know how many children every year are *not* being born as a result of VIS?"

"Yes, I do. It's estimated at about 160 million."

"And these are mostly the poorest, most vulnerable members of the global community, right?"

"By design, VIS infections are most prevalent among the poorest. Also, anyone with enough money can have fertility treatment done. So, yes, VIS is effectively blocking the birth of the world's poorest children."

"How many of those children would have died, if they had been born?"

"A certain percentage, no doubt."

"No doubt. In fact, according to this 2012 study, which you co-authored, and which was commissioned by the WHO, mortality rates were 25 per cent for children born into families with an income of below 2,000 dollars a year. And rising. By this estimate, we're talking about 40 million lives saved each year by VIS."

"But you can't talk about saving lives by blocking them from being born in the first place."

"And yet, the prosecution is happy to talk about *taking* lives by blocking them from being born in the first place! Surely, it cuts both ways, Doctor?"

Wang intervened again. "Are you asking a question, Counsel, or stating your own opinion?"

"Excuse me, your Honour. My question is this, Dr Polet, isn't it better to save a poor child from a certain life of misery and malnutrition? Isn't that a more responsible way to run the world, than to allow children to be born, who have no hope of anything beyond human misery?"

"It comes down to individual choices. Who are we to pass judgement on the value of human life, whether it be great or humble? We are not God. We cannot decide who deserves to be born and who does not."

Art paused and flipped through his notes.

"Dr Polet, you've worked for the WHO before, haven't you?"

"Yes, I have."

"Care to expand on that answer?"

"I was chairman of a committee responsible for overseeing evaluations of WHO coordinated programmes."

"Indeed. And in that role, do you recall overseeing the evaluation of a project called 'Africa Life 2000'?"

The witness shifted in his seat – imperceptible to everyone in the court, except perhaps Art Blume.

"It rings a vague bell," Polet answered.

"Well, I can refresh your memory. I have here a copy of the evaluation report your committee produced in May 2009, which lists you as an author. I can read some of the details to you, if you like"

"Oh, yes, yes, now that I think of it, I do recall that project."

"Good. So can you explain a little bit about it to the Court?"

"Well, as with most of the projects, we worked in cooperation with the health ministries of recipient governments, with NGOs, with USAID, and with the EU's DEVCO. This particular project sought to improve access to contraception in areas where HIV infection rates were high—"

"*—'or where fertility rates were high, and infant mortality rates were considered unacceptable.'*"

Dr Polet was silent.

Art looked at him for a second. "I'm not making that up. It's right here on page 43 of the report. Anyway, my question is, do you recall the conclusion of the evaluation?"

"Not precisely."

"Well, it says, right here, on page 395, that the project Africa Life has—and I quote—*failed to make a discernible difference in the high birth rates linked to areas of acute infant mortality in sub-Saharan Africa. Social factors and sexual practices make the promotion of high-quality modern contraception methods (including condoms) impractical. A more proactive approach, as well as a relaxation of certain restrictions placed by certain donor countries, is required to alleviate human misery in some areas.*"

Dr Polet remained silent.

"What did you mean by that, Doctor?"

"I was referring to the gag rule which USAID places on cooperation with NGOs that advocate or facilitate family planning solutions for women in crisis."

"By 'family planning solutions' you mean abortion?"

"Yes."

"So, in effect, your report is saying that a project designed to reduce fertility failed because it does not go far enough, and because it does not encourage abortion?"

"Because it did not include the cooperation of organisations that facilitate the full spectrum of family planning solutions."

"Including abortion?"

"Yes."

"So, you believe VIS is an immoral solution to the problem of overpopulation, but it is okay to encourage abortion to achieve the same aim?"

"Abortion is an individual choice, which women make depending on their individual circumstances. VIS infertility is imposed upon them by Brian Matterosi. The afflicted are left with no choice."

"You see, Doctor, I disagree. Poverty is not an *individual* circumstance; it is a social circumstance. And it doesn't leave you with very much choice. To fund abortions and call that moral, while calling population-based infertility solutions immoral, is just another example of the screwed-up, hypocritical thinking that defines the WHO's approach. No further questions, Your Honours."

» 58 «

The first half of my first year as a real university student passed in a kind of blur. I had managed to get a proper room in a flat share situation with a friend of James's from school. The place was a crumbling dump in the Portobello area of the city, a top-floor flat carved out of a lovely Victorian terraced house. Portobello had at one time been a fashionable suburb to the west of a much smaller city. In the 1990s, drugs and bad urban planning had reduced the entire neighbourhood to an inner city slum, in which students and welfare claimants scratched out a bare, but colourful existence, and the trendy professionals who would soon restore the area were still holed up in the eastern suburbs of Donnybrook and Ballsbridge. Our flat had no working shower and holes in the roof through which you could see the rain clouds. We maintained an elaborate system of buckets to catch the water as it spilled down through the broken slates on its way to soak the mouldy, filthy carpet.

I got a job in a coffee shop, and, together with the student grant, I had just enough to continue my meagre lifestyle and still pay my rent and the electricity for Drumnaslew. When the festive season started, I sold Christmas trees from a lot on the corner of the South Circular Road.

So it was, in the perpetual darkness of an Irish winter evening, that I stood outside in the blistering cold amongst the pine needles, rubbing my hands vigorously to get some life back into them, when out of a car popped Máiréad Hannigan, with her father and younger brothers. I had seen her once or twice around campus, but always at a distance and never in a way that suggested I could actually talk to her.

Even now, when she came right up to me in this very un-Trinity environment, I felt a strange kind of shyness grip me, and I think I would have ignored her altogether, if it had not been for her warm greeting.

"How have you been?" she asked me, while the rest of the family inspected various specimens of tree, testing them against the standard criteria of bushiness, uniformity of branches and ability to fit in corner of living room.

"Yeah, grand."

"Where are you staying?"

"Just down the road actually. Curzon Street."

"Really? That's cool."

"Yeah, myself and another guy managed to get a flat. It's grand. Well, it's a bit of a kip, actually, but it'll do."

She smiled. I couldn't tell if it was condescending or expressive of genuine warmth.

I scratched my scraggly face and touched my hair, suddenly conscious of the fact that I hadn't showered in three days. Our flat had no working shower, and Trinity charged fifty pence for the pleasure of using the facilities in the Sports Centre. To put that in perspective, fifty pence was the price of *half* a bag of chips.

"So," I asked, in that perverse way of prodding an open wound, "how's Rob getting on?"

"Dunno, I haven't seen him in ages" she said simply. That was enough. My heart warmed up at this stroke of good fortune. We shared a smile. We were interrupted by her dad ambling over to negotiate a price on a particular tree they had selected. Because Máiréad was no longer going out with Rob, I knocked an extra five pounds off the price. When the deal was struck, I helped strap their purchase onto the roof of their car. We said a quick and awkward goodbye, but not before agreeing to have coffee some time at college.

As the family got into the car I could hear her little brother teasing, "The Christmas tree man is Máiréad's *boyfriend!*"

Christmas proved depressing yet again. Thoughts of my mother and my father gripped me and forced me to realise how alone and isolated I was in the world. James said I was welcome at his house for Christmas dinner, but I declined the offer. His brother was back from Australia for the first time in two years, and the sister had just got engaged to a thick Cavan farmer, whom James hated with a passion. There was so much life and unity in that family, even in the way they fought, that being around them just made me feel more alone than if I stayed on my own.

The veil of grey descended again, robbing me of my self-belief and of my hope for a better life. I felt suddenly consumed by the loss and emptiness of my existence, the pointlessness of all my endeavours. The fire seemed cold and mean and insufficient. The cottage dirty and humble. The driving Leitrim rain battered my spirits and extinguished any passion that remained. I could not believe Máiréad, or any girl for that matter, would ever want me. I could not believe that anyone would ever love me, or that the world would ever come to grant me a true place within it.

Even my science seemed unimportant to me. I wasn't looking forward to the start of term. The classes in Trinity were boring, and I was rapidly losing the desire to continuously push my boundaries. I felt I had reached a kind of plateau, on which it was easy to coast along, but there was nothing left to challenge me.

It was somewhere in that empty period between Christmas and New Year—which James in his wonderfully poetic way used to describe as the "Festive Perineum"—that I lay in bed, too uninspired even to get up and light the fire. A copy of a journal I had borrowed from the Trinity Library lay on top of a pile of dirty clothes on the floor next to my bed. *American Microbiology*. It was the most recent volume, but I had not even looked at it yet. My eye lingered just long enough to read the name of one of the paper's authors. Gustav Gudjohnsson. I rose and picked it up. He had called the paper, *A New Approach to Systems of Bacterial Formation*. I flipped to page 493 and read the abstract.

"Motherfucker," I whispered under my breath. It was the paper I had written for Mr Green's science class. As I read on, I realised Gudjohnsson had completely copied my work, only taking the trouble to correct some of the naive writing of a fourteen-year-old, and embellish it with a few superfluous graphics.

My brain was spinning with pride and fury. I recalled his patronising smile and his faux benevolence. The cheating, lying Scandinavian shit!

I began to recall the evolutionary game theoretical models that underpinned this approach. It was a rather complicated model, I realised, as the memory of the paper came hurtling back into my mind. Really, I was quite impressed with the complexity of the abstract reasoning my fourteen-year-old self had attained. But there was a flaw, I felt. Somewhere in the model there was a mistake. Hastily I scrambled in amongst the dirty dishes that littered the kitchen table, in search of blank paper and a pen that would write. I needed to work this through on paper.

At some point, hours later, physical sensation forced me to get up from the table. My body was shivering with the cold, and my feet had passed from pain into numbness. As I lit the fire and the turf slowly came to life, casting its dim glow into the tiny cottage sitting room, I realised, in a burst of joy, that my depression was gone.

» 59 «

Rachel Hyberg lay naked in his arms. She was tracing circles around the pitch-black nipples that adorned his massive, muscular chest. This was the first time they had had sex with the drapes open. The drapes covered the ceiling-to-floor plate glass windows which wrapped around the suite on two sides. Normally, Leeton closed them before she came over, but tonight he had deliberately left them wide open, as a sign to her that it was finished. And, yet, when the passion took hold of them, she had stopped him from drawing them closed. The feeling of being on display was like an aphrodisiac. It had made her only more wild and irresistible; their lovemaking had become even more manic than before.

Now that it was over, the very wildness of it filled his heart with regret. He itched to get up and close the curtains: to hide away from what he had done.

"I love being on view to the world," she told him now. "I imagine the sparkling lights that glitter across the skyline are thousands of glowing eyes. The eyes of our own secret audience. They're watching our perfect bodies perform. They envy us, and they lust after us. We are like gods to them."

The sound of her voice was grating in his ears. He wanted to tell her to shut up, but he did not dare.

"It's mirror glass on the outside. No one can see in."

She laughed. "I know. It's just a fantasy, silly." She craned her lips up to kiss him, but he turned his head to the side. And so she returned her attention to his nipples.

"What are you thinking about?"

He started and gazed at her for a second. In the half-light of the room, her features took on a sinister aspect. The fine cheekbones were cast into a cleft by the shadow, while the eyes sparkled with an unnatural brilliance. And the smile was ever so slightly twisted. She knew full well what he was thinking about. She was a white demon, and she had seduced him. The very white demon he had been fighting against all his life. Anger bubbled up inside him. Anger mixed with fear and shame. Unconsciously his right hand formed a fist and an image—a gruesome image—flashed up in his mind of beating the white demon senseless, in order to free himself of its power.

He rose suddenly, and, without answering her unspoken question, went to the bathroom. He splashed cold water on his face until the fire within him was extinguished. With the calm now returned to his mind, he knew what he had to do. Go back in there, tell her he was very sorry, but he was a married man. That this was a mistake: a horrible mistake. That it was over, and they just needed to continue to play their separate parts to ensure justice was done. From that point forward, they would be colleagues, nothing more.

When he returned the room was brightly lit. Rachel was standing at his desk, still completely naked. The desk drawer was open. In her hand she was examining the photograph of Caddie holding Robert.

"She's very beautiful," she said, twisting a lock of her fine, blonde hair. She spoke as if that was the most natural thing in the world.

In an instant he was upon her, snatching the framed picture from her grasp and pushing her back, away from his family.

"Get out," he said. "Get out of here." His fists clenched.

There was no shock in her eyes. Neither was there fear. He could easily have killed her with his bare hands, but she was not the least afraid. Only a knowing smile crept across her face. Her eyes roamed the length of his body. Although he had put on underwear and a bathrobe, he felt exposed under her gaze.

"Such a frail little creature," she whispered, almost to herself. "So many big muscles, and yet so very weak. Too weak to be a part of bigger things, I'm afraid." And that was it. She turned and began dressing herself calmly, as if no one else was in the room.

When she'd gone, Leeton sat brooding for a very long time. He drank a cognac. Then another. Then he dimmed the lights and played the most recent video she'd given him of Brian Matterosi's biographical recording. As Matterosi sat in his little cottage and pondered biological theory, warmed by the turf fire against the penetrating cold of an Irish winter, Leeton had the feeling he was there with him. Despite the effect of the alcohol, he could almost feel the cold Irish air on his own body.

   The night dragged on.

» 60 «

The energy with which I attacked the start of 1992 was infectious. My flatmate, Ciarán, felt it; the people in the coffee shop in which I worked felt it; James felt it on the weekends he came down to Dublin to party with us; and, most especially, the staff in the TCD Department of Science felt it. Whenever you exude that kind of energy, whatever walk of life you are in, you attract people to you. They feel your energy and want to benefit from it. Good things happen when you're in that state of mind.

A few weeks into term, the Head of the Department of Science took me aside and asked me if I would do him a personal favour. A visiting German Professor in Microbiology would be coming to work on a joint research project in which Trinity was hoping to become involved, and he wanted to know if I would act as an "academic guide". This dubious distinction usually meant showing some doddering old git how to get from his rooms to the Science building on campus, making him cups of tea and fetching him books from the Library. But the fact that I was being asked was an honour, as it was usually post-grads who did this work, and I was only a First Year undergraduate. Even so, I was so arrogant, so sure of my academic superiority, and so absorbed in the Gudjohnsson paper, that I nearly turned the offer down.

But, of course, I did say yes. And anyone who knows anything about my academic career will know what a monumental decision that proved to be. Because the professor in question was none other than Heinz Lindemann.

My first impressions of Heinz? Well, let's just say I was fired up and full of myself after the Gudjohnsson discovery, to the point that I was probably a lot more concerned with how I appeared to him, than with how he appeared to me.

Heinz later told me how that first meeting went from his point of view. He said he got into Dublin exhausted, after finishing work in

Göttingen and hours of flight delays in Frankfurt, to be met by a wiry-looking, half-bearded youth of twelve-going-on-fifty: "a coat hanger with a mop stuck on top of it!" as he later described me. He said I never stopped talking the whole taxi ride into town. Apparently, I babbled in my school German, throwing in as much microbiology jargon as I had gleaned from various German sources, just to impress him. I even quoted extensively from one of his recent papers.

I have no independent memory of any of that, but I do remember that I finally got to discuss the Gudjohnsson affair with him, about two weeks after his arrival. I had mentioned it to a few of my lecturers before, and received nothing more than cursory smirks, but from Heinz, I got a very different reaction.

"Brian," he said with a sigh. "Now listen. We only have three more days to get the draft of the project proposal agreed, so I really don't have time to talk about this now. But on Saturday, *ja*? Then you come to my office with all your notes and your paper by Johannson—"

"Gudjohnsson."

"*Ja*, him. And then we talk, for sure. Okay?"

And Heinz was as good as his word. I brought reams and reams of my material—everything I had been working on since Christmas—and we went over the paper, equation by equation, line by line. He probed me with questions. Got me to rethink some of my assumptions. We worked on an alternative hypothesis, ran some Monte Carlo simulations and compared the results with our *a priori* assumptions.

It was not until a security guard, on a routine patrol of the building, opened the door and wished us "good morning" that we realised it was Sunday. We had worked twenty-two solid hours. And although I did not know it then, we had just forged the most significant working partnership in the history of modern microbiology. Unquestionably, millions of cancer survivors out there, and, I would argue further—the entire human race—owe their lives to the partnership Heinz Lindemann and I forged that weekend in 1992. All built around disproving Gustav Gudjohnsson's stolen theory, which in turn had been developed with the sole intention of embarrassing an American high school science teacher named Bill Green.

None of this I knew while walking home that afternoon, as the daylight faded away, and I turned the key in the partition door that led into our dingy apartment in Portobello.

"Oh, *His Majesty* deigns to grace us with his presence!"

"Was she that nice that you couldn't tear yourself away?"

I saw James and Ciarán, but was too exhausted and elated to cop what they were saying.

"What? No, I wasn't with a girl. I was doing research work. A biology project. Working with a world-renowned professor from Göttingen University."

They looked blankly at me. A half-lit cigarette dangled from James's mouth. Utterly baffled.

"On Sunday?"

"All fuckin' day long?"

"And all night," I replied. "And all day yesterday." And I let out a big yawn just to prove it.

"Right, well, you're a sad bastard, that's all I've got to say."

"And there's only one cure for it. C'mon, we're going out." James grabbed me by the collar.

"What? I can't. I'm knackered."

"You can and you will. I'm after comin' all the way from Athlone, and this here fucker's after comin' all the way from Cavan, boy."

"Don't you know!"

"So now, the first round's on you, Yankee Doodle."

A band was playing, and the piss-swill beer they served to us students in plastic cups was flowing freely. I drank and danced, and drank and danced some more, until the evening became night time and the exhaustion went right back out of my body, as it can only when you are seventeen.

I saw her in the eerie clarity that comes after drowsiness has been overcome by sheer force of will: Máiréad Hannigan was at a corner table, chatting to a few of her girlfriends. They had been watching me dance and were giggling. Under normal circumstances, embarrassment and self-doubt would make me question myself, and I would slink off to the bar or something.

But that was a magical night. All my fear was gone. I walked over, my eyes fixed only on Máiréad, and took her hand without saying a word. She rose and followed me, and we went out onto the dance floor and danced. It was the year of Nirvana's *Smells like Teen Spirit*. Ciarán and James joined us on the dance floor. Then others. Soon the whole place was on its feet, raving to the music.

The next thing I knew, it was just Máiréad and me again. We were leaning against a wall; my teen spirit was pressed into hers, and our tongues took up the dancing where our bodies had left off.

The venue eventually closed, but the night went on eternal. We felt young and powerful, and the city's cold, clammy streets belonged entirely to the four of us. We passed a late model Audi with a UK registration, and James climbed onto the roof. As he patriotically relieved himself onto the bonnet, the rest of us stood around and solemnly sang the Irish national anthem. I recall us stopping at the coffee shop where I worked and borrowing a tenner off the guy I worked with to buy teabags and bread and cigarettes, before stumbling back towards the flat on Curzon Street. Now I was arm in arm with James and Ciarán singing Red Hot Chilli Peppers; now I was holding Máiréad around the waist and we laughed together at our own complicity. She was already mine by the time we turned the key in the door. My girlfriend. As the sun rose that Monday morning in February, I fell asleep with her wrapped in my arms, as vibrant and as happy and as full of belonging as I had ever felt in my entire life.

» 61 «

"Dr Nguyen, you are an economist with the World Bank. You have served on the Board of the Federal Reserve Bank of San Francisco and hold a chair at UCLA Berkeley; is that all correct?"

"Correct."

After the witness's response, Leeton paused for a second longer than he needed to. He had caught sight of Hyberg from across the room. She was standing next to Camera Five, wearing a dress that was so tight and revealing as to be almost indecent. Unless he was mistaken, she had on an even more aggressive shade of red lipstick. She was staring at him, smirking, as if they were the only two people in the court.

Leeton forced himself to look back at his notes. "You're also a specialist in Computable General Equilibrium modelling, or 'CGE' modelling? Can you tell the Court what that is?"

"Basically, we make a model of the economy, taking into account all the factors like the level of employment, the wage rate, the amount of savings, levels of export, imports, taxes and expenditure by government. Everything, or at least, as much as we can. It's a model of the economy, but it's a very complicated model. One that we need a computer to solve. Then, we look at what happens to the economy when things change. This allows us to evaluate the benefits of a policy change, but also to look at the effects of a change in demographics, crime, effects of global warming—anything we can account for in the model."

"Can you model changes in populations, such as the projected change in populations caused by infertility?"

"Oh, yes. In fact, a big part of what our team is doing now is looking at the economic consequences of VIS infection."

"Can you give us a sense of what the results are showing?"

"Right now, we're really focusing on India and China. Across the world the analysis will be quite different. It depends a lot on how advanced the economy is; what the ratio of capital to labour is; how well developed insurance markets are; all kinds of different factors."

"Let's talk about China."

"China's a particular case. Because the Chinese government had adopted a one-child policy even before the outbreak of VIS, the economy was already adjusting to these kinds of demographic effects, so you're not seeing a huge drop in growth there."

"What about India?"

"Yes, India is more the classic case. And there, the projections are quite stark. With the increased dependency ratio, and the abrupt collapse in the size of the labour force, we expect key industries in India to capitulate completely. Agriculture, which is still quite labour-intensive, will face an almost insurmountable challenge in terms of labour supply. Rising staple food prices are inevitable, causing shock waves of inflation throughout the Indian economy.

"The worst part is, because of the difficulties with the caste structure in Indian society, labour mobility will remain low. So with the collapse in industries, despite the acute labour shortage, there is likely to be high unemployment also.

"Even as the population shrinks, *per capita* GDP will be falling hard. From its current level of 3,500 dollars, we see it falling by 200 dollars a year to somewhere around 1,000 dollars by the middle of the century.

"By 2060, the dependency ratio in India is projected to hit its peak at twenty-five seniors and two children to every one worker in the economy, and this is assuming a 25 per cent prolongation in working age. The sheer magnitude of this dependency ratio will make investment in the economy almost impossible, so a return to positive GDP growth, in absolute terms, cannot be expected realistically until 2070 or 2080.

"By then, the population will have shrunk from its current level of 1.4 billion to around 120 million, and that could be an overestimate, depending on migration patterns and the effects of increased crime and suicide. Existing infrastructure will be completely depreciated, and the economy will be starting almost from scratch. Essentially, the country will have returned to where it was in the eighteenth century."

"So it is fair to say, that the economic consequences of VIS for India will be devastating?"

"Devastating is an understatement. Before VIS infection, India was one of the global economy's points of pride. A developing country, a democracy, which was providing more and more opportunities for its people while fuelling growth elsewhere through healthy trade in goods and services. Now ... well, we've already seen a collapse in its government. As for the economy, it is hard to think how the Indian economy could have been any more undermined, short of dropping nuclear bombs on every major city."

"Thank you, Your Honours. No further questions for this witness." Without meaning to, he glanced in the direction of Camera Five. But she was gone.

» 62 «

Leeton sat back and crossed his arms as Art Blume began his cross-examination.

"Okay, Dr Nguyen, I'm just going to start by saying, I'm not an economist."

"I know, Mr Blume, you're a lawyer."

"Right, and I find it difficult to get my head around some of this stuff, so you'll have to take things really slow with me, so I don't get lost."

"I have all day."

"Great. Okay. Let's start from the top. This CGE model you use, it predicts how the economy is going to do, based on what happens if certain things—like population—change. Is that about right?"

"Yes, that's one application."

"So can it also tell us what would happen to the economy if nothing changes?"

"Yes, of course."

"Let's do that. Tell me what happens to India if Brian Matterosi had never spread VIS? What's the baseline scenario?"

"Well, in the medium-term, it looks pretty good. For India, we were predicting 3 to 5 per cent GDP growth from 2020 to 2025."

"And beyond that?"

"Beyond that, most developing countries are assumed to have reached the technology frontier, so growth rates are assumed to converge to their steady state potential output of 2.5 per cent per year."

"What factors drive that growth?"

"Mainly growth in the labour supply. But also we assume a slight improvement in technology."

"So the labour supply in the VIS-free world is assumed to grow? Then what are your assumptions about global population in 2100?"

"We assume population would peak at just over ten billion in 2100 and slowly decline thereafter."

"And how many of these people would be living in abject poverty?"

"I don't ... our model doesn't define a concept of 'abject poverty.'"

"But could you? For instance, the World Health Organisation has guidelines for minimum standards of living; the EU defines things like consistent poverty, material deprivation—"

"It could be done, yes. But it's not something we would normally include in our model."

"I have to say, I find it strange that you don't model poverty. Anyway, for the sake of argument, if poverty rates were to stay at current levels, how many more people would be in poverty, given that most of the population growth is happening among the very poor?"

"I can't answer that question off the top of my head."

"Would it be about 2.5 billion? Roughly eighty per cent of the total population growth?"

"I don't know. Possibly."

"What about resource constraints? Do you consider them?"

"No."

"No? Because I read that peak oil, pre-VIS, was predicted to happen around 2055. Now, because of the population fall-off and the reduction in demand, peak oil may never happen. Is that right?"

"Well, the assumptions about peak oil are pretty static—"

"So what are the consequences for an economy of running out of oil? Pretty drastic, I would think? I mean, that's gotta push up poverty further and reduce GDP, and all that?"

"Yes, but peak oil may never be reached. There's pretty much a limitless supply of oil out there, in the form of shale oil, and in the oceans. We just need to find ways of getting at it."

"Right," Art interrupted, "We all know about the environmental costs of shale oil. And isn't it true that the deeper you have to drill to get at the oil, the more money it costs to extract it, especially if you price in the environmental costs of extraction? And if the extraction costs are always greater than the burn value of the fuel, it isn't really an available resource, right?"

"Correct."

"So when we say 'peak oil', we really mean 'peak *available* oil', and that must represent a resource constraint in your model?"

"Except that new technologies are being invented all the time which make extraction cheaper."

"So in your baseline scenario out to 2100, you have implicitly assumed there will be new technologies to get around the hard resource constraints imposed by 'peak available oil'?"

Dr Nguyen paused to think for a second. Art waited patiently. This was the moment he loved. When the witness fell into his trap and began to thrash around to free himself. Which, of course, only made things worse for him.

"I ... I would say ... yes. I mean, I'm not an expert in this, but there are also bio-fuels, cold fusion; there is lots of research going on."

"But in this VIS model you created, did you assume any technologies to get around the demographic bottlenecks that you say will create such hardship in places like India and Sierra Leone?"

"What sort of technologies?"

Art shrugged. "I don't know. Telehealth solutions? Better medicine which allows older people to be healthy longer and stay in the labour force. Robots, maybe? There are all kinds of ways you can make the demographic challenges of a falling population less onerous on the current generation of workers. So why didn't you put any of them in your model?"

"You can't just imagine robots will be invented to do all the work for us. That's not credible."

"Oh, but it's credible to imagine cold fusion will be invented, to conveniently take away the problem of resource constraints and allow us to assume economic growth can continue at a linear pace indefinitely?"

"I said cold fusion was one of many possible solutions."

"And I'm saying robots are one of many possible solutions!"

Here Chief Justice Wang tapped her microphone in what had

become a customary warning to Art Blume that he was drifting too far into speech-making. Art smiled and gave her the thumbs up.

"What about climate change, Dr Nguyen? Does your model take that into account?"

"No."

"No? So you don't think burning the oil required to feed and clothe and shelter an additional three or four billion people will add any CO_2 to the atmosphere?"

"It's not that. It's just that the effects of climate change are too difficult to predict for inclusion in the model."

"But if they were to be included, could they potentially have a big effect on GDP?"

"Potentially. But climate change can also have positive effects. It's just too difficult to say with any certainty."

Art looked across at the judges, and at Wang in particular. It was almost as if he was pleading with her, personally, to help him come to terms with the nonsense this witness was spouting. Then he turned and addressed his final comment, not to Dr Nguyen, but to the gallery of observers behind them. He knew Camera Three would capture a full body image of him, with a defeated Nguyen in the background.

"It seems to me that when we break it down, what your model is really telling us, is that we just don't know what the heck is going to happen. No further questions for this witness, Your Honours."

» 63 «

My first ever academic paper, co-authored with Heinz Lindemann, was published as a National Scientific Council working paper in the summer of 1992. It came out in an "online" version on what was then a very primitive version of the Internet. Its findings had caused something of a sensation in the world of microbiology long before the paper was formally accepted for publication in the *Zeitschift für Biologie*, where it eventually found its place in the Autumn 1993 volume. Gustav Gudjohnsson published a retort in one of the Harvard journals, and we published an answer to that a few months later. I won't go too much into the details of the debate, but basically it was pretty rare in our discipline that leading academics went head-to-head in that "you're wrong—no, *you're* wrong" sort of way.

Without Heinz on my side, I would have stood no chance in the debate: not for want of having good arguments, but because I simply lacked the reputation to have my arguments credibly accepted. But Heinz was already as well respected as Gudjohnsson, and his seal of approval and name on the paper were enough to get people listening.

The definitive proof would come a few years later, with extensive lab work that showed bacterial conjugation patterns consistent with our calculations. One practical application of that research has been a substantial improvement in waste treatment processes which allow for increased biomass retention from human excrement through aerobic granulation. Beyond merely humiliating a Harvard professor, Heinz and I had written a new chapter in the science of shit.

The scientific world was awake to our work, and also to me, the new *Wunderkind* of microbiology. On a personal level, it was the vindication of everything I had worked towards and believed in. I thanked Gudjohnsson for stealing my work, and I thanked my fourteen-year-old self for making a crucial mistake that allowed me to correct the thief and win the war.

My moments of self-doubt were now utterly banished. I threw myself into my work harder than ever before. I forgot the depression and listlessness that had haunted me in Drumnaslew. I forgot my isolation and my troubled past.

Unfortunately, I also forgot about the people in my life. Máiréad, who had fallen completely in love with me, I treated with indifference, even contempt. I grew condescending towards Ciarán and James and the one or two other friends I had made in Dublin.

My hunger for knowledge became its own kind of addiction. I would regularly spend twelve or fourteen hours a day in the lab in Trinity, now that the Head of the Department of Science had agreed to grant me pretty much open access.

However, even that was not enough for me. It did not take long before I became frustrated with the state of Trinity's instrumentation. Electron microscopy was insufficient for the pursuit of my viral interests. I wanted access to a scanning confocal microscope to create depth-accurate imagery of viral infected tissue, and at the time there were only four places in Europe where I could get this: Cambridge, Amsterdam, Heidelberg and, of course, Göttingen.

Again, it was Heinz who helped me. By September of that same year, I had left Trinity and was a paid researcher at the University of Göttingen, which would remain my home for the rest of my adult life. I believe I was the youngest researcher ever to be employed by the university, having just turned eighteen, without even an undergraduate degree to my name. In fact, I was younger than most German kids in their final year of secondary school. Without Heinz's influence and belief in me, none of this would have been possible.

The material conditions of my life were now utterly changed. I had a salary of three thousand Deutschmarks a month, an apartment in a comfortable building close to the university that cost me a fraction of that amount, and no immediate need to worry about how or when I would eat.

The eating thing slowly became a problem. I remember it was the first thing Máiréad did when she came to visit me in Germany that

November. She poked me in the belly and said, "You're getting fat."

I was late meeting her at the train station because I had been working, and had, quite simply, forgotten her arrival. This set the tone for the visit.

As we walked through the town, it felt like there was a shadow hanging over us. Still, we held hands as we paced through the historic cobbled-stoned streets and admired the wooden-beamed fairy-tale architecture of the town. And yet, there was a tension, a coldness, between us, I could tell.

"I met James the other day, you know," she said to me at last, when we'd finally settled into a café overlooking the town hall square.

"Oh, yeah? How's he getting on?"

She shrugged. "He dropped out of college. He failed his exams and his repeats, so he would have had to repeat the year. He said his father's raging with him and won't let him back into the house. I think he's been doing a lot of drinking and, you know, drugs."

"Where's he living?"

"With Ciarán in Curzon Street. In your old room."

"Drawing the dole?"

"Yeah, I guess so."

I nodded absently. Máiréad looked down into her coffee and poked at it with her fingernail, playing with the foamy milk on the edge of the bowl-sized mug.

"He says he hasn't heard a word from you since you left."

"I've been very busy."

"You should write to him. He really misses you, you know."

A sudden pang of guilt shot through me when she said this. I suppose I knew deep down that I had run away from my life—once again—and been disloyal to my friends. But I lacked the emotional maturity to acknowledge this, and so instead I told her, "Okay, Máiréad, you might not comprehend this, given you are only an Arts student in a second-rate college, but I am paid by this university to do very important research. I don't have time to worry about people who can't get their lives together and waste themselves on drugs."

She withdrew her hand from mine. I sulked at this. We left the café and walked along through a park that connected the old town with the university.

"Here," I said when we had got that far. "This is where my lab is. See up there, the second window on the right? That's my office." A feeling of pride flowed through me as I said this. I was, after all, only eighteen and already had my own office in the university.

She looked up at it and nodded.

"If you want I can show you around. I have a swipe card for twenty-four hour access. I can show you all our instruments."

"No, that's all right. I'm too ignorant to understand about scientific instruments, anyway. I'm only a second-rate Arts student, remember?"

I sighed.

"Look, I'm sorry I said that. I didn't mean it like that."

She looked away.

"I'm sorry, okay?" I said again.

"Okay," she answered eventually. But it really wasn't.

That night I tried to get her to come to bed with me, but she quickly declined the offer in favour of the couch. During the night I couldn't sleep, so I got up and peered back into the living room. In the faint light that shone through the curtain, I could see her lying on her side, with her knees tucked up into her stomach. Her eyes were open, staring blankly into space. The street light glistened on her cheek, which was wet with tears.

In the morning she told me she was going to see her best friend, Eimear, who was doing an exchange semester in Cologne.

"Really? Eimear's in Cologne?"

"I told you that yesterday."

"No, you didn't."

"Yes, I did. You weren't listening."

I walked with her back to the train station, feeling sorry for what was happening, but equally unable to do anything about it. On the platform, Máiréad gave me one brief look filled with the old tenderness. But it was already nothing more than a memory, and we said our final goodbye.

She turned back to face me from the step of the train. This time, her face was impassive and distant.

"Good luck, Brian. Take care of yourself."

When she was gone I surprised myself by not being at all sad about what had happened. I just felt relief that it was over. I was eager to get back to the lab, to gorge myself once again on the drug that was my work.

I only ever heard from Máiréad once after that. It was a month after Christmas. She wrote me a very brief note on the back of a postcard, sealed in an envelope. The note said James had taken his own life on Christmas Day.

» 64 «

"The new Indian Prime Minister, Veedala Jhumi, is a lightning rod for anger on all things to do with VIS. He shot up from the obscurity of the grassroots of the Left Alliance's Mumbai branch office. After making a name for himself by organising some rallies in support of quotas for lower-caste Hindis, he spent the next ten years in search of an issue. When VIS erupted, he found his cause."

Peter paused and flicked to the next screen. It showed Jhumi being sworn in as Prime Minister. Then a shot of him signing the Abuja Treaty. Finally it showed him as chairman of a meeting of the "Alliance of VIS Victim Countries".

"VIS brought Jhumi into office, and, in return, Jhumi brought VIS into public debate in India. Long before any other afflicted country realised what was going on, the Indians were looking for blood. While never formally accusing the US of being behind the disease, he has always blamed 'the Americans', and in his rhetoric has often connected their refusal to ratify the Abuja Treaty with the individual actions of Brian Matterosi."

"He should be down on his hands and knees thanking Brian," Art interjected. A few pieces of half-chewed croissant were ejected as he spoke with his mouth full. "Whatever happens, Jhumi's a winner. If Brian walks free, Jhumi can claim it was all a set-up by the evil Westerners. If Brian gets fried, Jhumi can claim his fiery rhetoric delivered some justice for the people. Speaking of which, where is our favourite mad scientist today? Wait. Let me guess— upstairs recording his memoirs?"

Lisbeth nodded and returned to her file. Instinctively Art peered over to see what she was reading. It was the file she had prepared on Lord Richard Tournay, their next witness. Art remembered her talking about him before. He was her old economic geography professor at Oxford. It sometimes seemed to Art that England was run by a handful of people who all went to the same high school and the same college.

"So this Tournay guy? Any last-minute 180 degree turns in his research we should know about?"

"Lord Tournay's solid," Lisbeth answered.

"What about his elitist background? Any chance Kgabu'll try to use that against us? You know, privileged, white colonialist preaching about how there are too many savages cutting down rain forests ..."

"Not a chance. Lord Tournay's career has been impeccable. His credentials in terms of supporting development and foreign aid projects are second to none. If Kgabu tries that, Richard himself will have him for breakfast, never mind the media."

"So are we done with the press?" Peter interrupted. He was still standing in front of the projector with the image of the Indian Prime Minister behind him.

"Sorry, Pete, I'm all over the place here. Yeah, please, continue."

"Jhumi's latest action is to create a link between the next round of trade negotiations and the indictment of Brian Matterosi. The emerging market economies do not have the force to bring down the Western economies, but people are worried that Jhumi has managed to find common purpose with so many disparate nations across the globe from South America, Africa and Asia. VIS has forced them together, even as it has divided the West, and now Jhumi is getting his side thinking about supply cartels for semi-precious metals and other raw materials. The fear is, and this is what is coming out in the media now, that a failure to convict Matterosi could really solidify that cause and create a new economic counterweight to NAFTA and the EU."

Wonderful, Art thought. *I'm not just defending him against a few UN do-gooders. I'm defending him against the economic interests of half the planet.* He stuck his hand into his suit pocket and clenched the USB stick Jeroen had given him. It was his trump card, and the way things were looking now, he might end up having to play it.

"Okay, I think we get the picture; thanks, Pete." He glanced at his watch. 10:45. "All right, folks, let's get this done."

On the way into Court One, Lisbeth caught his arm and handed him another of her carefully prepared folders.

"What's this?"

"The file on Medi-Discover Technologies." She responded to his blank look by reminding him he had requested it a few days previously.

"I did?" Then he remembered: it had to do with Rachel Hyberg's previous work for pharmaceutical companies. Could be useful, though probably nothing compared to what Jeroen had provided him with. He tucked the file into the mess that was his briefcase. "Thanks, I'll have a look at it later."

Lord Richard Tournay wore his suit with no tie and the collar open. He was a tall man, with receding blonde hair and that slightly elongated face of the Norman English that always made Art think of period costume dramas made by the BBC. Only Tournay was the real deal.

"Lord Tournay, you are one of the world's leading social activists on development issues, is that right?"

"I suppose you could say so, yes."

"To be a little more precise, you're on the board of the UK's largest registered development aid charity and you also consult for the European Union's DEVCO programmes."

"That's correct."

"You also have a PhD from Cambridge University in England and you are a professor at Oxford. In which field?"

"Development economics. My particular area of expertise is the interaction of climate change effects and the global food supply chains."

"Let me cut right to the point. Tell us why Viral Infertility Syndrome will save the planet."

"The way I like to explain things, the planet's welfare can be best understood as a three-way trade-off between human population, human welfare and environmental degradation."

Lisbeth signalled to Rachel Hyberg, and the screens illuminated with a diagram from one of Tournay's papers. It showed a 3D graph with axes labelled "Poverty", "Population" and "Environment", connected by a concave shape.

"The concave shape on the diagram you see there is the 'welfare cap' as I call it. Our planet must be at a point on that surface. If one of the three variables changes, say population increases, then it forces a reduction in one or both of the other two. We can keep human beings as well off as they are now and not reduce the population, but to do so will degrade the environment. We can improve the environment—perhaps by designating the Amazon basin as a nature reserve—but only at the cost of human welfare; for instance, the farmers who depend on those resources for their livelihoods. And if we want both human welfare and the environment to improve, we can only achieve this by reducing the human population."

"So give us an example of this. What if the world's population were only 300 million, or about the population of the United States of America?"

"In that case we could have a planet in which global warming would no longer be an issue, the very concept of endangered animals would become a historical curiosity, while at the same time every person on earth could be—if not wealthy—then at least comfortably middle-class. We could all have large homes, cars, our own private gardens, not to mention clean water and nourishing food. No one would have to suffer."

"Sounds like a paradise. And all that would be needed is a drastic drop in population?"

"Yes."

"And is population control the only way to achieve this paradise?"

"I think so, yes. Certainly on this scale."

"But what about technology? Surely if we have better crops, for example, which use fewer resources ..."

"Well, that's true. Technology is an independent force which, if you like, is capable of shifting the entire welfare cap outwards, resulting in a higher level of human welfare for any given amount of environmental damage and population. The problem is that the shifts in technology are far less significant than is commonly imagined. Unfortunately, we tend to see technology as a panacea. And because it is driven only by market forces, it tends to grow simultaneous to environmental degradation. Given the scale of the population problem, it is unlikely, I might even say impossible, that we can rely on technology to bail us out, as it were."

"So without VIS, we'd be totally stuck, right?"

"I don't suppose it's a matter of being 'stuck'. One could equally well imagine wars and genocides, which would do the job of VIS, but in a far more brutal manner. Or else more and more environmental degradation. But the most likely outcome, in the absence of VIS, is that the world would continue along its current path, with the largest percentage of our species living in utterly deplorable conditions. Their chances of improving their lot would grow ever smaller, as the stock of ready land and resources reaches a point of exhaustion."

"But with VIS ..."

"With VIS, the world's very poorest, who after all are the people we should be most concerned with, will at last have an opportunity to see their children and grandchildren prosper."

"Of course, there won't be nearly as many of those children left to prosper ..."

"No, indeed. And that's the whole point. There are quite simply too many of us. And not enough of the planet's riches to go around."

"Thank you, Lord Tournay. Your Honours, I have no further questions for this witness."

» 65 «

The lab was empty. Earlier in the day, it had been full, and I had to wait to get at the refrigerator because some PhD student was standing with the door open, fiddling with her stupid samples. This was annoying because I had tissue samples that needed to get into the fridge, and I didn't want any unintended temperature variation to mess up my test results. I remember it because I had an irrational desire to grab her by the pony tail and fling her bodily out of my way. But that was hours ago. She was gone now, and so was everyone else. I liked it like this. No one got in my way or asked me stupid questions about my work.

A short time later, the peace of the empty building was disturbed by the sound of a door opening, and when next I raised my head Heinz was standing in front of me.

"All work and no play makes Brian a dull boy." He smiled down at me. Heinz was a big man, with a rather Prussian-looking moustache that had gone white with age.

I glanced up and forced myself to reply. Even Heinz was irritating sometimes.

"I'm still trying to isolate the VT5 from the BTV samples we got yesterday."

Heinz gave me a worried look. "Brian, there's no rush on that work. Those samples weren't even supposed to get here until January. It's Christmas Eve. According to Wesson's latest paper, bluetongue was present in the blood of ruminants two million years ago. That's a virus with a lot of history behind it. I think it can wait another two weeks, don't you?"

I looked down at my notes, and began retracing the protein sequences in my mind. VT6. VT7. VT1. All the proteins on my screen ran together into a vast blur, somehow moving to the tune of *Jingle Bells*. I fucking hated Christmas.

"I was already at home, you know. Jutta told me to drive back here and get you. She says you are to have dinner with us tonight."

I knew this was coming. And I didn't want to go to Heinz's house for dinner. I knew his wife, Jutta, was inviting me out of pity, and that bruised my ego. She also asked awkward questions about my family. And Christian, Heinz's stupid son, would be home from Hamburg. I hated him.

"I'm okay, Heinz. I have some food back in my flat."

"What food?"

"I dunno. Toast and cheese. Or else I'll go out and get a Döner Kebab."

"All the Döner shops are closed. It's Christmas Eve. You can't eat toast and cheese for Christmas. Jutta is making roast goose and red cabbage with dumplings."

I hesitated. That sounded good. Food was my one true weakness.

"And apple strudel with ice cream for dessert," Heinz said, clapping me on the shoulder. "C'mon, let's go."

Christian treated me better than I had remembered from our first encounter. I think his mother must have had words with him; in any event, he was quite civil. Over dinner he told me about the city of Hamburg and its various attractions; he even invited me to come and visit him when I had time off work.

After dinner we sat in their sitting room, and Jutta served up some brandies. The room was comfortable and tastefully furnished. It had exposed wooden beams across the ceiling and the centrepiece was a big, glass-fronted wood stove through which you could see oak logs burning. The fire made me think of Drumnaslew, to which I hadn't been back in three years. I had abandoned it—the Whelan family cottage—my last link to my own real family.

Jutta and Christian were busy remembering past Christmases. He threw his big arm around his mother, and she curled up with her feet on the sofa, as they gazed at an old album.

"Ah, that was the year you got the red bicycle, don't you remember, *Mäuschen?*"

It occurred to me that no family pictures of my own childhood

Christmases existed. I had left the photo albums back with my dying, alcoholic mother. Did those albums still exist? I very much doubted it. That was eight years ago, I realised with a shock. Eight years since I had left Watertown. What had become of her? It was impossible to ask this question without feeling an incredible surge of guilt. And yet, why should I be the one who felt guilty? My parents had failed me, not the other way around. I had merely saved myself, and had done an admirably good job of it. It angered me that, in addition to fucking up my entire childhood, my mother should also have the power to make me feel so guilty.

When I looked up from the flames I had been staring into, I saw that Jutta was watching me intently.

"Have you heard anything from your family in Boston, Brian?" It was as if she could read my mind.

"No," I answered curtly, hoping that that would end the discussion. But the sudden silence had drawn the men's attention, and now everyone was staring at me. This was exactly what I had been dreading.

I stood up abruptly. "I have to go. Thanks for dinner, Jutta. It was delicious."

"But it's only nine o'clock."

"I'm very tired."

"But we haven't given out the presents yet." I had forgotten—the Germans always unwrapped their presents on Christmas Eve.

"Oh," I felt more embarrassed than ever. "Well, I'm sorry. I didn't get anyone anything."

"We didn't get you anything either, Brian," Jutta said, handing me a beautifully-wrapped rectangular package. "This is a present from the baby Jesus, which was delivered by his faithful servant, *Knecht Ruprecht*. He comes to our house every Christmas Eve and leaves presents. He must have come while we were eating dinner."

"I think I caught a glimpse of him as he was heading back out!" Heinz added merrily, emptying his brandy.

"Go ahead, unwrap it."

I did. It was a set of little framed pictures. One of Faneuil Hall in Boston, one of the Ha'penny Bridge in Dublin and one of the town hall square in Göttingen. The final picture was of me and Heinz, at an award ceremony in Hanover the previous August. The Lower Saxony Science Foundation. I had received an award for my most recent work on dsRNA viruses. There was also a pack of picture hangers.

Jutta smiled. "It must be for your apartment. The baby Jesus wants you to make it feel a bit more like home."

I gathered the pictures together, grabbed my coat and said another confused goodbye. Christian offered to drive me back to my flat, but I said I'd prefer the walk. I was at the door before they could object.

Outside sleet had turned to rain, penetrating the white blanket of earlier snowfall with deep, wet cavities, like pockmarks. Slush made the footpaths greasy and slippery. All along the way from the Lindemanns' house back into town, the lights from the Christmas trees in family homes cast their glow out onto the empty streets. A smell of firewood hung everywhere in the still air.

In the abandoned centre of town, I turned down an alleyway behind a restaurant and opened the plastic lid of their dumpster. I threw the pictures in, where they lay amongst food waste and old plastic wrappings. Then I gave the side of the dumpster an angry kick.

Back in the flat, I lay in bed and unsuccessfully attempted to masturbate. Eventually I gave up and just lay there, staring at the bare walls of this place that was so completely not my home.

I dreaded crying and resisted it the way people often resist the impulse to vomit. But it was no good. Tears began to flow down my face. Once it began, emotion choked every part of my body.

It was the fourth anniversary of James's suicide.

» 66 «

Leeton Kgabu attempted to focus on the Richard Tournay file his team had prepared for him, but the words were swimming on the page. He glanced up at the judges' bench. Their gaze was fixed on him, like five inquisitors. For a moment, he thought it was his own trial. A painful memory of a police interrogation, a long time ago in Durban, forced its way into his mind. A shudder passed through his body. Instinctively, he gripped Umama's necklace and risked a glance at the tablet device he kept hidden under his papers, which was live-streaming the trial. The CNBC news camera was on him, and, for a brief second, the dreadful thought ran through his mind, that the world would see him sweat. But on screen, it appeared only as if he was adjusting his tie while reading his notes. To the world he still appeared calm, in control and powerful, which was all the reassurance he needed. He relaxed his grip on the necklace and turned his attention to the Court. They were waiting for his cross-examination; now it could begin.

"Mr Tournay," Leeton said, as he rose. A thrill passed through him at the deliberate use of "Mr", instead of "Lord". He wanted the world to know that he rejected the colonial legacy, and especially the royal titles which the whites—most of all the British— used to set themselves above the rest of humanity.

"Call me Rick, if you prefer."

A little laugh went up from the gallery behind him; a laugh in which Blume allowed himself to share. Leeton felt it was at his expense, and he burned in a flush of anger. But he regained control and forced a smile.

"I prefer to stick with *Mr* Tournay, if it's all the same."

"As you choose."

"You mentioned that overpopulation has forced people into poverty."

"Overpopulation and a certain level of environmental protection, yes."

"But what I found absent from your analysis was any notion of inequality."

"That's because it *was* absent from my analysis."

"But surely, if we reduce inequality we can reduce poverty, without hurting the environment or cutting the population?"

"I don't believe so. For one thing, there is no certainty that reducing inequality through redistributive policies actually achieves the goal of alleviating poverty. Taxing the rich to give to the poor won't work, if it hurts investment and overall economic growth. And even if it does work, it can only achieve poverty alleviation when that comes at the expense of the environment, because carbon intensity is greater at the lower tiers of Maslow's hierarchy of needs. For example, if you take resources from one rich person and distribute it evenly to one hundred poor people, the rich person will still likely have his share of carbon-intensive consumption. But the poor people, who might previously have eaten only a vegetable diet, will now have the resources to demand meat. Net carbon intensity will rise."

"But it's all right for the rich to eat that share of meat? And drive big cars and live in their big homes in the English countryside. Is that what you're saying?"

Tournay shrugged. "I don't claim that the starting position is particularly just, Mr Kgabu. But it is the reality we have inherited."

Yes, Leeton thought. That's the excuse they always give. Our colonial ancestors might have been at fault. And we might owe our current status and privilege to their past misdeeds, but well, that's all history. We are where we are!

"And what colour are these rich people?" Leeton was only barely aware that his voice was rising.

"I'm not sure that's really the most important question, sir."

"Just answer the question, please, witness."

"There are rich people of all ethnicities and races. Though if we insist on seeing the world in black and white, more of the rich are white, like myself. And more of the world's poorest are black, like you. Which I believe is what you are trying to get me to say, is it not, Mr Kgabu?"

"So by that token, if our goal is to protect the world's environment, would it not make more sense to release an infertility virus that targets only the rich, the ones who consume the most resources? What about a virus that targets white people? Would that not have been more effective?"

"I'm not sure it would. The capacity of the afflicted countries to adjust to the consequences of VIS will surely depend on the skills transmission of the current generation of the well-educated to the next generation. If we were to eradicate only the future populations of the developed world, we would be culling a future generation of engineers, doctors, programmers, and thereby likely creating important gaps in knowledge transmission. The current demographic projections for Europe, Japan and America which are based on a VIS infection rate of about 30 per cent, are about optimal, I should think."

"Are you suggesting Africans are incapable of engineering or medicine or computer programming?"

"Certainly not. But their most educated are mainly at work in America or Europe. Even at home, the skilled classes in developing countries have the lowest rates of VIS infection. You seem to imply that the effects of VIS are ubiquitous outside of the white world. But there are fertile people in Africa, South America and Asia. When the initial shock of demographic adjustment subsides, they and their children will be uniquely placed to inherit vast wealth and opportunity in their home countries. By 2060 Nigeria will be as rich as Switzerland, thanks to VIS."

"Do you have any idea how ruthless, how cruel and demeaning it is for the world to hear you say that? To say, in effect, that while their cultures and families will have been wiped off the planet, the few remaining survivors will inherit what the rest have had stolen from them?"

"No crueller, I suppose, than the alternative. Which is to know that if Brian Matterosi had not done what he has done, we would in effect have been condemning ten billion people to a poverty so bleak that it would last them not only their lifetimes, but also those of their children, and grandchildren, and onwards until the world's scarce resources were utterly exhausted. Only then would their lines be extinguished, in war and in famine."

"Easy to say from the position of privilege which you have inherited from your white, upper-class father, *Lord* Tournay."

Leeton felt the white man's eyes boring into him. Tournay's voice dropped and the tone remained flat, yet somehow was full of passion. "As you ought to know, my father was murdered in Zimbabwe when I was only a boy, by the same kind of bigots who insist on painting all members of a certain race or class with the same brush. I have dedicated my life and all of my inherited wealth to improving the living standards of the very people who took his. And as regards the use of my title, as I told you before, you're free to call me Rick."

"I have no further questions for this witness, Your Honours."

"Then the Court is adjourned. Thank you, witness. You may step down."

As he left the courtroom, Leeton felt the eyes of a hundred people were on him, although no one said anything. He needed some space, and the toilets were the only place to which he could escape. But he stopped short in front of the door. Something told him not to go in there. Instead he walked down the hallway and across the foyer to where the reading tables under the high glass ceiling overlooked the entrance foyer below. There were more toilets down that end, tucked around a corner. Two photographers, Italian or Spanish, were idly chatting nearby. They just had time to get their cameras out and snap the flash in his face, before he ducked to safety.

In front of the mirror Leeton peeled back his jacket and felt his cotton shirt. It was sticking to his skin. He splashed water on his face, but it did nothing to stop the sweating. He took out his iPhone and read the Skype message that appeared on the screen. "*I just want to know that you are okay, my Sunshine. Please call me. Please.*" He had not rung Caddie in four days, because he couldn't bear to look her in the eyes.

On its way back into his pocket, the phone slipped out of his hand, bounced off the edge of the sink and smacked against the polished tiled floor. The screen cracked into a million pieces. As he put it back into his pocket, gripping it perhaps a little more tightly than was necessary, a shard of glass pierced his finger.

He was busy washing the blood clean when he heard the door open. Sobiewski's face appeared in the mirror. Dread engulfed Leeton.

"Blood on your hands, eh?" the Pole said.

Leeton ignored him.

"I would say so, at any rate. Race wars in South America. Riots in London. The possibility of a global trade war. You've ignored every good piece of advice you've been given so far, Attorney Kgabu. Now is your final chance: recall the subpoena for Laura Schneider."

"Are you threatening me?" Leeton spun about, causing the little white man to cower, if only for a moment. That was satisfying. It made the sense of dread go away.

"I'm warning you, not threatening you. There's a difference."

"And I'm warning you, that if you keep on threatening me, I'll be telling the press afterwards how you attempted to interfere in the decisions of the prosecution, and pervert the course of justice."

Leeton left without looking back. A certain wildness welled up from inside him, and with it a determination to do something he knew he shouldn't.

» 67 «

If there is one thing in my life of which I am truly and utterly ashamed, it is how I treated Heinz towards the end of our professional collaboration. As my publications record began to pile up, and I was awarded honorary PhDs and given a full professorship in the university, I began to believe in the hubris of my own infallibility.

There was one particular paper on viral treatments for cancer cells, which I had started with Heinz back in 1998, but which for one reason or another, we had never completed. I took the raw idea and claimed it as my own; I finished the paper without giving Heinz any credit; without even telling him I was working on it. The paper, of course, was a sensation, a foundation stone upon which most of this century's cancer research has been built. And while Heinz was the first to congratulate me, I could tell he was hurt. His sad blue eyes told me what I already knew: that he would have freely given me all the credit, all the money, anything. He only wanted my trust, and I had withheld that gratuitously. Heinz was now Chair of the science faculty, and he was the only reason I was staying loyal to the university. When our relationship started to cool, I found myself thinking more and more of going commercial.

The incident with the cancer paper created a lasting rift, mostly because I wasn't able to admit my own fault. I think it was this that pushed me to open the BetterWorld laboratory. There were other factors too. I had grown more and more arrogant and found the constraints of the university irksome. Lecturing was something I had to do from my days as *Dozent* onwards, and while initially I really enjoyed it, by the late 1990s it had become tedious. I found the students to be mostly idiots, who just wanted to get drunk and live away from their parents and meet the opposite sex. Wasting my time explaining the same basic material over and over again to yet another vintage of spoiled, middle-class brats made me increasingly cranky. It was also annoying that big companies were taking my research findings and making millions from them, or that the university was getting paid for the patents and only paying me my normal salary. It wasn't that I wanted to buy expensive consumer items, but I would have liked to be able to upgrade my instrumentation without having to submit purchasing orders to the central procurement authority of the university. I wanted absolute freedom and control over my work.

In retrospect, I wonder why I didn't just quit the university altogether and set up anew somewhere else. Perhaps a part of me wanted the confrontation. Or, perhaps, I was simply too damn lazy to move out of my apartment and my messy office in the main science block.

And so I opened BetterWorld in 2004 in an industrial estate, just outside of the city of Göttingen, in complete breach of the terms of my contract with the university. I guess I knew this would put Heinz in an impossible situation, but I simply didn't care. That was how I behaved.

When the confrontation finally did happen, I felt ready for it.

"Brian, we have to talk."

"I'm pretty busy at the moment, Heinz, sorry."

"Now! Enough!" He slammed his fist on the table in an uncharacteristic expression of anger. I jumped to attention.

"What are you doing with this laboratory you've created?"

"It's called BetterWorld. Because that's what I want to do. Make the world better."

"You're an employee of this university. You can't start up your own research company. We have our own commercial partners. It's a clear conflict of interests."

I scoffed. "Do you know what I'm working on over there? Cancer! I'm going to develop viral treatments for skin cancer. It's going to be a cream you can spread on your skin and the virus will just eat away any cancer cells you might have. Even better, I'm going to make it an active ingredient and sell it to companies that make suntan lotion. And with the money I make off this, I'm going to find a way to cure every other type of cancer on the planet. Now, are you going to stand there and tell me that because of some stupid clause in a contract, I can't rid the world of cancer? Is that what you've become in your old age, Heinz, a fucking bean counter? I thought you were a scientist."

Heinz's eyes hardened against me. "And I thought you were a friend, Brian."

I didn't know what to say to that. He turned his back to me and walked out of my lab, but not before saying, "You're suspended with immediate effect. A notice of termination for breach of contract will follow in a few days. You have five minutes to pack your personal effects."

Great, I thought. *Now I'm free of this university.*

Of course, I soon discovered that the business world is not a place where you get absolute freedom or control over your work. If anything, the terms and conditions of the joint ventures I entered into with pharmaceutical and biomedical multinationals were more restrictive than anything I had faced in Göttingen University.

I had no experience running a company, and it soon showed. The personal fortune I had amassed from savings, prizes, awards, publications and fifteen years of very frugal living amounted to four hundred thousand euro, all of which I threw into the lab, borrowing another million from the bank, on the strength of my reputation alone. This was still not sufficient to buy the instrumentation I needed, and so I embarked on joint ventures. By 2006 I was heavily in debt and practically penniless. The rent on my apartment was past due and for the first time since I was a teenager, I had no money for food.

There was the string of employees I hired, many of whom were too bad to mention. In fairness, some of them might have been decent workers, if I had known how to manage them properly. The worse things got, the more bitter and resentful I became, and the worse I was at managing the lab.

This was the state of affairs when I met with Laura. She was sent to be my business manager, as a condition of a renegotiated capital deal with the Swiss multinational Zextra, one of my pharmaceutical partners who had now acquired a controlling share in my insolvent company. Laura later told me it was touch-and-go; that Zextra was very close to cutting its losses and winding up BetterWorld altogether. She had convinced them to give her a chance to put things right.

"The first thing you will do is go home and take a shower and put on some clean clothes," she told me after we had shaken hands.

"Excuse me?" I looked at her in shock. I was used to bossing around lesser scientists who held me in awe. No one talked to me that way. But Laura was unfazed.

"You stink, Professor. Go home and clean yourself up. I need to ask you a lot of questions but I'm not going to sit here in this filthy office and smell your body odour. I've also hired cleaners to come in and make this place presentable. They should be here any minute."

I wanted to tell her to go fuck herself. I wanted to remind her that I was a world-renowned scientist, a genius, on track for a Nobel prize, and that she was a little corporate nobody in a suit dress. But the Zextra people had made it very clear who was now in charge. I had no choice. And so I went home and took a shower. I even put on deodorant.

That first day set the tone for our working relationship. I continued to resent Laura's authority, but despite myself I had to recognise that most of the decisions she made were the right ones. Even so, I think I would have tossed the whole thing away in a fit of pique, but for two factors.

The first was that, although she took control of the business end of BetterWorld with an iron fist, she never attempted to interfere in the scientific end of things. My research was still my own. When it came to discussing actual research work, her attitude changed and she deferred to my judgment completely. Even when the people in Zextra headquarters in Basel were pushing one way, I knew that on the research end, Laura would have my back. By degrees I came to trust her.

The other factor, which took longer for me to acknowledge, had to do with the way her nose twitched ever so slightly at its tip when something amused her. She was not what you might call a classically beautiful woman, and so I didn't realise how attracted I was to her until I found myself dreaming about her little nose, in the middle of the work day.

We were in her office one day going over the latest patent contract. Laura was supposed to negotiate the deal with me on Zextra's behalf.

"They're trying to swindle you, Brian," she told me. "Here, read clause six. It says they can resell the patent rights to one of their competitors and, if they do, you lose your interest."

"But why would they want to resell a patent to a competitor?"

She looked at me like I was an idiot. "Because that way they can screw BetterWorld out of millions of euros."

"But then they don't get to develop the product."

"No, but they get the money. This is business, Brian. It's all about money."

"So what do we do?"

"You mean what do *you* do. I work for Zextra, remember?" There it was! The nose twitch. My heart jumped in my breast. She smiled as if she knew exactly what effect she had on me.

"Here, I drafted an email response for you. It suggests a bunch of tracked changes, but the only one that matters is right here. You see, I've added the word *'einvernehmlich'*. In Swiss German, that's legally watertight. Just send this email from your own inbox. And cut and paste! Whatever you do, don't forward my mail to them!"

That night, after she'd gone home, I went into her office. Her light grey cardigan was hanging on the back of her chair. She always complained the office was too cold. I touched it gently. Then I picked it up and held it to my face.

» 68 «

"I need to see you alone." Matterosi spoke as soon as the security guard had left, and the door closed behind him. He shot looks at Peter, Chun, Anna and Lisbeth. The first time he had acknowledged them as human beings, and it was only to tell them to get the fuck out, Art thought.

When they were gone, Brian stared at him and said, "Did you know about this?" The paper Matterosi thrust in front of him was similar to the one Art had received that morning.

"Where did you get this?"

"Never mind where I got it. When did you know this was going to happen?"

"Calm down, I only found out this morning. The team you just chucked out was busy working up our defence strategy. Anyway, I warned you this could happen."

"No! No! This wasn't supposed to happen. You have engineered this!"

"I engineered nothing. Kgabu called her as a supplementary witness for the prosecution. I told you he might. And now he's done it."

"Why, Art, why? She has nothing to do with VIS. Nothing. I told you that, and I told you that was what our testimony had to demonstrate."

"And we can tell that story, if that's what you want—"

"It's not a *story*, it's the truth. And I don't want you to tell any story; I want her removed as a witness."

"We can't do that. She's not our witness to remove."

Brian shook his head. He grabbed the paper and crumbled it into a ball. The anger, the agitation. This was what Art had expected to see. This was the Brian Matterosi he had been looking for. It had taken the love of a woman to bring it out.

"Make sure your people do everything they can to keep her name clear."

Art nodded.

"I have got one other card up my sleeve."

Silence. Brian stood waiting, still clutching the ball of paper in his fist.

"Sit down, Brian, please."

Art opened the folder and showed him the first of the photographs.

"Jesus Christ," the scientist said, as he flicked through the pictures, which had been ordered from the mild to the outright obscene. "Is this woman, the one from—"

"Yes," Art answered. "I told you right at the beginning Kgabu would make mistakes. And now he's really gone and done a doozy. We've got him by the balls. Right ... " He stabbed one of the more graphic images in the appropriate location, "... here. This is big, Brian. I'm talking mistrial."

"Mistrial?"

"At this stage, I think it's the best we can hope for."

"No!" Brian slammed the folder shut.

"What?"

"No mistrial."

"But we can discredit the ICC. We can have you extradited to the US. Your chances of a 'not guilty' verdict would be twice as high."

Brian stared up at him with those focused brown eyes that seemed to see so much. Cold and clinical. The scientist had already retreated, once again, into that distant place where Art could not reach him. The shield was back up again.

"There will be no mistrial, Mr Blume. Burn these pictures. It ends in this court with this judgment."

» 69 «

I was madly in love with Laura long before anything ever happened between us. And Laura knew it too. By degrees, my behaviour changed in ways that I imagined would please her. I improved my dress style. I joined a gym and started working out. I even redecorated my flat in the hope that she might one day come over. It seemed that she felt the same way, for there was a sort of complicity between us that transcended mere business interests. When she talked about BetterWorld and Zextra, it was in terms of "us" and "them".

One complication was that she had a boyfriend. It was a sort of on-off relationship. I couldn't stand the guy, who in my view obviously didn't love her and wasn't worth the tip of her pinkie finger. She didn't love him either, and I think it would have been clear to anyone that the relationship was all wrong. But I suppose that is always easier to see from the outside.

It was late March, the Holy Thursday of 2008. I came up to her office door for a chat. I suppose I wanted to see her before she went off for the long weekend.

"So, any plans for the weekend?"

"Nope."

The blunt reply took me aback.

"Oh," I answered slowly. Personal conversations were still a bit awkward between us. "I just figured maybe you and Jochen might be going away or some—"

"Nope."

"Oh."

She swivelled away from her computer and looked at me.

"We were supposed to go skiing. But we broke up."

My heart jumped with joy. "Oh, I'm so sorry."

"I'm not," she responded. "And, actually, you're not either."

The nose twitch! I couldn't help smiling.

"So, this weekend, did you want to ... I dunno, maybe ..."

"Yes," she answered, with a smile of her own.

"Yes, what? You don't even know what I was going to say."

"Neither do you. But the answer is yes."

And that was the strange way we began. Two days later, we met for our first real date, which turned into an epic walk in the woods of Lower Saxony. It was one of those paths that led up over villages and through the forest. We stopped in a café in a little Grimms' Fairy Tale town on the border with Hesse, where we warmed our fingers and our faces over big generous bowls of *Milchkaffee*. Then, back in the woods, along a forest path which our map told us would lead to a train station on the Kassel-Göttingen line, I worked up the courage to ask her why she had broken up with Jochen.

"Here's why," she answered. She took hold of my face with her little freezing cold hands and kissed me quickly on the lips. As soon as I had recovered from the shock, I kissed her back, and we kissed for a long, long time. The cold, crisp, spring day; the sunlight dancing amongst the still-bare branches of the beech trees that encompassed us; the daffodils shooting through the dank winter earth in triumph; all these beautiful things melted away into a single, wonderful, kiss. It awakened in me feelings that had been in hibernation for many, many years. Since I was a teenager.

» 70 «

"By early 2017 VIS was already a pandemic. And yet it took months for the world to even awaken to the fact that the virus was there. They were so far from knowing what it was, who had engineered it. This was partially because the WHO's credibility had been so badly damaged over their handling of the Ebola outbreak of 2014. And partially because of the war in Ukraine; the euro currency crisis; tensions between the West and Russia and the caricatures of Mohammad inflaming Muslim anger. The things that divided the world back then which had seemed so important.

"As we look back on it now, it seems ludicrous to think there was almost a nuclear exchange over three hundred and fifty square kilometres of impoverished industrial wasteland in Donetsk. It will only take a generation before the whole of Eastern Ukraine becomes an empty nature reserve. Then only the wolves will fight each other for control of Donetsk.

"Equally amazing was how fast the world pulled together, once the shocking truth of Viral Infertility Syndrome became fully known. Muslims and Russian separatists. Radical anti-austerity activists in Athens and bankers in Frankfurt. Suddenly there was something that the whole world could agree on: the fact that everything would change.

"And a new fault line emerged, which cut across all the previous divisions. Whether Brian Matterosi was the hero he pretended to be. Or the mad scientist, the murderer of the future, the bio-terrorist, which most of the world believed him to be. In the shock and confusion that followed the full realisation of what had happened, there was one man who captured the raw anger, and channelled it into a coherent voice: Veedala Jhumi. It was a voice that was potent enough to bring governments in the West to their knees; to unite three quarters of the world behind a common cause. A voice that united Christians, Muslims and Hindis, even atheists, in a call for something as simple and as straightforward as justice. As the trial of Brian Matterosi heads into its final stage, the world cannot help but wonder what form that justice will take.

"Whatever the outcome of the trial might be, one thing is for sure. This is only the first chapter in the story of VIS. As we watch the demographic *pyramids become more and more top-heavy, as we watch our cities die and our fields turn to wilderness, we are still writing this story.*

"*Tune in next week, when* Behind the Story *takes you to meet the victims from the small West African country of Guinea-Bissau, where VIS infection rates have reached a shocking 97 per cent of the population.*

"*Until then, goodbye from The Hague.*

"*For GlobalSix News, I'm Simon Collins.*"

» 71 «

Heinz already had cancer in 2006, when we had our big fight. But he didn't mention it to me. It was a tumour in his liver. The doctors said it could remain in remission for many years. I only found out about it years later, when the cancer was well out of control. The medication they gave him to retard the growth was a cure almost as bad as the disease. It was the reason why he had become so weak and had distanced himself so much from the day-to-day work of the laboratory.

Looking back on it now, it all seems so crushingly ironic. My only friend left in the world, my mentor, the man who believed in me when no one else did, was abandoned by me precisely because he suffered from the very disease I was trying to cure. And I was so busy with my head in a microscope that I didn't see the symptoms of the very real cancer patient in my life, who needed my support.

With shame, I now realise how he must have struggled with the Board of the University to keep my name clear, and avoid even worse professional consequences for me. And, all the time, his body was failing him. Not only did I betray him, but I added so much more to his burden.

And yet, when I finally did build up the courage to go and visit him three years later—coaxed into doing so by Laura, I must say—Heinz was nothing but glad to see me. There was not a trace of bitterness in him.

"How is the research going? Have you found a cure for me yet?" They had shaved off his moustache for hygiene reasons, and his face was sunken and hollow-looking. But his bright blue eyes still smiled up at me, the same as ever.

"Not yet, old friend. But we'll get there. And when we do, it will be your work that saves millions of lives."

He reached out his big hand to me, which though still large, was now weak and frail.

"I hear you have a girlfriend now?"

"Yeah. More than a girlfriend. A life partner. Her name is Laura. I'm totally in love with her."

"Tell me about her."

And I did. We talked for hours. I told him how Laura and I had met. How she had saved BetterWorld, then quit Zextra and joined the company with me. How the company was solvent again and making handsome profits. How we had moved in together to a new house. How she helped me and completed me in so many ways. How she made me a better man.

"It was Laura who urged me to come here and tell you ... how sorry I am for the way things ended at the university. How sorry I am for the way I treated you."

He just waved his hand dismissively. "Brian, I know what you are. You're a scientist. I knew it from the first day I met you—you were just a twiggy little boy trying hard to grow facial hair. But even then I could see it in you; that you had the passion. Everything you've done, you've done out of passion for science. How could I, of all people, ever be angry at that?"

"So you forgive me?"

"There's nothing to forgive. Now, get the hell out of this dismal place, go back to your lab and find a damn cure for cancer!"

Heinz would die a few weeks later, and though I saw him again, he was too far gone on the morphine to recognise me. So those were his last words to me: "find a damn cure for cancer".

That night in bed I laid my head on Laura's shoulder, and she ran her fingers through my hair. As I told her all about Heinz and what he had said, she held me close to her and told me it was all right. Laura had taught me it was okay to cry sometimes.

Afterwards, I noticed the tears had stained Laura's nightdress. I apologised for messing up her nightie, anticipating a smile and some more platitudes which would allow us to transition smoothly into sex. But in that way she had of sometimes being unexpectedly stern, her voice changed, and she said something I wasn't expecting.

"You know, it's not the fact that Heinz is dying of cancer that's making you cry."

"Of course it is."

"No, it isn't," she replied, in that definitive tone of hers.

I lay silent, braced for what she might say.

"You're really crying for your own parents. Mostly for your mother."

"You don't know what you're talking about." My family was the last taboo subject between us. I don't know why, but it was.

"Yes, I do. I'm a woman, and a woman feels these things instinctively. Every night when we go to bed, your mother is lying right here, taking up this enormous, invisible space between us. You have so many issues around your childhood, and it's holding you back. It's holding us back."

"Sorry, Laura, no. I don't know what bullshit pop psychology you've been reading, but I am a scientist. A real scientist. I don't buy into that stuff and I'm not going to go there, okay? Goodnight." I switched off the light and turned my back on her.

We lay motionless in bed for a long time, without even the pretence of sleep. I felt angry at her for not simply allowing me to wallow in my grief and self-pity for Heinz, for turning this into something about me and about our relationship.

Eventually I heard her say, in a whisper that was almost inaudible, "I want you to be a father for my children. So you're going to have to come to terms with your childhood, in order that you can become that man. You owe that much to our future children."

"*But I don't want to have children,*" I very nearly replied. "*The world is already grossly overpopulated. My legacy is my science.*" I had been thinking about this in the context of a lecture on climate change and resource constraints I had seen at the university a month previously. It would probably be an exaggeration to say that environmental concerns were a deep conviction of mine at that stage. Perhaps it was more of a convenient rationalisation for an instinct within me that resisted the formation of a family with Laura.

In any event, something in me knew better than to say that to Laura directly. I knew she saw our relationship the same way as she saw BetterWorld: a fundamentally sound investment that she was capable of turning around, through careful and good management. I think a part of me allowed her to believe this was true, even though deep down, I knew it was a lie by omission. There was something deep inside of me that was broken, and that could not be fixed. As I fell asleep that night I remember thinking, *"I should let her go now, before it's too late."* But I was far too much a coward to do that. And I still am.

» 72 «

That evening, Leeton found a white envelope taped to the door of his hotel room. She had marked the envelope only with an "xxx", written in what must have been her lipstick. Without even opening it, he knew what it contained: a USB stick with an MP4 file on it. The latest instalment of the Matterosi recording. A shiver went through his body. Leeton hastily tore the envelope down and glanced about him. Who else had access to that floor of the hotel? One or two security men? Perhaps the cleaners?

Still, Hyberg's lack of discretion didn't stop him from plugging in the stick and listening to the recording. This segment had been recorded from a hidden camera somewhere in Matterosi's hotel suite. Matterosi was on his bed, chin resting on his hands, with the Dictaphone in front of him. He was reading from his messy bundle of notes. When he reached the end, *"I remember thinking 'I should let her go now, before it's too late.' But I was far too much of a coward to do that. And I still am."* and switched off his recording device, Leeton hit the pause button as well.

He poured himself a cognac from the minibar and played the file again from the beginning. And again. He looked at the picture of Laura Schneider, which he had taped to the side of his laptop. What did she know? And the picture of Heinz Lindemann. What secrets had that old shit taken with him to the grave? How much did he really know about VIS? Whatever the briefings from the ICC investigators said, Leeton refused to believe Lindemann was as innocent as Matterosi made out.

As Brian Matterosi switched his recording device off for the fourth time, the clock on Leeton's laptop displayed 01:54. He noticed there were still another few minutes of recording on the MP4 file. It would have felt wrong under normal circumstances to spy on a man like this, in his most intimate moments. But Leeton reminded himself that this was no ordinary man. Matterosi was not entitled to dignity, to privacy, to anything, really. Not after what he had done.

And so Leeton watched on, as Matterosi rose and sauntered over to his window. After a while the scientist returned to the bed and switched on his television, flicking idly through the channels. From the camera angle, it wasn't possible to see what he was watching. But eventually he seemed to have found something that held his attention. He let the remote control fall to his side and his hand moved up his leg. Eyes fixed on the screen, he began rubbing his crotch. Eventually he opened his trousers, shimmied them down a bit and began stroking his penis, just as the file reached its end and went black.

Leeton left the desk in disgust. Despite a shower and another cognac, he couldn't get the image out of his head. Anger filled him again. It was two in the morning, he was half drunk and all he could think of was Brian Matterosi masturbating. *I have to sleep*, he thought to himself.

But wanting to sleep is not the same thing as being able to sleep. Leeton lay in the dark, in his bed, and tried not to think about the fact that he too had masturbated, in that same position, in that same hotel, in what looked like it could have been the very same bed. The same bed in which he had had sex with Rachel Hyberg. With a jolt, he was bolt upright.

He switched the light back on and looked around. He got up, paced to the corner of the room. He moved back again, pulled the desk chair across and stood on it. From that angle the television was still too visible. He dragged the chair a little further to the right and stood on it again. Just about there. He turned his head and looked up behind him.

There it was, tucked in to the shadow of what looked like an air vent: a black glass bulb stuck to the inside of the vent cover. Leeton yanked on it, hard enough to tear out the little piece of coaxial cable which connected the camera through the ventilation system to its source, deep inside the hotel's endoskeleton. On closer inspection, there could be no doubt as to what he was looking at: a microcamera.

"*You fucking, insane, bitch.*" he thought to himself, as wave after wave of horror at the realisation ran through his body. Instinctively, he grabbed his chest to feel Umama's necklace. It wasn't there. He'd forgotten to put it on that morning.

» 73 «

Like so many scientific discoveries in history, the Hydra began as an accident. I first stumbled upon it when we were working on the H354 mRNA beta virus, better known as Traxamat. We were testing it on lab rats, and the reduced fertility was noted in one of my assistant's reports on the current strain. I tested the rat sperm and saw how, in certain strains, the proto-Hydra had developed its unique structure to bind with the flagella and render them immotile. Instantly, I saw how I might tweak it further and enhance the infertility effects.

My first idea was to develop it as a sort of vermin control product. I think there were even notes seized by the German police which can prove this, though, of course, our defence strategy has not been to deny the deliberate nature of VIS. But it was the truth, nonetheless. I might very nearly have gone down in history as Professor Matterosi, the mastermind behind the viral drug Traxamat that cured cervical cancer, and who then went on to invent a virus that rid the world of its surplus rat population. There followed a strain that targeted possums, moles, and anything else that could be classed as vermin.

Once the innovation—what I think of as the "real work"— was done, I lost all interest in Traxamat. Actually, making it a commercial success became a chore; one I did out of love for Laura more than anything else. It was she who reminded me that just because I *knew* it would work, didn't mean anyone else would believe me. And so the drudgery of clinical trials commenced. By the time the fanfare hit, and we'd sold the patent, I was already deep into research on the skin cancer viral agents which had defeated me back in 2006. Laura dragged me along to the award ceremonies. She forced me to give keynote speeches at universities. I know they've released unflattering footage of me saying rude, dismissive things at this point. An arrogant, self-absorbed git. At the time, I wasn't very aware of my behaviour, but looking back on these videos, I guess there was some truth in it. The footage of me accepting an honorary PhD from Princeton is especially embarrassing.

I recall reading that C. S. Lewis was once asked why it was that God, if He loved us, allowed so much human suffering to take place. Lewis's answer was that suffering was necessary, because it was the only way to make us empathise. We needed the pain in order to learn to love each other.

The fiction around "God" notwithstanding, I think there's something to that. My life at that stage was so easy, I had forgotten what suffering even meant. I had so much success. I had the love of Laura to keep me happy. We had a comfortable, wonderful home in the outskirts of Göttingen. I had become an internationally acclaimed scientist. Heinz's death, when it did come, was sad. But I dealt with that the way I dealt with all my other problems: I buried myself in my work and forgot about it.

Maybe that was why the "having children" issue bothered me so much. I was afraid, perhaps, that the change would upset this perfect balance. I knew having kids meant a change in priorities. And my priorities suited me perfectly. More than just suiting me perfectly, I could rationalise them by noting how they made the world a better place. If Laura had been willing to take my sperm and leave the rest as it was, perhaps I would have cast aside my beliefs about overpopulation and accepted the inevitable. But she wanted much more out of me than just biological material. She wanted me to confront my inner demons and emerge a stronger man.

That, I think, is what caused me to conceive of the Hydra as a tool for achieving human infertility. At least, as a tool for making myself infertile, in a way that could never be tested or traced to any known cause. It was cowardly I know, but I felt I had no other option. I could not lose her, and I could not face having a baby with her. Even so, I do not think I would have been driven to this extreme had I not seen the therapist.

I hated that therapist, and I knew from the beginning she hated me. To my mind, at least, she was probing at my feelings and emotions not out of any desire to help me overcome my issues, real or alleged, but because she derived a sick satisfaction in exposing me; bringing me from the intellectual level on which I liked to operate, far superior to her own, down to a level where she had the power. The sticky, opaque world of psychology, where nothing was ever completely true or false.

"Do you feel guilty for leaving your mother alone?"

"No." I found one-word answers were a good way of defending myself.

"So, why do you think it is that you have never tried to contact her?"

"Who says I never tried to contact her?"

"That's what you told me that last session."

"What I *told* you was that I hadn't actually ever ... succeeded in getting through to her."

"So you have tried to contact her?"

"I didn't say that either. Fact is, I don't have the number. There is no number anymore. That doesn't mean I haven't tried. I mean, I tried to get the number ... You also have to understand how incredibly busy I am. I work an average of sixteen hours a day. Do you have any idea what that means, to actually work intensively at something, for sixteen hours every day?"

She looked at me for a moment in silence before asking her next question.

"Why do you feel so reluctant to discuss this?"

"Because, I ..." I took a deep breath, "I'm not reluctant. It's just ... I don't see the relevance of any of this. It feels like I'm wasting time that I could be spending on actual productive things."

I realised then I would much rather have spent the hour telling her about these actual productive things, but she would not allow me to steer the conversation back to my work.

"How do you feel about your mother? I mean, you're obviously still thinking about her ..."

How I felt about my mother? I felt she had never taken care of me, and yet at the same time she refused to let go of me. Dead or alive, it didn't matter: she was a ghost that had robbed me of my childhood. But at the end of the day, none of that mattered. So why even talk about it? From somewhere inside me, some place I couldn't identify, anger welled up.

"I'll tell you what I'm thinking," I answered. "I'm thinking you are yourself an emotionally manipulative, jealous person who can't come to terms with the fact that a man like me can actually be fine without all your psycho-meddling. Let's talk a bit about your mother, shall we?"

"Where is this anger coming from, Brian?"

I took another deep breath. "You know, this whole therapy thing was Laura's idea. She's the one who thinks I have an issue here, but I don't really. I'm going to be honest with you. I think psychology is mostly a load of bullshit. Psychologists are scientists who didn't do well enough in school to study real science at university. I'm coming here, because I have to."

Her face hardened even further.

"In that case, there's really no point in us continuing."

"Well, true. But we have to. We're going through the motions, but I promised Laura, so I have to keep pretending to do this, I'm afraid. An hour a week."

"Not with me," she said. "I'm not going to waste my time with you, so that you can tick a box for your partner. That's not helpful for you either; it's an unhealthy way to conduct your relationship, and it's frankly demeaning to me as a professional."

"You're not 'wasting' your time. I'm prepared to pay you. You're in it for the money, aren't you?"

The therapist looked at me in disgust and told me in a perfectly calm voice to please leave her practice immediately.

I never told Laura how it ended. There was something about that meeting that bothered me so much I wasn't even prepared to try with another therapist. Instead I lied to Laura and told her the therapy was going fine. Then, every week, I told her I was going to the session, when actually I spent the hour in the library in the university doing more research work.

This lie was like fertiliser for the seed that had been growing within me. Imperceptibly, little lies sprang up around it, which gradually drove a wedge ever wider between us.

I arrived home one night to find Laura had made us a romantic dinner, complete with candles. We chatted about the office for a few minutes, then talked a little about household matters. There was a certain glow to her, and I noticed her nose twitch just like it used to in the old days, when our relationship was still young. In bed she surprised me with a fresh set of sexy lingerie and did things to me that I regarded as particular treats.

Afterwards, still panting, I let my spent body collapse on her, with my head in the usual position just below her shoulder.

"Why the special treatment tonight?" I asked, as she ran her fingers through my hair.

She took my face in her hands and gazed into my eyes, in that way she always did when she felt she had something important to tell me.

"Because," she said. "I stopped taking the pill last month. And yesterday, I ovulated. So this is the first time we could actually be making our baby." Her eyes were glowing. "I could be getting pregnant right as we speak. Just imagine all the little Brian-fish swimming furiously towards my Laura-egg." Her nose twitched in silent laughter, and she added, "I know! They're not technically 'fish'. Don't correct me Mr Biology Genius. I like to think of them as fish." She placed my hand down there, to feel the semen soaking out from within her. "For once I don't give a damn about messing up the sheets!"

I forced a smile and kissed her, to avoid having to make actual eye contact. The wedge of dishonesty was thick between us. Two weeks previous, I had already injected myself with two separate strains of the Hydra. A week later I had masturbated in the toilet stall at the lab and tested my own sperm extensively. The Hydra worked exactly as I had hoped it would.

Which meant there was no more chance of my sperm getting her pregnant than if I had filled her with a glob of mayonnaise.

» 74 «

"...*live from Mexico City, where the siege on the US Embassy has entered into its third day. Mexican media have been reporting that Secretary of State Nelson has been in emergency communications with his Mexican counterpart all day, but it appears now that the US side is abandoning any hope that the Mexican security forces can restore order. Reports of US Apache helicopters crossing the border and on their way to the Mexican capital would seem to indicate that the US is taking the safety of its staff—and those two hundred American citizens who have sought refuge inside the embassy compound—into its own hands. Live from Mexico City, for GlobalSix News, I'm Tom Steward. Back to you, Mandy.*"

"*Thanks, Tom. Meanwhile, over in The Hague, Netherlands, where it is now early morning, the trial of Brian Matterosi is set to enter its final phase, with more witness testimony live on GlobalSix in just under two hours. This comes amid formal submissions to the ICC by a dozen heads of state that the process be further speeded up. However, they insist the trial should be fully independent. Speaking in the margins of the summit of the Alliance of VIS Victim Countries yesterday, India's Prime Minister and Chair of the Alliance, Veedala Jhumi, reiterated, 'What we want is justice. Nothing more, nothing less.' But as the wave of anger mounts, the feeling now is that nothing short of a guilty verdict will stop the tide of violence that has swept across the developing world this week.*"

Art silenced the television and stared out the plate glass windows of his hotel suite. The wet weather had set in now, and the empty cobblestones of Middelplein glistened as they reflected the milky light of a morning sun that fought to break through the clouds. The Dutch police had extended the cordon around the Paleis Hotel, after the most recent incidents with Molotov cocktails, so that it was hardly possible to see the protestors any more. But they were out there: in greater numbers than before. You could feel their anger like an ever-beating pulse.

GlobalSix might already be signing Brian Matterosi's death

warrant, but so far the US had not cracked. They—alongside China and Israel—remained the only three countries in the world which had not ratified the Abuja Treaty. The pressure on them had become intense. Jhumi's Alliance of VIS Victim Countries controlled oil and other natural resources, and they weren't afraid to wield it. The Indian Prime Minister had turned moral outrage into a political and economic bazooka. Europe—divided and leaderless as usual—had been the first to crumble. In their hypocritical way, they had even pretended to retreat onto the moral high ground that was the Abuja Treaty. The fact that they were effectively signing up for a death penalty they had abolished sixty years previously was conveniently forgotten by all but a few civil rights activists, who themselves risked being lumped into the pro-Matterosi crackpot camp.

Art grabbed the file which, in one stroke, could discredit GlobalSix and the ICC in the eyes of the international community. This trial had not yet been lost; it was still all to play for. Art only needed to do two things. First, pick up the phone and call *The New York Times*. And second, which was the hard part, convince his client to play along.

The buzz of his mobile phone awakened Art from his trance. He realised he was late—again—for the morning briefing and answered instinctively, "Lisbeth, sorry, I'll be there in ten minutes."

"Dad?"

His heart jumped at the sound of Jessica's voice. "Jessica? Is everything okay?"

"Yeah, everything's fine."

"Great. That's great. Listen, thanks for returning my call."

"Sure."

"So ... how've you been?"

"Um ... well, a little bit sick, actually."

At precisely the word "sick", Art's phone emitted a tiny electronic signal. The screen showed a second call—which this time *was* from Lisbeth—in the call-waiting queue. He looked at his watch: 07:23. Shit.

"Sick, huh? Sweetheart, I'm really sorry to hear it. Summer colds are the worst, they say. Good thing you're married to a doctor, though, huh?"

"Yeah, it is. A really good thing. Listen, Dad, I'm calling because I have something to tell you."

"Can this possibly wait until this evening? It's just … I've got the trial and I'm kind of running late …"

There was a pause on the other end of the phone. Art knew he had said the wrong thing. He vowed to make it up to her. Just as soon as he could he would head down to Paris and make her some chicken soup, and learn all about feminist lesbian sculpture, or whatever else she was interested in. But right now, the timing could not have been worse.

"Just forget it," Jessica said. "It's not really that important. Good luck in court."

Click.

Damn. Art tried to switch to the waiting call, but it was too late. Lisbeth had already rung off. No time now; he'd call her back from the car. He rammed the Laura Schneider briefing into his case and gathered up his overcoat from the floor. Jeroen was already waiting outside the hotel room door, wearing his perpetual sarcastic grin.

» 75 «

The next six months passed in a kind of a blur. I worked mainly on the Hydra, perfecting it so that it would impede female fertility as well as male fertility. It was partially the joy of solving the puzzle; partially the sheer beauty of creation. I had come to see viral engineering not only as a technical challenge, but also as a type of artistry. And the Hydra was my masterpiece: a virion whose morphology was so complex it could achieve two distinct effects—both utterly unique in nature—and yet so parsimonious that it was small enough to work in conjunction with a larger, more infectious pathogen, such as influenza.

Not without irony, it was the hour in the library on Thursdays, when I was pretending to be with the therapist, that I began researching the overpopulation problem in earnest. With my usual diligence and sense of application, I read broadly in the fields of demography, economics, food science and climatology and came to the obvious conclusion that the human overpopulation problem evinced all the characteristics of an inherently degenerative system. Without a positive aberration, a fluke perturbation in the system, we were trapped in a downward spiral that would lead to destruction of our species, taking with us all our symbionts.

Still, I would be lying if I said now that I was a true environmentalist in all this. The fact of the matter was, and is, that my concern about the overpopulation problem was a justification that I hastily concocted, like a postdoc's badly written research grant application. I made VIS not so much to save the planet, but because I wanted to see if it would be possible.

And what is perhaps even more disturbing is that a part of me—the socially retarded part I guess you could say—actually wanted to share the discovery of the Hydra with Laura, to give her an opportunity to marvel at the genius of my creation, as she had done many times in the past with the cancer stuff. But not even I was that stupid. Somewhere in my obsessive, scientific brain I understood that the idea of me developing an infertility virus, when we were supposed to be having children, would have been a slap in the face for any woman. Still, I can't imagine I was overly careful with my notes. My private lab was the same mess it had always been.

At home meanwhile, the domestic bliss of our lives was starting to show hairline fractures. It came out in little ways: fights over who did the dishes, over bills, over what television show we should watch. Our Sunday walks in the woods had stopped, and I noticed she was spending more and more time with our neighbour, Frau Zanderer. Maybe she noticed the change in my behaviour, my guilt at living the lie of trying to get pregnant. Or maybe it was just the frustration she must have felt at not getting pregnant after six months of trying.

Of course, instead of dealing with the problem head on, I did the only thing I was capable of doing. I buried myself even deeper in my work. This was the first of a long series of attempts at getting the Hydra launch pad right. I'm not sure how much of the technical details I should get into, but finding the right stage two carrier for the Hydra—something I expected to do in a fortnight—proved to be the hardest part of the entire project.

It was a cold, dark evening in November, but I was only vaguely aware of the rain drilling against my head as I walked my usual route from the lab, across the *Bundesstraße*, through the sports complex and into the settlement of 1970s houses where we lived. The RNA strands for the latest candidate launch virus were running through my head like the sheet music of a symphony, in which the orchestra consisted not of brass or string, but of proteins. And I was the composer, the conductor, the soloist.

Laura was sitting in the kitchen. It wasn't until I saw her face that the viral music stopped. Tears were streaming down her cheeks. She clutched in her hands a bundle of my notes. My first instinct was to deny everything. After all, Laura's grasp of virology was middling at best. But then she spoke, and I knew there was no point in pretending.

"Every single moment of intimacy we have shared ..." Her voice was hoarse and choked. Her chin quivered. "... the most precious memories I own ..." She forced herself to unfold the paper. It was a sketch I had done, months ago, of the Hydra. "They have all been lies. If you had cheated on me with another woman, I could perhaps have forgiven you. If you had hit me, perhaps there might still have been a way back. But this, this is beyond forgiveness."

» 76 «

Dressed in a tight-fitting, black business skirt and a shapely pin-striped blouse, Rachel Hyberg sashayed down the hall of the ICC building, away from the crowds. Leeton spotted her, broke away from his team, and followed. His plan was simple: he would confront her. Ask her who in hell she thought she was, spying on him like that. Was her intention to blackmail him? He would let her know in no uncertain terms that it would not work.

Now she was moving at remarkable speed, twisting and turning along a network of corridors Leeton had not noticed before. The chase continued, dragging him deeper and deeper into the building. Hyberg glanced back at him, a knowing smile painted onto her bright red lips. Only then did he realise the business skirt was actually made out of latex, and her stockings, which he had taken for fishnet, were steel mesh. The pinstriped blouse was see-through, and she wore no bra underneath. Her nipples, plainly visible, were pierced with steel rings.

Open office doors on both sides of the passageway caught his attention, and he peered through each one to see who was inside. Occupying one of the larger offices was an older white man dressed in a suit. He turned his head as Leeton passed. Instantly, Leeton recognised the face. It was Geert Steen, an infamous agent from the NIS who had been implicated in the torture of black South Africans under apartheid. He had escaped prosecution and fled South Africa, and his whereabouts were unknown.

The shock of seeing Steen there, employed by the ICC, caused Leeton to stop in his tracks. He turned again, realising with a growing sense of dread that he had lost sight of Hyberg. Further down, the corridor twisted to the left. Leeton followed. A fire alarm went off, and red lights flashed from the ceiling. He somehow knew Hyberg had pulled the alarm, and that only added to his panic. He had to find her now, before it was too late. In desperation, he threw open the office doors on both sides, but she was nowhere to be seen.

Finally, the corridor came to an end at a set of double doors. Leeton pushed them open, and found himself in a small, windowless room which he recognised as a torture chamber: the kind the NIS used in makeshift facilities outside Cape Town. Crude implements hung from the bare, breeze-block walls. The sound of the fire alarm increased. In the centre of the room, Caddie was strapped to a chair, naked, with electrodes prodding at her body. To her left, Brian Matterosi was standing in a lab coat, about to administer a drug in a syringe. To her right, stood Rachel Hyberg, holding his son, Robert, in her arms. Hyberg was looking at Caddie in a way that was almost lewd.

"She's very beautiful," Hyberg mused, as she twisted a lock of her own fine, blonde hair. A second later, the syringe plunged into Caddie's bare arm.

"No!" Leeton screamed, and attempted to run to her.

His body twitched and shuddered, and he awoke.

It was 07:00 in the morning. Leeton reached across and silenced the alarm clock. It felt like he hadn't had a wink of sleep.

On the way in to court, his team members tried to brief him about the morning's breaking news. He waved them away with a "not now". News was a distraction: idle gossip that would get in the way of examining his new witness— Laura Schneider. Leeton's poker instincts told him now, more clearly than before, that she was the key. That putting her in the witness box was crucial to this case, in a way he had not yet fully understood.

Laura Schneider looked a lot older, and, perhaps, a little heavier, than she had appeared in any of the pictures Leeton had seen of her, including those in yesterday's newspapers—the headline underneath had read: 'THE NEW EVA BRAUN?' But those pictures were all at least three years' old at this stage. A lot had happened since then, and it showed. The woman in front of him now wore every one of her forty years on her face. Her brown hair, tied up in a bunch behind her head, was fissured with strands of grey. She barely wore any make-up. And although she was well dressed, there was none of the sense of "no nonsense" businesswoman about her, which Leeton had imagined as he listened to Matterosi's description of her. Her sense of composure was that of someone who was about to crack. He would have to be careful not to be too rough. Not until he knew his angle.

"Ms Schneider, you were an executive director and co-owner of BetterWorld GmbH from 2007 to 2017, is that correct?"

She had the headset on for simultaneous translation, and yet when she answered, it was in almost flawless English. "Yes, but the company had effectively ceased to operate by 2016."

"And you were the partner of Brian Matterosi from 2006 to 2015."

"Yes."

"During your relationship with him, did Mr Matterosi ever express to you his concern about the human overpopulation problem?"

"No."

"Did he ever express a concern about poverty in developing countries?"

"No."

"What about global warming?"

"No."

"Your relationship ended in 2015?"

"Yes. On the thirteenth of November, 2015."

"What happened on that precise date?"

Laura Schneider stared vacantly across the courtroom.

"Ms Schneider?"

"That was the date he betrayed me. That was the date I found out."

"Found out what?"

"That he had infected us."

"Us?" Leeton recalled what he had heard on the recording. In Matterosi's version of events there had been no mention of Laura being infected. It was also nowhere in the reports. Her deposition should have included a medical report. How had he missed that?

"With VIS. Or some primitive strain of VIS, I don't know. He made us into his very first victims."

"And when you discovered this, you ended the relationship?"

"Yes."

"Then what did you do, after the relationship ended?"

"I went home to my parents' house in Konstanz. I cried. I lay sleepless in my bed and thought the world had ended. "

"Did you not return to the BetterWorld lab?"

"Not right away, no. Not until the following ... April, I believe."

"So you don't know what Matterosi was working on from August 2015 through to April 2016 at the BetterWorld facility?"

"No."

"And you felt no responsibility to the rest of humanity to stop him, given what he had already done to himself and to you?"

Schneider stared blankly across the room. Her lower lip quivered as she spoke. "On the thirteenth of November 2015, my world collapsed. The man I loved, the man I was prepared to die for, had taken away my future. I didn't know what to think at that stage. My only concern was staying alive."

"I find it hard to believe that a successful businesswoman like yourself would just turn her back on her company, her twenty employees, her home, simply because of a relationship problem ..."

Laura turned to him with a fierce stare in her tear-filled eyes.

"Maybe you can't understand what it means to be betrayed by the person you love, but, imagine it was you, Attorney Kgabu; imagine how your wife would feel when she discovers you have betrayed her."

A murmur went around the courtroom. Leeton felt a rush of blood to his face. He needed to steer this back.

"When did you first become aware that Brian Matterosi had been engineering the retrovirus behind VIS?"

She cleared her throat and thought for a moment.

"After he had returned to the university, the task fell to me of clearing up the laboratory. That was when I entered into the Delta part of the facility, where Brian had done all his private work. It was the first time I had been in there. Before that, I had always let him keep his own private space. I never interfered. He worked best on his own.

"Then I saw some of the notes and knew he had been working on something else. Something not at all related to the cancer research. But I still had no idea what it was."

"Did you not report this to the police?"

"There was nothing to report. As far as anyone knew, he had done nothing wrong. It was all just crazy notes."

"But you knew he had already infected you? Surely you must have suspected he would try to infect others? Why didn't you at very least report the infertility virus he had infected you with?"

She was staring blankly across the courtroom. Tears ran freely down her cheeks, and the pain of memories made the wrinkles in her face seem more pronounced.

"Because I loved him."

"And do you still love him now, Ms Schneider?"

"No."

"When did you stop loving him?"

"The day I read in the newspaper that billions of people had been infected with an unidentified infertility virus. At that stage, the world still had no idea that VIS had been deliberately engineered. I was the only one who knew. I was the only one who realised what he had done."

"When exactly was this?"

"July, 2017. I can't remember the exact day anymore."

"And what did you do?"

"I went to the police."

"What did you say to them?"

"I gave them the notes I'd found in the lab."

"And what else?"

"I told them VIS wasn't a natural phenomenon. That it has been engineered on purpose. And that I knew who had done it."

Commotion. The voice of Art Blume called out, "We need a doctor here!" Several of the defence team were gathered around in a circle, looking down at the floor. The cameramen were quicker than Leeton to get in on the action, and soon an impenetrable circle had formed around the defence bench. Leeton glanced at his tablet to watch what was happening on the live-stream.

Brian Matterosi had fainted.

In the confusion, Chief Justice Annabelle Wang called for an adjournment.

Where was Hyberg? Leeton wondered. It was the first time she had been absent from the court. Laura Schneider's remark had stuck in his mind, and the nightmare about Rachel and Caddie had unsettled him.

He decided he would use the break to check the news after all. He found a quiet spot, just outside Court One, which for the moment was free of reporters and crowds. He pulled up *The New York Times'* website on his tablet and read the headline. But there was barely time enough to make sense of the words that appeared on the screen. A second later he felt cold steel touch his wrist.

In front of him were three Dutch police officers. The biggest of them pushed Leeton's other arm until the tablet fell to the ground and the second handcuff clicked onto his wrist, trapping his hands behind his back.

"Leeton Kgabu, in the name of the *Openbaar Ministerie*, you are under arrest, charged with the sexual assault, rape and grievous bodily harm of Ms Rachel Hyberg." These words were spoken by a fourth man in a suit, who appeared to be a police inspector.

Leeton forced himself to be calm, and said, in what he hoped was a sanguine, but authoritative voice, "As an official of the International Criminal Court, I hereby invoke my rights to diplomatic immunity under Article 28 of the Abuja Treaty."

"Mr Kgabu's employment has been terminated on grounds of gross misconduct, with immediate effect. As he is no longer an official of the ICC, he enjoys no diplomatic immunity." It was Michal Sobiewski who spoke. He stepped forward from a gathering crowd and handed a piece of paper to the Dutch police inspector.

The inspector scanned the paper and said something to his colleagues in Dutch, which was close enough to Afrikaans for Leeton to understand.

"Get this rapist monkey the hell out of here. Come on, let's go!"

Reporters were everywhere. Cameras flashed on all sides as he was led out of the ICC building by the main entrance, but Leeton Kgabu barely registered them. All he could think of was what Laura Schneider had said. And that Caddie would know he had betrayed her.

» 77 «

I perched on the narrow ledge of the viaduct and stared down into the rushing water of the River Weser, fifty metres below. Why didn't I jump? I don't know. There was nothing more to live for. I had lost my partner, the woman I loved, my best, my only friend, my dearest confidante. I had also lost my home. And now, according to the letter I'd received from the lawyer, I was going to lose my laboratory too: the last thing that kept me sane.

More than losing Laura, I had watched her transform into something I could only describe as a monster. With no mercy whatsoever, she twisted my words against me; she filed injunctions, sold shares and pulled strings I did not even know existed. It was only after the events unfolded, one by one, that I realised how utterly I had put myself at her mercy. She controlled the company, the household, the bank accounts.

It was not just about the money, although she took all of that. It was also about hurting me. By taking away my lab, she took away from me the one thing that could have consoled me, that could have helped me to get through it all. This was calculated to further weaken me, to further rob me of my defences.

I consulted a lawyer briefly. He would sit impassively, very much the German, and wait 'til I finished crying, then he would give me good legal advice about how to protect my interests. I followed none of it, because I still loved Laura, and I was afraid that by doing anything to oppose her I would destroy whatever chance remained that she might take me back.

Like a fool, I kept returning to the house and standing, looking longingly through the window in hopes of catching a glimpse of her. I don't even think she was there. That went on for some time, until a restraining order was filed against me by the neighbour.

The miserable little room I ended up living in stank of filthy clothing and rotting food. I could not sleep, but would lie awake half the night, listening to my heart beat, replaying in my head imaginary conversations I would have with Laura, just as soon as she was willing to hear me out; to listen to my apologies; to give me a second chance.

Without Laura and without my work, I had nothing to live for. The only thing that bound me to this world was the fear of taking my own life. And so I perched on the high bridge above the furious, ice-cold river and begged a God I didn't even believe in to take me to Him. To end my miserable life, without me having to do it myself.

Unlike previous episodes of depression there was no solace for me, no magical moment when someone came to lead me back into the light. I simply floundered on in a state of intense anxiety, from tearful episode to tearful episode. No one came to see me, no one cared if I lived or died. Bitterly, I thought of all the fawning academics, all the smartly-dressed pharmaceutical reps, all the millions of cancer patients whose lives I had transformed. None of them cared whether I lived or died.

Months went by like that. How it would have ended I don't know. The person who did come in the end was the unlikeliest of saviours, an anti-saviour, really. It was Christian Lindemann, Heinz's son.

I was lying on the filthy mattress in my studio apartment when the buzzer sounded. I opened the door and saw him, but did not recognise him for the longest time.

"Christian?"

I had met him once in the hospital just before Heinz's death, and he had treated me coldly. That had been my excuse for not going to the funeral.

Now he handed me an envelope, containing a bundle of folders.

"These were found among my father's papers. It seems they belonged to you."

"Thanks for bringing them all this way."

"Don't thank me. Thank my mother. She asked me to bring these in person. So that I would see you. Although I have no idea why."

"Well," I shrugged. "You've seen me."

"Right." He turned and began walking away. I was about to close the door when he turned back. "Actually, I do know why. Two years ago my wife left me for another man. She took our two children, the house, everything. And I was left with nothing. I thought I was going to die. But I didn't. I survived." Then he turned and was gone.

My first instinct was to bin the envelope he had given me. But maybe Christian's little speech had had an effect on me. Despite myself, I opened the bundles and perused the old notes it contained. I vaguely remembered them as unwanted cerebral detritus which I'd left in the lab at Göttingen University. For the most part, they were ideas, half developed. Some I had forgotten about entirely, and with good reason. But some seemed genuinely novel, truly brilliant, in fact. It was not the first time in my life I had looked back over my old work and felt a surge of pride at the brilliance of my former self, rather like a parent's pride at the achievements of his child.

It was not much, but it was a spark. A spark that I felt I could build on. Maybe there was something in the coldness of Christian's attitude that awakened in me a stubborn desire to fight on, I don't know. The next day I went back to the university, armed only with the bundles of folders, and asked to meet with the Vice Deacon.

To my astonishment, my professional reputation was still entirely intact. It was only then that I realised the true value of Heinz's friendship and his intervention on my behalf. He had managed to steer everything to absolve me of any professional misconduct whatsoever.

And so when the Vice Deacon met me and I asked if there were any positions available as *Dozent*, he replied,

"No positions as *Dozent* at the moment. But the Chair is open, Brian. Why don't you apply? We've been interviewing, but frankly no one of your calibre is even out there anymore. Very few people of your calibre even exist."

The timing could not have been better; two days beforehand the *Gerichtsvollzieher* had been rummaging through the lab, carrying away computers and slapping official tape on all my dearest instruments.

He made it very clear that if I touched anything, I was going straight to jail.

This only added to my anger and bitterness. Once I was set up at the university, I threw myself into my work. Everything else besides work and junk food ceased to have any meaning to me. I hated having to sleep. I hated the sunshine. I hated having to talk to students, security guards, shop assistants.

My misanthropy reached its apex in those spring months in which I began working nights and sleeping in the daytime, just to avoid other people. I say "misanthropy" now. But oddly, that's not at all how I viewed myself at the time. I remember seeing clearly a vision for a truly "Better World", one in which only scientists or members of a chosen intellectual elite would live, and that the rest, the great hordes of humanity and the beast-like women who bore children and suckled them on their apish breasts, would wither and die away within a single generation.

In much of that vision I saw a vast world, forested and beautiful, resplendent with unspoilt nature. There were cities, but only a handful, and they bustled with discovery and science and a new ethic of knowledge that would replace all the old superstition and sectarianism that had caused so much misery amongst our species. It was truly a Utopia that I dreamt of in the shifting hours between my work and my sleep.

What is ironic, perhaps, is that while I dreamed of saving the planet and creating a paradise, I shunned the very beauty that was in the world around me. The spring of 2016 passed unnoticed. I hardly went out at all. I had become a creature so far removed from the young man who wandered the woods and swam in the lakes. I was a broken and bitter little beast, in all but one dark corner of my mind.

The Hydra was the first step to realising my vision. And though I had not kept any samples of it from the cold room in the Delta section of BetterWorld, I knew very well that didn't matter. The Hydra lived and thrived inside me. I only needed to draw my own blood and a million specimens of the most complex virus ever engineered by man were at my immediate disposal.

I began work on the rest of the retrovirus without delay. And while it is true what Art Blume said during the trial last week—that I actively attempted to create a strain that would be as mild as possible—it is not true to say I did so out of any compassion for the victims I would infect. I merely calculated, correctly as it turned out, that a milder infection would be less likely to encounter medical resistance and would therefore progress along a more successful contagion vector.

But the mRNA stubbornly refused to do exactly what I wanted: which was to replicate the symptoms of a very mild, but very contagious flu that would then release the provirus during Stage Two lysis, activating the Hydra.

I was careless with my own body, giving it nothing more than what was strictly needed to carry on working. By November 2016, the first strains were ready. They were not quite as safe as I would have liked, but I was impatient. That was when my now infamous world tour began. Seminars, conferences, research missions. Even holidays. And everywhere I went I spread VIS. In airports, in universities, in train stations. Into water supplies and into office buildings. It was so easy; I could do it right under the noses of police, of doctors, of other scientists. While little old ladies were having their knitting needles confiscated at airport security checkpoints, my scientific credentials allowed me to carry dose after dose of the virus right across the planet, with perfect impunity. Mogotio, Kenya, was where it started. Then a few other places in Africa, before I found what they keep calling the gamma strains, the ones that went pandemic. That was when I went to India.

How much of it was done because of Laura? I don't know. It sounds less than noble to admit that in the end my whole life's work and the fate of the planet were decided by one relationship gone horribly wrong. At the time I believed I was saving the world. But now I can see there was also so much hate inside me. So much anguish.

Most of it was spent in a fever. Even when I travelled I was constantly thirsty, using a potent mix of painkillers to control the swelling. Around and around the world I went, and one four-star hotel room blended into another. There were times I was barely coherent, but the research assistants who led me around still treated me with veneration. There was one research assistant who was so slimy, so obviously false in his praise of me, so obviously disgusted at my slovenly appearance, so obviously awaiting his first opportunity to tell his friends what a disappointment was the great Brian Matterosi, that I actually slipped a few drops of the virus directly into his glass of water. I remember thinking: *no one that mediocre and venal should have the right to breed.*

Looking back over the records the prosecution has prepared I can't even remember half of it. But it must have been true. It passed like a furious dream.

And then I was back in the university lab, killing myself with viruses. My life's work was concluded, and I had nothing more to live for. Still my mind raced onwards, in more and more incredible pursuits. I had vague ideas of developing other viruses, to lengthen human life, to make our bodies stronger and require less nutrition. In the end, all the strands of reasoning and complex experimentation blended into oblivion. When I read back those latter notes now, they make no sense even to me. The babblings of a madman. Ironically, if they had not found me that day, huddled on a metal shelf in a lab to which only I had access, badly dehydrated and with week-old diarrhoea encrusted on my trousers, if they had never arrested me, I think I would have died that way.

To know now that it was Laura who reported me to the police, is to know that it was she who saved me. And it will likely be her testimony which will see me die. And, yet, I would have given anything to keep her away from all this; not for my own sake, but to spare her this one last ordeal. It's only now, at the very end of my life, that I have learned what it means to truly love another human being.

And it's only now after hearing her speak that I can fully accept just how dead I am to her. There is no way back and no forgiveness for what I've done to her. My life's work is complete, and the only person I have ever loved is forever lost to me. All that remains now is to do my penance. I know what I have to do now.

» 78 «

"Your Honours, the extraordinary actions we have witnessed this morning leave us doubting the integrity, credibility and impartiality of this Court. Until we have some clarity on whether Mr Kgabu's alleged actions amount to a perversion of justice for my client, it will be necessary to demand an adjournment. I don't wish to pre-empt the decision of his criminal case in any way, but questions have to be answered as to whether Attorney Kgabu's relationship with Ms Hyberg may have been used to influence the administration of the trial to my client's detriment. Pending a full investigation into all improprieties and criminal acts which have been alleged by the Dutch Prosecutor's Office against Mr Kgabu, the defence further requests that Mr Matterosi be transferred out of United Nations jurisdiction and into his home jurisdiction of the United States of America."

"Mr Blume," Chief Justice Annabelle Wang began, sliding her reading glasses halfway down her nose so she could fix Art with what was supposed to be a withering stare. "Our role is to interpret the Treaty and to ensure the effective operation of this Court. We cannot and will not be drawn into—"

"Your Honour."

Wang broke off immediately. Cameras swivelled and pointed at Brian Matterosi, who was standing, and had just spoken.

"Sit down," Art hissed.

"I would like to change my plea, Your Honour."

Shit. He never should have let Brian out of his sight after the faint. He'd insisted on going off to his goddamn crucible afterwards and chewing whatever cud he'd been chewing. Now he'd worked himself into some kind of state.

"Your Honours, my client requests an immediate recess for legal consultation."

"No, he doesn't," Brian said.

"Yes, you do."

"No I don't, Art. Your Honour, I wish to change my plea. I engineered VIS, I released it and the truth is I did so as much out of a sense of misanthropy as out of any desire to help and to save. I've been a coward all my life, but now I can perform one act of bravery, at the end. I declare myself guilty of all charges that have been placed against me."

"Are you certain of this, Mr Matterosi?" Wang asked him.

"Yes, Your Honour."

» 79 «

The cell in the main police station in The Hague was nothing like the cells Leeton remembered from South Africa. The Dutch concept of jail was bright and clean, with a tidy stainless steel sink and toilet discreetly tucked into the corner. The bed was made with a fresh, crisp, white sheet. In fact, it was probably nicer than the homes to which most black South African men could hope to return, if they ever escaped the hell that was prison in South Africa.

And yet, for all these little comforts, Leeton was gripped by the same feeling of dread and panic, as he had had back then. The same restless anger consumed him at being bound up like a chained beast. His Zulu spirit could accept defeat, fatigue, pain. But not this. Not being left in a cage and forgotten. It was almost as if he could feel the cold metal of invisible past shackles digging into his flesh. Involuntarily, his muscles flexed, as if to burst out and free himself.

How many days had it been? So hard to say when you weren't sleeping, when you had nothing to do. Time was an elastic band. Change the tension and its measurement becomes meaningless. Was the trial over? There was one guard he liked, an Arab. This man had given him a newspaper out of pity two days ago. That was how Leeton knew about the plea change. And it was the one thing he was clinging to. The fact that his decision to put Laura Schneider on the stand was what had pushed Matterosi over the edge. In the end, he had won. Even if it had cost him everything.

If he craned his head out the little mesh window in the cell's steel door, he could even see down the hallway and as far as the television the guard had set up on his desk. The fat one was on duty again. The one who put his feet on the desk and watched soccer matches until it got late, when he would switch on the pornography and masturbate furiously. But it must still have been early, because "Fatso" had on PSV Eindhoven versus some Eastern European team, in a first round match of the European Club Cup. Fatso had given no indication that he knew who Leeton was, or that he even cared. It was a shock to Leeton, to think there were people like that, who took such small interest in the big things that were happening around them.

An indefinable number of minutes or hours passed. Leeton pulled his head up from the pillow at the sound of the steel door to his cell swinging open. Fatso stood looking at him. With an indifferent nod of his head, he ushered Leeton towards the visiting room.

"*Bezoeker*," he mumbled. Visitor. The slob spoke English fluently, Leeton was sure of it. But he made about as much effort with his language, as he did with his physical appearance. The buzz of the electronic release and the clank of another metal door which led out of the holding area heightened Leeton's sense of anticipation. It was only his second visitor in four days. The first had been a Consular Officer from the South African Embassy, assuring him that everything was being done, blah, blah, blah. Leeton knew before the woman had finished speaking that every word of it was a lie. South Africa had quickly decided he was toxic and given up on him.

He allowed himself to imagine the visitor would be Caddie, in tears. She would tell him all was forgiven, or better still, would look at him with her soft brown eyes and wait to be reassured of the fact that he was innocent. "*I'm innocent, my Moonlight,*" he would tell her, and she would believe him.

Even in fantasy the lie rang hollow. He might not have raped Rachel Hyberg. But he was certainly not innocent.

As he passed through the final metal door and the visitor area came into view, his anticipation was so far piqued that he could almost see her sitting there. But it was not Caddie. It was, in fact, the last person on earth Leeton was expecting to see.

"Art Blume. What are you doing here?"

"Leeton," Blume rose to greet him and extended his hand.

"No touching," a guard intervened. That suited Leeton just fine. He certainly didn't want to shake the American's hand.

Blume sat down and after a while Leeton did likewise.

"What do you want?"

"I guess congratulations are in order."

Leeton's reaction must have given away the fact that he hadn't been able to follow the news.

"So you haven't heard? They accepted the plea change and returned a unanimous guilty verdict."

They both knew what that meant. Article 63, Section 1 of the Abuja Treaty. Sentencing to be carried out in accordance with the national laws applicable for that crime in the designated victim country. There were, in fact, seventy-two designated victim countries listed. But India topped the list. So they had first dibs on Brian's execution. It would be an execution by lethal injection. Live, on television, for every victim to watch. Veedala Jhumi had already promised the world as much.

"Are you pleased?"

"Yes," Leeton answered, quickly, and with a certainty that felt somehow forced. Was he pleased? For months he had imagined the satisfaction he would get from watching the mad scientist die. But now that it came to it, the only image he could muster of Brian Matterosi was as a boy, walking alone down the snow-covered streets of Boston, friendless, hungry and cold.

Blume, meanwhile, was staring intently at him, in a way Leeton found unsettling. He placed something on the table between them.

"What's this?"

"My card. I know you're not guilty of rape."

"Really? And how do you know that?"

"Let's just say I'm a very good judge of character. They set you up, didn't they?"

"If you already know, why are you asking me?"

"Because what I don't know is *why*." The American leaned towards him, almost conspiratorially. "I want to help you, Leeton."

"And why would you want to help me?"

"Because I believe in justice. And because I believe these phoney rape charges are just another part of the hoax that was this trial. It's all somehow related. I feel like we've both been played. If you help me, I can help you get out of here."

"You're seriously asking me to help you appeal the conviction?"

"I'm asking you to help me find some justice here."

The invisible shackles burned into Leeton's wrists. It was a good thing for Blume, too. Because he might otherwise have hurt him badly. Instead, he forced out a derisive laugh and used his words to strike the blow instead.

"Maybe I got you wrong, Blume. You're not really motivated by money, are you? You're motivated by a desire to win, at all costs. You're an egomaniac, just like Brian Matterosi. Maybe that's why you can't see the evil in what he did, when all the rest of the world so clearly can."

"Leeton, listen—"

But Leeton had already risen and nodded to Fatso, who awoke from his standing slumber, hit a button on the wall and waited for the electronic lock to be released. Before the door slammed closed behind him, he heard Art Blume's voice, calling out to him.

"Call me if you change your mind!"

» 80 «

It was only after formal sentencing that the amorphous network of media, pundits and politicians that collectively constitute the "international community" seemed to awaken to the fact that Brian Matterosi was going to die a painful, brutal and very public death. The civil libertarians, who until then had directed all their indignation at the crime of VIS itself, now began to plea for a lesser sentence. The solidarity between the self-righteous Europeans and the brown- and black-skinned victims—a cornerstone of political support for the whole Abuja construct—began to break down. It wasn't long before the protestors who had once stood side-by-side during the whole trial found themselves facing off across police cordon lines. Placards on one side read: 'TWO WRONGS DON'T MAKE A RIGHT.' And on the other side: 'OUR VOICE SHALL BE HEARD!'

Art watched it all with sickening disbelief. He watched the Dutch Minister for Justice explaining on CNN, most diplomatically, that he had no power to stop Matterosi's extradition to India, where he would face sentencing "in accordance with national laws." They never said, "painful, murderous death by chemical injection." No, it was always "in accordance with national laws."

"This does not mean the Netherlands condones the death penalty. Quite the contrary. However, the design of the new international criminal architecture has had to take account of the fact that we in Europe have one view of how justice should be administered. But it is not the only view. And we must also accept that there is anger, very legitimate anger, out there right now ..."

"Fuck you," Art shouted at the television and switched it off.

He had attempted to lodge an appeal, of course, but without the cooperation of his client, there was no legal basis for it. He had even tried to have Brian Matterosi declared incompetent to plea; the ICC was having none of it. At first it was Brian refusing to see him, but in the end the ICC secretariat even stopped returning his calls.

Maybe what Kgabu had said was true, Art reflected, as he stared once again at the piles of notes before him. *Maybe I'm just a sore loser.*

And yet there was something about this case that he couldn't bring himself to accept. Something which was not quite right. He cast his eye across the stacks of files. The endless papers. He had been over it all a million times, and in the end there didn't seem to be anything more to say.

Frustrated, he threw on his coat and headed out into the Dutch streets for a walk. It was not safe to do so, but Art didn't care. He needed to get out and think.

The air was warm. Too warm for September. It was as if the autumn refused to come, not until the Matterosi trial had reached its bloody, vengeful, conclusion. Art passed down the quiet streets behind his office, along the canal and up into the old town. The still, heavy air encouraged the protestors to take to the streets. A convoy of riot police in armoured vans trundled across the cobbled streets right in front of him.

In the square in front of the now infamous Paleis hotel, he saw a band of New Earth Zealots, pounding on their drums and chanting. The NEZ belonged to the more radical fringe of the pro-Matterosi campaign; religious environmentalists who believed Brian was, quite literally, a saviour. For them he had been sent by God to cleanse the world of human overpopulation. The inconvenient fact that Brian was an atheist was overlooked, of course. The Zealots dressed in tunics and carried oak sceptres on the tops of which heavy wooden spheres were attached, all hand-carved. These sceptres were more than a means of proclaiming their faith: they could be used as bludgeons, against the anti-Matterosi side.

As Art approached he could make out what it was they were chanting—the text of Brian's autobiographical recording. They were repeating the words he had spoken into his little Dictaphone and which had been published by God-knows-whom on the Internet the day after the plea change. A chill ran down Art's spine as he realised these lunatics had no interest in saving Brian's life. They wanted him to die. His martyrdom would become an essential part of their cult.

In just five days, Brian would be transferred from ICC custody and handed over to the Indian government. Then it would be only a matter of hours before the New Earth Zealots, and everyone else, got their wish. Disgust mixed with panic in his heart, and he returned swiftly to the office, more determined than ever to stop the madness.

Art spent the next two days holed up inside, surviving on nothing but stale pastries and cold coffee. He listened, over and over again, to the recording. Brian's childhood, his career, the details of the virus. It was eerie to hear Matterosi speaking so freely, so passionately, when all throughout the trial he had remained so composed, so reserved. This more than anything, led Art to believe there was something in the recording that would give him some kind of a clue. There *had* to be. He even had the voice recordings sent off to a crime technician buddy of his in the NYPD, just to make absolutely sure nothing had been edited, manipulated, fiddled with. And still, nothing. No leads. Nothing to suggest he had missed any clues.

On the third day, Lisbeth came to see him.

"Oh, there you are," he greeted her without looking up from the screen. He was reading an academic paper by an Australian pro-Matterosi activist, which attempted to make the case that the ICC's use of television cameras during the trial was in violation of the International Bill of Human Rights.

"C'm'ere, this is kind of interesting stuff. Once you're finished reviewing those depositions you gotta take a look. I've just forwarded you a link."

"I came to say goodbye."

Art turned and looked at her.

"Goodbye? As in, you're leaving?"

"The Dutch police have given me the all-clear to travel home. I'm returning to England this evening." She must have seen the shock in his face. "Peter already left two weeks—"

"I don't care about Peter. Peter's a *schlemiel*. You, on the other hand, you're my best asset. I *need* you now more than ever, Lisbeth!"

"The trial's over, Art. We lost."

Art had to swallow the lump in his throat before he could answer her.

"In two days Brian will be loaded on a plane and flown to India, at which point he will be butchered live on TV, to satisfy the bloodlust of the masses. This *will* happen, Lisbeth, unless we do something—you and I—right now, to stop his extradition. Do you get that?"

"What I *get* is that I've not seen my boyfriend in three months, except as a grainy image on a computer screen. And I miss him awfully. I'm a person, Art, with an actual life beyond this case."

Art looked at Lisbeth and realised, perhaps for the first time, that she was a person. A woman, even. In fact, she was probably quite attractive. But more than that he saw her as privileged. Very privileged. An image flashed through his mind of her walking through one of those Oxford quads, holding hands with some squirrel-faced academic boy she'd met in college, on their way to the commons dining hall to drink sherry and schmooze with the dons. It struck him how different her world was to his. His own gritty fight to get into NYU. Endless subway rides in from the Bronx. Driving a taxi at two in the morning, with law books borrowed from the library, open on the passenger seat of one of those old Checker cabs. In some ways he had less in common with her than he did with Brian Matterosi. Or for that matter, with Leeton Kgabu.

"Fine," he said at length, almost spitting. "Go home to England. Who needs you anyway?"

» 81 «

The reporters surrounded his bungalow on Benedictus Kok Street, like a swarm of insects. Someone had obviously tipped them off to the fact that his car had left the airport and was on its way back to the Universitas neighbourhood of Bloemfontein where he lived. There was no way to get into the drive without running down a half dozen of them, and as the driver from the Ministry stalled, unsure what to do, they began clambering around the car, taking pictures of him from every conceivable angle.

"Just park up on the curb," Leeton growled. The driver obeyed.

As soon as Leeton opened his door they pounced on him.

"Mr Kgabu, can you respond to the accusations made against you by Rachel Hyberg?"

"Did President Kimsaka put pressure on the Dutch government to release you?"

"Despite all the controversy, do you consider your role as prosecuting attorney to have been a success?"

"Why did Rachel Hyberg drop the charges against you?"

He worked his way through them and towards the door, mumbling "no comment", while trying to look as if he hadn't seen any of the cameras.

"Was the extradition of Brian Matterosi to India the reason why the charges were dropped?"

"*Did you rape her?*"

Leeton turned and faced this final journalist. A white woman. He opened his mouth to speak. Before the words had a chance to come out, a thicket of microphones were thrust into the space in front of him.

"I never raped anyone."

"So are you saying the sex between you and Ms Hyberg was consensual?"

Behind the thicket of microphones, behind the piercing eyes of the reporters, the beady eyes of the news cameras formed another density of intrusiveness. They were many eyes, but it was as if they were all part of one big eye. Like an enormous housefly, buzzing in front of his face, waiting to feed on any excrement it could find.

"No comment."

Once inside, he shut the door behind him, and with it the reporters vanished from his mind.

Marambu stood in the hall, in the spot next to the coat rack. She stared at him. Leeton remembered how it was back in the old days, before his appointment to the ICC. Whenever he returned home from the Supreme Court of Appeal, Marambu used to stand in exactly that spot and greet him with a "Good evening, Mr Kgabu," and a broad smile that showed off her golden front tooth.

But now there was no greeting. And no smile. She just stared, coldly, as he took off his jacket.

"Where is Caddie?"

"Missus not home," Marambu answered in her thick, Xhosa-inflected English.

Leeton walked into the lounge. It was strange how very unchanged his home was, when outside everything was unutterably different. The sofa with the three cushions was exactly as before. The television. The ferns in front of the ceiling-to-floor beige drapes. The Zulu shield and spear decoratively adorning the wall next to the framed panoramic photo of the Umgeni Valley, where he was born.

Yet there were things missing. Little things that it took a minute to notice. Robert's baby toys weren't there. The magazines Caddie always left scattered on the coffee table were sorted into the rack. And the family photographs she had had framed and arranged on the end tables were gone.

He had thought it would be a relief to escape the trial, to return home and get on with his life. But now as he sat there, the weight of silence crushed him. The trial was all he had left. Leeton turned on the television and switched to "0-0-6". Live from New Delhi. The pre-execution coverage was in full swing.

» 82 «

Art told himself he wasn't going to watch it on television. Indeed, in some countries live viewing of the execution was technically illegal, and so could not be broadcast on the mainstream news channels. Ironically, the Netherlands was one such country. Not that it mattered: hundreds of Internet channels would be live-streaming it.

As the hours ticked away, Art found himself unable to resist the urge. Eventually, he threw open the first web channel on his desktop and began watching the coverage. Maybe he felt he owed it to Brian to be there. Maybe it was guilt after all. Art tried to tell himself Brian had brought about his own destruction with the plea change, but he knew that was a lie. His client was going to die because he, Art, had failed him.

It was 1 October 2020, the birthday of India's Prime Minister, Veedala Jhumi.

As soon as he opened the channel, Brian Matterosi filled the screen. The first public image of the scientist since he'd left the Netherlands. Live from New Delhi. The Indians had been keeping him under tight wraps.

Brian was now bearded and unkempt. It looked like they had been depriving him of sleep and food. Or else he was doing that to himself. Art had wished at least that he'd be calm, maybe even at peace with himself. But the opposite was true. Brian was shaking, tears were running down his face. The Indians hadn't even given him a tranquilliser. No, the bastards wanted him to feel every second of his last moments on earth, as they strapped him to the chair and used a surgical scissors to cut a patch out of his shirt, right below the shoulder. Then the doctor, whose face was covered with a balaclava to protect his identity, rubbed yellow disinfectant on the naked skin of Brian's arm. Disinfectant, so he wouldn't get an infection? Was this their idea of comedy?

"No," Brian pleaded, when he saw the syringe. He whispered

something which the microphone did not pick up, but which appeared as subtitles a second later. *Brian Matterosi: "I don't want to die."* Tears ran down his face. All the aplomb and arrogance of the trial was gone. He was like a little boy, shivering in fear.

Then it all went quickly. The syringe containing the lethal dose of pancuronium bromide mixed with a sodium chloride solution plunged into his arm. Brian let out a scream, but it wasn't clear if that was the drug or just the shock of the needle. For a moment he was still, and it seemed as if, at last, he had found his peace. A second later his body seized up, then went slightly limp, and began to shake as if in a seizure. His eyes grew wide in obvious pain. He screamed for about ten seconds, until a gargling sound choked out the screams. A strange foam-like substance was expelled from his mouth with every gasp of his dying body.

This went on for three eternal minutes, during which Brian's face turned an unnatural shade of blue. Finally the twitching stopped, and his limp body sank down against the straps. As the doctor picked up his wrist to feel for a pulse, Art switched off the television, returned to his computer and hit the "Publish" button on the blog post he had prepared that morning. The title of it read: 'OBITUARY OF AN INNOCENT MAN'.

There was more on the news that evening. Images of Brian's body, as it was taken to an incinerator at the facility's crematorium. Later they showed a masked Indian commando spreading his ashes across the Indian Ocean from a helicopter. No trace of Brian Matterosi's physical being remained. There would be no shrine for his supporters to gather round.

Art looked around the office he had been occupying since the trial had ended. The place from which he had launched his own personal campaign to prove Brian's innocence. There were files everywhere, some dating back to the summer, which had been prepared by Lisbeth and the team. Others, more recent, which he had prepared himself. All for nothing. A sickness filled his heart.

"Fucking shit!" He kicked one of the desks, causing half-full coffee cups to spill over papers. Stupid fucking cups. He picked one up and threw it against the wall. Then he grabbed a ream of files and threw them too. He grabbed more and more and threw it all into a mess, until he himself collapsed among the pile of papers on the floor and began to cry. It was the first time in his long career that he had cried for a client.

That was when he saw it. The file on Rachel Hyberg's former employer, Medi-Discover Technologies. The one he had asked Lisbeth to prepare, but which he had forgotten to read. On an impulse he picked it up and began perusing it. He was about to toss it back into the pile when, on the very last page of the briefing, he came across a name he'd seen before. Dr Tadeki Mateki.

"No ... fucking ... way."

In a second he was on to Google. Then back to the files he had on Matterosi. He read for hours, digging through stuff he thought he would never read again. Art paused only to check the calendar on his computer for dates.

At 08:17 in the morning, Art slammed his fist down on the stack of papers in triumph.

"Bingo!"

He picked up the phone and dialled Lisbeth's UK mobile phone number.

Her boyfriend answered.

"Can I speak to Lisbeth?"

Silence. Art could hear the young man whispering his annoyance. In the background Lisbeth was whispering her placation. *"He's upset. He hasn't got anyone else to phone. I'll just be a minute, darling. Go back to sleep."*

"Art?" She answered into the phone.

"I need you to do me one last favour."

"What?"

"I need you to find Tadeki Mateki."

"Why?"

"You still know who that is, right?" As soon as he asked the question, Art realised it was a stupid one. Of course Lisbeth remembered. She remembered everything. That's one of the things he liked best about her.

"Yes. What about him?"

"Turns out he used to work with Rachel Hyberg. Not far from where you are, in Milton Keynes, England. For a company called Medi-Discover Technologies."

There was a pause before Lisbeth answered. "That's not such a coincidence. The med tech industry in Europe isn't that big. Researchers do tend to move around."

"Right. But on a hunch, I checked the BetterWorld accounts to verify his payslips."

"And?"

"And, according to the accounts he was paid on the last working day of the month, just like all the other employees."

"So?"

"So Mateki was paid on Tuesday, the twenty-ninth of February, 2016."

Pause. "Are you saying 2016 wasn't a leap year?"

"No, it was a leap year, that's the point."

"So then, the twenty-ninth of February would have been the last working day—"

"Right. Except everyone else in BetterWorld got paid on the twenty-eighth. That's because the accounting software they used in 2016 didn't recognise leap years. So it paid everyone a day early, on Monday the twenty-eighth of February. Everyone that is, except for Tadeki Mateki, The one employee who has a link to Rachel Hyberg. His payslip was recorded in a way that was impossible for the computer to produce."

"What are you suggesting, Art?"

"Simple. Someone faked Mateki's pay records for BetterWorld. They knew he was supposed to get paid on the last day of the month, but they forgot to skip the extra day in February. They made a tiny, little, mistake that almost went completely unnoticed."

"But why would they—"

"That's what I need you to find out. From the deposition, Mateki has an address in England. In Bletchley, which is right back near Milton Keynes, in fact. It's real close to Oxford, isn't it?"

"Twenty miles."

"So will you do it?"

"Art, this is all coming too late. They executed Brian yesterday."

"You think I don't know that already? I'm not a moron," he snapped, realising just as quickly how the lack of sleep was making him cranky. He sighed. "Listen, we owe it to our client, to the world, to find out what dirty games the ICC has been playing here. Brian won't be the last innocent man they put to death. Please, Lisbeth, just do me this one last favour."

"Why don't you find him yourself?"

"Because you're good. And because I have to find someone else." Art glanced down at the page on which he had written Laura Schneider's new address and waited for Lisbeth to give her answer.

"All right, I'll do it."

» 83 «

His mind ran like a river. Pieces of the trial floated along the surface, but underneath, in the murky undercurrent, were the skeletons of his past. The river was amber, turning a deep gold in its depth, exactly the colour of good Scotch whisky. He poured another one; the rapids filled the glass, gushing across the ice cubes and from there into his mouth, into his mind. His mouth was the mouth of the river. His mind was the sea. And everywhere, all around him, Caddie's absence was draped, like the sky.

The spirits of his ancestors had tried to warn him, like seagulls squawking. Umama's very being had supplicated him to stop. But he had been weak. So weak. The whisky ran and burned away the lump that was forming, once again, in his throat. How quickly the bottle had gone from full ... to ... empty.

He reached across and answered the phone, because he thought it had been ringing. Only after saying "Hello?" five times did he realise he was talking to a dial tone. Either he'd missed the call or the ringing had just been in his head. Anyway, who cared? The only calls came from media people, looking to get him to appear on some fucking panel show and talk about the trial.

Outside, South Africans were still celebrating Matterosi's death. Dancing on the streets with joy, because justice had been done, and one of their people had achieved it. A black man had for once had his way against the injustice of the whites.

"Fucking idiots," Leeton said out loud, as if they could hear him. "You're cheering because one man died. Don't you realise you're celebrating the loss of your entire future?"

He lifted the empty whisky bottle and tried in vain to pour a few extra drops into his glass.

Celebrating the loss of their entire future.

An object, flat, rectangular and white, came into focus as he put the bottle down on the table. It was a business card which had travelled with him all the way from a Dutch prison cell.

They played us, Leeton. Art Blume had said to him. Leeton searched his poker instincts for the bluff that must have been in Blume's voice, but couldn't find it. And what was it she had said to him, the last night they were together? *That he was too weak to be a part of bigger things.*

He played the recording again. And he listened, this time not as a prosecuting attorney looking for evidence, but as a poker player looking for the bluff. Hours later, he picked up the phone and dialled the number on the business card. In poker, there is a time to fold and a time to call. And a time to go all-in.

"Leeton?" Blume answered the phone, without a whisper of surprise in his voice, even though it must have been three in the morning.

"Where are you?"

"In Konstanz. I'm trying to find Laura Schneider."

"You're wasting your time, Blume. She's not the woman you need to see."

» 84 «

Art Blume sat in the rental car outside the little block of modern, Swiss apartments and waited. It was eight in the morning. He rubbed some warmth into his hands then switched the engine on. The air here was chilly, perhaps because Basel was so much closer to the snow-filled mountains, or maybe because October had finally broken the back of the Indian summer which had drenched Europe in sticky heat for so long. In any event, being cold made the task of sitting in a car waiting for Godot incredibly tedious. *I could never be a cop*, he mused.

It was made all the worse by the fact that he had no idea what he was supposed to be looking for. The address had come from Lisbeth. She had found a record of it during her fruitless search for Tadeki Mateki. It was attached to a credit card that had been used to pay for the lease on the apartment in which Mateki was supposed to have lived in Bletchley, England. The apartment wasn't even furnished. The credit cardholder's name was Laurence Defrasne, whoever that might be.

Art had checked for names on the buzzers but there was no "Defrasne" or any other name. Only apartment numbers. Four of them. And so far no one had gone in or out. All he could do was sit and wait.

By ten o'clock he was seriously considering taking a little break and getting a coffee at the bakery he'd seen two blocks away. And he needed to pee. He was just about to switch the engine off, when the garage door opened and a Porsche sped out in front of him. The glass was tinted, but his instincts told him to follow it. Plus, it was about the only lead he had left.

He put his rented Peugeot into gear and took off after the Porsche. It drove fast, changing lanes dangerously and often, almost as if it knew it was being followed. But Art had thirteen years of Manhattan taxi driving under his belt. The car had not yet been invented that could outmanoeuvre him in city traffic.

It pulled into the garage entrance of an inconspicuous office block close to the centre of town. His heart jumped when the window descended, and he caught a glimpse of the driver, as she inserted a key card into the security panel. Good, he thought, at least my ten grand wasn't a complete waste.

The main entrance to the building had no company sign on it. He walked straight up to the reception desk and asked the smiling receptionist to announce his arrival to Laurence Defrasne.

"I have an appointment with her," he explained.

"I'm sorry," she answered, in a crisp Germanic accent. "We have no one by that name here. Are you sure you have the right address?"

"Absolutely positive. And I'm also sure she's in this building right now. Though I'm not sure of the name. But, you know, a rose by any other name and all that."

The receptionist gave no sign of recognition.

"I'm sorry. I can't help you, sir."

"Then call someone who can." He took out his phone and began taking pictures of the lobby. "Meanwhile, I'll just be generating some photographic evidence of this hidden corporate ... establishment."

"What did you say your name was?" Her tone had changed when he took out the camera phone. She flipped through the desk directory without looking up.

"Romeo Montague."

She dialled a number and spat something in Swiss German into the phone. Normally Art was good at German, which was pretty close to the Yiddish his grandmother spoke to him when he was a boy. But the young woman's Swiss accent was so strong, he only managed to pick up *"der Herr"* and *"ungemütlich"*. "The gentleman" and "uncomfortable".

"Take a seat. Someone will be right down to help you."

Art smiled. "Thanks, I prefer to stand."

When the elevator door opened, Art was prepared for just about anything. Muscle-bound thugs stuffed into security uniforms. Swiss bankers. Hell, he wouldn't have been surprised if a trio of juggling circus monkeys danced out to the tune of accordion music. But the person who appeared in front of him took him completely by surprise. It was the last person in the world he expected to meet in an office building in Basel, Switzerland.

"Jeroen?"

The Dutchman's sarcastic grin was the size of a windmill.

"Long time, no see, Art. I have to say, you look terrible."

"What the fuck are you—"

"Come on. I'll explain on the way."

Art paused. "Where?"

"To get answers. That's why you came, isn't it?"

On the way past the receptionist, Jeroen gave the girl a knowing wink. Once inside the lift, he inserted a key card into the lift's control panel and pushed a "down" button. Down? Art wondered at this. From the outside, he had counted at least four floors above them, why would they be going down? Were they going to the underground parking he had just seen the Porsche drive into?

The doors opened onto a carpeted hallway, whose walls were adorned with pictures of the ICC General Committee. On the left was a signed, original copy of the Abuja Charter, exactly the same as the one that hung on the wall of Court One. This was definitely not the underground parking garage. Jeroen led Art to a set of conference room double-doors at the end of the hall. He threw them open and a luxurious meeting room appeared. Flag of the United Nations on the right. Flag of the International Criminal Court on the left. In the centre, a polished wooden table.

Art instantly recognised Michal Sobiewski, the ICC General Secretary. He was puffing on one of his trademark cigars. Next to him was Rachel Hyberg, still wearing the jacket Art had glimpsed through the window of the Porsche.

Sobiewski stared hard at him with those cold blue eyes of his.

"Sit down."

"That's okay, I'll stand."

"Suit yourself." Sobiewski took a leisurely puff of his cigar before continuing. "Well, here we are, wasting time with a shyster turned human rights activist. Now, what is it you want, Mr Blume?"

"I want answers."

Hyberg looked amused. The smile she wore now in no way resembled the phoney media smiles she had maintained all the way through the trial. It was the same aggressively beautiful red lipstick he had seen a thousand times before; the same perfect posture; the same automatic flick of her blonde hair with her perfectly sculpted fingernails. And yet something about her was completely different. Art realised what it was: now she was being herself.

"I have to say," she said, her cold eyes fixed on him. "I underestimated you."

"You sure did. I didn't walk in here unprepared, you know. I'm ready to go live with this story."

Hyberg laughed at this, but Sobiewski merely leaned in to the table and frowned.

"I'll ask you again, what is it you want?"

"I want justice to be done."

"I thought," Hyberg continued, as if she hadn't even been listening to the two men, "that when the media attention died down, the execution was carried out, and there was no more glory to be gained, you would go back to New York and start to get excited about your next big case. Which is the only reason you didn't have a tragic accident months ago."

She sipped at her coffee, leaving a trace of red on the white porcelain lip, before continuing. "And then when you began sniffing around in business that was clearly not your own, I realised my mistake." Her gaze shifted momentarily up to Jeroen Clijvers, who was still standing over Art's right shoulder. "That was the point at which you came very close to dying, *most* tragically. In fact, I think it's fair to say that four days ago was the closest you have ever come to losing your life. That is, until right now."

"Are you threatening me?"

Hyberg laughed again. "Not really, no. *Threatening* you would suggest I wanted you to do something in particular or else suffer the consequences. Personally, I don't really want you to do anything, except to die. Fortunately for you, I don't make that decision."

"The fact is, Mr Blume," Sobiewski interjected, "you have one, and only one, ally right now. Lucky for you, he happens to be quite a powerful ally. He is the reason you are meeting with us right now. To give you one final chance at walking out of this building alive."

"Would you like to meet him?" Rachel smiled, reverting for a second to the fake, media voice she had used during the trial. It sent a chill through him, the way she spoke. He thought of what they had done to Brian and his own fear of death kicked in, stronger than he imagined possible.

Before he could muster any kind of a reply, the door behind him opened and he heard a voice he thought he recognised.

"Hi, Art."

Art turned around and saw him. The shock nearly caused him to faint.

"It can't be," Art said, staring at the man who had entered the room. His mind refused to accept it as real. Because it could not possibly be real.

"You're a ghost!"

» 85 «

Brian Matterosi, whose ashes Art had watched being scattered across the Indian Ocean, not fourteen days ago, appeared as alive as ever he had been.

"Sit down, Mr Blume," Sobiewski advised. "You don't look especially well."

Jeroen grabbed Art Blume's shoulders just before he collapsed and helped him into a seat.

"What's going on here?" Art managed to get out, once he had recovered a bit.

The ghost who looked like Brian Matterosi said, "First of all, I want to personally thank you for doing such a good job defending me. We had hoped you would go all out, and you certainly did."

"No," Art shook his head and rubbed his eyes, then stared again at the impostor. "Brian's dead. I saw him die on live television. Two billion people saw him die on live television."

"Don't believe everything you see on TV, Art," Brian answered.

"You must understand, Mr Blume," Sobiewski continued. "We needed a conviction. We needed a sacrificial lamb. It was the only way to restore some semblance of order to a badly fractured world."

"So you faked the whole execution?"

"That's right. It was also the only way to ensure Professor Matterosi's safety. After all, if he had been found innocent, can you imagine the death threats? There are people out there who would never stop hunting him. Now, with a bit of plastic surgery and the right home environment, he'll be free. Nothing makes you more anonymous than being dead, cremated and having your ashes sprinkled over the Indian Ocean."

"But why?"

"Because Professor Matterosi is a genius and a hero. His solution, fully embraced by a select group of scientists and politicians at the very highest levels, is the only conceivable way we have of managing the population pressure in the twenty-first century. You can't imagine we could let such a man be killed for the part he played in what was ultimately an internationally agreed solution."

Art's head was spinning. It all began to make sense. The link between Rachel Hyberg and Zextra. GlobalSix and the ICC.

"So it was all a conspiracy? The whole trial was faked?"

Sobiewski shrugged. "I wouldn't say the whole trial was faked. There were elements of truth in it. Much of the testimony on the effects of VIS was accurate. And Professor Matterosi was a formative figure in developing the virus, so he is, strictly speaking, not entirely innocent."

"But I didn't act alone," Brian added, as he slid into a seat next to Hyberg. "In fact, I don't think I could possibly have managed the logistics without some support. Quite a bit of support, actually. Everyone in this room, a half dozen prime ministers and about ten scientists are guilty to some degree or other."

"But we needed to distance ourselves from it. We needed to have someone—some evil genius—on whom the blame could be pinned. By agreeing to play this part, Professor Matterosi has done the world yet another invaluable service."

Art turned to Brian. "You lied to me the whole time?"

"I'm sorry, Art, it had to be done. We needed the lawyers to play their parts perfectly. Most people in the trial, in fact, had no idea of what was going on. But you especially. It was very important you believed in what you were saying."

"If you want to keep a conspiracy quiet, Mr Blume, you generally tell as few people as possible."

"And what about the recording? Was that a fake too?"

"As much of it as possible was true," responded Brian. "A painful amount of my life was laid bare, because it had to sound authentic. Still every word was read from a script. It was written by a scriptwriter, an English guy called Thomas Christie."

"Why go to all that trouble?"

Sobiewski answered, "Because it was a way of protecting a great many people who cannot simply disappear. Other scientists who worked on the project, for instance. Their role in the creation and spreading of VIS has been carefully edited out of the narrative, as it was from the trial."

"Like Tadeki Mateki's?"

"To name but one person, yes. But even more important than protecting our researchers, the recording tells a story that people need to hear. It makes it human and personal. Just think about the alternative, Mr Blume. Imagine the world wakes up to VIS and then discovers it was deliberately engineered and released by a team of international scientists working in conjunction with the CIA, MI6, FSB, Mossad and a handful of officials in the UN. Imagine they found out their hero, Veedala Jhumi, was as much a conspirator as the US Secretary of State. Then who's the bad guy in that scenario? How do all these hurt and angry people achieve the sense of justice they need in order to get on with their lives and cope with the massive social and demographic changes that are coming? We're doing all this for them. And for the planet."

Art turned to Jeroen. "And you? You knew all this?"

"I'm paid to forget things when it's not my job to know them any more."

"So then why did you help me to unveil the Kgabu-Hyberg affair? Why did you take those pictures?"

Jeroen just shrugged and smiled. It was Sobiewski who answered. "Kgabu proved to be too volatile. The very thing we wanted him for, his charisma and personality, was also the thing that made him too hard to control. When he started to go over the top, we needed to step in. We needed less rhetoric. And then he began to subpoena the wrong people. Bringing Laura Schneider to the stand was not part of the plan. It forced us to ... improvise."

"Which we did really well," Brian interjected.

"I had asked Kgabu nicely to stop, but when he refused to cooperate, we needed a way of controlling him. That's why Hyberg was charged with seducing him."

"So you arranged the leak of the affair in order to silence him?"

"We arranged the leak of the affair in order to discredit him. Despite our best efforts, it has transpired that America just isn't ready to ratify the Treaty. Discrediting Kgabu was a way of justifying that decision."

"We wanted the leak to come from you," Hyberg said. "But you hesitated too long, and eventually we were forced to take matters into our own hands."

Art thought of when he'd met Kgabu, sitting in the prison cell, having won the case, but lost everything else.

Sobiewski appeared to read his mind. "Don't feel too sorry for him, Mr Blume. He got his execution. We dropped the rape charges, and he's walked free. And now, as far as his countrymen are concerned, he's a hero. He could become the ANC's next prime minister."

"Except that he has lost his wife ..."

Sobiewski puffed on his cigar and shrugged.

"No one forced him to sleep with the pretty blonde."

Art gazed from one conspirator to the next, still trying to piece together the puzzle. "So why tell me all this now?"

"Because," Brian interjected, "you were getting too close. Already there's a growing number of people starting to question whether I acted alone. Fine if it's just the tinfoil hat brigade. But you add credibility to the whole thing. Then you even started digging around the Medi-Discover stuff ..."

"How do you know that?"

Rachel Hyberg smiled. "We know an awful lot. Maybe not everything, but an awful lot."

"The fact is we need you as an ally, not an enemy. Listen, Art, the world needs the UN now more than ever. Not just the Abuja Treaty, but a whole raft of international agreements that will help the planet adjust to the effects of VIS. We need you to be on board with this."

"And what if I say no? What if I blow the lid on this conspiracy?"

The men across the table sat in silence and waited for Rachel Hyberg to speak.

"Your daughter Jessica lives in Paris, doesn't she?"

"If you lay one hand on my daughter, I'll—"

"You'll what? Call *The New York Times* on us?" Hyberg laughed. "You'll be dead before you touch the green button." Her eyes continued the laugh from over the rim of the coffee cup, which her delicate little fingers now cradled.

Brian struck a more conciliatory tone. "Art, don't you want to be there for Jessica when she gives birth?"

"What? What are you talking—"

"You're going to be a grandfather, Art. The baby's due in a couple of months. And the scary part is, you didn't even know it. Talk about losing Jessica! You're already losing her as it is."

Brian sighed, reached across the table and placed a hand on his arm. "Go—be there for your family. Stop fighting other people's battles. It's over, it's done. I'm dead and you're free to bask in the humility of having lost a case for once in your life. But you've won something too. You've got a chance now to be a grandfather. While you're at it, maybe you can even become a father."

Art's mind was spinning with all the new information.

"You've played us both for fools."

"That's one way of looking at it. Another way is this: you've both won the case. You got Professor Matterosi off, scot-free, while Kgabu gets to celebrate a glorious execution. And in sixty years, the planet's population will be sustainable, at under a billion."

Art's pocket began to ring. He took out the phone and saw the UK number flash up on the screen. Jeroen was standing directly behind him.

"Go ahead," Sobiewski said. "Answer it."

"Lisbeth?"

"*Art, it's me. Listen you were right. I have been looking into all the employees of Medi-Discover Technologies. There's at least four more with false addresses in or near Milton Keynes. And I've found links to Laurence Defrasne in every single case.*

"Lisbeth, stop! Listen to me for a sec—" Art looked across the table at the three conspirators watching him. "I found out who Laurence Defrasne is. It's totally above board. Well, kind of. Turns out it's a tax thing."

"*A tax thing? Are you certain?*"

"Very certain. Looks more like avoidance than evasion. Probably not even illegal. Medi-Discover is a brass-plate cover for another company, with links to Zextra. So it really has nothing to do with the Matterosi case. I'm sorry for sending you on a wild goose chase. Fact is, I've been crazy these past months. I guess I just wasn't prepared to accept that I lost a case this big."

"*Well ... you have been a bit odd lately.*"

"For which I'm sorry. But hey, you know, I got some good news. I'm going to be a grandfather!"

"*Congratulations.*"

"Yeah, and it's made me realise there are more important things than work. We lost Brian, but it was always going to be a tough case. Anyway, you're young. Just chalk it up to experience."

"*All right. Well, if you need me again—*"

"I won't, Lisbeth. I'm going to take a little break now. You should do the same. Go out and live your life a little."

When he looked into the faces across the table, he realised he had given her a chance to do just that.

» 86 «

Brian Matterosi followed the sailor up the steel ladder, rung by rung, and emerged on the submarine's deck under exploding light and blazing sunshine. The last time he had seen the light of day had been three months ago in a port on the Black Sea, but it had been cold and cloudy and miserable. This was the other end of the world.

When his eyes adjusted to the light, he could see the island ahead of him, a low, flat atoll on which palm trees gave way to heavier forestation in the slightly raised centre. There were no signs of human settlement. This was Pickett Island. One of the most remote locations in the South Pacific. Nominally uninhabited, and protected by the US and British navies from any nosy yachts that might get too close, Pickett had been kitted out as a secret research facility during the Cold War. Now it was to be his retirement home.

The CIA man who led the mission ushered him into a dinghy, and they motored to the island's only dock, a single wooden pier invisible from a few hundred metres out.

"This is as far as I'm authorised to go," the man told him, after unloading the six cases of supplies onto the dock. Then he left Brian with a handshake. "Good luck."

Hitching the first of the cases onto the two-wheeler trolley, Brian followed the only visible path for a kilometre or so. It led into the forest. The raucous sound of tropical birds ripped through the air on all sides, as taller trees encompassed him. Then suddenly the path turned, and a house came into view. Its walls were whitewashed rendering, under neat wooden gables and a clean slate roof, somewhat British colonial in its style. It reminded Brian of Drumnaslew.

Before he got there, the door sprang open, and Laura rushed out to greet him.

"We've got our own hot tub!" she shouted excitedly. "I've been dying to tell you."

Brian frowned. "What about the lab? Is the lab set up properly?"

Laura rolled her eyes. "Yes, everything's there. Lots of fun microscopes for you to play with. It's all underground, so I can lock you in and go back to sunbathing any time I want."

They shared a laugh, and another wave of joy swept over them. They kissed until it became passionate. She began undressing him.

"Wait, shouldn't we go inside?"

Laura's nose twitched in that delightful inflection that signified she was internally laughing at her own joke. It always made him crazy for her.

"Yes, because our nearest neighbours, who are five hundred kilometres away on a different island, might see us doing something naughty!"

Afterwards as they lay in the warm, white sand, sunshine dappling on their bare skin, Laura suddenly removed her fingers from his hair and asked thoughtfully,

"You know the recording you made? You told me before it was written by some script guy."

"Correct."

"What exactly did you tell him?"

Brian stiffened, "So you listened to it?"

"I couldn't help myself. I had to know what you'd said about me."

He craned his head and looked at her. She had a strange look in her eye that made him afraid.

"It was all written to create a distorted image of me, as a mad scientist. All carefully chosen lies."

"Not entirely lies. Just some lies, interwoven with an awful lot of truth."

"That was his job. He did a lot of research. He had to make it sound authentic."

There was something in the script that had bothered her. Some detail, he guessed, that was too personal. That she would have wanted them to edit out. Brian couldn't remember exactly what he had told Christie. The Englishman had asked a lot of questions.

And he was insightful.

"It was written to protect you, Laura. To make it look like you despised me."

She smiled and resumed stroking his hair.

"I only despise you when you fling your underwear on the bedroom floor."

"So you're not angry?"

She sighed. "No woman would be happy with those kinds of things being said about her by the man she loves, in the knowledge that millions of people were listening to it and believing it. But I know you did what you had to do, Brian. And I'm proud of you. Come on, let's go inside and I'll show you our new home. The hot tub is amazing!"

It wasn't until later that Laura remembered the post they had left for him. Most were copies of scientific journals and correspondences from a select group of research associates. But there was one that was just a photo, stuck on cardboard to make it into a postcard. In the background it showed the Palace of Versailles. In front of the palace stood Art Blume, dressed in shorts and a blue polo shirt. He was holding a chubby little baby and standing next to two younger women, one with long, dark hair, the other with shorter blonde hair and glasses. On the back, Art had written: *I took your advice. This is me and my grandson out enjoying climate change.*

As Brian looked at it, Laura appeared over his shoulder. When he turned to her he saw that same strange look in her eye. Then he knew what it was in the recording that had troubled her so much.

She smiled away the sad look, and turned towards the kitchen.

"Cute baby."

Brian followed her and placed a tender hand on her shoulder.

"Laura."

She turned in response to his touch and looked him deep in the eyes.

"It was just a recording. A story we had to spin."

"I know," she said at length. "And I guess there's a sort of justice in it, somewhere. But that doesn't change how I feel."

The light from the window caught her in profile as she turned back towards him. Her face had aged, but she was still the most beautiful woman in the world to him. She had given up so much, out of love for him. He held her in a tight embrace, full of love and joy and gratitude for the fact that after all they had been through, she was still in his life.

That evening, was Brian's first chance to immerse himself in his lab. All the sample boxes had been placed in the storage room, exactly as he had instructed. He dug in amongst the sealed boxes labelled 'bio-hazard' until he'd located one in particular. Inside was the suitcase. He opened it and rooted around amongst the relics of his past—his Dungeons and Dragons character sheet; the photograph of himself as a boy taken by gay Matthias; his old *Compendium of Advanced Mathematics*—until he found what he was looking for. The plastic leprechaun he had taken from his mother's mantelpiece, with 'HAPPY ST PADDY'S DAY' written on its base.

He held it to his lips and bowed his head. And said a prayer for his mother's soul.

Printed in Great Britain
by Amazon.co.uk, Ltd.,
Marston Gate.